THE LACEMAKER

Silver Linings Mysteries Book 2

A Regency Romance

by Mary Kingswood

The Lacemaker: Silver Linings Mysteries Book 2

Published by Sutors Publishing

ISBN: 978-1-912167-28-9 (paperback)

Cover design by: Shayne Rutherford of Darkmoon Graphics

Version 6

Author's note:

this book is written using historic British terminology, so *saloon* instead of *salon*, *chaperon* instead of *chaperone* and so on. I follow Jane Austen's example and refer to a group of sisters as the Miss Wintertons.

The Lacemaker: Silver Linings Mysteries Book 2

About this book: *A traditional Regency romance, drawing room rather than bedroom.*

Caroline Milburn and her younger sisters live in two cramped rooms, struggling to survive by their skills in lace making and weaving. When their previously unknown grandfather drowns on the Brig Minerva and bequeaths them a cottage in the country, their lives seem set to improve. But where will the daughters of a linen draper fit into rural life, now that they are better off? How will Caroline find husbands for her younger sisters? Why have purses of money been buried in the garden? And why are the neighbours so interested in them?

Charles Leatham was happy in the army, where all he had to do was to follow orders. With both his older brothers dead, he's forced to return home and he knows where his duty lies - he must marry, and soon, to secure the inheritance. He doesn't care who he marries, but why is his step-mother so keen to pair him with the ill-bred linen draper's daughter? She's a termagant and a shrew, but he always follows orders so he resigns himself to the inevitable. At least she'll be grateful for the offer... won't she?

This is a complete story with a HEA. Book 2 of a 6 book series.

Isn't that what's-his-name? Regular readers of my books will know that occasionally characters from previous books pop up again. There are a few in this book. Lord Randolph Litherholm, the new Duke of Falconbury, made a brief appearance in *The Clerk*, the prequel to this series; his story will be told in book 6, *The Duke*. Lawyer Mr Willerton-Forbes and his flamboyant sidekick Captain Edgerton have been helping my characters solve murders and other puzzles ever since *Lord Augustus*. Keep an eye out for Mr and Mrs Elkington, unobtrusive guests at a dinner party here; you'll be seeing more of them in the next book, *The Apothecary*.

About the Silver Linings Mysteries series*:* John Milton coined the phrase 'silver lining' in *Comus: A Mask Presented at Ludlow Castle*, 1634

> *Was I deceived, or did a sable cloud*
> *Turn forth her silver lining on the night?*
> *I did not err; there does a sable cloud*
> *Turn forth her silver lining on the night,*
> *And casts a gleam over this tufted grove.*

Ever since then, the term *'silver lining'* has become synonymous with the unexpected benefits arising from disaster. The sinking of the *Brig Minerva* results in many deaths, but for others, the future is suddenly brighter. But it's not always easy to leave the past behind...

Book 0: The Clerk: the sinking of the *Minerva* offers a young man a new life *(a novella, free to mailing list subscribers).*
Book 1: The Widow: the wife of the *Minerva's* captain is free from his cruelty, but can she learn to trust again?
Book 2: The Lacemaker: three sisters inherit a country cottage, but the locals are surprisingly interested in them.
Book 3: The Apothecary: a long-forgotten suitor returns, now a rich man, but is he all he seems?
Book 4: The Painter: two children are left to the care of a reclusive man.
Book 5: The Orphan: a wilful heiress is determined to choose a notorious rake as her guardian.
Book 6: The Duke: the heir to the dukedom is reluctant to step into his dead brother's shoes and accept his arranged marriage.

Want to be the first to hear about new releases? Sign up for my http://marykingswood.co.uk/.

Table of contents

The Litherholm family

Hi-res version available at http://marykingswood.co.uk/.

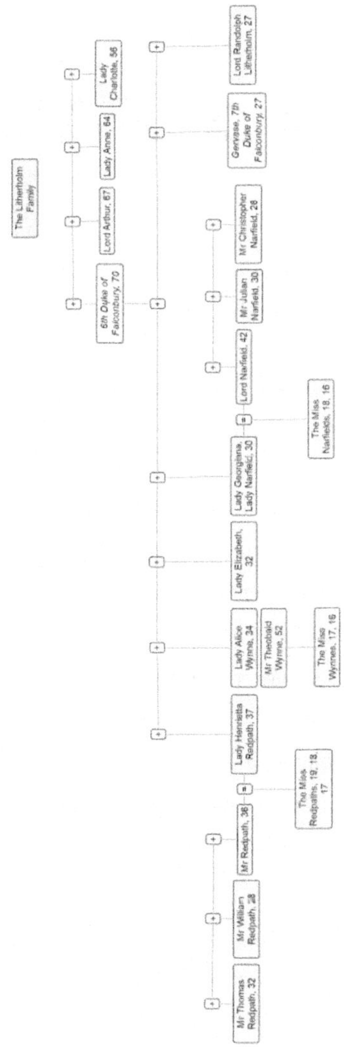

1: A Letter (March)

Caroline laid the strip of lace flat on the counter, smoothing it carefully. Mr Turner, the linen draper, placed a neat pile of shilling coins beside it, while his sister looked on suspiciously. She was always suspicious, that one, suspecting Caroline of some subterfuge, even when the price was clear to see before her. Mr Turner, however, was old-fashioned. He still paid the traditional way, with the number of shillings that could cover the lace.

With delicate fingers, Caroline began to place the coins on the strip of lace, placing them as tightly as she could. Eventually, when not a scrap of lace remained uncovered, she stood back.

"That one is over the edge," Miss Turner said in her sour way, pointing to one of the shilling coins.

"It is just the angle from which you are looking," Caroline said easily. "The light is not the best just here."

"I can fetch a lamp," Miss Turner said, the fire of battle in her eyes.

"No need, Elspeth," Mr Turner said. "Let us not argue over a shilling. You know Miss Milburn's work is worth it. I never have any trouble selling her pieces, and this is a very pretty one."

Almost five guineas for three weeks' work — not a great deal, but much needed. Quickly, before he could change his mind, Caroline scooped up the coins and tucked them into her purse, hiding it away in a pocket. There was a great deal to be said for the old-fashioned fuller skirts, which had room for the concealment of pockets. She strongly disliked the new fashion for a reticule held in the hand. With a nod of the head and a quick bob to the Turners, she hurried out of the shop.

The rest of her day's business was more pleasurable. Winchester had shops in abundance, and her steps took her to the grocer for tea, cheese and spices, the apothecary for Lin's herbs, the silk merchant for more thread for her lace and — an indulgence — the milliner for a new bonnet for Poppy. Gradually her basket filled with neatly-wrapped packages. Only when she heard the clock strike the half hour again did she hasten back to the White Hart to catch the return stage to Romsey. She had no time to buy food at the inn, but she had had the foresight to buy a pie from a stall in the market, and that sustained her for the journey home.

Caroline was squeezed into the middle of a seat designed for two, but that didn't matter. She had seen the passing scenery many times before, and besides, she was busy designing her next piece of work in her head. She could already see the cushion laid out in her mind's eye, the placement of the first pins, the strip gradually growing under her nimble fingers. Mama might lie in the Abbey graveyard, but her skills were still alive in her daughters.

With a great racket as the guard blew his horn, the stage coach turned in to the crowded yard of the White Horse Inn in Romsey. Caroline never rushed to alight, waiting for the dust to settle and the initial confusion to dissipate. When she descended, she picked her way past the carts and wagons, skirted the groups of people greeting arrivals or bidding farewell and made her way through the arch to the Market Place. From there it was only a short walk to the house she shared with her sisters, three other families and a linen draper's shop. The shop had once been her father's and the whole house theirs, but when he had died and everything had to be sold, they had squashed into just four rooms, and since Mama's death, it was only two, with the use of an attic room for the looms. Still, it could be worse, she supposed. They had a roof over their heads, and enough money for their modest wants, and today they had fresh cheese and a new bonnet for Poppy.

Lin was bent over the worktable, absorbed in her task, one fair curl falling unregarded from her coiled hair. "Gracious, are you back already?" she exclaimed, as Caroline set her basket down on the table. "Did you catch an earlier stage?"

"The coach was, if anything, a little late," Caroline said. "It wants but an hour until dinner. Have you finished the scarf already? I thought it needed two more days of work."

"Oh... oh, well, I *meant* to, but I had this wonderful idea. Peg dolls." She held up the work on which she was engaged, showing a clothes peg dressed in rather a fetching gown and bonnet. "We can sell them, you see, dearest," she went on eagerly. "It's another way to make money. You're always asking us to think up new ideas, and so I have. Don't you think it's sweet?"

"It is, yes. Very pretty. How much would you be able to sell it for — a penny? Tuppence? And how long has it taken you to make it?"

"Oh, not long... an hour or two... once I had got the idea." Sheepishly, she held up several failed attempts. "But... you mean we cannot make a profit by them? Oh… I am very sorry, Caro. It seemed like such a good idea."

"So it is, or would be if we didn't have Mrs Hasbroke waiting for that scarf."

"I am very sorry," Lin said again, hanging her head. "I am a great trial to you, I know. Shall I go and help Susie now?"

"No, I'll give her a hand. You can get an hour's work done on that scarf while the light is still good."

Lin nodded and rushed away to the loom in the attic, leaving Caroline shaking her head ruefully. Lin was a hard worker, and enthusiastic, but too easily distracted. And yet it was so disheartening to watch her youth draining away in the hours spent bent over her loom. That attic was sweltering in the summer and freezing in the winter, and exhausting all year round. Lin was too pretty to be wasted in that way. Some rich young man should sweep her up and dress her in silk and diamonds, and allow her to spend her days creating peg dolls or painting portraits or whatever her project of the moment was. She was nineteen already, and should be dancing at night, not huddled over a single candle with a needle.

Caroline hung her cloak and bonnet on a peg and took her basket through to the back room, where Susie was stirring a pot on the range.

"Had a good day, Miss Milburn?" Susie said, with her wide smile. She had been their nurse in the prosperous days, and still addressed the sisters with the formality their mother had insisted upon, even though she was now as much friend as servant.

"Good enough," Caroline said, as she always did.

"Winchester busy, was it?"

"As always. I bought some of that tasty cheese you like to melt onto toast. Our usual tea was far too dear, so I had to get something cheaper. Mm, something smells good."

"Made a seed cake."

Caroline tied on her apron, and settled at the table to pare vegetables. "These carrots are so old they almost bend in two. Was there nothing better in the market?"

"Not within the price you set, Miss Milburn, no. They'd keep better if we still had the use of the cellar. Gen'leman called to see you today."

Caroline laughed. "I don't know any gentlemen, Susie, not any more. I never knew many, and now there are none."

"Well, he looked like a gen'leman, right enough. Said he had somethin' to your 'vantage."

"Oh, selling some kind of patent medicine, was he? Only a guinea a bottle, and cures gout, freckles, the bloody flux and leprosy."

Susie chuckled, a low rumble that made her ample flesh wobble. "Nothin' like that. Attorney, he was. Card's over there, by the clock."

"An attorney?"

That was different. Caroline abandoned the carrots, and reached to the high shelf where the clock stood. Beside it was a neat rectangle of card. *'Mr L Stratton,'* she read. *'Stratton, Walsh, Stratton and Stratton, Attorneys At Law'.*

"I know Mr Stratton," she said thoughtfully. "A portly old gentleman, with a great white wig and a fondness for snuff."

"This one were a thin, *young* gen'leman," Susie said. "Fine lookin' man, for a lawyer." She sniffed disparagingly. "Left a letter for you. Now where did it go to? Miss Poppy had it in her hand, I reckon."

"Then it has been cast aside somewhere, or thrust into a pocket," Caroline said. She sighed. "Ah well, it will turn up, I dare say. Where *is* Poppy, though? Is she in the loft?"

Susie looked sheepish. "Don't know, Miss Milburn, and that's a fact. Haven't seen her for hours, but then you know what she's like."

Caroline did know. "Well, I'd better go and find her. If I have to go out to look for her, I'll send Lin down to do the vegetables."

"I can do them no bother," Susie said. "Mutton's stewing and everything else is ready. Off you go."

It was three flights of stairs up to the loft where their looms were. On each floor, she asked for Poppy, but was met with shakes of the head. In the attic, Lin was hard at work but there was no sign of Poppy.

"Mrs Bright has a new baby," she said.

"Ah. I'll try there."

Back down the stairs again, and out past the main kitchen to the yard, threading her way through Lin's pots of herbs and the lines of washing strung between posts. When Papa was alive, the laundry had gone out to the washerwoman and the yard was a pleasant, flower-filled place to sit, but with four families now sharing the house, there were always sheets and chemises hanging.

At the back of the house was a narrow alley, foul with discarded refuse, scavenging dogs and trickles of malodorous liquid. Crossing carefully, Caroline pushed open a gate and entered another yard. And there was Poppy, without her cloak and still wearing her working apron, the baby in her arms, crooning gently. She looked up at Caroline with a beatific smile on her face, tendrils of soft brown hair curling around her face. She looked angelic in such a pose, an enchanting Madonna. Almost sixteen, with sweetness of countenance and an innocence of such purity that Caroline feared for her future. Lin was a beauty too, but she had a deal of sense and knew how to keep out of trouble. Poppy had no such instincts.

"Isn't he sweet, Caro? So good — he's been asleep all afternoon. He is to be Baptised John — that's a fine name, isn't it?"

"A good, Biblical name," Caroline said, softly. "I'm afraid you'll have to give him back to his nurse now, dear. It's almost time for dinner, and Susie needs some help."

"Of course. Sally!" she called, and the maid's face appeared from an upper window. "I have to go now."

The maid nodded, and emerged into the yard a few moments later. Gently, Poppy laid the sleeping baby in her arms, then skipped away and out through the gate.

"Don't be cross with her, Miss Milburn," the maid said. "She loves babes so, and she's ever so good with them. Besides, I got the whole nursery cleaned, from top to bottom, so she's been a big help."

"I'd like her to be a big help to her own family sometimes," Caroline said. Then, since that sounded ill-humoured, she added, "I could never be cross with her, Sally."

And it was true, she reflected, as she followed Poppy back across the alley. No one could ever be cross with her, for whenever such a thing were attempted, she would gaze at the scolder with huge, reproachful eyes, and instantly all annoyance dissipated. Lin was remorseful and downcast when any neglect of duty was pointed out, but Poppy was simply incredulous that anyone could admonish her. How could it possibly be wrong to do whatever her heart told her was needful?

It was not until the three sisters sat down to their dinner that the letter from Mr Stratton finally emerged from its hiding place in Poppy's pocket. *'To the Miss Milburns'* it said, and so Poppy, with her own form of logic, had decided that it could not be read until they were all three together. Caroline could not remember the last time they had had a letter to open. A few condolence letters, after Mama's death, and how expensive that had been. One had come all the way from Scotland and had cost a shocking one and tenpence. But this one was a pleasure to open, for it had been delivered by hand, and therefore had cost them nothing.

"Read it, Caro," Lin said. "It must be important, seeing as he's an attorney."

'To Miss Milburn, Miss Elinor Milburn and Miss Penelope Milburn. It gives me great pleasure to inform you that I have some tidings to impart to you of the most interesting kind, which will be greatly to your advantage. Please call on me at the offices of Stratton, Walsh, Stratton and Stratton at any time convenient to yourselves. I am readily available between the hours of eight and two, but may be obtained at other hours by appointment. Yours in anticipation of an early meeting, Lester Stratton.'

Caroline laughed out loud. "Now I imagine him sitting behind an empty desk waiting for us to appear and give him something to do. I have never heard of an attorney who was readily available before. Papa always had to make an appointment to see the elder Mr Stratton. It will be some scheme or other — some investment he wishes us to participate in. He's misinformed if he thinks we have money to spare for such nonsense."

"But it could be something wonderfully exciting!" Poppy said, her eyes aglow. "A prince wishes to marry one of us, or... or... a long-lost relation wishes to claim us. A duke, perhaps, and we should go to live in his castle and eat peaches every day."

"Then you would be very ill, eating so many peaches," Caroline said.

"But you will go to see this Mr Stratton?" Lin said anxiously. "So little ever happens to us that, even if it's a mistake, it will be amusing, won't it?"

"Oh, yes, and the letter is addressed to all of us, so we may all go and meet this young Mr Stratton, and hear his tidings of a most interesting kind. In fact, let us attend him promptly at eight, so that we may have the rest of the day to do our work. I have a new piece to begin and I should like to make a good start tomorrow."

The following morning, therefore, as soon as the Abbey clock had struck eight, they donned their cloaks, bonnets and gloves and walked the short distance to the premises of Stratton, Walsh, Stratton and Stratton. The door was locked and the shutters were closed.

"Typical," Caroline muttered, but even as they loitered uncertainly, debating whether to go home again or to wait, the clerk arrived with a rush.

"Good day, good day, good day, ladies! Miss Milburn..." He bowed perfunctorily to Caroline. "Miss *Elinor* Milburn." Another, much lower, bow. "Miss... um... um... Do come inside, ladies. You will be wishful to see the younger Mr Stratton, I perceive."

He unlocked the door and they meekly followed him inside. Caroline could not help smiling. Every clerk and apprentice in Romsey knew Lin's name and face, and accorded her that special courtesy reserved for a beautiful woman. Caroline was known to most of them only as Lin's older sister, and Poppy was of no account at all. If only Lin could attract the notice of a gentleman, someone of independent means who could afford to marry her and perhaps support her two less pretty sisters. One day, perhaps, but the months and years were passing by, with no sign of such a person.

Not two minutes later, the elder Mr Stratton arrived, accompanied by a younger man, unknown to them. Caroline had to agree with Susie's description of the stranger as *'a fine looking man'*. He was slender and not above average height, but he had a charmingly pleasant countenance, which was currently wreathed in smiles, as if his day afforded him no greater delight than to meet three uninteresting spinsters with neither money nor prospects. He dressed well, like a gentleman, and... yes, he had noticed Lin. They always noticed Lin.

"Well now, how delightful to see you all again, and under such happy circumstances," the elder Mr Stratton said. Happy circumstances? For the first time, Caroline felt a flicker of interest. "Miss Milburn, may I present to you my nephew, another Mr Stratton you see, who has just joined us from Portsmouth now that my father is unhappily not able to undertake as much of the business as was his wont. Nephew, this is Miss Milburn, and Miss Elinor Milburn, and Miss Penelope Milburn."

"Delighted! Delighted!" he cried, executing his bow with a flourish. "So happy to make your acquaintance, especially with such wonderful news to impart. Such an exciting day for you all, and for me also, for you are my very first clients. Do come into my office. Mind the rug! There is a worn patch just there, so do take the greatest care. My uncle will be just next door if you have any questions which I am unable to answer, but he is entrusting your case entirely to me. This way, ladies."

All the time, the wide smile on his face never wavered, and Caroline decided that his enthusiasm was genuine. Whether he was always thus, or it was related to the information he had to convey to them, or whether it was merely the effect that Lin had on him was uncertain. Probably the latter, she decided, for he could scarcely take his eyes off her.

The clerk followed them into the office, and fussed about arranging chairs on one side of the desk. When they were seated, the clerk withdrew and Mr Stratton took his own seat. The desk was entirely empty, and although the shelves lining the room were laden with serious-looking tomes, there was not a thing out of place, not a document or a pen holder or an opened book to be seen anywhere. Mr Stratton was indeed very new to Romsey if he had not yet had time to clutter his office with the detritus of his occupation.

"Now then, ladies, to business," he said, the smile widening even further. "There is good news, but, as is so often the case, there is some rather sad news for me to impart first." The smile faded, replaced by a solemn expression, and his voice dropped to a low, sympathetic tone. "I am very sorry to have to inform you that your grandfather has died."

There was a long silence in the room, as the sisters exchanged glances.

"This is indeed sad," Caroline said, "but it is hardly news, Mr Stratton. Both our grandfathers died some years ago.

Grandfather Milburn departed the world some ten years ago, and Grandfather Carter before Mama was even born."

"Ah," he said, and for the first time he looked uncomfortable. "Is that what you were told? I regret to inform you that you have been misled. Your maternal grandfather was *not* called Carter and he did *not* die until last month."

"That cannot be so," Caroline said. "His name was George Carter, and he was a soldier in the 37th Regiment of Foot. He was killed in action in India."

Mr Stratton gently shook his head. "His name was Abraham Wishaw. He was a hop merchant, primarily, although he dabbled in other commodities. He died just a few weeks ago when the ship bringing him from Ireland foundered."

And in that moment, every truth in Caroline's life crashed in pieces to the floor.

2: Bursham Cottage

"I don't understand," Poppy said.

"Nor do I," Caroline said sadly. "Was there ever a Mr Carter? Was Grandmama even married at all?"

Mr Stratton shook his head. "Lucy Carter, your maternal grandmother, was the daughter of a gamekeeper, and Mr Wishaw..." He eyed Poppy cautiously. "Let us say only that they had dealings together, and your mama was the result. Mr Wishaw was a wealthy man, and so he paid handsomely to establish your grandmother and her daughter comfortably and respectably. He provided an annuity. He had your mother educated, and when she showed aptitude as a lacemaker, he arranged for her to be properly taught. When she married, he saw that she had a modest dowry. That provides you with an income to this day."

"Sixty pounds a year," Caroline said hollowly. Her grandfather was a wealthy man. She could not quite believe it. Why had Mama never told them? Perhaps she had known nothing of it herself. Perhaps she, too, had believed in the fiction of the soldier killed in action. If the records were checked, would she discover that the 37th Foot had never been in India at all? Everything she had once taken as a certainty was a lie.

Mr Stratton leaned forward eagerly. "Clearly this has come as something of a shock to you, but it is not so bad as you might think. Mr Wishaw always took care of his daughter, and he has extended that care even in death. May I—?"

Caroline was not very interested in Mr Wishaw. "What about us?" she said brusquely. "We have always considered ourselves respectable, but if Mama was not... was not... then we are not... not *legal* either."

"Oh, no, no, no!" Mr Stratton said, flapping his hands in distress. "No, you are all perfectly legitimate. Your parents' marriage was completely valid in every way. The matter has been thoroughly gone into, very thoroughly, by myself and my uncle also. You need not have the least concern on that score, I do assure you. Up until the time of her marriage, Mr Wishaw had watched over your mother quite carefully, demanding an annual reckoning from my uncle, and my great-uncle before him, as to your mother's situation. But once she married... well, he considered that his oversight was no longer needed, for she had your father to look after her. But now... Miss Milburn, may I explain to you all that has occurred in the last few weeks to alter your situation quite considerably?"

She had barely taken in the revelation of her mother's status — she was *illegitimate*, a thing shocking to the church, to the world and to Caroline herself. Her grandmother had never been married, had given birth to a child outside the holy estate of matrimony — it was indecent! But he didn't wait for her answer.

"Mr Wishaw had business interests in Ireland, so from time to time he visited that country," he said. "He was returning from one such visit last month when he embarked on the *Brig Minerva* at Dublin. Have you heard of the *Brig Minerva*?"

Mutely, Caroline shook her head. To her left, Lin held her hands in a grip so tight that it must surely cause her pain, and Poppy was pale, frowning a little. She was but fifteen! How much of this was comprehensible to her? Not much, she must hope.

"The *Brig Minerva* hit a rock off the Cornish coast and sank with the loss of almost all lives," he said. "Mr Wishaw was amongst those unfortunates who drowned. But being a prudent man, he left a will. May I read you the relevant section?"

Again Caroline nodded. Although Mr Stratton's eyes strayed often to Lin, he deferred always to Caroline, as the eldest. She was used to that, but somehow today she felt quite unable to play the rôle of wise older sister. She was adrift and rudderless, all her surety swept away. She wished her mother were there. Had she known? Or would she have been as shocked as her daughters?

Mr Stratton opened a drawer of the desk and pulled forth a piece of parchment. "I need not trouble you with the preamble," he said. "There are some small bequests, and then the business interests and the contents of his principal bank account left to his partner. Ah, here we are, this is the part. I shall read it to you exactly as it is written, although you will find the language hard to understand, I daresay."

He cleared his throat. The wide smile was back. *'Having no wife or other children to consider, I hereby give and bequeath to my natural daughter Elizabeth Milburn wife of Henry Milburn linen draper of Romsey and her heirs and assigns for ever the messuage tenement or dwellinghouse known as Bursham Cottage situate standing and being at Bursham St Matthew aforesaid wherein I now live together with all my household goods furniture plate linen china and personal effects of whatever sort such as may be found within the said messuage tenement or dwellinghouse, to be hers for her own absolute use and benefit And I further give and bequeath to the said Elizabeth Milburn the sum of five thousand pounds to be put out to interest in the stocks called the Long Annuities which I desire she may have the interest of paid to her during her natural life and after her decease the same sum to be equally divided amongst all the children of the said Elizabeth Milburn.'*

He gazed at Caroline over the top of the document, eyes gleaming. "Do you understand any of that, Miss Milburn?"

"Five thousand pounds," she said slowly. "Invested in the stocks. Two hundred pounds a year."

He beamed at her merrily. "Very well done! Your ability with numbers is admirable, quite admirable. And also the house."

"Bursham Cottage," Lin said. "And all the household goods."

"A cottage," Poppy breathed. "I should like to live in a cottage. Does it have roses round the door?"

"Vegetables!" Lin said. "Is there a garden to grow vegetables? And a herb garden! We can make lavender pillows."

"Chickens!" Poppy cried. "We can keep chickens!"

"Wait!" Caroline said. "We don't know if—"

"Lambs!" Poppy shrieked. "Goats... piglets... kittens..."

Mr Stratton laughed in delight. "Ah, it sounds charming, quite charming! Let me tell you something about the property." He drew another document from the drawer. "Now then... let me see... ah, yes, it has four rooms..."

That was a disappointment. Only two rooms more than they presently had.

"...and four bedrooms, as well as the usual domestic offices — kitchen, pantries, cellarage, et cetera."

Better. Caroline adjusted her ideas somewhat.

"Outbuildings... although it does not say what. Approximately two acres of land about the house itself, including a good orchard."

Two acres... "How big is two acres?" she said tentatively.

"About the size of a field... or two. I am not very sure," he confessed. "There is also pasturage in the form of two fields, presently rented to a neighbouring farmer for the sum of thirty two pounds a year."

"Thirty two... and two hundred... and Mama's sixty... that is almost three hundred pounds a year," Caroline said wonderingly. "Not including whatever we can earn from our usual occupations."

"My dear Miss Milburn," he said, laying down the paper and leaning back in his chair, the smile wider than ever. "With an income of three hundred pounds a year, and the produce from your own garden to reduce your expenses, you will not need to earn anything. You will be ladies of independent means. You will be very comfortably situated. Very comfortably indeed."

"Comfortably situated," she echoed wonderingly. She could hardly believe it.

~~~~~

A few days later, Mr Stratton hired a small carriage and accompanied them to view their new house. Lin and Poppy twittered happily of all that they would do when they were living
~~~~~

there — the animals Poppy would keep, and the vegetables and herbs Lin would grow. Mr Stratton joined in enthusiastically, for he was enthusiastic about everything, even turnips. Caroline watched the countryside roll by and wondered what they would find. Perhaps the house would be too dilapidated to live in. A leaking roof or sagging floors would be beyond their means to repair, and then she would have to play the rôle of parent-figure and tell her sisters that it was impossible. Sometimes she felt as if she were forty instead of only two and twenty.

Eventually they came to the village of Bursham St Matthew, a prosperous looking place with several houses of some size, and rows of neat cottages with well-kept gardens and chickens scratching energetically.

"Chickens..." Poppy sighed happily.

"The church and parsonage... a baker... an apothecary..." Lin cried, peering through the carriage window. "A smith... a chandler of some sort... a butcher and poulterer... Oh. No grocer."

"I believe there are several villages in close proximity," Mr Stratton said. "There will be a grocer in one of the others."

As they drove out of the far side of the village, they passed two substantial entrances, their drives curving away to unseen houses some distance away.

"Your neighbours," Mr Stratton said. "Ah, I believe we are arriving."

The carriage slowed and then stopped, and they peered out at a pair of tall stone gate posts, with the words *'Bursham Cottage'* painted on them. Metal palings and high iron gates, padlocked shut, protected a proper carriage drive leading to a solidly substantial house, not a cottage at all, and much bigger than Caroline had envisaged.

"I cannot unlock the gates," Mr Stratton said. "The Salisbury solicitor has the full set of keys, and he is not here yet. I have only a key to the front door."

They clambered out of the coach and descended to the road, looking about uncertainly. To one side of the main gates, a small side gate stood invitingly open, and with a cry of joy, Poppy ran straight through it and vanished from view.

"Poppy, wait!" Caroline called, but she was long gone.

"I'll look after her," Lin called back, as she set off in pursuit.

Caroline sighed.

"She is a free spirit," Mr Stratton said, his smile sympathetic. "Let us examine the house, shall we?"

The drive was not long, ending in a circular sweep before the front door. The house was neatly proportioned, with a bay window either side of the entrance, another floor above that, and attic windows protruding from a roof in good repair. The shutters were all closed and there were no broken panes in the windows. The garden, however, was in a sad state of neglect. Brown grass grew waist high, and here and there overgrown and weed-infested clumps of shrubs suggested the remains of pleasure grounds. Poppy and Lin had disappeared into the wilderness.

The front door yielded at once to Mr Stratton's key, and they stepped into a large and well-appointed entrance hall, fitted out with old-fashioned but solid oak furniture. High ceilings and a branching staircase gave it an airy feel.

"All the contents are yours, of course," Mr Stratton said, gazing about him. "Shall we explore?"

The first room was clearly a study or office, perfectly tidy and the bookcases empty, but with dust on every surface.

"Mr Wishaw's business partner has taken all the ledgers and documents," Mr Stratton said, gazing around at the forlorn bookcases. "There is not much left, is there? I suppose Mr Wishaw was not a great reader."

Opposite it was a parlour. It was not quite grand enough to be called a drawing room, but it was clearly a place for receiving callers. Then a dining room, and finally a room in a state of disorder, filled with boxes and bolts of fabric, bottles and heaped-up chairs, candlesticks with stubs of candles and all the detritus of a household not too particular about tidiness.

"A morning room?" Mr Stratton suggested.

Caroline shook her head. "The light is wrong. Perhaps in high summer, but I would prefer the parlour to work in, I think, and the looms... there are windows in the attic, so that may be the best place for them. Four bedrooms, I think you said, so we may have a room each, even Susie."

"Miss Milburn," Mr Stratton said tentatively, "I wonder if you have considered inviting a female relative to live here with you? An older woman — an aunt, perhaps. A widow, or some such. The world might look askance at three young women setting up house together."

"I have considered it, for about two minutes," she said, with a smile. "We have no aunts or cousins or widowed relations that I would not be pulling caps with inside an hour. I've been the head of our small family for two years, ever since Mama died, and I am loath to surrender my position now. Besides, we are not gentry, Mr Stratton. We work for our bread, and although that no longer has the urgency it once did, we shall not be sitting about embroidering fire screens or paying morning calls on the ladies of the parish."

"I understand that," he said. "However, if you place yourselves in a lower level of society, then that is where you will stay. It will reduce your prospects considerably."

"By prospects, I presume you mean marriage prospects," she said. "They are not very great, with or without a widowed aunt. We are the daughters of a linen draper, Mr Stratton. Our place in society is settled, and our reputations will not be damaged by living alone."

He nodded, and said no more on the subject.

In every room, Mr Stratton had folded away the shutters and peered through grimy window panes into the garden. Now he said, "I cannot see your sisters. Would you object if I were to go looking for them? You may be used to Miss Penelope's sudden starts, but I confess to a touch of anxiety on her account."

"Pray go, Mr Stratton. I shall have a look upstairs."

But after he had gone, she walked around the downstairs rooms again, more slowly. All the furniture was of the same solidly serviceable style as the hall, plain oak or beech rather than mahogany or rosewood, and the rooms were cold, fusty from lack of use. In the parlour, she cleaned a patch of the sofa with her handkerchief and sat gingerly, gazing around her domain. Only two paintings on the walls, neither of interest, and few ornaments apart from some plain candlesticks here and there. A sofa to one side of the fire, and two chairs the other. A scattering of other chairs around the walls, stiffly aligned. Two small tables, and a writing desk by the window, but no paper, pens or ink. It was at present a cheerless, unwelcoming room but with fresh paint on the panelling and paper on the walls, a few of their own knick-knacks scattered about and a good fire blazing, it would be charming.

The study was less interesting. The drawers of the big desk were locked, its leather chair polished to a pale sheen by Mr Wishaw's rear. Beside the fire, a leather wing chair was likewise worn and cracked from use, while its twin, the visitor's chair, was pristine, apart from the layer of grime that coated every surface. There was a window seat that would have looked inviting, had it been cleaner.

The dining room furniture was a little better, the table and sideboards polished beneath the dust, but the cupboards were empty, with not a bit of silver or glassware to be seen. Probably there was a silver safe somewhere about the place. She counted the chairs — sixteen. A dining table big enough to seat sixteen people! She could not quite imagine entertaining so many. Even in Papa's day, they had never sat down more than ten at table, and that was rather a squeeze.

This was a gentleman's house, she realised with a start. Or rather, a wealthy man's house, for Mr Wishaw had not been a leisured gentleman. But neither would they be ladies, and sit around doing the boring things that ladies were expected to do — embroider unwanted cushions, net purses or paint indifferent landscapes. No, that would never suit her. At all costs, she must be busy. She would still make lace, and earn a little extra money by so doing. As for Lin... well, Lin would marry. She was too pretty to dwindle into spinsterhood. And Poppy? Caroline sighed. There was no knowing what Poppy would be when she grew up, or if that time would ever come. There was too much of the perpetual child in her for comfort.

There was still no sign of her sisters from any window, but perhaps the view would be better from upstairs. The bedrooms had a sad, neglected air. There were four large rooms, the beds all stripped down to the mattress, but they were good, solid beds, with matching good, solid washstands and dressing tables and wardrobes. Mr Wishaw liked his furniture to last, clearly. There were two smaller rooms, which might be box rooms or dressing rooms, or perhaps a nursery. A door revealed narrow, uncarpeted stairs leading up to the attic. Not being equipped with a candle, she deferred further exploration for another day.

But there was another door which led to a corridor under the apex of a roof, above the kitchen wing, perhaps. Skylights covered in green mould let in an eerie light. Another attic space, then, but divided into small rooms. One door led to a twisting stair. Servants' quarters, she guessed. Susie might like a room here, instead of her pallet in the kitchen.

A noise... What was that?

Caroline stopped, listening. There it was again, and emanating from within the house, in fact from the room at the furthest end of the attic. Cautiously she crept nearer... a deep rumble, regular and steady. A dog, perhaps? It could not be a horse, not here on the first floor, but perhaps some kind of wild beast wandering in while the house was empty... no, that was a foolish idea. A hornets' nest, perhaps. Or was it too early for such things?

There was only one way to find out. She strode down the corridor and thrust open the furthest door.

The room was in darkness, the shutters closed, but the noise was loud here. As her eyes adjusted, she examined the floor but could see no sign of a dog. There was a line strung across a corner of the room with a couple of shirts hanging on it. In another corner was a chamber pot. And there was a bed, with two large lumps in it.

As she watched, one of the lumps stirred, shifted and opened one eye.

Then it screamed.

3: A Ride In The Woods

The figure in the bed sat bolt upright, still screaming. A grey-haired woman, in a nightgown. The rumbling snores of her companion ceased, and he stirred.

"Shut yer wailin', woman!"

Abruptly, the screams ceased, and Caroline and the woman stared at each other, transfixed. It was hard to say which of them was the more astonished.

Caroline regained her wits first. "What are you doing here?" she said.

The woman's companion lifted himself on one elbow. "'Oy! What *you* doin' 'ere!"

"I asked you first," she said crisply.

"We live 'ere," he said indignantly. "We're the servants 'ere. Oo are you?"

"I am Miss Milburn, one of the new owners of Bursham Cottage. We were not informed of any servants, and besides, your master has been dead for weeks now, so I have no idea why you're still here. And if you *are* servants, which I beg leave to doubt, you are very poor ones. I never saw such a neglected house. There is dust everywhere, the windows are filthy and the carpets need a good beating."

"We've 'ad no 'structions," the man said belligerently. "'Ow's we s'posed to know what to do if no one tells us?"

"You are not twelve," Caroline said sharply. "You must know how to keep a house clean." Abruptly she realised the futility of arguing with servants. "Get dressed and come downstairs, and then we will decide what must be done about you."

"Oh, please don't turn us off, miss!" the woman cried, panic in her voice. "We've nowhere else to go, and we'd be 'appy to work for you. Please don't send us to the workhouse!"

"We will talk about it when you are dressed," Caroline said more gently.

Downstairs, there was no sign of Lin, Poppy or Mr Stratton, so Caroline ventured into the kitchen, which was in a sad state of disarray, the fire almost out, used pots and dishes everywhere, and the table covered with dirty plates, a half-eaten cheese, most of a loaf and three mice, who scattered at her approach. From above came the sounds of two reluctant servants rising from their bed in the middle of the day. Caroline could not help but smile at the man's indignation at being expected to do his job. Indolence was not a sin she could in any way condone, but such brazenness was amusing too. The neglect everywhere did not dismay her. There was nothing she liked better than hard work, and with Susie's help, the four of them would soon set Bursham Cottage to rights. If the two sleepers were prepared to work, then perhaps they could stay on. There was enough money to afford more servants, she thought.

The scullery door was unlocked, so she ventured outside to find the others. Almost at once she heard voices coming from a low, barn-like outbuilding nearby. They were all inside, Poppy ecstatically stroking the soft mane of a horse. At the other end of the barn was a two-wheeled chaise with a folding roof. Despite the lack of care within the house, the stable was in good order, and the horse looked to be healthy.

"Look, Caro — a carriage!" Lin cried. "We shall have transportation. Won't we be grand?"

"I'm not sure we can afford to keep a horse and carriage," Caroline said. "Papa always said it was too expensive."

"But they are here already," Lin said. "We do not have to buy them."

"No, but think of the cost of hay and oats and shoes, and... and whatever else horses need," Caroline said vaguely, not having much idea about such things.

"There is also a tax payable on horses and carriages," Mr Stratton said. "Besides the expense, there is a great deal of work required to take care of a horse, or else you would need to employ a groom. You would not want to undertake such a responsibility without much thought."

"I believe there is already a groom," Caroline said. "There are two servants resident in the house, and one of them must have been looking after the horse."

"Female servants?" Mr Stratton said.

"One man, one woman."

"There is a tax on manservants, too. I will let you have the relevant amounts so that you may decide what you can afford. However, your other expenses will be low, and you may find the gig useful to get about. There are several villages within walking distance, but if you need to go into Salisbury, it will be convenient to have your own vehicle. There are stairs at the side there, so probably there are rooms above to accommodate a coachman." He paused, frowning. "Two servants in the house? Then why did they not make themselves known to us when we arrived?"

"They were fast asleep," Caroline said.

"At noon? Good grief! Fine servants they will make."

"We shall see," Caroline said. "They have nowhere else to go, so the threat of the workhouse may inspire them."

~~~~~

Two weeks later, a wagon laden with all their possessions, with Lin's herb pots balanced precariously on top, made its ponderous way to Bursham St Matthew. Preceding it was a post chaise containing the Miss Milburns, in varying degrees of excitement and anxiety, and Susie, in phlegmatic acceptance, together with Mr Stratton, who had insisted on accompanying them. Poppy was the most excited, for she now had two acres of land to be filled with all manner of baby animals. They would start with a cat for the kitchen mice, and then chickens, Caroline had promised her, and then see what would be practical after that. Privately she suspected that Poppy would soon tire of the daily chores of feeding and egg-collecting and cleaning out the coop.

Lin was excited in her quieter way, for she planned to grow enough fruit and vegetables to keep their table supplied. She already had lists of seeds to buy, and charts of the best sowing times, and had bought a stout book which described in excessive detail the requirements for every kind of produce. It all sounded very complicated to Caroline. But Lin was also rather subdued to be leaving Romsey and all their friends. Or rather all *her* friends, most of them male, it had to be said. Her departure had thrown all the apprentices and tradesmen's boys of the town into the
~~~~~

utmost distress, and the sisters' preparations had been severely hampered by the constant appearance of one or other of Lin's admirers, to congratulate her on her good fortune and to lament the fifteen miles which would now separate them.

"I would not mind if even one of them could afford to wed her, but they none of them have two farthings to their name," Caroline grumbled. "It is all very well for the apothecary's apprentice to profess his undying love in the most poetic terms, and declare on bended knee that he cannot live without her, but whether she is in Romsey or Bursham St Matthew, he is going to *have* to live without her, and there is an end to it."

Susie, to whom these thoughts were offered, laughed and said, "Ah, you're awful hard on them, Miss Milburn. You make no allowance for the pain of young love. Besides, an apothecary's apprentice will one day be an apothecary himself, and then you'd be glad enough to have him hovering around her."

"And when will that be — years from now! She is nineteen, Susie. She should be going to balls and evening parties, as I did until Papa died. And there will be no one suitable at Bursham St Matthew, not even an apothecary's apprentice. It is such a small village, and we will know no one and go nowhere."

"You worry too much," Susie said. "There's a church, isn't there? Well, then. That's where you'll meet people. It won't take long, you'll see."

Caroline herself felt no excitement about the move. Anxiety gnawed at her insides, making her nauseous. What if the money ran out? Could they afford three servants, a horse and a gig on just three hundred pounds a year? How would she sell her lace and obtain new supplies once they lived such a distance from Winchester? How would they make new friends? Where would they fit in to the local society? Would the villagers treat them with respect or despise them? And how on earth was she to find a husband for Lin in such confined society?

Their arrival at Bursham St Matthew on this occasion was more auspicious. The drive through the village was enlivened by an audience of cottagers' wives, who emerged from their various abodes to point and stare and bob little curtsies as the procession passed by, and a horde of small children, who waved cheerfully and then raced the carriage all the way to Bursham Cottage. The padlock had been removed from the gates, which now stood wide open to welcome them. The two servants, Martin and Molly, emerged to greet them formally. Caroline had to admit that they looked more promising now. They were both clean and tidy, Molly attired in a business-like cap and apron, and Martin wearing a worn but respectable coat. Molly described herself as the cook/housekeeper, and Martin as groom, coachman and general manservant, so it had been decided that Molly could keep the kitchen, and Susie, who had struggled as a cook, would take the housekeeper's rôle.

Caroline introduced them to each other with some trepidation. If they could not get on, or if the two older servants could not manage the work, then they would have to go. However, Mr Wishaw had left them one hundred pounds apiece, and they had sons living in Salisbury, so they were in no danger of the workhouse. The three greeted each other stiffly, but with civility, so Caroline was cautiously optimistic, and even more so when she entered the house. It would be putting it too strongly to say that the house was immaculate, but the dust had gone, there were fires burning and the beds were made up ready for them. The choosing of rooms took some time, but Caroline left her sisters to settle the matter between them. For herself, she had no interest in where she slept, for having a bed once more must be an improvement on the pallets brought into the parlour each night for herself and her sisters, while Susie had had to sleep in the kitchen.

Now that she had the full set of keys, Caroline was eager to explore the more interesting parts of the house — the linen cupboard, the store for silver and plate, the wine cellar and the safe. She was pleased to find the house very well supplied with all the necessities, and there was money, too. A box in a locked drawer of the desk contained over a hundred pounds, and in the safe was a delicately netted purse containing notes to the sum of five hundred pounds.

Caroline looked at the money heaped on the desk and sighed wistfully. “I suppose this must go to Mr Wishaw’s business partner.”

“He has already retrieved anything related to the business,” Mr Stratton said, with his beaming smile. “Everything left in the house is yours.”

“I have never seen so much money in my life before,” she said.

He laughed. “You are a wealthy lady now, Miss Milburn, but do not grow too attached to all this. It will soon be Lady Day, and you will have the servants to pay and all the tradesmen’s accounts to settle. No, no!” he said, seeing the look of horror on her face. “All the late Mr Wishaw’s bills were settled by the executors of his will, so you will not find yourself with a vast debt for barrels of brandy or anything of the sort. No, the only bills will be those you and your sisters incur. You should probably call upon the tradesmen yourself quite soon, to assure them of your custom.”

"How will I know where to find them?" she said, feeling as lost as if she were in a foreign country.

"The servants will tell you, or it will be noted in Mr Wishaw's account books, which are..." He rummaged about in cupboards and drawers, eventually emerging triumphant, a pile of leather-bound notebooks in his hand. "...here, you see. These will also give you an idea of likely expenses."

"Yes," she said. "Thank you. You are very kind, Mr Stratton. I don't know what we would have done without you."

"You must not worry so much, Miss Milburn," he said gently. "You will soon grow accustomed to your new situation, I assure you. I shall call upon you in a few days to ensure that you are settling in well, but until then, might I recommend that you keep all this money tucked away in the safe?"

Even as she followed his advice, and closed the cupboard door that hid the safe from prying eyes, she was filled with foreboding that could not be assuaged. They had given up everything that was familiar and moved to a strange house, in strange country and surrounded by strangers. However would they manage?

~~~~~

Charles Leatham found his step-mother already at the breakfast table, and resigned himself to the inevitable tirade. He was not disappointed.

"You *must* marry, Charles, and the sooner the better," his step-mother said.

"I know, Mama. I understand my duty, but I am only just returned home. Let me have a little time to catch my breath, at least."
~~~~~

"You have had plenty of time to catch your breath," she said firmly. "It is more than a year since Alfred died, after all, and you could have extricated yourself from the army sooner, if you had set your mind to it."

Yes, he could have resigned his commission earlier had he wished to, that was true. A younger son who suddenly found himself the heir was always allowed to leave as soon as he liked. But he had had duties and men he felt responsible for and a career he loved, and no wish at all to hasten the moment when he must return to Starlingford and do his duty. His wretched duty! It must be done, he knew that. He was the last son, and he understood what was expected of him.

He sipped his coffee and gazed at his step-mother over the rim of the cup. He was fond of her, and could not blame her for nagging him. After all, he had been shockingly dilatory about the business, he accepted that.

"I promise you I will marry this year, Mama, and it matters not a jot who it might be, so you may choose my bride for me, if you please. All I ask is that you do *not* haul me off to London or Bath to be paraded about like a prize bullock, and that you do *not* expect me to marry—"

"Good morning, Mrs Leatham, Mr Leatham."

And there she was. Mildred Beacher, aged eight and twenty, and as deeply worthy a lady as had ever existed. The daughter of a highly-regarded man of the cloth at Salisbury Cathedral, she had been betrothed to the middle Leatham brother, Benjamin, for several years while he awaited a living. When he had died, she had been affianced to the eldest brother, Alfred, and now he, too, had died. Of a putrid fever, said the physician. Of boredom, and in terror of a lifetime with Mildred, more likely. Charles did not care to whom he was married, so long as it was not Mildred.

He rose politely, and held her chair for her. "Good morning, Miss Beacher. I trust you are well?"

"I am always well, Mr Leatham."

No putrid fevers for her, unfortunately. He immediately chided himself for such unworthy thoughts, and bowed his head as she made her usual morning prayer to thank the Good Lord for food and the roof over their heads. Mildred was tedious company with her preaching ways, but he wished her no harm. She had moved to Starlingford after her father had died, and she provided companionship of a sort for Mama.

As soon as Mildred's prayer ended, and the footman had poured coffee for her, Mrs Leatham said, "Have you seen the new occupants of Bursham Cottage yet, Mildred?"

"I? How should I have seen them?"

"You were in the village yesterday, so I wondered... well, no matter. I shall call upon them today. Do you wish to come with me?"

"I planned to take some pork jelly to the chandler's wife whose baby just died."

"Oh. Oh, well, in that case... Charles, do you—?"

"No, thank you, Mama," he said firmly.

"I shall go myself, then. But just think, Charles — three young ladies, all unmarried. One of them will be sure to do for you, and no need to look to Bath or... or anywhere else," she said hastily, with a glance at Mildred, who was fortunately engrossed in buttering her bread with methodical precision.

"You want me to marry Wishaw's natural daughter?" Charles said in surprise.

"No, no! Their mother was his natural daughter, but she married very well. A linen merchant from... somewhere, I forget where."

"Romsey," Mildred said. "And he was a linen *draper*, I believe. A shopkeeper."

"Well, well, we must all buy our linens somewhere," Mrs Leatham said equably. "I am sure he was a very respectable linen draper."

"I heard he left the family destitute," Mildred said. "Living in two rooms, according to Mrs Christopher. Inheriting Mr Wishaw's property is a great piece of good fortune for the daughters. I hope they are grateful for God's mercy on them. Far be it from me to offer you advice, Mrs Leatham, but for myself I would not presume to call upon them until it is clear that they are sober and modest people, suitable to be acquainted with persons of quality such as yourself."

"Oh, do you think—? Well, perhaps you are right. We shall see them at church, I daresay."

"If they attend," Mildred said darkly, biting crisply into her bread.

Charles escaped as soon as politeness allowed. If his father were there to exert a moderating influence, he could cope with his step-mother's matchmaking and Mildred's piety with tolerable equanimity, but Papa was feeling his age and rarely emerged from his bedchamber before noon now. Then he would summon his son to his book room, and there would be a tedious hour with the bailiff or the gamekeeper or the secretary, discussing the management of the estate, after which Charles would be dispatched to inspect roofs or fields or barn walls or, even worse, talk to tenants and farmers, and what could he say to such people? He had enough trouble making conversation with people of his own station, but discussing escaped pigs and crops that failed to grow was not something that came easily to him.

But until his father rose from his bed, he was free, and his feet took him, as so often, straight to the stables. There was nothing like a hard, fast ride to chase away his megrims and regrets. For a brief time, he could imagine himself back in the army, his fellows around him, united in a common purpose of the utmost importance. How could he ever have imagined, as the third son, that he would be needed for the succession? It was a cruelty of the harshest kind. No, again he had to chide himself for the thought. He was luckier than most, for he was young and healthy and the heir to a comfortable manor house and a substantial fortune. Unlike his brothers, he was alive. He had enjoyed five years of freedom, and now he would do his duty without complaint.

He rode hard across their own fields, then cut through Valmont's Low Mead, and into Corran Woods. At first, the track wound about, overhung by low branches, and he rode with caution, allowing his horse to rest somewhat. But then he came to his favourite part of the ride, a wide, straight track a full mile long where he could allow his horse to have his head and gallop flat out. That was more like it! The thunder of hooves, the beast beneath him as exhilarated as he was, and his own pulse racing with excitement...

The only warning he had was a flash of white very close — *too* close — then his horse was rearing, hooves flailing the air, almost unseating him, then twisting in mid-air, plunging, kicking...

For a few moments, he was fully occupied, first in trying to stay on the horse, and then to bring him under control. But when he spun the beast around, there was the burst of white again — a sliver of pale gown visible beneath a dark cloak, and above it the terrified face of a child. No, not a child, he realised, a young woman standing on the track, her clothing so dark that she was impossible to see until the last moment. Only that quick flash of white as she moved had saved her life.

"What the *Devil* are you playing at?" he yelled at her, his anger at the near-disaster making him brusque. "What are you doing here?"

"There was a mouse!" she said. "You've scared him away now."

"A mouse? For goodness' sake, do you realise—?" Then, puzzled, he said, "Who are you, anyway?"

"Poppy Milburn, if you please, sir."

"And where do you live, Miss Milburn?"

"Bursham Cottage, sir."

He sighed. One of the linen draper's daughters. "Then I shall take you back there directly," he said in resignation.

4: Callers (April)

Caroline had had a difficult morning. Or *another* difficult morning, if she were being quite truthful. Only three nights spent in their new home, and already the cracks were showing. Molly and Susie were bickering, Martin was quite happy to spend hours in the stables grooming the horse but considered that gardening was beneath him, and Poppy kept disappearing. Poppy disappearing was nothing new, of course, but in Romsey that meant that she was at one of the neighbour's houses, whereas here there were woods to get lost in, streams to fall into and, for all Caroline knew, cliffs to fall down and wild beasts to be attacked by. The countryside was a nerve-wracking habitat for three young women who had never lived anywhere but in a town, not to mention muddy. Never had she seen such a quantity of mud.

It would not have been so bad if Caroline had been able to sleep at night, but the soft bed, not shared with her sisters, was so unfamiliar that it kept her awake. And then there were the frightening sounds of the darkness — odd hoots and yowls and rustlings in the undergrowth, the wind howling round and rattling the windows, and Martin's snores, audible even from the other end of the house as she lay fretfully awake.

Today had started badly, for Molly had let the kitchen fire go out. That meant that there was no hot water for washing, and no coffee, either. Then breakfast was late, and when Martin returned from the village with their mail, there were three more bills, and a letter from one of Papa's brothers wanting to know more about their legacy and peevishly querying why he had not been consulted on the matter, as the head of the Milburn family.

"Possibly because you have ignored us ever since Papa died," Caroline muttered, tearing up the letter and hurling it onto the fire in disgust. "If he had ever offered us the least help in the past, I might have asked for his advice."

"We had no need of his advice in this case," Lin said. "We had Mr Stratton to help us, and Uncle Claud wouldn't have wished to travel down from London, would he? I don't know why you wanted to tell him anything about it, Caro."

"Mere courtesy," she said. "I shall not bother again."

They were engaged in sorting through the multitude of items heaped up in the morning room. It was no easy task, and Caroline was already hot, dirty and longing for an opportunity to resume work on her lace again when there was a sharp rap on the front door.

"I'll go," she said eagerly, grasping the opportunity for a distraction.

A strange man stood there, respectably if drably dressed. In Romsey, Caroline could identify the profession or trade of everyone she met, but here she could not guess who the man might be. A farm worker of some sort, she supposed, by the mud caking his boots. She could recognise his expression, though, which was decidedly hostile.

"Miss Milburn?" His voice was local, she thought, but not well-educated.

"Yes. How may I help you?"

"You can help me, miss, by staying off his lordship's land. I've strict instructions to shoot poachers on sight, and we wouldn't want any misunderstandings, would we?"

"His lordship?"

He stared at her, as if astonished that anyone might not know who his lordship was. "Lord *Elland,*" he said, as if explaining to a child. "His lordship's land begins just across the road, and you'd best keep off, if you know what's good for you."

"And your name?" Caroline said, trying to suppress the anger that rose inside her.

"Grison. His lordship's head gamekeeper."

"Well, Mr Grison, if you or any of your underlings mistake me or my sisters for poachers, then your eyes must be poor indeed. I don't think poachers roam Lord Elland's estates in long skirts and bonnets, do you?"

"What about your manservant, eh? What about *him?"*

"I am sure Martin is no poacher," she said disdainfully.

"Aye, well... mebbe remind him. That's all." And without another word, he turned and stalked away, leaving Caroline in no very good humour.

Then, not half an hour later, she heard the steady clop of hooves on the drive. Looking out of an upper window, she saw another stranger arriving, with Poppy sitting before him on his horse.

Caroline flew down the stairs and flung open the front door. As she did so, Poppy raced past her into the house.

"Is that young woman in your charge?" said the man on the horse, his eyes hard as iron.

"She is my sister," Caroline said.

"Then you should keep a closer watch on her," the horseman said, his mount dancing beneath him, as if in a hurry to be away. "I almost ran her down in Corran Woods."

"Then you were riding too fast or too carelessly," Caroline said at once.

"I was no such thing," he spat back. "That track is wide and open, perfect for a gallop. Your sister should be more aware of the possibility of a rider there."

"Or a rider should be more aware of the possibility of someone afoot."

His face reddened with anger. "She should not be there at all! Those woods belong to Lord Elland, and his gamekeeper is well armed to deter poachers, and perfectly willing to shoot trespassers. Tell your sister not to go there again."

"I shall tell her no such thing!" Caroline said indignantly. "Lord Elland should not be permitting his gamekeeper to shoot anywhere likely to be used by local people. Do not defend him in such a strategy, if you please."

For a moment, she thought he would explode, but then, with a great effort at civility, he said, "I beg your pardon, madam. My advice was intended to be helpful."

He wheeled his horse, and took off down the drive, scattering gravel from his beast's hooves as he went.

"Insufferable man!"

Caroline shut the front door with rather more force than was necessary. Nevertheless, she talked to Poppy and impressed upon her the need to keep away from Lord Elland's land. A gamekeeper willing to shoot at anyone on his land was not something to be taken lightly.

~~~~~

APRIL

They had not been in the house three days when Molly found a couple of large fish outside the kitchen door. Two days later, it was a bag of rabbits, and then some pigeons. It was only on the fourth visit, a gift of more fish, that Martin managed to intercept the culprit and brought him to Caroline. He was a pleasant-faced young man, eyes shyly lowered, twirling his hat nervously in his hands. Since he carried a gun and various bags, just like Mr Grison, Caroline assumed he was another gamekeeper.

"This will not do, Mr... erm..."

"Carter, miss. Tim Carter."

"Well then, Mr Carter, Mr Grison has warned us off his land and—"

"Oh — no, no! I work for His Grace, not Lord Elland. I'm one of the Valmont gamekeepers. All the Low Mead and the Hanging Woods are my responsibility... the whole southern end, in fact, and I'm allowed to make gifts if I want to. Not to everyone, mind, but you're different."

"Why are we—? Wait... Carter? Our grandmother was a Carter... the gamekeeper's daughter. You're a *relation!*"

"Yes!" He beamed delightedly. "Informally, of course, but that never mattered to us. I never met Great-aunt Lucy, but we talked about her and the babe she had by Mr Wishaw. He took good care of them, too, so there was never any bad feeling about it, not on our side, although he pretended not to know us." He
~~~~~

laughed. "But then he left the house to you! We must be second cousins… I think. My grandfather was brother to your grandmother."

"That's amazing. So a Carter is still the gamekeeper. Delighted to make your acquaintance, Mr Carter."

He grinned at her, willingly came in for ale and a chat, and in not much more than an hour they caught up with fifty years of family news.

Their earliest formal callers were the local clergyman and his wife, rather drably dressed, their clothes faded and carefully mended. Mr Christopher was a bluff and hearty man in his forties, while his wife was a quiet creature some years younger than her husband. He chatted easily about the village, the local tradesmen and the late Mr Wishaw. His wife said next to nothing, but there was a look about her that made Caroline suspect that she ruled the roost at home.

When he mentioned Mr Grison, Caroline pulled a face and said, "He warned us off Lord Elland's land, and since we don't want him shooting at us—"

"You need not fear Grison's gun," Mr Christopher said. "Lord Elland would never allow him to shoot wildly at people, not even poachers. It suits Grison to allow people to think he would, but you need have no alarm for your safety. Grison may seem unfriendly, but there is no harm in him."

Caroline doubted that, but felt it polite to keep her thoughts to herself.

"How are you finding Wishaw's servants? I was glad to hear you had kept them on."

When Caroline told him about Martin refusing to work on the garden, Mr Christopher laughed. "He is not much of a one for hard work, but so long as you allow him to go down to the Wheatsheaf on a Saturday evening to meet all his cronies, he will serve you well enough. For the garden, you need a strong young man. Might I suggest my eldest son? Just the type of work he enjoys. Offer John a shilling a day, or even ninepence, and he will gladly scythe your lawns and dig over your kitchen garden for as long as you want. He helps out at the Starlingford Home Farm from time to time, but it is seasonal work, and you know what young men of sixteen years are like — they have so much energy to burn that they need to be kept busy all the time. We should be very happy to offer his services to you for as long as you need him."

Caroline was equally happy to accept, for she could see no other way to bring the garden back into some semblance of order.

The second caller, just a day later, was a Mrs Leatham, who arrived in a carriage complete with a footman on the back to deliver her card. *'Mrs Ambrose Leatham, Starlingford'*, Caroline read. She knew from the helpful vicar that the Leathams were one of the two important families of the neighbourhood, second only to Lord Elland, but she had not expected notice from either of them.

"Well, well," she said to Lin as they stood in the hall examining Mrs Leatham's calling card, the footman standing woodenly in the doorway. "Are we at home, do you suppose?"

Lin giggled. "I am not sure. What do you think, sister?"

"I think perhaps we might be, once we have got rid of these aprons."

Poppy was not to be found, so only Caroline and Lin sat in the chilly parlour, the fire newly lit, to receive their visitor.

Mrs Leatham turned out to be a pretty young woman of not much above thirty, who offered condolences on the death of the grandfather they had never met, and enquired with minute interest into their arrangements at Bursham Cottage. She was not very interested in Lin's plans for the garden, but their linens, plate and servants all came under her scrutiny, with a great many hints for the management of their household. This led without a pause for breath to her own family. She told them at once that she was her husband's second wife.

"I was never blessed with children myself," she said, "but I love my step-children just as much as if they were my own. I took the greatest pleasure in seeing the girls well settled with good husbands, and have always intended to do the same for the boys. Both Alfred and Benjamin were on the brink of matrimony when they died, and—"

"How sad!" Lin cried. "What a great tragedy, to lose two sons at once."

"Oh... no, they did not die at the same time, no. The middle one, Benjamin, died first, but he was always sickly, even as a boy, so it was no great surprise. But Alfred — such a great, strong fellow, one would not have supposed... but there you are, there is no knowing when one may be struck down by a putrid fever, which is why we would so like to see Charles married before too long. You have met Charles, of course?"

"Um... have we?" Caroline said, floundering rather.

"Oh, yes! He found your young sister wandering in Corran Woods, and saw her safely home."

Ah, she remembered *him* — the very rude young man. His step-mother was optimistic if she imagined any woman brave enough or foolish enough to take him on. "He forgot to give us his name," Caroline said blandly. "I wish you good fortune in your search for a wife for him."

She beamed happily. "Why, thank you, Miss Milburn." Her eyes slid to Lin, then back to Caroline. "I am sure we shall have no trouble in that regard. Such a handsome boy, and the heir to his father's estate now, of course." Again she glanced at Lin and back. "Not the least trouble in the world."

Caroline's spirits rose after this visit. Perhaps there was hope of a husband for Lin yet, although Mr Leatham would have to improve his manners markedly before she could be comfortable about such a match.

If she was surprised to receive a visit from Mrs Leatham, she was even more surprised when, only an hour later, another carriage rolled up the drive, this one with two footmen on the back. *'Lady Elland, Corranswater'*, read the card. Once more Caroline and Lin found themselves receiving a caller in the parlour.

Lady Elland was very different from the sociable Mrs Leatham. She was a sour-faced woman of an indeterminate age somewhere between forty and fifty. Caroline was unfamiliar with the peerage, but she suspected that Lady Elland's vast array of jewels, furs and lace was excessive even for a baron's wife. It was not even very good lace, and her hat was so over-burdened with feathers it looked as if it might fly away. The visitor gazed around the room with disfavour.

"Hmpf," she sniffed. "This room is very cold."

"If we'd known your ladyship planned to call, we'd have started the fire earlier," Caroline said.

"Today is Friday, is it not? Friday is your day to be at home. Bursham St John on Tuesdays, Bursham All Saints on

Wednesdays, myself and Mrs Leatham on Thursdays and Bursham St Matthew on Fridays. Valmont is Tuesday or Friday, but I daresay you will not be calling there."

"Valmont?" Caroline said.

"The Litherholms. The Duke of Falconbury."

"Oh no, we will not be calling there," Caroline said. "Indeed, your ladyship is mistaken in imagining us to be persons used to making or receiving morning calls at all. We are not gentry. I am a lacemaker by trade, and my sisters are weavers and painters."

"Hmpf," she said again. "That is honest, in any event. Very well, let us dispense with the pleasantries."

Caroline had not noticed any pleasantries, but she inclined her head in acknowledgement.

Lady Elland shifted a little on her chair, her cheeks slightly flushed, and if Caroline had not thought her incapable of such emotion, she would have suspected her of being embarrassed.

"Mr Wishaw, your late grandfather, held certain documents in his safe keeping," she said, her eyes not quite meeting Caroline's. "Important documents relating to my husband's family. Naturally, Lord Elland would like them back. Did you find any such documents about the house?"

If Caroline thought it odd that Mr Wishaw had been holding important documents belonging to Lord Elland, she decided not to say so. Best with such neighbours to accept the enquiry at face value.

"We have found no documents of any sort in the house," she said. "Mr Wishaw's business partner took everything related to the business, and we have found nothing else, apart from a few bills and personal letters."

"Have you examined the desk? Wishaw's bedchamber? The bookcases?"

"The desk drawers and shelves in the study were empty, except for writing things and sealing wax and such like items, and there were no documents in the safe. The bedchamber held nothing but clothes and personal effects."

"Hmpf." She gazed at Caroline with narrowed eyes, as if unsure whether to believe her or not. "Well... if you should happen upon such documents, you will remember that they are Lord Elland's property, and must be handed back to him forthwith."

"They would hardly be of any use to us," Caroline said, in surprise. "If we find anything relating to his lordship, you may be sure we will return it promptly."

"Make sure that you do," she said. "They have... no value in themselves, you understand, but my husband is sentimentally attached to any detail of his family's history. He would be very grateful to have them returned to him. Very well, we understand each other, I am sure. I bid you good day, Miss Milburn, Miss Elinor."

Caroline and Lin accompanied her to the door and watched her assisted into her carriage by the two footmen, who wrapped furs around her as tenderly as if she were a piece of porcelain.

As the carriage bounced away down the drive, Caroline said thoughtfully, "That was odd, but I daresay we shan't see her again."

"I hope not," Lin said. "I didn't like her at all. What do you suppose these documents are that she is so keen to recover?"

"No idea," Caroline said, "but I wonder greatly why Mr Wishaw should have had them. However, if they are anywhere in this house, they are too well-hidden for us to find. I expect the business partner scooped them up. He seems to have taken everything else in the way of papers and books. We had better keep an eye open for them, but I doubt we will find anything."

~~~~~

The Leathams met in the saloon before dinner. Charles's father was always the first down nowadays, to have his traditional sherry before Mildred and her censorious eyes arrived. Not that she ever criticised openly, but her lips pursed in a certain way that was enough to sour a man's pleasure in his favourite tipple. Mr Leatham was approaching seventy years old, a kindly man who looked fondly on everyone, and would not for a kingdom distress a lady by his actions. Charles was not quite so honourable. He was not over-fond of sherry, but since Mildred had descended upon them, it had amused him to join his father at the sherry decanter, and if Mildred disapproved of such a harmless activity, there was nothing he could do about that.

"Well, Charles," his father said, as he accepted his sherry from the footman. "Did you have a look at the smithy roof?"

"I... had a look at it, yes," Charles said cautiously. "Hapgood thinks it will do for another year or two yet."

"But what do *you* think?"

"I am not sure. It does leak sometimes, but only when the rain is particularly heavy and from the east, and Hapgood says that—" He broke off at his father's raised eyebrow. "The trouble is, we have already committed ourselves to the new windows for the dairy cottages, and there is the work on the upper fields. I am very mindful of the expense. You always say that we have to balance the immediate needs against the long-term management
~~~~~

of the estate." When his father still said nothing, he went on, "I beg your pardon, sir. I am not very good at this."

His father's eyes twinkled. "You are not very *experienced* at it, that is all. Hapgood is a great one for putting off the repairs for a year or two, and sometimes that means that there is a great deal more work to be done and expense incurred to set it to rights. If the leaking roof damages the roof struts, it will cost far more than a few tiles and half a day's labour. We cannot afford to have the smithy out of action for long or all his customers will go elsewhere and then we shall have less rent from him. Do you see? All these things must be taken into account."

"I do see, sir, yes. It is just... so *complicated.*"

"You will get used to it." The door opened to admit the two ladies, and the elder Mr Leatham swallowed the rest of his sherry at a gulp, thrusting the empty glass hastily into the hands of the footman. "Ah, there you are, my dear, as lovely as ever. And Miss Beacher. You are well, I trust?"

"I am always well, thank you," Mildred said. "How are your rheumatics today, sir? Will you not ease your joints and sit? Let me fetch you a footstool and arrange a cushion at your back."

Obediently he did as he was bid, and allowed her to fuss over him, although he declined a shawl, protesting that there was a good blaze in the hearth and he was not in the least chilled.

"Well, Charles, I have found just the wife for you," his mother said, drawing him aside. "I called upon the Miss Milburns and the elder will suit you admirably, I believe."

"The elder?" He had a vague memory of an argumentative young woman. "You like her?"

"Very well indeed. The middle sister is prettier, but empty-headed, more interested in her garden than anything else, and the youngest is but fifteen. I did not meet her, but she is too young to be considered. Miss Milburn impressed me most favourably as a very sensible, practical sort of person."

"Practical?" he said with a sinking heart.

"Practical," she said firmly. "The worst possible wife for your position is an over-refined person with finicking ways and expenses to match. Miss Milburn may not be a gentleman's daughter, but she struck me most forcibly with her command of domestic matters. Knew to a nicety every candlestick in the house and barrel in the cellar. That is what you need, Charles — a woman of sound common sense, not someone with high-flown ideas above her station."

"Miss Milburn," he said gloomily. There would be no comfort to be had from such a woman, he was sure.

Mrs Leatham laughed merrily. "Now do not look so dismal, dear boy. Believe me, it is for the best. Men are too inclined to fall for the first handsome face that comes their way, and it does not answer. You want a woman who will be a help and support to you, not a flighty creature who will over-spend her pin-money every quarter. Trust me, practical is better than pretty."

"Is it so?" he said, smiling down at her. "I shall point out to Father what a mistake he made in marrying you, then."

She had the grace to blush. "Oh, well... a *second* marriage is quite different. A man may please himself then, you know. But for a first marriage..."

"I take the point." He sighed. "Miss Milburn, then."

5: Chance And Good Fortune

Charles had a chance to view his prospective bride in happier circumstances at church on Sunday. All three sisters attended, arriving just as the Starlingford carriage was disgorging its occupants. His eye was instantly drawn to the pretty middle sister, clutching a handful of primroses, which she arranged carefully on a freshly-dug grave near the lych gate. Pretty and sentimental, then, for old Bill Smith, the present smith's grandfather, could mean nothing to her. The youngest sister bore a vacuous expression, so his gaze passed swiftly on to Miss Milburn. She was studying him with some intensity, and not with favour, to judge by her unsmiling countenance. His step-mother diverted his attention, and when he next looked, the sisters were halfway to the church door.

The angle of the Leatham pew was such that he could see nothing of the sisters during the services, but there they were outside the church as the worshippers spilt out into the churchyard, the vicar busily introduced them to the worthies of Bursham St Matthew. His step-mother bustled across to the trio straight away, gesturing to him to follow. Reluctantly, his heart sinking at the prospect of three simpering females, he did so.

"Miss Milburn!" his step-mother called breezily. "Do let me introduce you to my son. Come along, Charles, and meet the Miss Milburns. This is my son Charles, who would much rather be off with the army than lounging about at home, I am sure. The country is very dull for an active young man, but your coming is just the thing to liven us up. Charles, this is Miss Milburn, Miss Elinor Milburn and Miss Penelope Milburn."

He bowed, they curtsied and he waited politely for Miss Milburn to speak first.

"How do you do, Mr Leatham. Have you run down any more young ladies lately?" Miss Milburn said.

If she had smiled he might have thought it a jest, but her expression was anything but friendly. "I do not make a habit of it, madam."

"I am very glad to hear it. It would be shocking indeed if we could not walk about the footpaths and byways of Hampshire without the fear of being mown down by gentlemen riding too fast."

"I was not riding too fast!" he began, before catching his step-mother's delicately raised eyebrow. Quickly, he turned to the youngest sister. "I trust you suffered no harm from our unfortunate encounter, Miss Poppy?"

"Oh no, except that the dear little mouse ran away. I do so love mice, don't you?"

"Erm… I cannot say…"

"Although Caro says that we must let the barn cat roam the house and it kills all the dear little mice. That is such a pity, isn't it? Susie screams when she sees one, but I like them. Such funny little creatures, with their tiny noses! But we are to have chickens soon, just as soon as Caro can arrange it. Baby chickens are such darlings, aren't they?"

"Erm..." He looked helplessly round for support, but found his step-mother engrossed in a discussion with Mr Christopher. Miss Elinor had wandered off to fiddle with the flowers she had left on Bill Smith's grave. Only Miss Milburn remained. Desperately, he said, "And how do you like this part of Hampshire, Miss Milburn? It is very different from Romsey."

"Oh, very. I have never seen so much mud in my life before."

Again he looked for any sign of humour in her manner, but could see none. "It is an inevitable consequence of wet weather," he said coldly. "You will grow accustomed."

"I am sure of it, but that does not make it an attraction. The town is superior to the country in every way, in my opinion."

"That is because you know nothing of the matter," he said hotly. "The country has so much beauty in its woods and fields, so much open space and good, clean air, so much freedom to move about untrammelled by crowds or a press of vehicles. There is no comparison."

"Indeed there is not. Towns have convenience, cleanliness and every want within easy reach. The country has wild animals everywhere, hostile gamekeepers, pleasant walks made dangerous by young men riding too fast, and mud. Inordinate quantities of mud."

"Miss Milburn, it is disingenuous to—" His eye was drawn by the younger Miss Milburns, who were now in animated discussion with several members of the Smith family at the flower-strewn graveside. "Do tell me, why has your sister laid flowers on the grave of a man she cannot have known?"

"Oh, that is Lin's latest scheme to make money," Miss Milburn said calmly. "She thinks if she makes up posies of pretty flowers, she can sell them to grieving relations."

"But why could they not pick their own flowers?"

"They could, of course. Lin will work that out, in time. For the moment, she is happily occupied scouring our wilderness of a garden for wild blooms and tying them into pretty bunches with ribbon."

He could think of no sensible answer to this, so attempted none. He threw a helpless glance at his step-mother, who at last recognised his dilemma and came to his rescue, sweeping him off to their carriage, where his father waited patiently for them.

"They are crazy, those Milburn girls," Charles said, as he helped his step-mother to her seat. "Are you quite sure you want me to marry one of them, Mama?"

"Perfectly sure," she said. Then, as he tucked a rug around her against any chills, she added, "Not the younger ones, for they would not suit you at all, but Miss Milburn will do admirably. I shall call upon her again this week, and you may accompany me, like the dutiful son you are, and then you will see."

"Will I," he said, not in the least convinced.

But as he watched Mildred break off her earnest discussion with Mr Christopher on the nuances of his sermon text and approach the carriage, Miss Milburn, for all her antipathy towards him, seemed very much the lesser evil.

~~~~~

John Christopher arrived at the kitchen door promptly at seven o'clock the following morning, armed with his own scythe and whetstone, and was directed at once to the neglected lawns.
~~~~~

"Aye, I knew you'd be needing me," he said smugly. "Mr Wishaw always did the garden himself, but he were never interested in the lawns. Always let them get long. Now the kitchen gardens, he'd be there digging and hoeing and weeding till all hours, but the lawns he cared nothing for."

When she took a tankard of ale out to him mid-morning, Caroline said, "Why are you not at school, Mr Christopher? With your father a clergyman, I'd have thought you'd have been chained to a desk with your Greek primers."

He laughed. "Nay, I'm no scholar, and Father never expected it of me. There's no money for schooling, Miss Milburn, not at the parsonage. Father's taught us our letters and some numbering, but that's the extent of it. Tossed out at twelve to make our way, we are. Anne and Lucy are in service, and I help out at the Starlingford Home Farm in the summer. Now Walter — he shows some cleverness. Father's teaching him Latin and a bit of Greek. Might get a scholarship, who knows? He's ten, and maybe he'll make something of himself, but the rest of us are only good for scything."

He laughed, not in the least discomfited, and Caroline left him to it. He was a good worker, and fast, for the garden quickly emerged from its wrapping of long grass and weeds. It was surprising how much better the house looked when the ragged, brown grasses surrounding it were scythed down to the ground and the green spring shoots were visible. Before long, a path to the kitchen garden had been uncovered, and Lin was able to don her stoutest boots and gloves, and begin work on her project of supplying the house with fresh vegetables and herbs. First, however, they needed seeds, and the helpful Mr Christopher informed them of a lady in Bursham All Saints who could supply them with several of their most urgent requirements. Since

Bursham All Saints also contained a grocer and a haberdasher, it was no hardship to decide that an early visit was very necessary, despite the mud on the lanes.

Bursham All Saints was a rather larger village than their own, and the home of the local physician, although Caroline felt that the apothecary in their own village and Lin's herbal remedies would be sufficient for most needs. She vividly remembered the costs associated with Papa's last illness, and again with Mama. Such expense was not to be thought of except in the direst of situations. After a pleasant hour at the home of the wheelwright's mother, filling their basket with seedlings and cuttings and small packets of seeds, followed by visits to the haberdasher and grocer, they turned their steps towards home.

They had just passed the Starlingford farm when the noise of horses and rumbling wheels drove them to move to the side of the lane. A splendid procession drew into view, comprising two curricles, one drawn by a pair of black horses, the other by white ones, followed by a small carriage with two gentlemen sitting rigidly inside, looking neither to right nor to left, and then no fewer than two luggage wagons and finally, some distance behind, two outriders. Only when all the carriages had gone by and the outriders drew nearer, one on a fine white horse, the other on a black, and both outlandishly dressed in the fashionable style, did Caroline begin to suspect that the gentlemen in the carriage might be merely valets and that these two smart young men were the owners of so much grandeur.

They drew their horses gently to a halt alongside the sisters.

"Well, well, what have we here?" said one.

"Three fair maids all in a row," the other said, as in unison they doffed their hats and bowed.

"Whither bound, fair maids?" said the first, his white horse pawing the ground beneath him.

"And who may you be?" said the second.

"And by what happy chance comes there such an assembly of beauteous maidenhood?"

They were perhaps five and twenty, very handsome and as like each other as they could stare. Caroline was not inclined to answer such a nonsensical opening, especially as she had no idea who the two men might be, and she could see Lin's doubtful expression mirroring her own.

Poppy, however, had no such inhibitions. "We are the Milburn sisters, and we are bound for our home at Bursham Cottage. But who are you?"

The two men, who must surely be brothers, exchanged surprised glances, and then both dismounted, one to the left of his horse and the other to the right.

"Why, you must be the new tenants—"

"— in Mr Wishaw's house. We heard he was drowned and dead—"

"—in the *Brig Minerva*."

Poppy shook her head, her delicate curls bobbing around her face. "No, we own it. He left it to us, because Mama was—Ouch! Why did you kick me, Caro?"

"Too forthcoming with strangers," she said sharply. Poppy subsided, but with large, reproachful eyes.

"Oh, how remiss of us—"

"—not to introduce ourselves! I am Edward Alsager and this is—"

"Elliott Alsager of Corranwater. Edward is the elder by less than an hour, but I do not mind, for—"

"—we share everything equally. We are the very best—"

"—of friends!"

They beamed at each other, and even Caroline's natural hostility towards the new and unknown could not withstand their good humour. They were Lord Elland's sons, she presumed, and two more easy-going young men it would be hard to meet. They walked the rest of the way home with the sisters, chattering readily on all manner of subjects, and commenting on minute changes as they passed through Bursham St Matthew — "Why, look, brother, Jeremiah Pierce has—" "—painted his door red!"

They made Caroline laugh, but when the brothers had escorted them to their gate and ridden away, and the sisters were walking up the drive admiring their newly-shorn lawn, she said to Lin and Poppy, "They are very affable, I dare say, but they are the sons of a baron and not for the likes of us."

"Of course not!" Lin said at once.

"What do you mean?" Poppy said, wrinkling her nose bewilderedly.

"Do not let yourself become fond of either of them, that is all," Caroline said.

"She means we must not think of marrying above our station," Lin said, with unwonted seriousness. "We are not of the gentry, and so we should not aspire to marry gentlemen. Men with a respectable trade or profession, that is where we should be looking for husbands."

In principle, Caroline agreed wholeheartedly, and the barony would be ambitious indeed, but Mr Leatham? That was certainly a possibility for Lin, so beautiful as she was. So she said cautiously, "Of course, if a gentleman should fall in love with one of us... that would be different. We might consider it then."

"I shouldn't like to marry too high," Lin said. "It would be uncomfortable, I think. But someone like Papa — a linen draper, or... or something of that nature... that would be very acceptable. I should know how to behave in such a situation."

That did not sound too promising for Mr Leatham. Caroline sighed. Where in this corner of Hampshire were they to find a husband for Lin? They were surrounded by the out-of-reach sons of the nobility, or else the sons of the soil, the farmers and millers and carpenters who were very good and worthy people, but not at all the life she wanted for her sister. It was very difficult.

Susie greeted them on the doorstep in great excitement. "Mr Stratton was here again and—"

"Mr Stratton!" Lin said. "How kind of him to call!"

"Aye, with three other gen'lemen, lawyers like hisself. You not being in, they've gone to the inn to see about rooms, since they'll likely not get back to Romsey tonight. They're to come back in an hour. Left cards on the mantel."

She nodded towards the parlour, and with only the briefest pause to remove muddied boots, the three sisters rushed in to retrieve the cards. Mr Stratton's they were already familiar with, but there were three new ones. *'Mr P Willerton-Forbes, of Markham, Willerton-Forbes and Browning, Gray's Inn, London'* and *'Captain M Edgerton, late of the East India Company Army'*, Caroline read. The final card said only *'J Neate'*, with a London address.

When the gentlemen arrived, Caroline took them into the study, its masculine air seeming more appropriate for what sounded like a matter of business. Mr Willerton-Forbes and Captain Edgerton looked nothing at all like lawyers, to Caroline's mind. At least, when placed alongside the plain, sober clothes of Mr Stratton they looked nothing like lawyers, their attire being of a sort which might have graced the streets of London. Mr Neate was a slender man dressed all in black, who was a secretary to the other two.

Mr Stratton was his usual beaming self, introducing his colleagues briskly, but then allowing his eyes to stray towards Lin. "Delighted to see you again, ladies! Quite delighted! You have been greatly in my mind, wondering how you go on, you see. But look how cosy this room is already, with a lace cloth here and a vase of spring flowers on the mantel. There is nothing like the feminine touch, I declare, to make a house into a home, and as for the garden — now there I see the artistry of Miss Elinor at work already."

"Lin's artistry, perhaps, but John Christopher's scythe," Caroline said crisply. "Please sit, gentlemen, and tell us how we may help a London lawyer and a captain of the East Indian Army."

"Ah, but they are here to help *you*," Mr Stratton said, his grin so wide that it reached almost from one ear to the other. "I have told them who you are and they are quite satisfied— I beg your pardon, Mr Willerton-Forbes. You must tell the tale in your own way, of course."

The London lawyer had done no more than raise one finger, but it was enough to subdue Mr Stratton.

"Miss Milburn, Miss Elinor, Miss Penelope, thank you for receiving us without prior notice. We are obliged to Mr Stratton for his good offices in introducing us to you, and also for furnishing us with the proof of your identity which we required for our purpose. It is most convenient for us that he has already made those same enquiries into your family in order to fulfil the terms of the late Mr Abraham Wishaw's will. I congratulate you on your good fortune! This is a splendid property, and I trust you will enjoy your residence here."

"Thank you, sir," Caroline said. "We are indeed grateful for Mr Wishaw's benevolence, and are very happy to be settled here."

"I have more good fortune to impart to you," Mr Willerton-Forbes said. "Mr Wishaw was tragically drowned in the sinking of the *Brig Minerva* off the Cornish coast two months ago. Three and twenty souls were lost in the disaster, but one of them was the Duke of Falconbury, and so the event drew notice from higher levels than would normally be the case, and was much reported in the newspapers and discussed in the London saloons and clubs. As a result, one person in particular was very moved by the loss of life, and decided to assist the few survivors and the next of kin of those drowned. This person, whom we call the Benefactor, knowing no other name, wishes to give you, as Mr Wishaw's nearest kin, one thousand pounds, free of all restrictions."

Mr Stratton, who had been practically bouncing with excitement on his chair, now burst out, "Is that not wonderful news? One thousand pounds to add to the five thousand that Mr Wishaw left you — a tidy sum! A very tidy sum! This must set your mind quite at rest, Miss Milburn, as to your ability to meet the additional expenses of your new home."

They all gazed at her, Lin and Poppy too, waiting for her to express her pleasure at the unexpected largesse. One thousand pounds. Another forty pounds a year, if invested prudently. A dowry, perhaps, of two thousand pounds apiece, if it should be needed. The formless fears of future poverty receded slightly. Yes, even Caroline could not be displeased by the increase in their wealth.

She laughed. "There is some Madeira in the cellar, gentlemen. This might be an appropriate time to sample it, do you not agree?"

6: Searching

One morning, Lin and Poppy were out in the garden, Susie was humming upstairs, and Martin and Molly were in the kitchen preparing breakfast, so Caroline set out her lacemaking cushion for the first time since the move. She looked at the half-completed piece in dissatisfaction. It was a narrow strip, only good for trimming or perhaps an elegant fichu, but ever since Mama's death that was all she had felt able to work on. Quick pieces that could be traded for the much-needed coins at Mr Turner's shop every two or three weeks. Before that she and Mama had worked side by side on much finer pieces, like wedding veils, collars and caps, and Caroline's favourite, fans. There was nothing like a lace fan for adding elegance to a lady.

Resolutely, she finished off the current piece. It was not up to her usual standard, so perhaps she would keep it for herself, as a smart fichu. Then she began to dress her pillow for a new piece, a fan, but something more elaborate, in Mama's delicate style. Breakfast was a brief interruption before she went back to work in the parlour. Oh, the joy of making lace again! Her worries about their new life had receded somewhat, for they had enough money to live on, her sisters were safe in the garden, Susie was happy since she had learnt to leave the kitchen to Molly, and even their inherited servants had settled into some semblance of usefulness.

She was startled out of her absorption by the sound of carriage wheels and hoof beats. With a sigh, she pushed away her pillow stand, and went to the window. Mrs Leatham's carriage, and this time two cards were handed to the footman to be delivered to the door. *'Mrs Ambrose Leatham'* and *'Mr Charles Leatham'*, Caroline read, when Susie brought the cards into the parlour. Well, these morning calls were tedious, but perhaps this one had possibilities.

"Show Mrs Leatham and Mr Charles Leatham in, wait to see if they want any tea, and then run and fetch Lin from her patch of dirt in the garden."

"Not Poppy?" Susie said, then got the point. "Ah, Lin."

Susie dashed out to the hall again, and Caroline had no time to do more than check in the mirror over the mantel that nothing was askew before the visitors were upon her.

"Ah, Miss Milburn... all alone?" Mrs Leatham said.

"My sisters have been drawn out by the fine weather to do a little weeding in the kitchen garden."

"Well, no matter. I would not disturb them for the world. I have brought my son to see you today, Miss Milburn. He has been most anxious to further his acquaintance with you, have you not, Charles?"

He bowed, saying nothing.

The offer of refreshment was made and accepted, and Susie bobbed a neat curtsy and disappeared to attend to it. She was rather well suited to drawing room appearances, Caroline thought. She had been a kindly if haphazard nurse and an indifferent cook, but was turning out to be an efficient house maid.

Caroline and Mrs Leatham sat decorously on facing chairs, while Mr Leatham milled about the room, slapping his gloves against his thigh as he walked. Caroline waited politely for Mrs Leatham to begin the conversation.

"And how are you settling in, Miss Milburn?" she said, not waiting for a reply. "Mr Popham tells me that you are buying your tea from him, but I must advise against it. He is a very good sort of grocer for ordinary wares, such as flour and sugar, but I would not buy tea from him. He does not look after it well, and that affects the taste. You must go to my fellow in Salisbury, Higgins. He is very good, and will not overcharge if you mention my name."

"I should hope he would not overcharge at any time," Caroline said indignantly.

Mrs Leatham stared at her, then said, "Oh! Oh, I see what you mean. I mean only that you will be offered his best price if he understands that you are a neighbour of mine." Then, without pausing for breath, she said, "I trust your visit from the London lawyers went off satisfactorily. Oh, you need not look so conscious, and I shall not pry, although one might guess their business with you."

"Might one?" Caroline said faintly, trying to work out how Mrs Leatham even knew they were from London.

"Oh, yes. The Benefactor's purpose is in all the newspapers. It is quite a puzzle as to who might be giving such large sums to those connected with that poor ship that went down, but I expect it must be something to do with the dear Queen, do you not think? Ladies are so readily affected by a sad story, and who else would have so much money to hand?"

"The new Duke of Falconbury," Mr Leatham said. He had been gazing vacantly around the room, but he snapped back to attention abruptly at this new subject, lounging against a window frame to face his mother.

"Oh. Do you think so? Distress at his brother's death, I suppose?" his mother said. "And he is very rich, naturally... a duke, after all... and his estates are vast. Why, part of his land borders yours, Miss Milburn, and Valmont is more than ten miles away from here. Beyond Corranford one is entirely surrounded by the duke's property. Have you settled on a coal merchant yet, Miss Milburn? We get ours from Powney, and it is always of excellent quality, although he is not terribly reliable as to deliveries. He never quite appears just when one expects him."

"Mr Wishaw got his coal from Dunn's," Caroline said. "I see no reason to change. Unless he overcharges us, of course."

"Oh. Oh well, Dunn's is reliable enough, I daresay."

Susie returned with the tea and cakes. Caroline mouthed *'Lin?'* at her, but she gave a slight shake of the head. Mrs Leatham talked and ate and talked and drank, without much pause for breath. Fortunately, she required little in the way of response, but Caroline, her fingers itching to get back to her lace, heartily wished her long gone. Mr Leatham settled on a chair, accepted a cup of tea, gulped it in three mouthfuls and then resumed his restless prowl.

After a few minutes, he stopped, gazing out of the side window towards the kitchen garden. "Whatever are your sisters doing?" he said. "They appear to be chasing butterflies."

Caroline laughed. "So they may be. Poppy has always been fascinated by them."

"How delightful!" Mrs Leatham cried, springing up and rushing to the window. "How charming! Charles, you will not mind if I go outside and further my acquaintance with the younger Miss Milburns? You may stay here and drink your tea with Miss Milburn."

She left the room, leaving Caroline bemused. Mr Leatham scowled as if he had been sucking lemons, but he made no protest, sitting down on his chair again, playing idly with the gloves he had discarded on the table beside it.

"More tea, Mr Leatham?" Caroline said.

"Thank you, but no."

What on earth was she to say to him? His brooding silence had not mattered when his mother had been there to fill the void with her chatter, but Caroline had not the least idea how to make conversation with such an awkward man.

Eventually she said, "We made some new friends yesterday — the Alsager brothers."

He grunted, but made no comment.

"You must know them very well, being neighbours."

"Not really."

"Oh... but surely, when you are much of an age—"

"Just because we are the same age does not mean we have to live in each other's pockets, you know," he said angrily. "I have nothing at all in common with those two wastrels, I am happy to say. *They* may spend their lives sweet talking every female within a twenty mile distance, but some of us have better things to do with our time. Never was a pair so spoilt! Every whim gratified, every extravagance permitted and every folly indulged. I am sure you found them very agreeable—"

"Very," she said at once. The contrast between the amiable twins and the ill-mannered Mr Charles Leatham was striking.

"—but do not be fooled and get your hopes up, Miss Milburn. They have both been betrothed these three years or more, but do they show the least sign of settling down? Not a bit of it! Instead they gad about the country with no thought of their responsibilities."

Caroline was incensed by his presumption that she might have set her cap at one of the brothers, but couldn't think of a sufficiently cutting response on the spur of the moment, which only made her the angrier.

"*Some* of us know the meaning of the word *duty*," he said. "Ha! Some of us know what it means to suffer obligation and deprivation."

That was too much to be borne. "What have you ever known of deprivation!" Caroline cried, jumping to her feet in rage. "You were born rich! When have you ever had to decide whether to eat meat or buy new shoes? When have you had to go to bed at five o'clock because you couldn't afford candles, or wood for the fire? When have you ever worked from dawn till dusk without a break because you needed the money? You know nothing of suffering!"

He shot to his feet too, his eyes narrowed as he looked her up and down disdainfully. "And what do *you* know of the obligations of rank? Of tenants and servants and entire villages looking to you for help? Of having to decide whether to repair a roof here or improve the drainage there? Of not being *able* to work, even if you want to, because you have to be a landlord and magistrate and figurehead for the parish? Of having to marry without affection or even liking, because of *duty?* What do you know of *that*, Miss Milburn?" His face was contorted with anger. "Pa! It is useless to argue with someone like you! You know nothing of the realities of life."

And so saying, he stormed out of the room, leaving Caroline seething. When Mrs Leatham returned some minutes later, however, she only laughed.

"Poor Charles! He has been like a bear ever since he came home from the army. He will be much more settled once he is safely married."

"Oh, is he engaged?" Caroline said.

Mrs Leatham smiled at her. "Not yet, my dear, but he will be before long, I am certain of it. We shall have him married before the summer is out, I expect. Well, I shall take my leave of you, Miss Milburn. Do remember that we are at home on Thursdays. I shall expect to see you at Starlingford on Thursday next."

"But—"

"No, no, I positively insist. You must not be shy, you know. Even though you have not been used to these morning calls, you are in a different level of society now. You may bring your sisters with you, if you wish."

So saying, she swept out, leaving Caroline with very mixed feelings. Although she automatically sat down at her lacemaking chair to begin work, she could not clear her mind sufficiently to pick up the bobbins. Making morning calls was for ladies who had nothing better to do. A different level of society? She had no ambition for it. Lin, perhaps... she was too beautiful to have to spend the rest of her life working for her bread, or grubbing in the dirt like a peasant, although any hope Caroline had harboured of Mr Charles Leatham appeared gone. He was already spoken for, it seemed. She could only hope that his wife might teach him better manners, or else plague him to death. Or both, and serve him right.

It was just as well she had not begun to work again, for no sooner had the dust settled behind the Leathams' carriage that Lady Elland's rather grander one rolled up the drive. With a sigh, Caroline prepared to receive another morning caller. This visit was rather pleasanter, however, for her ladyship brought her two sons with her. They bounced in, dressed as extravagantly as if they were in London, as excitable as before, gaily wandering about the room examining this and that, finishing each other's sentences and making Caroline laugh with their antics. And, miraculously, their happy natures had even affected their mother, who smiled and chuckled at their jests and said, "Oh, you two monkeys!" at frequent intervals. Caroline could see at once how it was that Mr Leatham described them as spoilt and over-indulged, for in their mother's eyes they could do no wrong.

They stayed for almost an hour, sipping tea and crumbling cake, and after they had gone, Caroline discovered a small posy of flowers and a box of some sugared confection left on the hall console, with a little note saying, *'Welcome to Bursham St Matthew'*. Mr Leatham, however, had only left his gloves. So careless with their possessions, these rich people! She placed them on the console, and supposed she was now obliged to go to Starlingford, if only to return his gloves to the forgetful Mr Leatham.

~~~~~

That Sunday, Caroline began to feel for the first time that they were beginning to be part of the parish community. They were
~~~~~

greeted by so many people, and introduced to as many more, that it was hard not to feel that they were making friends. John Christopher, their gardener, was instrumental in drawing them into his extensive collection of youthful relations and friends in a way that his father, being a generation older, could not do. Poppy, in particular, seemed to relish meeting so many people of her own age, and since they seemed to be sensible people, Caroline hoped they would be a good influence on her dreamy young sister.

Not being able to work on a Sunday had not been problematic in Romsey, for they had sat out in their back yard, for once free of washing, gossiping with the house's other residents or passing neighbours, and when it was wet, they had collected in the big kitchen. Here they were stuck out in the midst of fields and woods with no neighbours, and only Susie, Martin and Molly to gossip with. Luckily, they now had a big garden, and Lin took Caroline all round their domain for her to admire the early apple and pear blossom, the emerging lawns and the newly dug vegetable bed. Only a small portion of the kitchen garden was yet reclaimed, but Lin had great plans for the rest.

"I'll make some early sowings tomorrow, and then begin work on this next bed. Mr Wishaw left most of it in good order, but of course it was neglected over the winter, and he left some portions fallow by intent. His notes are in the tool room at the back of the stables, and there are some seeds from last year, too, so I'm very well supplied. But Caro, Poppy wants her chickens as soon as may be, and there's an old hen house behind the stables that would do very well, if it could be repaired. There's spare wood there, and tools, and John will do it, and he can get some layers for us from his mother for a few shillings, or chicks if we prefer. Poppy wants chicks, of course, but then we'd have to wait for eggs. What do you say? May I tell John to do it?"

"By all means," Caroline said. "Yes, we promised Poppy some hens, and we must keep our word. Get chicks if that's what she wants, but she must take care of them herself. You two may have found new occupations for your hands, but I plan to continue making lace."

Lin looked slightly conscious. "You're very good not to nag us about getting the looms set up," she said. "At least my herbs and vegetables will save us some expense, and we can sell the surplus and Poppy's eggs, too, eventually. She wants to get a milking goat, too, but I think I've dissuaded her from rushing into that."

"Yes, one thing at a time," Caroline said. "Let's see how she gets on with the chickens first. She's not good at keeping to a task." A pause, then she added, "Where is Poppy, anyway? Has she wandered off again?"

"If she has, she'll be back for her dinner," Lin said with a slight shrug.

"Just so long as she doesn't go onto Lord Elland's land," Caroline said fretfully. "Mr Grison patrols in those woods very stringently."

"She won't," Lin said confidently.

A quick look around the house showed that Poppy was nowhere indoors, and neither Susie nor Molly had seen her. Caroline scanned the garden, but there was no sign of her, nor was she anywhere in the stables. The fear that Poppy had disappeared into the woods grew on Caroline, and once there, she could easily encounter Mr Grison and his gun. He was clearly conscientious about his work and accidents happened.

Her anxiety could only be kept at bay by activity. She left Lin to her contemplation of the garden, and walked across the road to the footpath that led into Lord Elland's woodland. It was a wide, open track and anyone on it would be clearly visible for some distance... surely even Mr Grison could not mistake Poppy for a poacher? But she recalled that Mr Leatham had not seen Poppy in her dark cloak, even on the track, and if she should see something in the undergrowth to either side... It did not bear thinking about. There was nothing for it but to go in search of her.

"Poppy? Where are you, Poppy?" she called out as she walked, but there was no answering cry.

Instead, a man popped out of the trees directly ahead of her, a shotgun under one arm, and a bulging bag over one shoulder.

"Oh, Mr Grison, you startled me," she said. "I'm just looking for my sister."

"She ain't here. I've been patrolling all day, and ain't seen a sight of her, and if I'd have seen her, I'd have told her to get off his lordship's land. And I'll tell you the same, Miss. No business here, any of you."

"Oh. Well, if you should see her, please tell her to come home at once." She looked again at the shotgun and the full bag. "Are you shooting things on a Sunday, Mr Grison?"

He grinned at her. "Rabbits, poachers and thieves don't take no notice of the Sabbath, Miss, so neither do I."

Caroline disagreed with him rather strongly, but she wasn't about to argue with a man holding a gun, so she turned round and went back to the house to await Poppy there. But as the hour for their dinner drew near, there was still no sign of her. She was nowhere to be found in the house, the outbuildings or the garden.

"She'll come home when she's hungry," Susie said.

"But when will that be?" Caroline said. "If Mr Grison—"

"She knows not to go onto Lord Elland's land," Lin said. "Besides, Mr Grison said she wasn't there. She likes the farm, where all the baby animals are. I expect she is there."

"Yes, of course," Caroline said, relief hitting her with force. "That's where she'll be, and no notion of the time. I'll just go over there and—"

"You worry too much," Lin said with a smile. "Poppy's not a child, and she's not stupid. She'll be home when she's ready, then she'll be wondering what all the fuss is about."

Susie laughed. "No use telling your sister not to worry, Miss Lin. She took on the responsibility for you two when your mother died, and she'll never stop fretting over you, so you might as well get used to it. The mutton'll keep for another half hour yet, Miss Caro, so you go and see if she's at the farm, petting the lambs or some such."

The afternoon air was cooler, so Caroline wrapped herself in a warm shawl and walked down the garden to the stile that led to one of their own two fields, now empty of crops or beasts. A narrow footpath led straight towards the farm, kept free of weeds by Martin's boots as he passed to and fro to collect milk or eggs and the odd duck or pigeon that happened to fall into his basket when Mrs Neilson felt generous towards her neighbours. The farmyard was deserted except for one man tending the animals, but when she asked after Poppy, he smiled and directed her to the kitchen door.

There she was, surrounded by various members of the Neilson family, and in her arms a tiny baby.

"Caro!" she cried delightedly. "Look, isn't she sweet? So tiny! Just three days old, and so good, not a whimper out of her all day. This is Ruby, her mother, she's Davy's wife, and you know Mrs Neilson, don't you? And Alice and Dora and..."

Caroline smiled and said hello and yes, she was a lovely baby and yes, she was very good and so like her father, and would Poppy like to hand the baby back to its mother now and come home for dinner?

"Oh, is it dinner time already? But may I come again tomorrow? You won't mind, Caro, will you? Ruby says I'm such a help, and I do love to hold her."

"You can come again if Ruby wants, and Mrs Neilson doesn't mind, but just tell us where you're going, won't you?"

"Oh yes, of course."

But she wouldn't, Caroline knew that. The urge to wander was too powerful and too instantaneous for Poppy to take thought of others.

That day, for the first time since their arrival, they sat down to eat in the dining room. At first it had seemed easier to eat in the kitchen with the three servants, but Martin and Molly had been uncomfortable with the arrangement and Susie had nagged them, too.

"You're not servants like us, you're the family, and you should eat properly with the decent spoons and plates, and crystal for your wine, and covers on the table, just like you did when your poor, dear papa was alive," she had said.

So today they sat in state in the dining room, although there was only one course with no removes and the meat had been carved in the kitchen. Still, Caroline felt it was right. They had sunk in the world since Papa's death, and now Mr Wishaw had raised them up again. They were not gentry, and never would be, but they were respectable and had their own place in the world.

"Let's have a glass of wine with our dinner, to celebrate," Caroline said. "There's some Madeira in the study still, from when those lawyers were here. I'll fetch that."

She made her way quickly to the study, picked up the bottle of Madeira and turned back towards the door. Only then did she notice that one of the drawers of the desk was slightly open. She frowned. That was not as she had left it, for she liked order and tidiness, and leaving a drawer ajar was not something she would ever do.

Alert now, she scanned the rest of the room. One of the cupboard doors was not properly latched, and a look inside revealed that the account books, left in a neat pile in date order, were now scattered higgledy-piggledy along the shelf.

There was no doubt about it. Someone had been there, searching in haste for something, since she had last been in the room the previous day. One of the servants? Or had they been burgled? And if so, why?

7: Locks And Keys

Two minutes were sufficient to determine that no one in the house had been rummaging about in the study. The servants were convincingly outraged at the very idea, and Lin and Poppy knew nothing of it.

"Why would I want anything from the study?" Poppy said, mystified. "If I did, I'd ask you."

"No one goes into the study but you," Lin said. "Well, apart from Susie, to tidy the fireplace and dust."

"Someone must have got in while we were at church," Susie said.

"But I locked the front door," Caroline said.

"Kitchen door's always open," Susie said. "No one'd bother to lock that, would they?"

After dinner, a search of the rest of the house revealed nothing out of place. The only room with any sign of having been searched was the study.

"I expect it was one of Lord Elland's sons," Lin said. "They leave little surprise gifts everywhere, seemingly. So Anne

Christopher said. They were not in church, after all. And Mr Leatham left his gloves. Maybe he came to find them."

"He was in church, and there are no gifts from the Alsagers," Caroline said. "More likely it was that gamekeeper, Grison," she added darkly. "He was wandering about the woods all day, so he said, and I can imagine him sneaking in and looking around for money."

But nothing had been taken. In the safe, the money box Caroline had removed from the locked drawer of the desk contained exactly the expected amount of coins, and the pretty netted purse with its five hundred pounds in notes lay untouched. She fingered the purse thoughtfully, admiring the expert workmanship in the delicate pattern. A very female pattern, she thought it. A strange purse to find in a man's safe, but perhaps it had been a gift from a lady.

It was unsettling, but, apart from resolving to leave all the doors locked when they went to church, there was nothing to be done about it.

~~~~~

Charles was never fond of Sundays, with the need for sobriety and church, and no pursuits of a frivolous and therefore enjoyable nature. He could not ride or play cards or read anything other than sermons, and if he tried, ever so surreptitiously, to open a novel, his father would say in his mild way, "Whose sermons are you reading today, Charles?"

Talking was permitted, if the subject were sufficiently serious, and his proposed marriage to Miss Caroline Milburn was serious enough even for his father to approve. After dinner, therefore, when Mildred had gone to her room to write her weekly duty letter to her sole remaining relative, a very elderly
~~~~~

great-aunt in Harrogate, Mrs Leatham laid out her strategy for a successful courtship.

"You should not visit her alone, for that would look far too particular," she said. "Nor can I visit again so soon. I have hopes, however, that she will call here on Thursday, so that Mr Leatham may meet and approve her."

"If she is your choice, my dear, I shall not have any grounds for disapproval, I am sure," her husband said, beaming at her. "She sounds a very pleasant girl, and although her mother's birth was rather unfortunate, she made a sound marriage, and the father was quite respectable."

"Respectable?" Charles said, eyebrows raised. "You find nothing objectionable in seeing your grandchildren raised by the daughter of a linen draper?"

"We are notare so high in the instep as all that, Charles. The children will live here where your dear mama will oversee their education, and ensure that your wife knows what is expected of her. No, I have no worries on that score."

"She has no dowry," Charles said.

"I am not quite destitute yet, you know."

His step-mother added, "It is simpler if she has nothing, for she will be so grateful when you offer that she will accept at once, and make you a docile and conformable wife."

"Do you think so?" Charles said dubiously. "She does not strike me as the docile and conformable type."

"She will be, once I have trained her for her position in society," she said complacently. "Better by far a girl from a lower level of society who has the potential to be groomed than one already decided in her opinions and manners. You would not be comfortable with anyone too grand, you know. Now, dear, she will call on Thursday, so you must be at home for that. Then you will see her at church on Sunday, and make sure you spend some time talking to her this time. You were far too slow to approach her today, and barely had time to exchange more than a dozen words with her. She will come to dinner next week, and she will be obliged to call to thank us, you know, but if she does not, because she might not know the proper form, then we will call on her again. The following week, you may offer for her, and that will be the worst of it out of the way. After that, you may leave everything to me, to arrange the wedding clothes and so forth. She will need an entire wardrobe, for I am sure she has not a single gown worth keeping. We shall have you married by Midsummer, never fear."

"Midsummer," he repeated, only half attending. "But what if she refuses me?"

"Why ever should she?" his father said. "You are the heir to my estate, and while it is not the largest such in the county, it is unencumbered and the rents are steady year on year."

"And you are a handsome fellow," his step-mother said, patting his cheek fondly. "That will weigh with her, you may be sure. All young ladies like to be wooed by a good-looking man. Besides, what other option does she have? Of course she will accept you."

"And if she does not, there is always Mildred," his father said, with a wry smile.

Charles shuddered, pulling a face. "What about one of the younger sisters?" he said.

"No," his step-mother said firmly. "Caroline is the practical one. The last thing you want is a wife without an ounce of common sense. Our income is not excessive, and an extravagant daughter-in-law would have us rolled up within a year. We can go to Bath, if you prefer," she went on brightly. "Plenty of young ladies to choose from there, and the waters would do us all good, I should think."

"Not Bath!" Charles said with resolution.

His father said, "Not the waters!" at the same moment.

"There is always London." She sighed. "I should dearly love to go to London again. The entertainments! The excitement and bustle!"

"The crowds, the expense, the hideous prospect of dancing every evening," Charles said. He exhaled slowly. "Well, it will have to be Miss Milburn, then."

~~~~~

Two days later, the study was again attacked, and this time it was during the night. Caroline left the room in perfect order at four o'clock when she went to tidy herself before dinner, and at seven the next morning the door to the cupboard hiding the safe was very slightly ajar, and a blob of candle wax on the floor betrayed the existence of a night-time intruder. The safe itself was still securely locked, the key one of those Caroline kept always on her person, nor was anything missing from within it.

"I don't like the idea of someone prowling about down here while we were fast asleep upstairs," Caroline said. "It's unnerving."

"We could have been murdered in our beds," Lin said in shocked tones.

"That seems unlikely," Caroline said briskly. "This person is looking for something, not bent on violence."
~~~~~

"No, but if we'd been awake and come downstairs for... for something to eat, as anyone might, we could have encountered him in the very act of breaking in and been hit over the head... or some such."

"And how did he break in, that's what I should like to know," Caroline said. "There are no open windows and both the doors were locked, so how we are to prevent him walking in any time he likes, I cannot guess."

They were still pondering this when a horse trotted up the drive.

"It is Mr Stratton!" Lin cried. "He will know what to do!"

Caroline would not normally regard it as necessary to have a man tell them what to do, except for poor, dear Papa, of course, but in this case she felt that Mr Stratton's advice would be beneficial. He immediately summoned Martin and Molly to the study, and asked them severely who else might have a key to the house.

"No one, sir, truly!" Martin said. "Mr Wishaw were very careful about such things, and had the locks changed regular, and when he were away, he had the gates padlocked, too. He were very particular about locking up at night, too — always did that himself, and drew all the bolts, and put a chain across the front door."

"And who does that now — locking up at night, that is?"

"Dunno, sir. Not me. Mr Wishaw never trusted me to do it, and Miss Milburn's not asked me to."

"I never imagined it to be necessary," Caroline said. "In Romsey a simple bolt was enough. I noticed all the extra bolts and chains, but I thought Mr Wishaw perhaps had valuables for his business to protect. Well, I suppose we shall have to be more careful in future. I'll lock up myself every night."

"That means securing every external door and ensuring the windows are securely closed and shuttered," Mr Stratton said. "It is a good habit to get into. You have some quite valuable silverware here that might attract a thief."

When the servants had been dismissed back to the kitchen, and the four of them had sat down to a belated breakfast in the dining room, Mr Stratton said, "What worries me most about this is wondering what your intruder was looking for."

"Money, surely," Lin said at once. "He tried the safe, after all."

"Money is not the only thing kept in safes," Mr Stratton said, sipping his coffee thoughtfully. "Documents, too, and—"

"Oh!" Caroline said. "Lady Elland asked if we had found any documents of Lord Elland's. Do you remember, Lin?"

"Something relating to his family," Lin said slowly, frowning as she tried to remember. "She didn't say what."

"Or why Mr Wishaw held them," Caroline said. "It seemed odd, to me. We told her to ask Mr Wishaw's business partner."

"Hmm... interesting," Mr Stratton said, then bounced to his feet. "Wait a moment..." He dashed off, returning a few minutes later, grinning from ear to ear. "That is *very* interesting. Martin tells me that the person who fitted the locks to the doors here, and changed them every few years, was none other than Lord Elland's gamekeeper. Grison? Is that the right name? So you see where my thoughts are going..."

"No," Poppy said, looking bewildered.

"Yes," Caroline said. "That Mr Grison kept a key for himself, and broke in. He was in the woods just across the road from here on Sunday, so it could have been him. I thought he was after money, but this makes more sense."

"With your permission, ladies," Mr Stratton said, his eyes gleaming with excitement, "I should like to investigate further. Mr Wishaw's business partner may know something of these documents, and why they are so important to Lord Elland. And while I am calling upon Mr Salter in Salisbury, I shall arrange for a locksmith from there to visit you, to change the locks and advise upon better security. I do not like to think of you all alone here, and a burglar at large in the house. Three ladies like yourselves — you should not have to suffer such distressing events."

But his eyes rested on Lin as he spoke.

~~~~~

The following day, Mr Stratton returned in a fine procession. His horse was followed by a rather splendid chaise and pair, with a postilion, two footmen behind and an outrider, and then, less spectacularly, a modest gig driven by a plainly attired man of middle age, together with a boy of twelve or so.

"Miss Milburn! Miss Elinor!" Mr Stratton cried, as soon as they emerged from the house to greet the arrivals. "Here I am again with company for you, welcome, I hope."

"You are always welcome, Mr Stratton," Lin said, before Caroline could speak. "And your friends, of course."

The friends turned out to be Mr Norrington Salter, an elderly man who had been Mr Wishaw's partner in their hop business, together with his wife, a little woman as round as a pat of butter.
~~~~~

"My dears, what a dreadful time you are having!" she cried, the carriage lurching as she descended without waiting for the footman's assistance. "My dear Miss Milburn!" She enfolded Caroline in her lavender scented embrace. "My dear girl!" Lin squeaked as she, too, was squashed to Mrs Salter's pillowy bosom. "Oh! Where is your youngest sister? Never mind, I'll see her later, I daresay. Oh, you poor things! Nothing is worse than a burglar breaking into one's home."

Caroline could think of many worse things, but she bit back her riposte, appreciating the sentiment even if it was slightly misplaced.

The gig belonged to a locksmith recommended by Mr Salter, and while he and his apprentice disappeared with Martin to appraise the outside of the property, the Salters followed Caroline and Lin into the study.

"Ah, this room is so familiar," Mr Salter said sadly. "Poor Abraham! And such a tragic end, to be taken by the sea when he was yet in the prime of his life."

"He was your age, Mr Salter," said his wife affectionately. "Well enough for his years, but a little past his prime, just as you are. As we both are. Now the Miss Milburns here are in the prime of life, and look at them — owning their own home and everything that's grand. Your father was a linen draper, I understand? Mine was a cordwainer, so I consider myself most fortunate to have caught a man such as Mr Salter, so kind and generous as he is. Do you girls have beaux left behind with broken hearts in Romsey? I'll wager you do! And no need to blush, missy, eh? But you'll find young men enough round here, I make no doubt."

Caroline smiled as best she could and let her rattle on, but she was pleased when Mr Salter brought his wife's chatter to an abrupt end, by saying, "That's enough now, Amabel, for goodness' sake! Don't assault the young ladies' ears any longer."

She subsided at once with a good-natured laugh, not at all put out.

"That's better," her husband said. "Now, Miss Milburn, tell me, if you please, about these documents of Lord Elland's."

Caroline raised her eyebrows. "Why, I know nothing about them. They're not here, that much is certain."

"Hmpf. Curious. Yet Lord Elland came to you asking for them?"

"No, it was Lady Elland. Family papers, she said. Did she come to you? I told her you had taken all the papers relating to the business."

He eyed Caroline shrewdly, as if weighing her up. She thought he would probably be a formidable man to deal with in business, both cunning and quick-witted, to judge by the sharp gleam in his eye, but she had nothing to hide, so she didn't drop her gaze in the slightest.

After a while, he grunted. "*He* came. His lordship. Very pleasant fellow, not at all high and mighty. Abraham had some family papers of his, he said. Wondered if they might have got mixed up with the business documents. Would like to have them back, if they could be found. Never told me what they were about, though. You any idea?"

"None at all."

He grunted again. "Well... if they do turn up, I've a mind to have a look at them myself. Just to make sure that they *are* his precious lordship's and not related to the business. Will you do that, missy? Let me see them?"

Now, Caroline knew of no reason why she shouldn't do as he asked, but there was something sly about his manner that set her back up. It was odd that Mr Wishaw had had Lord Elland's papers in the first place, and doubly odd that his business partner should also be interested in them. If she came across private papers of Lord Elland's, it would be right to return them to him as soon as possible, and not show them around to anyone who asked. So she said slowly, "If I find anything I can't identify, I'll ask Mr Stratton's advice on the matter."

Mr Salter's eyes narrowed suspiciously, but he could hardly press the point, so he said no more on the subject, and after that they talked only about the cottage and the village and nothing in particular.

The Salters stayed for barely an hour, but in that short time they managed to deluge Caroline and Lin with well-meant advice, as well as finishing the half-full bottle of Madeira and eating an entire pound cake. Mrs Salter took care of most of the latter single-handed. "Oh no, I mustn't... but if you press me... perhaps just one more slice," she said several times. Caroline didn't begrudge her the pleasure. There was enough money in the safe now to pay for an extra pound cake now and then.

The locksmith efficiently replaced the locks on all the doors and the desk drawers, and checked all the shutters for soundness, showing Caroline the slender metal rods that slid across to secure them. He fitted bars to the outside of the study windows as an extra deterrent. He examined the safe and its key, but declared that it had come from a very well-known firm in Birmingham, and the lock was the original one, and not one which could be replaced even by a man skilled in the ways of locks, such as himself, and certainly not by an amateur like Mr Grison.

"No, the only way to break into a device as strong as this is to copy the key, and I doubt the previous owner left it lying around, eh?"

"If our thief had had a copy made of the key, we should certainly have found the safe broken into," Mr Stratton said cheerfully. "So no need to worry on that score, Miss Milburn. Just be sure to keep the key on your person at all times, and if you undertake a journey, leave it with a responsible person like a solicitor, as poor Mr Wishaw had the foresight to do."

The locksmith stayed for hours, and Mr Stratton stayed, too. He said he was supervising the work on the locks, but he seemed to spend much of his time wandering about the garden with Lin, or sitting beside her on the seat beneath the twisted old apple tree. When the locksmith cheerily waved them farewell and rattled away down the drive in his gig, the apprentice squeezed in beside him, Lin turned to Mr Stratton and said, "You won't rush away, I hope. Stay for dinner, do."

"Oh... how very kind, but..." He glanced at Caroline.

It was not exactly what she wanted, but she could hardly refuse at that point. "Of course. You'd be very welcome, if you don't mind taking pot luck."

He beamed with delight. "How kind! How very kind you are. I should be delighted to accept. If I secure myself a room at the inn in the village for tonight, I shall not have to rush away straight after dinner and perhaps we could make up a card table."

"Oh, that would be fun!" Lin said.

"We are imposing rather on Mr Stratton's good nature," Caroline said. "He has already spent two days on our affairs, including an overnight stay in Salisbury. I should not be comfortable expecting him to sacrifice another night on our account."

"It is not the least imposition in the world, Miss Milburn," he said. "I assure you, nothing could delight me more than to spend an evening in your charming company. It is no sacrifice, I assure you." His eyes rested on Lin as he spoke.

Caroline had to admit that it was a very convivial evening. Poppy was retrieved early from the farm and the three ladies donned their best gowns in honour of the occasion. Mr Stratton ventured into the cellar and selected what he described as *'a terrifically decent Burgundy — not seen anything like this for years'*. The meal was adequate to the occasion, there being no additional dishes owing to the lack of notice to the cook, but Mr Stratton praised everything, and kept them entertained with a string of amusing anecdotes. Afterwards, he taught Lin the principles of backgammon, while Poppy looked on and Caroline mended stockings.

When he had finally taken himself off to the inn, although with many assurances that he would be welcome to join them for breakfast, the three sisters mounted the stairs to their bedrooms.

Caroline could not restrain herself from saying, "Lin, I hope you won't offer Mr Stratton too much encouragement. I shouldn't like the poor man to suffer a broken heart."

"Oh no, there is no danger of him suffering a broken heart, I assure you."

"That's good," she said, but she wasn't reassured.

8: Making Calls

Thursday arrived, to fill Caroline with gloom.

"Mrs Leatham expects us to visit today," she told Lin and Poppy at breakfast.

Lin pulled a face. "Must we?"

"I don't want to go either, but it would be rude to refuse when she's asked so pointedly. We have to keep on the good side of our neighbours."

"Do we?" Lin said. "Can't we just exchange bows after church and ignore them the rest of the time? They are far above us socially. I can't imagine why Mrs Leatham called on us at all."

"Nor can I, but she has, and she's made it clear she expects us to return the call," Caroline said crisply. "She will realise soon enough that we are not of her class. I shall visit her, certainly, but it would be best if we all go."

"Oh, but John is to set up the chicken coops today," Poppy said, her eyes brimming with tears. "He wants me to be here to show him where I want everything. I can't go, Caro. Please don't make me."

"It is best if we all go," she repeated firmly.

But in the end, Martin set that idea to rest. "I can drive you to Starlin'ford in the gig, right enough, Miss, but Mr Wishaw chose it just for hisself, y'see. Me drivin', 'im sittin' good and comfortable, like. Might squash two of you onto that seat, since you're thin as rails, but not three, not likely."

After some terse discussion, it was agreed that Poppy would stay behind, although Caroline charged Susie with keeping an eye on her. "Make sure she doesn't wander into Lord Elland's woods," she said anxiously. "Mr Grison—"

"Lord, Miss Milburn, you don't give the girl any credit for good sense," Susie said. "Stop fretting. She knows well enough not to wander there."

There was no more that Caroline could do. She and Lin put on their Sunday best gowns and cloaks, clambered into the gig on either side of Martin, and lurched away down the drive, waved off by John Christopher and Poppy. They drove to the edge of the village, and then halted at the high Starlingford gateposts, where the gatekeeper's wife rushed out from the lodge to open the gates to them, curtsying to them as they passed onto the long drive to Starlingford. To one side lay their own fields, leased to Mr Neilson, the farmer, where ploughing was underway, and on the other lay the farm itself. Somewhere cattle were lowing, and from the farmhouse, high and tremulous, came the wailing of Ruby Neilson's baby.

They plunged into a belt of large trees overhanging the road, sunlight sparkling as it filtered through the leaves, as the road curved around and began to climb a low hill. Onward and upward they went, as Caroline considered with wonder that this was all Mr Leatham's land. She tried to calculate its size, comparing it to their own two acres, but had to give it up. Her mind could not comprehend such vastness, and all of it in the possession of a single man. And Lord Elland's estate was even larger, and the Duke of Falconbury's larger still.

Abruptly, they emerged from the trees into brilliant light, and there below them was a sunny green valley with a shimmering stream winding its sinuous way through it. On a small hill opposite sprawled the house — or rather, the mansion. Its soft red stone glowed in the sunshine, and uncountable windows gleamed. On the roof, scores of tall chimneys stood in lines, like soldiers on parade.

"Ohhh..." Caroline breathed, awed. "What a beautiful house!"

Martin rumbled with laughter beside her. "Aye, it looks well enough from 'ere, but it's a rattly old place, not like Lord Elland's fine modern 'ouse."

They descended into shrubberies that hid the house from view, crossing the stream by way of a neat arched bridge, and then began to rise again. Only when they were almost upon the house did it emerge from its concealment. Close to, the building exuded warmth from its red bricks. Creepers softened the walls, and cheerful spring flowers framed the windows. The front door opened before the gig had stopped moving, and two servants, perhaps the butler and housekeeper, emerged to greet them.

"What will you do while we're inside?" Caroline said in an undertone to Martin.

"I'll wait 'ere, miss, just walkin' the 'orse now and then. You'll not be more'n fifteen minutes. 'alf an 'our at most."

"Fifteen minutes," she repeated uncertainly.

"Aye, for a first visit. No more'n 'alf an 'our. 'orse don't like waitin' longer. You never done this before?"

"With Mama once or twice. Condolences, bridal visits, that sort of thing, but not... not like this." *Not as if we were gentry,* she wanted to add. *Not as if we were quality.* Never had she felt so out of her depth.

The butler, or perhaps he was merely a footman, offered his hand to assist her to alight, which she felt obliged to accept. Then she was so unbalanced that she almost fell, and landed in a most ungainly fashion. Meanwhile, Lin had hopped down agilely from the far side of the gig, and smothered a laugh at her sister's inelegant descent.

"Your cards, madam?" the footman said.

"Oh... we don't have cards." She remembered then that Mrs Leatham had stayed in her carriage while the footman conveyed her card into the house. Should they then have waited in the carriage, and sent Martin in to... to what, if there were no cards? To find out if Mrs Leatham were at home. But she was, of course, since she had asked them to call today, and how would they manage the horse if Martin were not there? It was very confusing.

The housekeeper came forward to help out. "Would you care to step inside, madam?"

Caroline nodded, and the housekeeper and footman stood aside to allow the sisters to walk up the shallow steps and through the front door into the hall. It was like no hall Caroline had ever seen, for it was as large as the assembly room at Romsey. High above, wooden beams supported the arched ceiling. Painted wood panels covered the lower half of the walls, while the upper half was all windows, so that light poured in. The stone flagged floor was covered with colourful rugs, while a log burned merrily in a vast hearth.

"Oh, how lovely!" Caroline cried.

The housekeeper smiled. "The great hall is the oldest part of the house," she said proudly. "It's more than three hundred years old. The rest of it is not much more than two hundred or so. What name shall I give, madam?"

"Miss Milburn and Miss Elinor Milburn," Caroline said absently, her head bent back, the better to admire the painted ceiling. The housekeeper and footman disappeared through a door partially concealed by velvet drapery.

Beside her, Lin muttered, "Such an uncomfortable place! Not at all cosy."

"No, but... three hundred years old!" Caroline said. "What were people like, then? Did they have the same concerns that we do, or was life so different that we wouldn't recognise them?"

Lin shrugged. "There's enough for us to worry about today, without wondering about people dead for hundreds of years."

The footman returned. "The mistress is in the small parlour, if you would care to follow me."

They were led through the half-hidden door, down panelled corridors and through echoing apartments, before the footman threw open another door. "Miss Milburn and Miss Elinor Milburn, madam," he intoned.

The small parlour might have been small by Starlingford standards, but it was perhaps five or six times the size of the parlour at Bursham Cottage. The ubiquitous wood panels were here painted a pale shade of lemon, with gold-patterned wallpaper above them, so that the room seemed to be filled with sunshine. Like everything else in the house, it exuded wealth and an elegant manner of living which was quite foreign to Caroline.

What on earth was she doing in this place, visiting these people as if she were their equal?

Mrs Leatham came towards them, smiling warmly. "My dear Miss Milburn! And Miss Elinor! How delightful! Do come in."

In the far corner, lurking uncomfortably, was Mr Leatham, looking as if he would rather be anywhere else. On a striped silk chaise longue near the fire sat a person Caroline had not met before, although she thought she might have seen her at church. She was close to thirty, with the sort of long, joyless face that would make her formidably imposing in middle age, but looked incongruous in one relatively young. She wore a severe spinster's cap which did nothing to enhance her looks, and neither her dress nor her person bore the slightest ornamentation.

"Let me present to you both my young friend Miss Beacher, who has been betrothed to both of my older sons before their most untimely demises, and is now so kind as to bear me company. Mildred, here are Miss Milburn and Miss Elinor Milburn, of Bursham Cottage."

Miss Beacher rose, and made the smallest possible curtsy for politeness, before seating herself again, her lips pursed in seeming disapproval, although whether she disapproved of some element of their attire or the very fact of their existence could not be determined. She seemed inclined to ignore them, however, a state which Caroline had no desire to change. But here, at least, was the answer to a mystery. Mrs Leatham had hinted that Mr Charles Leatham would soon be engaged to be married, and who was better suited as his bride than the woman who had almost become Mrs Leatham twice before? Yes, it was very fitting, although it was to be hoped that the run of bad luck which had caused her to lose two potential husbands to untimely deaths would not continue for a third. Poor Mr Leatham! His bride looked sour-faced enough to plague him most satisfactorily. It was almost enough to make Caroline feel sorry for him.

Mrs Leatham directed Caroline to sit beside her, and called to her son, "Charles! Bring a chair for Miss Elinor, and come and make yourself agreeable to our visitors."

He brought the chair, and another for himself, but the making himself agreeable was not very noticeable. He sat in silence, his expression that of a long-suffering man who was doing his duty but without the least pleasure in it. He tapped one foot repeatedly, his lips twisting awkwardly, and said not a word unless prodded by his mother. Miss Beacher, meanwhile, sat rigidly on the chaise longue opposite them, not moving in the slightest, but just as silent.

Mrs Leatham chattered on in her artless way, and when Caroline, feeling obliged to say something, anything at all, to maintain her side of the conversation, made some remark on the house and how beautiful she thought it, its mistress clapped her hands delightedly.

"Oh yes, it is delightful, is it not? Very old and draughty, and mightily inconvenient, of course, but such a charming home. When I first saw it, I was so pleased that I had accepted my dear husband's offer of marriage, for I knew I should be perfectly happy here. And so I have been, and I know that my successor will be just as happy. Should you like to see some of the principal rooms?"

"I should like that very much," Caroline said.

"I do not ask you, Miss Elinor, for I know you to be more interested in gardens," Mrs Leatham trilled, "and perhaps on another day we shall venture out there, but there is such a sharp wind from the east today that it would be most unwise. Charles, you may stay here and entertain Miss Elinor. You might show her Mr Alman's landscaping drawings, which must be of great interest to such a keen gardener. Mr Alman redesigned the pleasure grounds in Mr Leatham's father's day, Miss Elinor, modelling his ideas on those of Mr Brown, for of course we could not afford the great man himself. Come along, Miss Milburn."

Rather bemused by these arrangements, which in a less gracious hostess might be deemed rude, Caroline followed Mrs Leatham through the succession of lovely apartments, the wainscoting gleaming, the colours warm and vibrant. Mrs Leatham never stopped talking, until Caroline's mind reeled from the battery of facts and dates and anecdotes of which her guide had a seemingly limitless supply.

"Is it not beautiful?" Mrs Leatham said several times. Then, without waiting for Caroline to compose her compliments, she rushed on, "It is a great privilege to live in such a wonderful old house, do you not agree? Now then, this is my husband's sanctuary — his book room. Let us just tiptoe into his domain and bid him a good day as we pass by." She rapped briskly on the door, and at once marched in. "Here we are, my dear," she said loudly. "Here is Miss Milburn for you to meet. Come, now, Miss Milburn, you must not be shy, you know."

Mr Leatham was much older than his wife, a white-haired gentleman with a rounded face, smiling gently on the world. "Ah, my dear! Delightful, quite delightful." He was sitting in a wing chair beside the fire, book in hand, although he seemed half asleep. He rose to greet them, however, bowing and speaking kindly to Caroline. She curtsied, feeling once again like an impostor in this luxurious place.

What would Mama have made of it, she wondered, their practical, down-to-earth mother who had liked to poke a little gentle fun at those of Papa's customers she called *'the carriage trade'*. What would she have said were she alive now, at finding herself mistress of a house in her own right, with an independence and a carriage of her own? How would she have coped with making morning calls as if she were gentry herself? She would have smiled and been civil and then laughed about these people later, most likely. And so Caroline smiled and was civil, but she was not sure there was anything to laugh at. She was too uneasy for humour.

When they returned to the small parlour, she was amused to see that refreshments had been laid out and Lin was tucking in as if she had not seen food for a month. Probably she had never seen food like this before — tiny cakes and pastries, bowls heaped with bon-bons and sweetmeats, strange dried fruits that she could not even identify. As she ate, she was talking rapidly, arms waving for emphasis, caught up in some detailed description of her plans for a medicinal herb garden.

Mr Charles Leatham sat on a chair nearby, nodding occasionally, stupefied by the outpouring of words. He looked up at his step-mother as she entered the room with clear relief on his face. Jumping to his feet, he said, "Ah, there you are! You will forgive me, I am sure, Miss Milburn, Miss Elinor, but... stables, you know... horse... overdue... must check..."

Mrs Leatham laughed. "Yes, yes, run away, Charles. Miss Milburn, do sit here. Some tea? And you must have one of Mrs Bendish's apricot fancies. *Such* a light hand with pastry."

Caroline sat and drank tea, although it had a queer taste she disliked, and ate an apricot fancy, which was delicious, and then a second one, while Mrs Leatham chattered away to Lin about the difficulty in obtaining reliable gardeners.

Miss Beacher, meanwhile, seemed not to have moved an inch since Caroline had left the room. Her sour expression remained unchanged, and the table at her side bore no tea cup or plate. She was not tempted, it seemed, by Mrs Bendish's fancies. Caroline had an image of Miss Beacher standing before the vicar for her marriage to Mr Charles Leatham with just such a discontented face, and there at last she found something in the day's visit to make her smile. Yes, she would make him a most fitting wife.

The clock on the mantelpiece struck the hour, and Caroline realised they had far exceeded the allotted fifteen or thirty minutes for a first visit. She rose to leave, mumbling something inane about not keeping the horse waiting. Mrs Leatham smiled and accompanied them to the entrance hall, but there she stopped, the door firmly closed.

"Now, my dears, I shall be sending you an invitation to dinner in a week or two—"

"Oh, no, we couldn't possibly!" Caroline said at once.

"Nonsense!" Mrs Leatham said briskly. "Just a family dinner, nothing too formal so no need to be shy about it. I tell you in advance so that you will have time to consider your gowns, you see. Your youngest sister is not out yet, I daresay, so it will just be the two of you, and—"

"We can't," Caroline said firmly.

"Nonsense," Mrs Leatham said again. "I shall not entertain any excuse, Miss Milburn, for you are part of the county's society now. You must accept invitations, for it would certainly give offence to refuse. You are not expected to reciprocate, so you need not concern yourselves with that, and I shall send the carriage for you. A pleasant evening amongst friends — why, what is so terrifying about that? Unattached young ladies are always acceptable dinner guests, you know, and we all want to get to know you better." She nodded to the butler, and the door was opened. "Ah, there is your driver waiting. Splendid. You will go on to Corranwater next, no doubt."

"I don't think so," Caroline said. "Lady Elland is not so friendly as you."

She laughed at that. "Nevertheless, you had better go. She will be very put out if she hears you have called on me, but not on her. One would not wish to offend such an important lady in the neighbourhood, would one?"

Caroline nodded, not wanting to go anywhere near the formidable Lady Elland, but also not liking to argue publicly with Mrs Leatham. She seemed like a pleasant, motherly sort of woman, but she was just as formidable as Lady Elland, in her way. She and Lin made their farewell curtsies to Mrs Leatham, and climbed into the gig, unassisted by the butler.

"Corranwater, Martin," she said, loud enough for Mrs Leatham to hear.

Martin rumbled with laughter and flicked the whip to stir the horse into motion. He was still laughing as they rolled slowly down the drive.

"Corranwater," he said, with another chuckle. "Lord, but you's gettin' grand."

"Just drive, Martin," Caroline said crisply, arranging her skirts more smoothly. "Please confine your remarks to the horse."

That just made him laugh all the harder.

9: An Invitation To Dinner (May)

Corranwater was the very opposite of Starlingford. Instead of a gently curving drive through rolling greensward, they passed along a road that deviated neither to right nor to left. Instead of the dappled sunshine through high leaves, they were shrouded in the gloom of closely-packed evergreen trees. And when they eventually emerged into the parkland itself, there was no vista across a stream-laced valley, just the house rising before them, grey and solid and monstrous, like the etching Caroline had once seen of a great castle somewhere, looming threateningly. Massive pillars reached from the top of the entrance steps all the way to the roof, which was lined with statues. Beneath it, huge doors opened as they approached and several men in livery rushed out to receive them.

They drew up at the foot of the steps, and one of the many manservants approached Caroline. This time, she remembered to stay in the gig, just in case Lady Elland was not at home. The servant held out a gloved hand for her card, but Caroline had had time to consider the problem.

"Miss Milburn and Miss Elinor Milburn to see Lady Elland," she said in a clear voice.

The footman betrayed no surprise, turning away at once and returning to the house. The others remained at their stations on the steps, ready to help them down from the gig or slam the door in their faces, as appropriate, and of the two options, Caroline rather hoped for the second. If her ladyship refused to see them, they could leave and need never return. But just a few minutes later, the manservant returned with the news that Lady Elland would receive them.

Caroline managed to descend a little more elegantly this time, even with the footman's aid. Lin had her own footman to assist her. The two sisters smoothed out their skirts and ascended the steps side by side beneath the towering columns. The entrance hall was another difference from Starlingford, for instead of warmly glowing wood, they were surrounded by cold, echoing marble and pale statuary of men in classically draped robes with stern faces and blank eyes.

Several footmen stood around the perimeter, but one wore a different livery. He had a dark face with eyes the colour of coal, and his black hair was worn long and tied into a queue, in the old style. Unlike the others, who stared impassively at the opposite wall, immobile as statues as they waited to be called into action, this fellow stood, arms folded, and stared openly at Caroline and Lin as they entered. It was not a comfortable stare, of admiration or interest. For some reason, she felt there was some hostility in his manner. He made her shiver.

A stately butler bowed and led them at a funereal pace across the hall. He showed them into a vast room filled with an assortment of furniture — small tables with curved legs, silk-covered sofas and chairs with gilt arms, stools and consoles and display cabinets all dotted about in small groups. The walls were covered with paintings in heavy gold frames of people in high wigs and colourful brocades. Caroline's feet sank into a deep-pile rug that was so luxurious she wanted to lie down and stroke its soft surface.

"Ah, how kind in you to call," Lady Elland said after the butler had announced them. She was smiling, so they were to see her friendly face today. "Do come in, and let me make you known to Lord Elland."

He was a pleasant-faced man of around fifty, still hale, who greeted them with civility but without warmth. The only other occupant of the room was a worn-looking woman of middle years in drab clothing, a Miss Pointing. "My relation," Lady Elland said dismissively. There was no sign of the two bouncy sons, which was rather a disappointment, for they would have lightened the atmosphere considerably. Caroline had no idea how she was to make conversation with people she had nothing at all in common with. To her surprise, however, within five minutes Lord Elland proposed a walk in the garden.

"Oh, yes, please!" Lin cried.

There was a slight delay while outer garments were found for Lord and Lady Elland, and then they were led through another, even grander, room to doors leading to a broad terrace at the back of the house. Beyond it, formal beds surrounded a wide reflecting pool which ended in a fountain.

"A parterre!" Lin exclaimed, and promptly set off towards it, with Lady Elland and Miss Pointer in pursuit.

Caroline was more interested in the fountain. "How does it work?" she said, enchanted.

"There is a reservoir on that hill over there," Lord Elland said. "The water runs down the slope in underground pipes and the pressure is sufficient to lift the water into the air."

"How ingenious! Modern engineers are so clever, aren't they?"

"They are, it is true, and we live in an age of wonders, but fountains are a very old idea, Miss Milburn. The Romans and Greeks both constructed them."

"Oh. That was a long time ago, wasn't it?"

"A very long time ago," he answered gravely. "Shall we walk beside the pool? Then you may examine the fountain from closer quarters."

The gravel path crunched under their feet as they walked, while Caroline struggled to think of something to say to him. Making conversation with a baron was not a skill which she had ever needed to develop before. She could hear Lin's high voice in the distance, and wished she had her sister's facility with strangers. Where there was a garden to be admired, or plants to be discussed, Lin could talk endlessly, but Caroline had no such topic to fall back upon. Household management and lacemaking were her only skills, and neither was of interest to a gentleman.

Fortunately, she didn't need to think up something to say, for Lord Elland soon began to speak again, although the subject was surprising.

"Miss Milburn, I believe Lady Elland approached you recently to enquire after some documents relating to my family which the late Mr Wishaw had in his possession."

"Yes, but we don't have them," she said. "There were very few papers in the house. Mr Wishaw's business partner took everything relating to the business, and all that was left were old bills and a few personal letters. Nothing about your family at all."

"I talked to Mr Salter, but he has nothing of the sort. He very kindly permitted me to examine everything he took away, and there was nothing there."

"Maybe Mr Wishaw had them with him when he went to Ireland, so they went to the bottom of the sea?" Caroline said.

"That is unlikely, because Mr Salter told me that all his friend's possessions were recovered after they refloated the ship, and he looked through them himself and found nothing. It is my belief that the papers are still in your house, Miss Milburn, but perhaps hidden away in some secret crevice for safe-keeping. Under the floorboards, perhaps, or behind the wainscoting or a loose brick somewhere. Or the attics?"

"I'll have another search, if you like," Caroline said. "It would help to know just what I'm looking for, though."

Lord Elland smiled. "That is just the problem, I have no idea! The documents came from Italy and relate to my mother's family, that is all I know. She is French, although she met and married my father in Italy, and they lived there very happily for many years. I and my sisters were born there, and I can still remember the heat of the sun, the scent of jasmine and the taste of fresh olives and figs. We only returned when my grandfather became sick, and wanted his son at home." He sighed. "The papers have no significance in themselves, but Mother is seventy now. She is very nostalgic for her French family, but we have quite lost track of them. These papers would be a great comfort to her, if they could be found."

"Why did Mr Wishaw have them, if they're yours?" Caroline said, wondering a little at so much effort for papers of no significance.

"Oh, one of his business associates came across them in Italy," he said airily. "Mr Wishaw thought they would be of interest, but for one reason or another they were never handed over. He never liked to entrust them to the mail service, and either he was away somewhere or I was. But having heard of their existence, Mother is fretting about them, you know how elderly ladies do. I would like to set her mind at rest."

"Well, I'll have another look," Caroline said. "I haven't gone through the attics properly yet, so I'll start there."

"You are very good," he said.

By this time, they had almost reached the fountain at the end of the reflecting pool, but running feet on the gravel heralded the arrival of the footman who wore the different livery.

"Mon seigneur! Mon seigneur! Un instant, s'il vous plaît. Excusez-moi, mais votre dame mère désire vous voir tout de suite. Immediatement, s'il vous plaît."

Lord Elland stopped at once. *"Oui, Lucien. Je suis en chemin."* The footman scuttled off as fast as he'd arrived. Lord Elland turned to Caroline. "Forgive me, Miss Milburn. That is my mother's personal footman, Lucien, informing me that she requires my attendance at once. If she has had another one of her turns—"

"Of course. Go to her, my lord. Don't worry about me. I'll find Lin over in the parterre."

"Thank you for your understanding." And without another word he hastened away.

So the sinister footman was old Lady Elland's personal footman, was he? What a strange household they were, to be sure.

~~~~~

MAY

The invitation arrived for dinner at Starlingford. *'The carriage will collect you at a quarter before five and bring you home at midnight,'* Mrs Leatham had added. There was no question of refusing. Lin could barely contain her excitement at the prospect of her first dinner as an adult. Caroline had accompanied their parents to a few dinners and card parties and even assemblies, and had been among the company when they returned hospitality, so although such occasions had not occurred often, she had some experience of them. Papa had grown too ill to accept evening invitations by the time Lin had reached the proper age, and after he had died Mama had not thought it proper to accept hospitality that couldn't be returned. Now there was no reason not to accept. Even Caroline confessed to some curiosity to see how the true gentry entertained. Only Poppy was long-faced to be excluded.

"Your turn will come," Caroline said, with more optimism than she truly felt.

"Oh yes!" Poppy said. "I shall be sixteen soon, so perhaps then...?"

"Perhaps," Caroline said, not wanting to give her too much hope. Who knew how many such invitations they would receive when they could not reciprocate?

"You must tell me *everything*," Poppy said, practically bouncing. "All the dishes and what everyone is wearing and the jewels! The ladies will all be wearing jewels, won't they?"
~~~~~

"Oh good grief, jewels," Caroline said. "We shall have to make do with Mama's few pieces. We didn't sell the pearls, did we? They will do for you, Lin, and I can wear the topaz cross. They will not expect us to be dripping with diamonds."

Three whole days were devoted to the delicious task of making gowns and hairpieces and trimmings, and this involved the ceremonial opening of Mama's Box. Even before Papa's death, Mama had begun setting aside lengths of silk and delicate muslin and fine wool for their trousseaux, and before the shop had been sold she had taken a great many more, so that they now had a whole box full of unused fabrics of the very finest quality. There was no discussion on whether they should be used or not, for they none of them expected to marry well enough to need so much finery. The only question was which would make the best gowns, and whether to assume that full evening dress would be required.

"Mama only ever wore half-dress," Lin said, as they fingered the silks reverently. The morning room had been cleared of detritus and a worktable set up in there, now that spring had brought better light for sewing.

"Different company," Caroline said. "We dined with grocers and apothecaries, not gentlemen. When we went to the assemblies, we wore full dress then. I wore the gown with a short tunic over the top for dinners. It was the cream sprig muslin that Poppy wears now on summer Sundays. It looks better on her than it ever did on me, but then everything does. I shall wear this apricot satin, I think, with my own net over it. If we add some spangles, it will look charming. And a demi-train." She sighed. "I don't like this fashion for trains, but we must make an effort, I think."

"Full dress, then," Lin said in a small voice. "Must I have a train, too, and show off… well, *everything?*"

Caroline laughed. "We may cut the neck as high or as low as you wish, and a tiny frill of lace will make you feel more comfortable. As for the train, a demi-train is not too difficult, so long as you remember not to turn round too quickly and stand on it. We'll practise a bit before the day. I think you should wear the white crêpe, dear, in a three-quarter length tunic, but the ice blue sarcenet will be perfect for the slip. We have nothing for our hair, but I can net something. Stockings we have a-plenty, but gloves—! We'll have to look through Mama's things and hope there is something suitable."

"We could buy some," Poppy said.

Her sisters stared at her.

"So we could," Caroline said, in astonished tones. "We are ladies of means now."

Thus it came about that they made their first trip to Salisbury. The gig was not large enough for all of them, but Caroline recklessly authorised Martin to hire a larger chaise from the inn. They departed at first light, had breakfast at the White Hart, tripped merrily from shop to shop, spent almost one hundred pounds and returned home exhausted, exhilarated and, in Caroline's case, full of guilt. One hundred pounds on fripperies such as kid gloves, satin slippers and tortoiseshell combs! Such expense would have been unthinkable just a few weeks ago, but their present income, and the largesse of the unknown Benefactor, made the purchases possible, so long as they were not repeated too frequently. She consoled herself with the thought that the mound of parcels filling the box of the chaise also included some more practical acquisitions — lengths of simple muslin and cambric, pins and thread, soap and some tea that was cheaper than Mr Popham's.

Caroline left Lin and Poppy to unpack and went straight away to the study to note down all their purchases in the accounts. She had not been there long when Susie came in.

"Beg pardon for disturbin' you, Miss Milburn, but Mrs Neilson is here and askin' to see you."

"Mrs Neilson? From the farm? I didn't hear the knocker."

"Came to the kitchen door. Askin' for you in particular. Show her in, shall I?"

"Oh yes, of course."

Mrs Neilson crept in, clutching the edges of her cloak nervously. Caroline had not seen her much, apart from church, but she had not set her down as a diffident type, in fact very much the reverse. Embarrassment, then. Caroline's heart sank.

"Come in, Mrs Neilson. Would you like some tea?"

She shook her head decisively. "No, no. Not... not a sociable call, Miss Milburn."

"Oh dear. Have we erred in some way?"

She twisted her hands awkwardly in her lap. "It's your sister, miss," she blurted.

"Poppy? Is she making a nuisance of herself?"

Mrs Neilson's face softened. "Oh, no, no! Not really, but... she's so gentle and kind and..." She heaved a sigh, falling silent for a moment. Caroline let her gather her thoughts. "Trouble is," Mrs Neilson went on, "she's so good with the babe... *too* good, really. Ruby's happy to let her do it, and then they sit there at my kitchen table gossiping, and really, Ruby needs to manage the child herself and learn to get on with her work while she's about it. It's not easy, but we've all had to do it. Ruby's not a lady like what you and your sisters are—"

"We're not ladies!" Caroline said, astonished. "We work for a living..." She tailed off, all too aware that they had passed the whole day in Salisbury spending money, and had earned not a penny piece since they had moved to Bursham St Matthew. They lived off their investments now, and that, to their neighbours, made them gentry. "I'll speak to Poppy," she went on more gently. "Shall I tell her not to visit at all?"

Mrs Neilson smiled. "No need for that. Maybe... if she comes home with us after church, say... she could stay for the rest of the morning and it wouldn't be stopping Ruby. You do understand, don't you?"

"I understand very well," Caroline said. "She is so powerfully drawn to babies that she just can't resist them, but now that she has some chicks to take care of, I'm certain she will be content with those. I'll make sure she appreciates the position, and if she turns up when she's not wanted, just send her home."

She had no sooner seen Mrs Neilson out, through the front door this time, and turned back to her accounts than there was another interruption, this time from Lin and Poppy. Lin bore a rusty old tin box in her hands, grimy with dirt. Clearing a space on Caroline's desk, she placed the box there. The two sisters stood watching Caroline, Lin grinning gleefully, Poppy wide-eyed.

"What's this?" Caroline said, eyeing the box warily.

"John found it in the garden this morning while we were out," Poppy said. "Dug it up, from the new rhubarb bed."

"Rhubarb! Why are we growing rhubarb?"

"Purgative. Come on, Caro, open it," Lin said, quivering with excitement.

Gingerly, Caroline took hold of the box and tugged at the lid. It refused to lift. Another, harder, tug, then a heave and it burst open, tossing something into the air, which fell back onto the desk with a resounding thump. Caroline jumped, her chair sliding backwards. Then she laughed at the nondescript grey lump that had given her such a fright.

"What is it?" she said, prodding it warily.

"Look and see," Lin said, giggling.

The outer wrapping was waxed cloth of some kind, made into a bag, stiff with age or dirt, it was hard to tell which. Loosening the drawstring, Caroline found a second bag inside the first. And inside that...

A purse, elaborately netted like the one in the safe, although this one was a dull, faded colour. Inside was a bundle of notes. Caroline didn't need to count them to know the amount.

"Five hundred pounds," she said thoughtfully. "Another purse, another five hundred pounds. One in the safe, one buried. What does it mean?"

Her sisters were mute.

Silently, Caroline rose and crossed the room to the cupboard where the safe lay hidden. Unlocking it, she deposited the purse inside, next to its twin. From the cash box, she counted out five sovereigns and gave them to Lin.

"Give that to Mr Christopher, as a reward for his honesty. If he should find any more such boxes, he will be rewarded in similar fashion."

Poppy clapped her hands. "Oh, yes! He's utterly honest, and should be thanked for his trustworthiness. May I tell him so?"

"Pray do, but ask him also not to speak of this to anyone else. We don't want half the parish furtively rooting around in our kitchen garden in the hope of finding another box of treasure."

Poppy nodded, snatched the coins from Lin's hands and rushed out of the room, leaving Lin and Caroline to muse on the oddity of a man who buried money in his vegetable bed.

10: Dinner At Starlingford

Charles could not foresee any pleasure in the evening to come. He had endured a miserable day, his horse having gone lame after a mistimed jump, and the rest of his morning had been spent closeted away with his father, as Hapgood, the bailiff, tried to explain the principles of four-field rotation to him. When that palled, they had moved on to the management of the succession houses. He had never bothered to think about fruits before, considering them basic foodstuffs which were simply there when required, but it sounded like an immensely complicated business. And now, having been bored all morning, he was to be bored all evening as well. Lord, if he could just escape! If only he could go back to the army and leave Starlingford for Cousin Will… But he could not. He must do his duty and suffer Miss Milburn's unwelcome presence at dinner.

It was all part of his step-mother's strategy, but he could not summon any enthusiasm for it. He was obliged to marry but he had no anticipation of happiness in the wedded state, and so courtship held no attractions, either. Nevertheless, he had been given his orders by his mother — to cleave to Miss Milburn's side all evening.

"Like a barnacle!" she said merrily. "Do not allow anything or anyone to detach you from your prey."

Poor Miss Milburn, to be viewed as prey. It made him feel less like a humble barnacle, clinging to the hull of a ship, and more like a hawk, digging his claws into his victim. Yet surely she would be less reluctant to be caught than a rabbit or mouse. All young ladies wanted to marry, so she would be willing prey, when the moment came. The moment that would require him to wind himself up to propose... he shuddered. He could face the massed French army with greater fortitude than an offer of marriage to a young lady. Still, no need to think about that for a week or two. He had a little time left before he must shackle himself for ever.

"Shall we attempt something a little more challenging with the neckcloth tonight, sir?" his valet said cheerily, as Charles dressed for the evening. "Mr Narfield's man has been showing me a new arrangement that is all the crack in London, I'm told."

"All the crack? When have I ever aspired to be all the crack, Roffey? You are mistaking me for a man of fashion."

The valet laughed, not at all put out. "The usual it is, then, sir. With the diamond pin? That adds such a refined touch, I always think."

Charles conceded that the diamond pin would not render him unpalatably fashionable, and a very few minutes later was making his way downstairs to the saloon. His father was there, enjoying his sherry before dinner.

"How is that horse of yours? Any heat in the leg?"

"A little. Whitelaw has applied his usual poultice, but I might ask Davy from the farm to look at it in the morning."

"Good idea. No point taking chances." He sipped his sherry, gazing at Charles over the rim of his glass, mischief in his eyes. "So we are to have the pleasure of your Miss Milburn's company this evening, I understand?"

"She is not *my* anything," Charles said gloomily, pouring a sherry for himself.

"Not yet, but she will be, in time. You must not look so miserable at the prospect, Charles. Smile a little, and charm her with those delicate little attentions that ladies love."

"Charm her? Is it not enough that I am prepared to marry such an ill-favoured woman without expecting me to simper and coo and fawn over her? Heaven knows I have never had the knack of flattering a woman."

His father smiled. "It is the easiest thing in the world. You have only to notice something about her that pleases you, and then you tell her so."

"But nothing about Miss Milburn pleases me," Charles said, crossly. His father only laughed at him.

Fortunately Mildred came in just then, to stiffen Charles' backbone. There was nothing like the sight of Mildred's dour countenance to throw Miss Milburn into a more favourable light. He could not be entirely displeased with the prospect of marriage to a linen draper's daughter if it saved him from a lifetime of facing Mildred over the breakfast table.

His step-mother arrived soon after, and Cousin Will, who was paying his twice-yearly visit. Will Leatham was a cheerful man of two and thirty, a clergyman who wore his piety lightly and was as good company as any Charles had known. He was a second cousin, and heir to the estate if Charles should fail to perpetuate the line. His step-mother was inclined to resent such encroachment, but Charles liked him and his visit was a blessed relief from the frustrations that beset him.

The Narfields were the next to appear, a couple whose estate adjoined Starlingford to the north. Narfield was the younger son of a baron, a rôle which would normally see him making a career in the church or law, but he had inherited a great deal of money from a nabob uncle and assumed the life of a gentleman. Like all the Narfields, he had married well, acquiring the well-dowried daughter of a viscount for himself, while both his older brothers had married into ducal families.

The carriage brought the remaining guests — Mr and Mrs Elkington from Bursham St John, Mr Barr from Bursham All Saints, and the Miss Milburns. Charles turned away from his conversation with Will and received the shock of his life. The dowdy, unprepossessing Miss Milburn he had encountered previously was gone, replaced by a young lady possessed of both style and an air that could only be described as self-assurance. He was no expert on female dress, but her gown seemed to him to be both elegant and restrained, not overly fashionable but very pretty. And flattering, he could not deny. He had thought her reed-thin, but her skirts flowed over attractive curves and the lacy frill at the top—

"Oh, how charming," murmured Will in a low tone beside him. "How perfectly delightful."

"She does look well, it is true," Charles said, surprised, unable to tear his gaze away. While the butler announced the new arrivals, her eyes roved about the room. When they met Charles's, they narrowed slightly. Still hostile, then.

"Such perfection," Will said. "Who is the dark-haired one? Her sister?"

Belatedly, Charles realised they were admiring different women. "The one with dark hair and eyes is Miss Milburn. The fair one is her younger sister."

"Fair indeed! Fair of hair, and of face and form."

"But bird-witted," Charles snapped. "Not a thought in her head apart from her wretched garden. I swear she talked unremittingly about rhubarb last time she was here."

"Rhubarb? Good grief! But the dark one is yours, is that so? The older one? She is the one Cousin Daphne wishes you to marry?"

Charles nodded curtly, unable to say more for his step-mother was bringing the two Miss Milburns towards them to introduce Will. As soon as that was accomplished, she deftly manoeuvred Miss Elinor and Will aside, leaving him facing Miss Milburn.

"How are you, Mr Leatham?" she said, her face unsmiling. "Run down any more young ladies in Corran Woods lately?"

"It is not something I do by habit, Miss Milburn," he said tersely, adding belatedly, "Besides, I did *not* run down your sister."

"Only by chance, I'm sure, the speed you were going. You ride far too fast, and she said you came upon her quite without warning."

"That was because she was not paying the proper attention," he snapped. "If she had been looking out—" He caught himself before his temper snapped altogether. It was hard to receive criticism of his riding skills when his favourite horse was at that very moment sorely injured, but quarrelling with her was fruitless and would hardly advance his cause. He could quarrel with her as much as he liked after they were married, but for now circumspection was in order. And perhaps her expression was not entirely serious? He lowered his voice and went on, "Well, never mind. No harm done, and it is all in the past, eh?" Then, with the faint memory of his father's advice still echoing in his mind, he said, "You look... very well. I... like... um... the way you have done your hair."

She laughed at him, and he could not honestly say that it was a companionable laugh.

"Oh, I must give you credit for trying, Mr Leatham. Have you been reading a book on how to be pleasant to people? It needs a little more practice, I think. You will not mind if I go and talk to your father? He is sitting all alone over there."

He would not have managed to sit beside her at dinner but for his step-mother's contriving, for Mr Barr seemed inclined to take that seat. But Mrs Leatham was not a lady to allow anyone to overset her careful plans, and so Charles found himself at Miss Milburn's side, in his barnacle incarnation.

He was determined to be pleasant, so as soon as she had taken two sips of the soup, he said cheerfully, "Is it to your taste, Miss Milburn? There is salt here, if you wish it."

She looked at him with amused eyes. Such dark eyes... the colour of treacle, to match her dark hair. "It is a very pleasant soup, Mr Leatham, and your cook has already added a great deal of salt."

"Good," he said. Then, when that did not seem quite sufficient, "Very good." After a pause, he added, "I am particularly fond of onion soup."

She laid down her spoon, and said, merriment brimming in her eyes, "As onion soups go, it is a very fine specimen, I must agree. I confess that I like a white soup as well as any, although I had a turtle soup once that was most excellent, and must rate as the most magnificent soup ever presented to me. However, I cannot like a curry soup. I have only tasted such a thing once, but I found it very disagreeable. Do you enjoy a curry soup, Mr Leatham?"

He found it impossible to be cross with her. She was teasing him, but ever so gently, so he replied in a whisper, "Do not tell Mama, but in truth I am not at all fond of an onion soup. It makes too much of itself, and lingers on the tongue long after it should be done with, and the memory of it endures for hours, I find."

"Oh, indeed," she said at once. "A very brash, underbred soup, I fear."

That made him laugh out loud. "Whereas turtle soup is excessively refined, I suppose?"

"Certainly. A turtle soup can never be ill-mannered."

"How absurd you are, to talk so of soup," he said.

"You began the subject," she said, but her tone was not combative.

She picked up her spoon and returned to the soup, but he was not displeased with the exchange, and when he caught his step-mother's eye, she was smiling and nodding encouragingly at him.

After that, Miss Milburn turned towards his father on her other side, and Charles was reduced to watching Will across the table, where he was seated between Mildred and Miss Elinor. The latter chattered away unstoppably, and from time to time he caught snatches of her discourse — *'... golden rod... night-shade... syrup of hore-hound... purgative... convulsions... hemlock...'* Poor Will looked dazed, as well he might, and after a decent interval turned with obvious relief to Mildred. At least they had something in common, and could discuss their favourite sermons without boring everyone else.

When the ladies withdrew and the gentlemen rearranged themselves, Narfield took Miss Milburn's seat, and Charles found himself the subject of gentle chaffing.

"So it is to be Miss Milburn, I understand?" Narfield said, smiling widely. "A pleasant young lady, but the younger sister is prettier."

"Mama says that Miss Milburn is more practical," Charles said, somewhat defensively.

"Ah, yes, and that is a very important consideration," Narfield said. "But she has no dowry, I understand?"

"I have no idea," Charles said stiffly, not liking the close questioning. What business was it of Narfield's who he married?

"You could do better," Narfield said thoughtfully. "I say nothing against the lady, nothing at all, but a month in London just now could see you betrothed to someone with connections, and perhaps a few thousand to add to the estate."

An acid response rose to his lips, but before he could utter them, his father came to his rescue. "Charles could have a wider choice elsewhere, but he is not minded to parade himself through the saloons of London or Bath. We wish him to marry quickly to secure the succession, and Miss Milburn is an eminently sensible choice. We shall be very happy to welcome her into the family."

Not minded to parade himself... he shuddered at the very thought. Lord, the morning calls, the routs and balls and card parties, the outings to Richmond and Vauxhall Gardens, the drives through Hyde Park to display oneself to the world, or at least the small fragment of it that was the Beau Monde.

Conversations with strangers and — oh, the horror! — dancing with insipid young ladies who had even less to say for themselves than he had. Or, which was worse, gabbled away in a constant stream of inanities. He could not bear the thought of it. No, Miss Milburn, for all her faults, was vastly preferable to the nightmare of the season.

And she would save him from Mildred. He must never forget that.

After they had rejoined the ladies, his mother hissed, "Barnacle!" at him as he collected his tea, so he dutifully found Miss Milburn and sat down on a nearby chair. However, he could not think of a single thing to say to her, and she seemed content to watch everyone else, sipping her tea thoughtfully. In the end, they sat for some twenty minutes within a few feet of each other without exchanging a single word.

But then, to his relief, his step-mother called for the card tables. Naturally, she contrived for him to partner Miss Milburn, against Mr Elkington and Mrs Narfield. He anticipated no pleasure in the game, for he knew their opponents to be experts at whist, but at least he was not required to make conversation, which was a blessed relief.

By the end of the second game, his ennui was quite driven away. Miss Milburn, it transpired, was a decisive and clever player, who somehow contrived to take tricks that common wisdom suggested were impossible.

"My dear lady, how did you do that?" Mr Elkington said at one point.

"Just remembering the cards," she said, with a smile.

Once, when Charles was dithering between two possible cards, she said briskly, "The ten of hearts, Mr Leatham."

"How do you know that I have the ten of hearts?" he said, genuinely bewildered.

"But you must have," she said, in a surprised voice. "Don't you?"

"I do," he said, laying it down.

Mrs Narfield laughed. "How fortunate that we are playing for fish and not guineas, or we should be quite rolled up, Mr Elkington."

The card tables only broke up when the butler announced that the carriage was at the door, as ordered. It was midnight already. The meal had been tedious, but he could have happily played cards with Miss Milburn all night. He would love to see her play a more challenging game, such as piquet, but he had an uneasy feeling that she would thrash him soundly.

But when he bade her farewell, he was able to say with perfect sincerity, "Thank you for your company, Miss Milburn. I have been greatly entertained by your exploits at the card table."

"Thank you, sir," she said, dipping a demure curtsy. "The onion soup was enjoyable too, wasn't it?"

Such behaviour left him with unexpectedly agreeable thoughts on fine curves and treacle-coloured eyes that twinkled merrily. If only she were always so affable, perhaps marriage would not be such a great trial after all.

But Miss Milburn could not leave without a final outbreak of spleen, to remind him of exactly why he so disliked her. As Charles and his step-mother accompanied the Miss Milburns, the Elkingtons and Mr Barr to the front door and waited for cloaks and hats to be brought, Mrs Leatham said brightly, "Mrs Narfield is to stay with her brother and his wife at Valmont next month, and she has asked me most particularly to call upon her there. I am not usually upon calling terms with the Litherholms, but one must make the effort for one's friends. It is a long way, however, and I should much appreciate a companion on the road. Would you be so good as to bear me company, Miss Milburn? Valmont is well worth a visit, I assure you."

"I?" she said, in astonished tones. "Why would you ask me when you have Miss Beacher?"

Mrs Leatham went slightly pink, but persevered. "Oh... well, Mildred, you know... she dislikes these grand houses."

"She cannot dislike them more than I do," Miss Milburn said robustly. "Valmont is where the Duke of Falconbury lives, isn't it? I have no business in such a place."

"Nonsense," Mrs Leatham said. "It will be a pleasant day out for us all. Charles will accompany us, you know."

Charles raised an eyebrow, not having heard of the scheme before, but said nothing.

Miss Milburn laughed. "Is that meant to be an inducement, ma'am? Because it's just as likely to harden my resolve not to go."

"Then Mama must hold me excused," Charles said at once, rather peeved. "Far be it from me to deter you from an excursion of pleasure."

"It makes no difference," Miss Milburn said. "You are very kind to take notice of us, Mrs Leatham, and I cannot thank you enough for this evening, but you mustn't treat us as equals. We are the daughters of a respectable man, but he was no gentleman. You cannot take a linen draper's daughter to the home of a duke."

"You are impertinent," Charles said hotly. "You think very well of yourself, Miss Milburn, if you profess to know propriety better than Mama. If she chooses to take you under her wing, then she imbues you with her own consequence, and may take you anywhere with her, even to a duke's home. It is ungrateful to refuse such a generous offer."

"Thank you for your advice, Mr Leatham, but your interference is uncalled for. Mrs Leatham and I are perfectly capable of discussing such matters without your aid. I dispute your accusation of impertinence, but if I am ungrateful, then it must be so, for I cannot countenance such a scheme. Good evening to you both."

She took her cloak from the wooden-faced footman, swirled it around her shoulders in one fluid movement and strode towards the open doors and the waiting carriage. The Elkingtons, Mr Barr and Miss Elinor scuttled in her wake, displaying various shades of embarrassment.

But when the carriage had left, the door had been closed and the servants had disappeared, his step-mother laughed.

"I shall bring her round, never fear. A little self-effacement is no bad thing. She is very aware that you are far above her present station in life, and once you are married that will make her perfectly docile, you may be sure."

Charles wished that he could be so certain. That night, after his valet had left him, he paced about his room restlessly. Back and forth, back and forth, like some caged beast in a menagerie. He felt rather like that poor creature, trapped in a rôle for which he had neither aptitude nor inclination. In the army, he had known his place, had followed orders, had enjoyed the comradeship of his fellows, had been happy. Here, in his own home, surrounded by those who loved him and wanted only the best for him, he was beset by uncertainty.

But he knew what he ought to do. He knew his duty. When the time came, he would marry Miss Milburn, even though he despised her and she despised him. However difficult, he would make the best of it, just as he was making the best of his unexpected elevation to the position of heir.

The bars of the cage closed in around him.

11: Mr Leatham Pays A Call (June)

Caroline was relieved that the evening at Starlingford had passed off with no more than a couple of spats with the obnoxious son of the house. Such an insufferable man! She sincerely pitied poor Miss Beacher, who seemed an inoffensive woman, for it seemed to be her destiny to marry the son of the house, at the third attempt.

Lin had enjoyed herself enormously. "Did you ever see such a fine spread? Turkey *and* beef, and did you try the gammon? It was cooked in wine, Miss Beacher told me. And pheasant ragout! Jaune mange! Asparagus! I am going to grow asparagus here, I think, if I have space. And three kinds of wine to drink, and all those cakes on the tea board. Lord, if only I could eat like that every day."

"I wish I could have gone," Poppy said wistfully.

"But you enjoyed dining with Mr and Mrs Christopher at the vicarage?" Caroline said.

"Oh yes, and it was so kind of them to ask me, knowing I would be all alone here. It was John's idea — he is so thoughtful, always looking for little ways to help. I had a lovely evening, playing spillikins with the children, and there was a leg of mutton in my honour, John said, because they don't usually have meat except on Sundays. There was wine, too, but Mrs Christopher only let me have the tiniest sip, with water in it, and after supper John walked me home to make sure I got back safely. What did they all wear at Starlingford? Were they very grand, with lots of jewels and lace?"

"Mrs Narfield was quite grand, wasn't she, Caro?" Lin said. "Those drops in her ears were emeralds, I'm sure. But their gowns… do you know, I think ours were as pretty as any of them, and prettier than Miss Beacher's, for she wore a very plain muslin, with no interesting ornament at all. And Mrs Leatham's lace was nothing like as fine as Caro's."

"No one makes lace as fine as Caro's," Poppy said, her huge eyes softening. "Except Mama, of course. But what of the gentlemen? Were they like that man we saw going into the assembly once? The one with the shirt points nearly above his ears and his breeches so tight I could not see how he would ever contrive to sit down."

The sisters giggled at the memory. "Nothing like that," Lin said. "They all dressed like gentlemen, but nothing to draw the eye."

"Papa always said that is one of the distinguishing characteristics of the true gentleman, that he doesn't draw attention to himself," Caroline said. "Although behaviour is more important. I liked Mr Will Leatham, didn't you?"

"Oh yes, very polite," Lin said, " although he didn't say very much when he sat beside me at dinner. I had to make all the conversation."

"Which you managed perfectly well," Caroline said. "Whereas I was stuck with the taciturn Mr Charles Leatham, and a man with whom I have less in common would be hard to find. Conversation with him was like drawing water with a leaky bucket — a lot of effort for very little reward."

"You seemed to be getting along quite well at one point, " Lin said. "You must have found something to talk about."

"Soup," Caroline said. "We talked about soup."

The others laughed rather uncertainly, as if not sure whether she was serious or not.

"But still, he is such a handsome man, isn't he?" Poppy sighed. "Quite stern looking, but very handsomely featured, and so tall and broad in the chest. So many gentlemen are not well-built in that way, because they never do any real work, do they? They never build up their muscles by digging or sawing or chopping, like John Christopher has. But Mr Leatham is well-built. I suppose that comes from his days in the army."

Caroline didn't think Mr Leatham was at all handsome, but that was because she'd never seen him when he wasn't scowling at her. No, that wasn't quite true. When they'd talked of soup over dinner, he had joined in the joke good-humouredly, and at the whist table... he had been handsome enough then, she conceded, his eyes blazing with excitement and his whole countenance lit up with smiles of glee. Yes, he was very handsome when he smiled, but that was an occurrence as rare as hen's teeth.

After writing a short note to Mrs Leatham to thank her for her hospitality, Caroline had presumed that would be the end of their acquaintance with the Starlingford family. She had no intention of prolonging it by reciprocating with a dinner at

Bursham Cottage, or by further morning calls, and hoped they would now be allowed to return to their usual activities. Lin and Poppy were busy in the garden with their plants and chickens, and they had been promised a goat and kid. Caroline herself returned with relief to her lace. A trip to Salisbury saw the sale of her first three lace fans, and orders for a dozen more, so she worked steadily each day for two hours before breakfast, and then for another two hours. After that, she kept her accounts up to date, or walked to one or other of the shops in the three neighbouring villages, or discussed the management of the house with Susie.

It was irritating, therefore, when the very next Friday saw Mrs Leatham and her surly son calling again. Not that she minded Mrs Leatham very much, for although it was a disruption, she merely chattered away in a rattle of genial inanities for half an hour and went away again. She never seemed to mind that Lin and Poppy were nowhere to be seen. The surly son paced about restlessly, spoke not ten words to Caroline and then meekly followed his mother back to the carriage. He seemed docile, and yet there was some barely-contained anger in the way he slapped his gloves against his leg as he strode about the room. Why was he so angry? Not at Caroline, surely, for she scarcely knew him. But she refused to let him unsettle her, and merely made polite noises until they went away again.

What was worse was that the sisters seemed to have been accepted into society more widely. Each Friday saw a steady stream of sedate carriages, disgorging all the matrons and dowagers that the three villages could muster. Sometimes they brought their sons or nephews or grandsons with them, and if Lin was nowhere to be seen, the young gentlemen would feel the need for a stroll about the garden, not returning until their female kin sent Susie in search of them.

Their persistence made her smile, for she was beginning to realise that their efforts were in vain, since their other regular visitor was Mr Lester Stratton. Every Saturday he rode out from Romsey to stay for two nights at the inn, and somehow he always managed to inveigle himself an invitation to dinner at Bursham Cottage. Lin would smile and blush just a little and lower her eyes demurely, and Mr Stratton would smile and contrive to sit next to her, and it was not at all difficult to see what was happening. Caroline could not object to it. She had once thought that Lin, with her looks, might aim for something better than a country town attorney, a proper gentleman, perhaps, but if her affections were engaged, then she would not stand in their way.

It was pleasant, she found, to have a man about the house to whom they could talk openly. Any difficulty or uncertainty could be put to him, and he would beam his warm smile and answer clearly, without evasion or being patronising. He was the only person beyond the family and John Christopher who had been admitted to the secret of the hidden boxes of money. Three had now been found, and with half the beds still undug, there was every expectation of more turning up.

"Mr Wishaw had a reputation as a careful man with his money," Mr Stratton said thoughtfully. "Perhaps he mistrusted banks, and preferred to keep some portion of his wealth hidden away where no thief or disaster could steal it away."

"But the net purses?" Caroline said. "A lady's hand made those, and they are very distinctive, are they not?" They had laid out all the purses for Mr Stratton to see, and they were indeed very unusual, with intricate patterns.

He shrugged. "I cannot see that the purses are significant. One has to keep money in something, after all, and net purses may be obtained anywhere. Are you comfortable keeping so much money in the safe here? Two thousand pounds is a considerable sum. Should you like me to take it to the bank for you?"

Gratefully, Caroline agreed, keeping only a little for their own expenses. Almost eight thousand pounds now invested, plus Mama's little annuity, and the rent from the fields... more than four hundred pounds a year, even if she sold nothing at all. It was very satisfactory.

There was only one worry to trouble Caroline at this time. John Christopher came diffidently to the kitchen door one morning asking for Caroline.

"Something to show you, miss."

He led her round to the outside of the house, where he had been engaged in trimming back the ivy that grew there. Without a word, he pointed to the study window.

"What am I looking at? Oh!"

The locksmith had fixed bars across the windows to protect the study from thieves, and the bars themselves were still intact. Some enterprising person, however, had been carefully chipping away at the fixings and gradually loosening them. Eventually, it would be possible to remove the bars altogether.

Mr Stratton was not concerned. "These external fittings are merely a deterrent. Even if a thief could remove the bars completely, there would still be the reinforced shutters to get past, and in any event, there is nothing of value in the study outside the safe and I do not believe a common thief will succeed in breaking in to *that!* Mr Wishaw must have paid a great deal of money for such a secure receptacle. You may be easy in your mind, Miss Milburn."

"I shall never be easy in my mind," she said with a laugh. "Not until I am beyond the mortal sphere."

"Have you thought of a dog?" Mr Stratton said. "No intruder could enter secretly with a dog about the house."

Caroline groaned. "Do not suggest it in Poppy's hearing, for there would be no peace until she obtained one. Naturally it would be a puppy, and not in the least house-trained. Then I should have the servants rebelling at the extra work, it would dig up Lin's vegetables and chase the chickens and we should be all in chaos."

He laughed, but said, "Very well, no dog, but in truth I do not think you need any additional security. We will check all the windows regularly, but I doubt the thief will effect an entry this way."

And with that she had to be satisfied.

One morning, Caroline was busy with her lace, using a black thread this time, when a carriage crunched up the gravel drive. She sighed. It was not a Friday, when they were expected to be at home to receive callers, and Lin's lovelorn swains would not arrive in a carriage. Nor was it to be a short, formal visit, since the carriage, after depositing the caller, had rattled away towards the stable. So it was a great surprise when Mr Charles Leatham was shown in, alone.

"Is Mrs Leatham not with you?" Caroline said.

He gave a slight lift of one shoulder. "Oh... not today. She is... busy."

"Oh. She is well, I take it? And your father?"

"They are quite well, thank you."

"And Mr William Leatham? Is he still at Starlingford?"

"He left yesterday." A long pause. "He was quite well then."

"Good, although I am sorry he has left. You will all miss him, I think. He is very entertaining company." He said nothing, so she laboured on. "And Miss Beacher? Is she well?"

"Mildred is always well. Nothing ever ails *her.*" Was that bitterness in his tone? Yet he was to marry her, wasn't he? How odd.

Caroline cast about wildly for some other topic of conversation, but her mind was blank. "Will you sit down, Mr Leatham? May I send for some tea? Or a glass of Madeira?"

"Nothing, thank you." He stood by the window, gazing moodily into the garden.

Caroline gave it up, determined to make no more effort with him. If he wanted to talk, let *him* open the subject. And if he should be determined to stay silent, she might at least make productive use of the time. She seated herself once more on her lacemaking chair and took up the pillow. Perhaps the clack of the bobbins attracted his notice, for he drew near to look over her shoulder as she worked. It was unnerving to have him standing just behind her, but she would not be intimidated! She worked on, her fingers deftly moving the bobbins in their rhythm, adding a pin, weaving the bobbins, another pin, another spell of weaving.

"That is very clever," he said. "Is it for one of your gowns?"

"No, as a spinster, I can't wear this much lace. It's a fan, do you see?" She spread out the completed section, so that he could see the curve.

"Do you need a black fan? You are not in mourning, are you?"

"It's not for me. I'll sell it to a shop in Salisbury. Ebony-framed fans are much in demand just now, seemingly, so I'll get a good price for it."

He made a sound that might have been annoyance. "Why do you want to do that? You are not any longer a poor orphan needing to make a living. You had best leave off this sort of thing."

She spun round in her chair to glare at him. "Not a *poor* orphan, no, but only a slightly better off one. We still have to watch the pennies, Mr Leatham, and any extra income is useful."

"Nonsense!" he said, and for a moment he sounded so like his step-mother that she was tempted to laugh.

"It may be nonsense to you, sir, but I assure you it is a very serious matter to me. I prefer to be beforehand with the world rather than in debt."

"Well, of course," he said testily. "Did I ever suggest otherwise? But you must have a good income by now, and your expenses must be low."

Carefully she set her lacemaking pillow back on its stand and stood to face him. Trying very hard to keep the anger from her voice, she said, "Mr Leatham, neither our income nor our expenditure is any concern of yours."

"Pfft," he said, slapping his gloves against his thigh. He walked across to the window again, then turned to face her. "Miss Milburn, my step-mother has tried her best to lift you into a higher level of society, but you seem determined to sink back to your former plane. It is not good enough. You had much better save your lace for your own adornment."

"What business is it of yours what I do?" she said hotly, no longer bothering to hide her contempt. "I will do as I please, without reference to you *or* your step-mother. I am perfectly content in my own level of society and have no wish to ape those above me."

"That is foolish beyond reason, to refuse to rise when you have the means to do so," he said. "You must stop this selling of fans nonsense at once. You may not be a lady, but you have the means to appear to be one."

"Well, of all the horrid insults!" she cried.

"It is no insult to speak the truth," he said angrily. "Those who know better must instruct the ignorant. I want your assurance that you will not sell any more fans, or anything else of that nature."

"I shall do no such thing! Whatever makes you imagine you have the right to lecture me on such matters?"

"Oh, this is ridiculous!" he said, tossing the gloves onto a table with some force. "Let us just get this over with, shall we? Miss Milburn, will you marry me?"

Caroline's mouth dropped open in astonishment. For a long moment she gaped at him, hardly able to comprehend his words. Then she burst out laughing.

"Don't be absurd!" she said, between gasps of laughter.

"What is so absurd about it?" he said stiffly.

"You must be insane," she said. "You don't even *like* me, and I certainly don't like you."

"What has that to do with anything?" he snapped. "We should learn to get along, I daresay, and if not, we will not need to have much to do with each other, apart from... you know, the begetting of heirs and so forth."

"For heaven's sake, what are you saying?" Caroline said. "I can't imagine what is going on in your mind. Aren't you supposed to marry Miss Beacher?"

His rage dissolved at once into an expression of absolute horror. "No, no, no! *Never!* Mildred would have done admirably for Ben, for he was ordained and as prosily pious as she is, but I would probably murder her within a month. I could not bear it. *Any* wife would be better than Mildred, even—" He stopped, and at least had the grace to look embarrassed.

"Even me? Well, you are full of compliments today, Mr Leatham. I cannot understand why you have evaded matrimony for so many years when you display such irresistible charm."

"I do not see the point in wrapping it up in fancy words," he said, but his anger had died down a little. "Not that I have ever had much of a facility with fancy words, so plain words will have to do. I must marry to ensure the line continues, and Mama has selected you as the best candidate."

"And you always do what your step-mother wants?"

"She is usually right," he said with a shrug. "In her view you are a sensible, practical person, which is better than some highly-strung society lady, and infinitely better than Mildred, so... Will you?"

"Will I what?"

"Marry me, of course. Lord, you are slow-witted today."

"No, sir, I will not marry you. I don't want to marry at all, but especially not you. Even if you had... what did you call it? Wrapped it up in fancy words, I wouldn't wish to marry a man who despises me so thoroughly. During the course of your proposal, you've managed to call me ignorant, stupid and not a lady. And to think I could avail myself of a lifetime of such insults. What an enticing prospect! How can I bear to refuse?"

"There is no need to take an offensive tone, madam."

"Oh, are you offended? Excellent. Perhaps you might now have some inkling of how *I* feel."

"You are rash to throw away such an offer, however bluntly expressed," he said. "You may not like me very much, but you would have my name and wealth and a position in society. The daughter of a linen draper is unlikely to do better. A little gratitude would not go amiss, yet you toss it back in my face."

"I cannot be grateful for an offer made with such obvious reluctance. You said I am not a lady. Well, you are right about that, I own it. But you, sir, are hardly a gentleman, and I will never marry a man who holds me in such contempt. Go away and find some other poor, ignorant, stupid female to importune. I hope I never set eyes on you again."

12: Of Purpose And Wisdom

Charles left the house without waiting for the maid to let him out, pulling the door shut behind him. He should have been cast down by his rejection, but instead he found it liberating. His mother would be disappointed and his father would be sympathetic, but for himself, he could see the funny side of the business. Whatever sort of man was he that even lowly Miss Milburn, an impoverished spinster and a lacemaker by trade, should reject him? He was not a gentleman, that was what, and those dark eyes had flashed at him contemptuously as she said it. He laughed as he remembered her, her back straight, her chin defiantly raised, her voice level and unafraid. She might not be a lady but she was magnificent in her disdain as she upbraided him.

But if he was not a gentleman, what then was he? He had been a child and a scholar and a cornet and latterly he had been a captain, but now? He was nobody. He was the heir to his father's estate, but he knew nothing of the management of land, and all attempts to instruct him had been in vain. One day, in the fullness of time, he would be *the* Mr Leatham of Starlingford, but would he be a gentleman then? In all honesty, he could not say. What was a gentleman anyway? Was it merely the owning of land, of living on income not earned by labour, or was there more to it? Miss Milburn obviously thought the epithet encompassed more than mere idleness.

He was so sunk in thought that he had passed through the gates to Starlingford and was beyond the farm before he began to take note of his surroundings. Only the high wail of a baby brought him back to awareness. He knew, however, where he was bound. If there was one person in the world who could tell him what a gentleman was, it was his father.

As so often these days, he was dozing beside the fire in his book room, but he woke at once and greeted Charles with apparent pleasure.

"What a delightful surprise. Do come in, Charles. Would you like some Canary? This latest supply is a very good sort, and I can recommend it."

He meant, of course, that he would like some himself. Charles poured two glasses, set one glass within easy reach of his father and then settled himself on the matching chair to his father's.

"I offered for Miss Milburn, but she would not have me," he said without preamble. "She said I am not a gentleman. What do you think she means by that?"

His father looked at him, lifted his glass and sipped, then set it down again. Finally, he closed the book that still lay open on his lap, put it on the table and carefully removed his glasses. Thus prepared, he said, "You are not... disappointed?"

"Disappointed?" For a moment he could not think why he might be disappointed, until he remembered that his proposal had been rejected. "I know Mama will be, but—"

"Mrs Leatham will have some strategy to help your suit to prosper," his father said. "She is of such an optimistic nature that failure does not enter her thoughts. But what of you? It is a blow to a man's self-esteem to be thus rebuffed."

Had his self-esteem been dented by his unceremonious dismissal? "I cannot say," Charles said slowly. "I believe I have always been prepared for such an eventuality, so it does not entirely surprise me."

"Ah." His father sipped his Canary thoughtfully. "So it is her opinion of you, that you are not a gentleman, which rankles."

"Rankles... not exactly. I am merely... puzzled. What does she mean by it? I am of gentrified stock, I am educated, I wear appropriate clothing for my station, I know how to behave in society and I carry out the obligations of a landowner. What more is expected of me?"

"Perhaps," his father said gently, "it was your manner of addressing her which fell short of her expectations. You can be... a trifle brusque at times."

"Hmm." Charles tugged at his ear thoughtfully. "She always rubs me the wrong way, that is the Devil of it. I never know what to say to her, and then, somehow, we end up at loggerheads. Do you think I should have sweet-talked her? Used flattery? For I am no good at that sort of thing, and I cannot think she wants it. She is too sensible to respond to high-flown phrases."

"Not flattery, exactly, but when a gentleman is offering marriage to a lady, it is customary to explain just why he feels she is the perfect wife for him. To expound on her many virtues, and so forth."

"Miss Milburn has no virtues, that I can see," Charles said gloomily. "She is a termagant."

"Now that cannot possibly be true," his father said, with his gentle smile. "Come now, tell me three things you admire about her."

"She can play whist," he said at once. "If ever she is desperate for the readies, she could make a handy living at the gaming tables, I wager."

His father laughed. "Very good. What else?"

"She takes care of her sisters. Mind you, they need the Devil of a lot of looking after. Elinor is full of wild schemes, and Poppy is so up in the clouds that her feet barely touch the ground. Caroline is a good protector, like a mother hen."

"A little too good, perhaps. It would do the younger girls no harm to take their share of the burdens of adulthood. That is two virtues. What else?"

For a moment Charles could think of nothing, until he remembered how she had answered him, not an hour ago. Those treacle-coloured eyes! How they had upbraided him. "She says what she thinks," he said slowly. "And do you know, I think she is mostly right. I *was* rude to her, and offered her insult, and that is no way to speak to one's future wife."

"No, indeed," his father said gently.

"I wish I knew how to talk to her… or to any woman, really, but they just seem like some strange creatures from another continent. Fascinating and exotic but impossibly alien. And incomprehensible."

"Ah, that is all because of family history," his father said sadly. "Because your poor mother died bringing Felicity into the world, and I could not look after all six of you, the girls went to your Aunt Jane, and you, Ben and Alfred went off to school. You were only eight, far too young, really, but I was distraught and not at all able to cope with you and... well, it was done for the best. But it meant that you grew up without very much contact with the female of the species. Until I married again when you were sixteen, I daresay you scarcely saw a single female from one month to the next. It does not lead to easy discourse with the other sex. And then there is the Leatham shyness. I had it in abundance, and your mother was a timid creature, too. We were well-suited in that regard! But such a marriage does not produce lively children. The girls had the benefit of Aunt Jane's outgoing nature and then your step-mother to introduce them to society, but you boys were left to my taciturn care, I regret to say. Ben found his strength in God, and Alfred in books, as I have, but I think you have not yet found yours."

Charles said nothing for a while, considering all that his father had said. Before he could get his thoughts in order, his step-mother peered round the door.

"Oh, Charles!" Her voice was surprised. "Heaton was right — you *are* back. But what have you done with the carriage?"

"The carriage? Oh! The carriage! I quite forgot I went to see Miss Milburn in the carriage. Oh Lord, I have left Whitelaw kicking his heels at Bursham Cottage. I had better go and fetch him."

"Let Edward do it. Tell me at once, did you offer for her? What did she say?"

"What? Oh, she will not have me. I will tell you all about it later."

So saying, he swept past his astonished step-mother, grabbed his hat from the hall table — where were his gloves? That was odd — and rushed out of the house. His long legs carried him back down the drive, past the farm where the baby still wailed, and onto the Corranford road in no time, where the first person he encountered was Miss Milburn herself, walking towards the village. She started when she saw him, then inclined her head the smallest amount in greeting.

"Your gloves are on the hall table, sir," she said.

"My gloves? Did I leave them there?" he said, too bewildered even to remember to bow.

"You abandoned them in the parlour. Good day to you." She began to walk past him.

His head was filled with the memory of her angry words to him, and he could not easily stand aside and watch her walk away from him. Perhaps she would rebuff him, but he *had* to say what was in his mind. "What did you mean?" he blurted. "When you said I was no gentleman, what did you mean by that? What embodies your concept of a gentleman?"

She turned narrowed eyes on him. "Do you care what I think?"

"I do! Truly I do. Miss Milburn, I have no idea what I am, but I should like to understand what I am not. Will you explain it to me? Please?"

Her face softened and he thought there was amusement in her eyes. "I have a letter to get to the Wheatsheaf before the mail cart leaves. You can walk with me, if you want."

He fell into step beside her. "Thank you." He hesitated, then added, "May I apologise for—?"

She waved him into silence with a short laugh. "If we're going to apologise for every insult we've hurled at each other, we'll be here all day. I don't bear grudges, Mr Leatham. If we can conduct a rational conversation without snapping at each other for the five minutes it will take to reach the Wheatsheaf, I'll be satisfied with that."

He laughed, too. "Very well. Then will you tell me, Miss Milburn, what is your idea of a gentleman?"

She sighed gustily. "I'm going to annoy you, so please don't get angry with me, but it's not something I can describe. I've not had much experience of such people, and certainly not socially until recently, but quite a number of gentlemen used to patronise Papa's shop to buy their neckcloths, or linen for their shirts. Papa used to say of them, *'He's not a* proper *gentleman'* or *'That one's a real gentleman'*, and sometimes I couldn't see at first what the difference was. I suspect that much of his approbation depended upon the speed with which they settled their bills. But there was one man... he was different. Even I could see that he was superior to the rest."

"In what way?" Charles said.

"That's just it, it's hard to say. It wasn't that his clothes were better, or his manners, or his way of speaking. He had an air about him, that's all I can tell you. Although he *did* have good manners. Mama always said that whenever he met her, he made her feel like a lady, even though she wasn't." She bit her lip, and glanced up at him mischievously. "So there is one difference. You not only don't make me feel like a lady, you tell me to my head that I'm not."

He pulled a rueful face. "That was very bad of me. I do not know what it is about you, but you bring out the worst in me. I am not normally quite so... so..."

"Obnoxious? Rude? Bad-tempered? Boorish? Abusive?"

A bubble of anger rose inside Charles, but those dark eyes were twinkling at him. She was right about one thing — she did not bear grudges. There was no hint of resentment in her manner. "I daresay I am all of those things," he said slowly.

"But not always," she said. "You can be quite polite when you set your mind to it, or perhaps when I am nowhere near you. Truly, Mr Leatham, I cannot imagine why you asked me to—" She broke off abruptly, for they had almost reached the inn, and there were several people about. "Never mind," she said hastily. "Thank you for your company, sir." She dipped him a farewell curtsy and vanished into the inn.

'I cannot imagine why you asked me to marry you.' That was what she had been about to say, and in truth he could not imagine himself, except that it was his duty to marry and his step-mother thought she was suitable. As always, he felt as if a lead weight were settling in his stomach at the thought. Being married, like managing the estate, seemed an impossibly confining business, choking all the joy out of his life. What would he not give to be back in the army and far, far away from all these dispiriting decisions. He sank onto the bench outside the inn. He would allow himself five minutes to wallow in misery, then he would get up and go home and pretend that all was well with him.

So he wallowed, and a few people tipped their hats to him as they passed by or offered him a respectful bow or curtsy, recognising him, and whispering his name to each other. He knew most of them, too, but nobody spoke to him, leaving him to his thoughts.

"Good heavens, Mr Leatham, are you still here?"

"Miss Milburn? That was quick. "He jumped to his feet, clutching his hat. Wherever were his gloves? They seemed to have vanished.

"The letter was dealt with quick enough, but I was talking to Mickey in the stables about the goat and kid his sister is to send for Poppy. I must have been twenty minutes or more. I thought you'd be long gone."

"I was just feeling sorry for myself." Impulsively, he offered her his arm and to his surprise, she took it.

"Now, what have you got to feel miserable about?" she said. "You have a fine home, a father and step-mother who are fond of you, enough money to live on..."

"I have no purpose," he said. "That is my problem. In the army, I knew who I was and what I needed to do. So long as I followed orders, everything would be fine. But now... there are no orders."

"Except from your step-mother when she tells you who to marry," she said, and the acid tone was back in her voice.

"Those are not orders," he said tersely. "Merely... suggestions. Strongly-made suggestions, sometimes, and taking no account of my objections, but in the end, the decision is mine."

"Is it?" Before he could answer that, she went on, "Do you miss it very much? The army, I mean?"

At her words, he was swept with such longing to be back that he was almost overwhelmed. Unable to speak, he merely nodded.

"What do you miss most? The killing? The screams of men dying? The blood?"

"The comradeship, the constant physical activity, the importance of the enterprise," he shot back. "A year ago I was defending this country, our whole way of life, from possible invasion by hostile forces. Now I am trying to decide between reroofing the smithy or a row of cottages. And then there is the fence to be replaced at Mr Ascot's field, because his cows keep wandering. It is all so *petty*."

"Not to Mr Ascot or the smith or the cottagers. It's not on the level of defence of the realm, I'll grant you that, but it's important to be a good landlord, and to be seen to be so. That's purpose enough for any man, I'd have thought."

These words seemed, in his present mood, to be so wise that he said impulsively, "What would you do, Miss Milburn? The smithy or the cottages? One family helped or six? And if Mr Ascot's fence is to be replaced, then there will not be enough money to fix the smithy until next year. What on earth is anyone to do?"

"Fix the smithy roof, fix the worst cottage of the six and send two men from the farm to patch up the fence."

He gasped at the speed of her answer, then his eyes narrowed. "Why?"

"The smith is too important a man to be left with a leaky roof. Even I have heard rumours of the smith and his discontent, and how much he dislikes Mr Hapgood. Not you, and not your father either, but Mr Hapgood is widely known as a nipcheese. As for the cottages, if you repair one of the six, everyone will be pleased that you are doing something at last and hope it will be their turn next. And Mr Ascot grumbles worse than an old spinster. There is nothing wrong with his fence that a few planks wouldn't fix. One cow escaped once, and now he wants the whole fence replaced."

"How do you know all this?" he said wonderingly.

"There are advantages to not being a lady, Mr Leatham. When I meet the apothecary's wife, or the baker, or the woman who does the laundry for Mr Ascot, they talk to me as an equal. Which I am, of course. No one would tell you any of this, although if you were to visit your tenants without Mr Hapgood, you might find them more forthcoming."

They had reached the gates to Starlingford by this time. "Yes," Charles said slowly. "Smithy, one cottage, patch up the fence. And talk to the tenants without Hapgood."

She chuckled. "Now you are following *my* orders, Mr Leatham. Please remember that until recently, my entire domain was two rooms and a shared back yard. It doesn't exactly qualify me to advise on estate management, although I do have some experience with leaky roofs, it must be confessed. I suggest you talk it over with your father."

"Yes, yes, but this is so *sensible*, Miss Milburn. How wise you are! I thank you most sincerely for your thoughts on the matter. I must talk to my father at once. I bid you good day."

He made her a most respectful bow, and set off briskly along the drive for home. He was within sight of the house before he realised he had forgotten to retrieve the carriage again. With a sigh, he turned round once more.

13: Mysteries

Caroline had another visit from the lawyers appointed by the Benefactor. This time they wrote to her to make an appointment, arriving precisely at the agreed hour. All three sisters were there to meet them, Lin and Poppy feeling that the occasion warranted a retreat from the garden and hen-house for once, and the effort of scrubbing muddy fingernails and donning a respectable gown. Was it possible that there might be another thousand pounds to be given to them?

The sisters sat in a row behind Caroline's desk, while Mr Willerton-Forbes took the primary visitor's chair on the opposite side, Mr Neate self-effacingly retreated to the window seat and Captain Edgerton lounged against the mantel.

"My visit is a matter of courtesy only," Mr Willerton-Forbes said when the preliminaries had been dispensed with. "We have been attempting to gain admittance to Valmont, but his lordship is not minded to see us. Since we were to be passing your door, we felt it the perfect opportunity to ensure that all is well with you, and to enquire if there is any other matter with which we may assist you."

Lin and Poppy sighed with disappointment. No more money, then. Caroline was sorry too, but they now had more than enough for their needs.

"Such as what, sir?" she said, puzzled.

"For example, the investment of your fund from the Benefactor, although I imagine that the estimable Mr Stratton has advised you in that regard. But any matter that has arisen as a result of the sinking of the *Minerva* which is troubling you, and upon which we might perhaps be able to render assistance."

"There is one thing…" Caroline said slowly. "We have found large sums of money buried in the garden, and—"

"Buried in the garden?" Captain Edgerton said, springing to attention. "Truly? That is extraordinary!"

"How large were these large sums?" Mr Willerton-Forbes said.

"Five hundred pounds in each," Caroline said. "We have found five so far. One was in the safe when we first moved in here, and four were dug up from my sister's herb garden, the latest only yesterday. Each was a roll of bank notes in a netted purse, and the ones in the garden were in a waterproof bag inside a tin box."

"Do you have any of this for us to examine?" Captain Edgerton said eagerly.

Caroline opened the safe to retrieve the latest find, and produced the other four purses, now empty of their contents, from a desk drawer. "I don't have the boxes any more, or the waterproof bags. They were too horrid to keep. But everything else was sound."

The three men peered at the bank notes and the purses.

"There is a lady's hand in the purses, I believe," Mr Willerton-Forbes said. "These tassels... they look complicated, but to me, all such creations look complicated."

"These really *are* complicated," Caroline said with a quick laugh. "The netting is straightforward enough — well done, but not anything out of the ordinary. But the tassels, and this stitchery around the opening are very elegant. It grieves me to think of them buried underground, left to rot away."

"Ah, but they were not left to rot," Captain Edgerton said. "They were carefully protected against damp and earth. I should very much like to see precisely where they were found."

"Let me show you," Lin said, jumping up at once. "This way."

"I can show you my dear little chickens, too," Poppy said.

"Chickens! How charming," Captain Edgerton murmured, following the two out of the room.

Mr Willerton-Forbes laughed. "Captain Edgerton does like a mystery to solve, but I do not believe this particular one will tax him too far."

"Mr Stratton thought the money was Mr Wishaw's nest egg," Caroline said.

"Ah." Mr Willerton-Forbes leaned back in his chair, steepling his hands. "A prudent man may well secrete a sum for safe-keeping if he mistrusted banks. But you do not find that suggestion convincing?"

"That's just it, he didn't seem to mistrust his bank. He kept meticulous accounts, which show every penny that went into the bank and every penny that he drew out, and everything balances. There are no spare sums of five hundred pounds unaccounted for. Besides, these notes are drawn on a different bank, from London."

"I had noticed the London bank. Also, the netted purses are a curious detail. How then do you explain these sums?"

Caroline frowned. She had puzzled over it for hours at a time, letting her thoughts meander as she worked at her lace, but she was no nearer a solution that satisfied her. "The one we found in the safe when we first moved here was the full amount," she said slowly. "It wasn't as if he was gradually accumulating notes until he reached five hundred, and then he'd bury it. More that it came to him like that, five hundred pounds in a purse, but he couldn't bury it straight away. Maybe the ground was frozen, since it was the tail end of winter then. So I think someone gave him that money. I just don't know why."

"That is logical," Mr Willerton-Forbes said. "It cannot be gambling winnings, not with such a regular amount, so perhaps a bribe? Perhaps someone wished to assure himself of Mr Wishaw's business."

"And he kept it off the accounts and buried it... yes, that makes sense," Caroline said. "A bribe... is that common in business? It seems rather unsavoury to me."

"And to me, also," Mr Willerton-Forbes said. "However, such things do go on. Five hundred pounds to ensure that Mr Wishaw and Mr Salter would buy their hops from one supplier in particular... such things do indeed go on. Mr Wishaw has his nest egg for his retirement, and Mr Salter is none the wiser."

A squeal of girlish laughter issued from the garden. Mr Willerton-Forbes smiled at the sound. "Your sisters are enjoying rural life, I think, Miss Milburn, but perhaps it is not such an easy transition for you?"

She shook her head ruefully. "I imagined a quiet life, not very different from Romsey except with clean air and water fresh from the well. We would continue to ply our trades, as we always have. But that will not do for our neighbours, who are determined to make gentry of us. One of them wishes to take me visiting at Valmont, if you please! As if I have anything in common with a duke! It is ridiculous."

He smiled, but said, "But if you go, then you will have succeeded where I failed, Miss Milburn. We are refused admission at Valmont."

"But why?"

"Who can say? These great men have their whims. I thought my name might allow me past the gates, for my head of chambers, another Willerton-Forbes, is the most senior lawyer advising the Litherholm family. But no. Even a letter of introduction from my uncle and another from Sir Lester Markham were not sufficient. Yet I cannot complete my assignment from the Benefactor without transferring one thousand pounds into the hands of Lord Randolph Litherholm."

"But he hardly needs the money, does he?"

"That is not the point," he said primly. "My terms of reference are to include the nearest relative of *every* victim of the *Brig Minerva*, no matter how high or low on the social scale, no matter how rich or poor, so that is what I shall do, however long it takes. Lord Randolph will see me eventually, I am determined upon that."

"You are very conscientious," Caroline said. "It must be very dull work, looking up relatives."

"Not so dull as you might imagine," he said, eyes twinkling. "Being conscientious makes it a great deal easier to alleviate the dullness. The sinking of the *Brig Minerva* has thrown up enough mysteries to please even Captain Edgerton. There is the man who has no history, but appears on the quay in Dublin sprung from the very air, seemingly. He *said* he had been raised in an orphanage in Carlisle, but, being conscientious, I dispatched Captain Edgerton to enquire, and he found no trace of such a person at any orphanage."

"People change their names all the time," Caroline said, laughing. "It hardly needs explanation."

"Ah. You think so? In the circles where I normally move, such things are highly unusual, but I suppose outside the highborn families it is a more common occurrence. Still, I should like an explanation all the same. I believe I may pay another visit to the gentleman, to see if I might winkle out the truth."

"Oh, he did not drown?"

"There were only three survivors, but he was one of them, and there is another curiosity — how was it that he survived, but others, more experienced at sea than he, did not? And yet another mystery that intrigues me, and you may tell me, if you will, if this is also a common event — one of the passengers, travelling under a man's name and wearing man's clothing, was in fact a woman."

"Oh, that is strange!" Caroline said. "I can't imagine… perhaps she had to travel alone for some reason and didn't wish to attract attention. A woman on board ship alone would be…" She broke off, floundering for the right word.

"Vulnerable?" the lawyer hazarded. "Indeed she might. Perhaps that was all it was."

"You sound disappointed," Caroline said.

"Not exactly, but I had anticipated some more devious explanation than simple concealment of her feminine nature. Yet I daresay that is the answer. How useful this has been, Miss Milburn. Your practicality is refreshing. You have my gratitude for your assistance."

"I'm not sure I've been much help," she said, chuckling. "After all, your mysteries are not all that great, are they? One man travelling under a new name, and one woman pretending to be a man."

"Ah, but there are other, greater, mysteries that interest me also. Why, for instance, a sturdy ship manned by an experienced crew and captain, travelling in calm seas and perfect weather, should drift onto rocks? What happened that night aboard the *Minerva?* I should very much like to know. Why was the Duke of Falconbury aboard, since he should have caught the packet two days earlier? Also, why the new duke refuses to see me... and refuses to claim his title, too. And one that is of the greatest interest to me personally — who is the Benefactor whose largesse I am distributing?"

"You don't know?"

"I have not the least idea. Curious, is it not?" And he beamed at her happily.

~~~~~

There was no relief from the stream of calls from their neighbours in the three Bursham villages, which Caroline felt obliged to return, and after that the invitations began to arrive. These were not landed gentry, like the Alsagers and Leathams, but even so Caroline was reluctant to accept.

"We'll be obliged to hold parties of our own if we go to these," she said. "I'm not sure—"
~~~~~

"It's only the Christophers, and Mrs Christopher says it's pot luck and just family," Poppy said. "Please may we go, Caro?"

"The Pierces' card party is very informal, and we can walk there," Lin said. "It will be great fun."

After pot luck at the parsonage and cards at the house with the cheerful red door, there was dinner with the Wenman sisters, the widows of two brothers who lived at the far end of the village. Poppy was deemed to be too young for that, but Lin and Caroline went, and Caroline had to admit that it was pleasant to be in company again, as they had not been since Papa had died. It was not elevated company, but it felt very fitting for the daughters of a linen draper. Their peers were an unassuming clergyman, a former attorney and the widows of two coach builders. If they wished to widen their circle of acquaintances, there was Mr Ascot, the apothecary, Mr and Mrs Dunn, the innkeepers, and Miss Porter, the former governess. And so, inch by reluctant inch, the sisters found themselves pulled into the upper level of society in Bursham St Matthew.

It was not long before Caroline felt the pressure to return the hospitality extended to them. Molly said enthusiastically that she could happily cook for a dozen or more if she had a bit of help in the kitchen, and Martin was happy to pretend to be a footman for the day and polish up the silver, while Susie opened a new jar of beeswax polish and set about the dining room furniture with a will. So it was that Caroline, who had never wanted to be anything but a lacemaker, found herself obliged to don an evening gown once more, and play hostess to a dinner at her own table. She chose a Saturday night, so that Mr Stratton could be of the company, and she sent out cards of invitation to the Christophers, the Wenman ladies, the Pierces and Tim Carter, their gamekeeper cousin, and his wife. By the time all was settled, they sat down fourteen at table, with two full courses, wines provided by Mr Wishaw's extensive cellar, fish by courtesy of Tim Carter and cheese from the Bursham All Saints dairy. The vegetables were not, sadly, from their own kitchen garden, for Lin said there was nothing ready, but there was no shortage, and all agreed that everything was cooked to perfection. Or, if they did not agree, they were polite enough not to mention it.

Lin and Poppy were in alt, Lin probably because Mr Stratton was there, and Poppy because it was her first ever grown-up dinner and must be accorded the accolade of perfection on that account alone. Caroline was forced to admit that the evening was a pleasant one, the food good and the company in lively spirits. The Mrs Wenmans could both play the pianoforte, so there was music after dinner and then cards, with tea and a light supper at the proper hour. Everyone left in time to be home before the onset of the Sabbath, and Caroline retired to bed with the comfortable feeling that they had, at last, found their proper level in society and might quietly forget about the grander folk at Corranwater and Starlingford.

This pleasant sensation lasted all of half a day, until they attended church and met with Mrs Leatham.

"My dear Miss Milburn," she called from some distance away. "Halloo there! Miss Milburn!"

Caroline broke off her conversation with the Mrs Wenmans to turn and make her curtsy, as Mrs Leatham bore down on her. "How delightful! Mr Christopher tells me you have begun entertaining at last. What a fine thing, to be sure! You should have let me know, for Charles would have brought you some game and fish for the table. He is always out shooting things, or fishing. Are you not, Charles? Where has he got to now? Foolish boy! He is always wandering off. But next time, do let me know and Charles will provide whatever you need."

"Thank you, Mrs Leatham, but Mr Carter is well able to provision us."

"Timothy Carter? The *Valmont* gamekeeper? You know him, do you?" Two elegant eyebrows lifted in surprise.

"He is our cousin," Caroline said patiently, wondering if she could escape in time to have a word with Mr Ascot, the apothecary. But Mrs Leatham was far from finished.

"Your *cousin?* But how—?" She stopped, worked it out and blushed slightly. "Well... well... that is very good." She cleared her throat, and renewed her smile. "Indeed, it is splendid that you are making so many new friends in the village, and having the courage to entertain. But now that you have got into the way of it, I hope you will not neglect your *other* friends." As she spoke, she simpered, so that Caroline was left in no doubt as to which other friends were referred to.

Not for the first time, Caroline heartily wished that the Leathams attended a different church, or that they were less regular in their observance of the Sabbath, for every Sunday she must endure the blandishments of Mrs Leatham. It was an effort to be civil to her.

"If you mean yourself, Mrs Leatham, we wouldn't presume to invite you to dine at the cottage. We don't have the standard of accommodations for a lady such as yourself."

"Nonsense!" she trilled. "Next time you entertain, I do so hope you will extend an invitation to us. I am not sure that Mr Leatham would wish to leave his own house unless the weather should be particularly favourable, but Charles and I should be delighted to attend."

"And Miss Beacher, too, I trust," Caroline added.

"Oh... of course, Mildred too. Now, my dear, I am so glad I caught you because our arrangements for the visit to Valmont are all in place. Thursday is to be the day, and—"

"But—"

"—it is all settled with the Narfields, so we shall be expected. Is it not exciting?"

"But—"

"You need not be overly concerned about your gown. Just wear the best you have, but nothing too elaborate. The Valmont ladies would not like it if we were to dress too fine, you see. One must have the distinction of rank preserved."

"Mrs Leatham, I—"

"The carriage will call for you at ten o'clock sharp, so be sure to be ready. Elinor may come too, if she pleases, but Poppy is too young for such company, I feel sure you will agree. Oh, I must just have a word with Mr Ascot about Mr Leatham's tonic. Forgive me if I dash away, Miss Milburn. Remember — Thursday at ten o'clock sharp!"

With those words she was gone. Caroline stamped her foot in frustration.

A low chuckle made her turn her head. Mr Charles Leatham stood not five paces away, grinning in delight at her discomfiture.

"You may protest as much as you please, Miss Milburn, but Mama is not a lady to be denied. No point making yourself miserable over it. In my experience, it is far better to accede gracefully from the start than to wage a long campaign and be forced in the end to surrender. Mama will have her way."

"Oh, so you always give in without the least fight, do you? How craven! A fine soldier you must have been."

He bridled at once. "I was an excellent soldier, if you must know, madam, in battle or elsewhere, but I had a thousand times sooner take on the French than Mama."

"Then you're foolish as well as cowardly, sir. Are you afraid of one woman?"

"When that one woman is my step-mother, yes."

"Why? You're a man, and may do as you please. What can she possibly do to you?"

"She can torment me," he said glumly, his irritation subsiding. "In desperate cases, she can cry, and there is nothing more horrifying than female tears." He quirked a rueful smile. "I know you think me a poor creature, Miss Milburn, and perhaps I am, but I like a quiet life. Since I have no idea what to do with myself, I am perfectly happy to let Mama order my life for me. It is what I am used to and trained for — to obey orders." He sighed, and she wondered if he were regretting the loss of his army career again. "So there it is. Mama tells me I am to accompany her to Valmont, and therefore to Valmont I am to go."

"Well, more fool you," Caroline said. "*I* shall not surrender so tamely."

"I have no objection to seeing one of our great families in their natural habitat," he said thoughtfully. "The house is magnificent, and the gardens— I have heard much of the wonders of the lakes and waterfalls. And..." He lowered his voice conspiratorially. "I am greatly looking forward to seeing Mama cowering in the splendour of Valmont. How else can we know our place in society, if we see nothing of those far above us?"

"I know my place in society perfectly well, thank you," Caroline said tartly. "I wish you joy of your visit to Valmont."

He chuckled. "Are you not even the slightest bit tempted? Is it my presence which deters you? If you come, I promise not to quarrel with you."

She gazed at him in amazement. "You could never keep such a promise. I'd wager you would be in a pelt inside five minutes."

"Oh? What would you wager, then, madam, if you are so certain of it?"

"Ten pounds," she said, without the slightest hesitation.

"Tame! Make it fifty," he said. "That would be more interesting, would it not?"

"Fifty! I cannot afford to throw away so much money."

"Come now, Miss Milburn, how hard can it be? Forget the five minutes — I will give you the whole day. Can I really last so many hours without quarrelling with you?"

"Of course you can't. Fifty pounds it is."

It was only after he had left, with a smug smile on his face, that she realised he had achieved what his step-mother could not — he had made her agree to go to Valmont.

14: A Visit To Valmont (July)

"Lin, you must come with me," Caroline said desperately. "Don't leave me to a whole day all alone with the Leathams."

"It was your own fault for allowing Mr Leatham to goad you," Lin said. "I'd rather be assaulted with red hot pokers than go to Valmont."

Caroline laughed. "No, you wouldn't. Red hot pokers... the horrors of the Leathams and Valmont can't be *that* bad, and I would have thought you'd have wanted to see the gardens there."

"Oh... these grand gardens... there's not much I can apply here, and I've enough to do with the herbs at the moment."

With a sigh, Caroline said, "Well, if you won't, you won't. Just don't go into the village on your own, will you? And keep an eye on Poppy. She hasn't wandered off for a while and—"

"Heavens, Caro, stop *worrying!*" Lin said crossly. "You're always fussing over us. I'm almost twenty and Poppy will be sixteen next Sunday. We're not children, you know."

"I know. Sorry." But even so, she gave Susie strict instructions to keep an eye on her two sisters.

~~~~~

JULY

There were three days of feverish needlework to attire Caroline suitably for the grandeur of a ducal residence. Mama's Box had yielded a charming organdy muslin for a round gown, a figured silk for a matching spencer, cap and reticule, and enough ribbons for some very pretty embellishments about the sleeves and hem. Her own lace provided a fichu, and she extravagantly bought new kid half-boots and gloves for the occasion. She felt like a child who has been playing in her mother's wardrobe, and yet she could not remember her mother ever wearing anything so stylish.

The only distraction from the frantic preparations came from John Christopher, who dug up yet another box. This one was a little different, being an ornately carved silver affair, and firmly locked. It was too good a piece to be forced open, so Caroline cleaned it up and locked it away in the safe until she could get it to the locksmith. Another five hundred pounds! She happily calculated the increase in income this new addition to their savings would bring.

She was ready and waiting at ten o'clock on Thursday. She waited. She continued to wait, as Poppy dashed in and out of the house to check the clock.

"Quarter past!" she cried gleefully. "They're not coming."

"Oh, where are they?" Lin said fretfully. "They are *so* late. I *hate* it when people are late. It's so nerve-wracking."

"Why are *you* so impatient?" Caroline snapped. "You're not the one kept waiting."

"You're very cross today," Lin said. "It's your own fault for agreeing to go in the first place. I'm not waiting any longer. I have things to do." She flounced away into the house.
~~~~~

Caroline knew exactly why she herself was cross. It was not the prospect of Valmont itself, for she had to admit to some curiosity about the place, however little right she had to be going there. No, it was her wager with Mr Leatham which preyed on her mind most forcibly. However could she have been so stupid as to agree to it? All he had to do was to curb his temper for a few hours, and she would have to pay him fifty pounds. Fifty pounds! It was an unthinkable amount of money to throw away. She would simply have to provoke him into an argument, for she would take no pleasure in the day otherwise.

Eventually, almost twenty minutes past the hour, the Leatham carriage turned in at the gates and drew to a halt, the door opened and Mr Charles Leatham descended to assist Caroline inside with a bow and a proffered arm.

"You see, I am determined to be charming today," he said with a wide grin. "Nothing can deter me."

"We shall see about that," she said grimly, taking her place beside Mrs Leatham, while Mr Leatham settled on the seat opposite, still grinning in the most infuriating manner.

"Well, now, is this not delightful?" Mrs Leatham said. "What a pity your sister is not with us, but I am sure she knows best. How charmingly you look, Miss Milburn. Is that a new cap? Did you make it yourself? So clever! We are going to have the most delightful day, and you and Charles may get to know each other a little better. Charles, be sure to take good care of Miss Milburn today. Now, Mrs Narfield will be there to receive us, and her sister-in-law Lady Narfield, who is Lord Randolph's sister, you know — Lady Georgiana Litherholm, as she was. As for the men, there is no knowing whether they might have gone off riding or shooting or some such thing. The gentlemen are so keen on their sports, are they not? So we may not depend upon them, but some of the other ladies might be there. His lordship has quite a large party gathered at the moment — all his sisters, and various aunts and uncles and cousins. Now, his lordship is the new duke, everyone knows that, for his brother is drowned in that terrible sinking down in Cornwall, just like Mr Wishaw, but he has not yet claimed the title. It is unlikely that he will condescend to honour us with his presence, but if he should choose to do so, he must not be addressed as Your Grace, but only as my lord. Poor man! He is so cast down by his brother's death, Mrs Narfield said. Dresses all in black, and has the mourning wreath still on the door, apparently. Ah, now this is Corranford, Miss Milburn. Just a tiny hamlet, nothing here but the mill. Once we are past the ford, we shall be entirely surrounded by Valmont land. The woods…"

Caroline's head was spinning. Fortunately, Mrs Leatham required no participation from her captive audience, being perfectly capable of maintaining the conversation single-handedly. Caroline began to get an inkling of why she had been invited, to provide a complaisant listener for her monologue, someone new enough to require explanation of every landmark of interest along the way.

If she had been less nerve-wracked by the prospect of losing fifty pounds, Caroline would have enjoyed the journey immensely. The weather was kind, the carriage was well-sprung and the roads not too badly rutted. As they drew nearer to Valmont, they came to the boundary wall of the duke's residence and then to the village that clustered around one of the gates. There were no fewer than eight entrances, the indefatigable Mrs Leatham told her, all with a lodge house built in the same style as Valmont itself. The village was a fine, bustling place, with a market under way in the centre of it, the square a mass of farmers and bleating lambs and pie-sellers shouting their wares. There were some pretty cottages and more imposing houses, as well as a number of interesting shops and inns, all of them bearing the Litherholm coat of arms.

"Does it mean something, the shield over the door?" Caroline said. "The pig seems an odd thing for a duke to put on his arms."

"Oh, it is all symbolic," Mrs Leatham said vaguely. "To do with a battle somewhere, I expect. Ah, here is the gatekeeper to admit us."

After a brief discussion between the gatekeeper and the coachman, the high gates were swung open for them and the carriage passed through into the hallowed grounds of Valmont. At once, the noise and commotion of the market was left behind, and they were surrounded by great tall trees, their leaves rustling gently far above. Spears of sunshine broke through the canopy to light their path. It was very tranquil. After a considerable time, they emerged from the trees to gain their first view of the house.

"It's enormous!" Caroline breathed. "And all for one man!"

Mrs Leatham chuckled. "I knew you would be impressed. Of course, his lordship is not alone here. Why there must be a hundred servants, at least."

"You'd need that many," Caroline said. "Think of all those miles of floors to mop and carpets to beat and windows to clean, and imagine how many grates would need to be black-leaded."

Mrs Leatham looked momentarily startled, as if the idea of black-leading grates had never crossed her mind. And perhaps it never had, since her servants seemed to know their business without much intervention from their mistress.

Mr Leatham chuckled. "How practical you are, Miss Milburn."

"Indeed," Mrs Leatham said, rallying. "That is what we admire most about you, dear Miss Milburn."

As the carriage rolled to a halt, a troop of footmen emerged from the house, resplendent in wigs, white gloves, black coats and silk knee breeches. Caroline had seen respectable merchants and bankers dressed less stylishly than these humble servants. The butler was even better dressed, and would have passed for a gentleman in any company. Perhaps he was, at that. It may be that the duke was so grand that mere gentlemen wanted to serve him. No, not a duke… he was just a lord, still. It was so complicated.

They were admitted to a great hall with marble tiles, white and a rich red in a checkered pattern. A staircase with banisters polished to a high shine led to a half-landing and then up to the next floor. Huge chandeliers sporting scores of candles hung on long chains, and more candles in sconces lined the walls. Every candle was brand new, and the housewife in Caroline was horrified at the thought that half-used ones were replaced before they were finished, just so that the duke… no, the *lord* could have fresh ones every day. What a waste! And if they were used in the servants' hall, that would be just as much of a waste. Wax for entertaining, Papa had always said, and tallow for everyday. Susie wouldn't know herself if she were burning the best beeswax in the kitchen.

A housekeeper, just as grand as the butler, awaited them at the far side of the hall, and led them through the house. The rooms were all connected one to another, so they walked from one overpowering chamber to the next, in relentless procession.

Mrs Leatham, who had only visited twice before, took it upon herself to act as guide. "This is the library, Miss Milburn," she said, waving an arm vaguely towards a bookcase.

"His Grace the Sixth Duke liked to call this the Royal Withdrawing Room," the housekeeper murmured. "It is only used in the winter, hence the warm colouring. The library is in the other wing, but Lady Narfield will be delighted to show it to you, if you have a particular interest in books. Now this is my favourite room." She threw open another door.

"Ah, the dining room," Mrs Leatham said.

"We call it the buttery," the housekeeper said. "A small room for a private party, perhaps. His Grace the Sixth Duke used to host his political dinners in here. Through here is the Queen's Room, where you will find the ladies, I believe."

Caroline felt small. Every room, every piece of furniture, every ornament was built on a larger-than-life scale. There were fireplaces large enough to walk into, vases the height of a man, ornately painted ceilings far above their heads and everywhere decoration, embellishment, ornamentation. She far preferred the plain oak tables and chairs at Bursham Cottage to this grandiose display of wealth.

The ladies were congregated in a small corner of the room, an array of muslins in the mourning colours of pale grey or lavender, elaborately decorated about the sleeves and hems, and some fine lace caps. Mostly Honiton lace, she thought, as she drew close, or possibly Bruges. One of the ladies wore an Italian style, which must have been an heirloom piece, perhaps made in one of the convents. Caroline's fingers itched to feel the delicate threads, and admire it from close quarters.

Mrs Narfield emerged from the throng to greet them, the ladies rose in a mass of swishing skirts and there was a great to-do of introductions. Lady Henrietta, Lady Alice, Lady Elizabeth, Lady Anne, Lady Charlotte... Some quite young, others much older. One elderly gentleman, Lord Arthur. Caroline smiled and curtsied and curtsied again, wondering what on earth she was doing there. She should have listened to her first instinct and refused. She should never have allowed Mr Charles to goad her into accepting. And then the fear washed over her again — fifty pounds!

By some unspoken agreement, the ladies began to drift towards a pair of doors. Two footmen in black sprang to open them, and the chattering group passed through. One elderly lady and the gentleman resumed their seats with relief, but everyone else followed along, Caroline last of all. They entered a smaller room which had doors to the outside. More footmen leapt to open them, and the group moved in stately procession out onto the terrace.

"We are to be given a tour of the gardens," Mr Leatham whispered in Caroline's ear. "Quite a privilege."

"Are we supposed to be grateful?" she whispered back. Her reserve of civility was already depleted by the prolonged introductions.

He chuckled, and said smugly, "*I* am suitably grateful, even if you are inclined to be perverse today."

"And you are never perverse, I suppose, Mr Leatham."

Another low laugh. "I admit to frequent perverseness, Miss Milburn, but not today. Today I am the epitome of unruffled composure."

"How annoying," she said, with great sincerity.

That just made him laugh the more.

The gardens, it turned out, were every bit as grandiose as the house. Long brick walks and winding gravel ones, arbours, grottos and cascades, statues and fountains and quiet pools, shrubberies and topiary and woodland paths, hot houses and cool houses and a kitchen garden bursting with exuberant growth. And every step of the way, Mr Leatham was by her side, smiling and exuding good humour. He stood quietly as she stared at the vegetables.

"Look at those beans," Caroline said crossly. "I thought Lin would grow some, but we have nothing like that. I must ask her why she hasn't sown any."

"I daresay she cares more for her rhubarb," Mr Leatham said.

"What do you know about Lin's rhubarb?" Caroline said suspiciously.

"Only that she talked incessantly about it when she called once. What do you do with it? Not eat it, I hope. Nasty stuff, rhubarb."

"It is medicinal, and although it has its uses, I would far rather have beans. It is very provoking to see such abundance when we have none."

"If the beans displease you, shall we move on?" he said in amiable tones. "I believe the ladies are returning to the house, and we cannot have you distressed by a vegetable."

"What do you care?" she said, quite aware that she was being petulant but unable to help herself. "Why are you still clinging to my side like a limpet, Mr Leatham? For you are not at all wanted, I'll have you know."

For a moment his face darkened and she held her breath. Was he about to lose his temper? But no. He mastered his anger, and even dared to smile at her. "Ah, you are trying to provoke me into dispute, but your trickery is in vain, Miss Milburn. I am determined to be chivalry personified today, and I am clinging to your side like a *barnacle*, not a limpet, so that you may have every opportunity to win your bet. It would hardly be honourable in me to hide myself away, would it? We cannot quarrel if we are not together."

"Oh... pfft!" she said, and stomped away. She was not managing to provoke him into anger, but he was certainly provoking her. And deep inside was the leaden ball of fear — fifty pounds! If she should lose...

The ladies gathered on the wide terrace, where the elderly lady and gentleman who had declined the walk joined them. The army of footmen had been busily engaged in setting out tables covered in snowy cloths, laden with bread and cake and fruit and cold meats. Caroline quickly chose a seat between two other ladies, but Mr Leatham brought up another chair and squeezed in next to her. Across the table, Mrs Leatham smiled knowingly, and nodded her head in seeming approval. Such irritating people, the Leathams.

More footmen arrived to serve platters of hot pastries and pour wine.

"How many footmen do they have?" Caroline said, overwhelmed by so much massed servitude.

One of the ladies overheard her. "Only twelve at the moment," she said. "The household is below full capacity until there is a duchess in residence. However, the valets serve at dinner, and the grooms help out when we have a large event, so we manage."

Only twelve. Below full capacity. Caroline could find no sensible response. Valmont was run on a scale her mind could barely comprehend.

The lady turned towards her and went on, "Such a pretty lace kerchief you wear, Miss Milburn! That is not patent lace, I warrant. Did you obtain it from a supplier in Salisbury?"

"No, my lady. I made it myself."

"How clever you are! Such a fine accomplishment, to make one's own lace."

"It's my trade, my lady. I beg your pardon, but I've forgotten your name."

She smiled, not offended. "I am Lady Narfield, but I was Lady Georgiana Litherholm before my marriage. The sixth duke was my father. So confusing, is it not, all these names? Let us speak of you, instead. Your friend said you have only recently moved to Bursham from Romsey. That is quite a change, but you have made an excellent choice. Bursham is very well situated, and so convenient for Salisbury. We are nearer to Andover, but the shops are not so good there."

"Oh, we didn't choose it, my lady. Our grandfather left it to us in his will after he drowned on the *Minerva*." Belatedly, she realised this was not a good choice of subject. "Oh, I beg your pardon, my—"

But her face lit up. "Your grandfather was on the *Minerva?* Alice, Etta, did you hear that? Miss Milburn's grandfather was on the *Minerva* too."

With murmurs of interest, they drew up chairs and gathered around her to hear more. The attention was embarrassing, not least because she had known nothing at all about her grandfather, or his travels to and from Dublin, until Mr Stratton had revealed the contents of Mr Wishaw's will.

"But how exciting," one of the ladies said. "To suddenly find oneself the possessor of a house in that way, quite unexpectedly! And you have sisters, you said? No doubt you will be very popular among the local swains with such a dowry."

"Oh, no, we don't have—" Caroline began, but then stopped. Between the three of them, they owned a house and several thousand pounds. That was indeed a substantial dowry for three women who had previously been living in two rooms, and scraping by on whatever they could earn by their own hands. Was that why Mr Stratton was so interested in Lin? And it was not just Mr Stratton, for there was always one or other young man popping up with offers of weeding the vegetable beds, or fixing a fence, or lopping off a dead branch in the orchard. Of course, Lin was pretty enough that there was no need to look for a mercenary motive, but it might be an added inducement.

Another man emerged from the house, and at first Caroline assumed from his black coat that he was merely another footman. But he began to mingle with the ladies, and when he was introduced to Mrs Leatham, she caught the name. Lord Randolph Litherholm. The new duke. He was so young! She hadn't realised, not being familiar with the family, that the duke was brother to the younger ladies of the party, and the older ones were his aunts. He couldn't have been more than seven or eight and twenty, handsome in an aristocratic way, although his face was solemn and unsmiling.

When he was introduced to Mrs Leatham, she blushed and stammered and curtsied twice, and seemed unable to finish a single sentence. It was strange to see her fluency desert her so spectacularly. She offered her condolences, which he accepted graciously, making polite enquiries about her husband, and their journey, all the conventional small talk of casual acquaintances.

After a few minutes, he moved on and Caroline realised her turn was coming. She quailed, having never even seen a duke before, never mind been introduced to one. She reminded herself sternly that he was just a man, for all his title and money and hordes of footmen, and he wasn't much older than she was. Nor did she depend on his goodwill for employment or social favour. She was just a passing visitor who would never be here again. With such thoughts, she was able to make her curtsy without agitation. Then she became stuck, her mind an utter blank. What on earth does anyone say to a duke? Fortunately, Lady Narfield rescued her.

"Ran, Miss Milburn's grandfather drowned on the *Minerva*, too."

At once his face changed, alive with sudden interest. "Indeed? Then I am very sorry for it, madam. We are united in our grief, for none can comprehend such depth of sorrow who has not suffered it. Please sit, Miss Milburn." He half turned and caught the eye of a footman, who somehow divined his meaning without any words spoken and brought forward a chair. The duke sat down beside Caroline. "Tell me of your grandfather, Miss Milburn, for I would know everything of my poor brother's sailing companions."

"I'm very sorry, my lord, but I know nothing about him, except that he was a hop merchant on business in Ireland. I didn't even know of his existence until after he was dead, and found out he'd left his house to my mother. Since she's dead, my sisters and I inherited."

"So the inheritance came as a complete surprise?"

"Absolutely."

"But how came you not to know anything of him? Did your mother never speak of him?"

"She never knew, either. She thought her father was a soldier who died in India, but in fact she was an illeg—" She stopped, blushing.

"Ah," he said, understanding. "Such things happen in the best regulated families, Miss Milburn."

"Even in yours?" she said, before she could stop herself. Across the table, Mrs Leatham's eyes widened in horror, but she heard a low chuckle from Mr Leatham, standing behind her.

The duke was not in the least disconcerted. He smiled at her, and his face softened from ducal dignity to impishness, which made him look even younger than his years. "Even in mine," he said. "It is the way of the world, but a natural child need not be any great disgrace, on either side. Your grandfather made provision for your mother, and that is as it should be. For you, then, the sinking of the *Brig Minerva* has been nothing but a blessing, bringing you unexpected good fortune, and I congratulate you. Whereas for me, it has brought nothing but grief and uncertainty."

Uncertainty? What uncertainty could there be, surrounded by such wealth?

He must have seen puzzlement in her expression, for he went on, "My brother was away in America for three years, Miss

Milburn. There is always the possibility that he has married and fathered a son who is now the duke. That renders the succession most uncertain."

"Would he do that without telling anyone?" Caroline said.

"Perhaps. He had a secretive nature, sometimes, and in his last letter to me he said that he had a surprise for me. I wondered then... but if he was bringing home a wife, she would have been on the *Minerva* too, and there was no woman on board."

"But there was," Caroline said at once, without thinking. "She was dressed as a man, but she was a woman. Maybe your brother married after all."

15: A Wager

For perhaps ten minutes, the duke and his sisters plied Caroline with questions, none of which she could answer. She could only refer them to Mr Willerton-Forbes, who had told her of the woman masquerading as a man. The duke leapt to his feet, intent on rushing away immediately to write to Mr Willerton-Forbes to obtain more information. He had actually turned and taken two steps away from the table when the horrible truth dawned on him.

"If that was Gervase's wife, then she is drowned too," he said in a hollow voice. "If she carried a child, it is gone. It is no use."

"Three years, Ran," one of the ladies said. "Ger was gone for three years. There could be a child left behind somewhere... too young to travel, perhaps. There is still hope."

"Still hope," he echoed, but his voice was bleak. "Three years... I shall write anyway, and find out what I can. You will excuse me, Miss Milburn... Mrs Leatham... ladies." He bowed, spun on his heel and strode away.

"Poor boy," one of the ladies said. "He has taken it very hard. They were very close, always."

"Was Lord Randolph's brother much older than him?" Caroline said.

It was Lady Narfield who answered. "Ten minutes. Twins, you see. Not identical, in looks or in temper. Ger was the mercurial one... up in the boughs one minute, sunk in gloom the next, and always restless. Ran was the steady, solid one. But inseparable as boys, until Father thought it best for them to spend some time apart. This trip to America was the final attempt to get all that restlessness out of Ger's system before he married and settled down to be the heir. And now this. Poor Ran. He cannot believe that Ger is dead and he is alone now." She sighed. "But enough of my brothers. Miss Milburn, I have a favour to ask of you. I shall be hosting my own party of guests later this month at Narfield Lodge. Mr and Mrs Leatham will be there, but I should like you to be of the company as well."

"Oh, my lady, I'm not fit to mingle in such society," Caroline cried.

"Let me be the judge of that," she said, with a smile.

"But I'm a lacemaker by trade, not a lady like you. I shouldn't even be here today, except that— Well, I shouldn't," she said, not liking to mention the wager. "I certainly shouldn't be staying as a guest. It's not right."

"You need not be ashamed of your origins."

"I'm not ashamed of them, my lady, but I know my place in society, and it's not mixing with the sisters of dukes."

"But you are a friend of the Leatham family." Did her eyes flicker to Mr Leatham for a moment? "That is good enough for me. Besides, you would be helping me out. We have a number of very young ladies staying this year, and I should dearly like to have someone with a touch more common sense to help me keep an eye on them and steer them out of trouble. You are such a sensible person, and not at all timid. You would be a great asset. Will you at least think about it?"

Caroline was too flustered to couch a polite refusal. She was distracted, too, by Mrs Leatham, who was smiling and nodding encouragingly. "I will think about it," she said.

"Good, good. And now I must go and make sure that Aunt Charlotte has taken her tonic and Uncle Arthur has gone off for his nap. He will be as cross as a bear if he does not get his hour of sleep." And with a rustle of muslin she rose and went into the house. Most of the other ladies had drifted away, too, either back inside to find a respite from the afternoon warmth, or, parasols aloft, venturing out into the gardens again. Mrs Leatham, too, murmured something about shade and a rest, whispered the word *'Barnacle!'* to her son, and vanished inside.

Caroline was left alone with Mr Leatham.

~~~~~

Charles had watched these exchanges with increasing irritation. First Mama had behaved in the most bird-witted way with the duke, twittering incoherently like a schoolroom chit. Then Miss Milburn, who ought to have been quite overwhelmed by such attention, had chatted away to him as if she had known him for ever. She had so monopolised him, in fact, that Charles had never even had the chance to be introduced to him. It was not pleasant to be overlooked as if he were of no consequence at all, while Miss Milburn, the linen draper's daughter, was treated like royalty. And now Mama had forced him to spend the rest of the day alone with the woman.

But he had a bet to win, and so he dredged up some semblance of a smile and offered her his arm. "Shall we walk,
~~~~~

Miss Milburn? We have not yet tackled the maze. It is a very fine specimen, it appears, inspired by the one at Versailles, just as Valmont was inspired by the palace there."

"I have no wish to get lost with only you for company, Mr Leatham."

"Now why on earth should we get lost?" he said testily, before remembering the need for calm. He must not allow himself to be provoked! More evenly, he went on, "One need only approach the matter systematically to be in and out in no time. A quick walk round the maze, and then we can find a cool spot beside one of the pools, or return to the terrace for lemonade."

She eyed him speculatively. "Very well, but you must be the guide. I'm sure you are much better at systematic approaches than I am."

He was suspicious of her sudden acquiescence, but he agreed to it and they set off for the maze. It was some distance from the main pleasure grounds, tucked away behind the stables, and he was uneasily aware that all the other guests had gone in a different direction. If they should happen to lose their way, there would be no one to help and they would not be missed until the hour for the carriage to be summoned. However, he had great confidence in his ability to find his way. He was a trained soldier, after all.

The stables were easy enough to locate, a splendid block built in a square around a yard. It was constructed in the same style as the house, complete with towers at each corner and a fine clock above the arched entrance. At the back of the stables, a wide gravel path led to the imposing hedges of the maze. They found one of the openings and passed inside, where the air was cool between thick hedges that towered over their heads. Almost at once there was a junction.

“This way,” Charles said confidently. “We are making for that pagoda in the middle.”

“That is no distance at all,” Miss Milburn said, gazing at the colourful tower that rose above the hedges.

“Indeed. This should not take more than five minutes, and another five to get out again.”

She smiled and followed him without a word.

He led the way, turning first one way, then another. From time to time they passed benches or statues on plinths, but after a while they all began to look the same to him, and he could not be sure that they were not doubling back and passing some that they had seen before. Still, he remained confident. “Are you confused yet?” he said to her.

“Completely,” she said, beaming at him cheerfully. “How glad I am that I have you here to lead the way, Mr Leatham.”

He had the annoying feeling that she was laughing at him. “Left at the next junction, I think. We should be almost at the middle.”

But they were not. They turned this way and that, and sometimes the pagoda seemed almost within reach, but always there was a solid hedge in between.

“Perhaps we should give up on finding the middle, and try to get out,” Miss Milburn said, with irritating cheerfulness.

He stopped, anger boiling up inside. As if she could have done any better! Recollecting himself, he took a couple of deep breaths, then said with more composure than he felt, “We took a wrong turn somewhere, but we are very close now, I am certain.”

"You said that ten minutes ago, and ten minutes before that," she said chirpily. "You're not very good at this, are you?"

"If you think—!" He caught himself just in time. Another deep breath. And another. "I am not as good as I believed, it is true, but I shall find the way in the end."

"Ohhh!" she wailed, flopping down on a convenient bench. "You're not going to, are you?" Her voice wobbled, almost as if she were about to cry.

Alarmed, he sat down beside her, and patted her gloved hand in what he hoped was a reassuring manner. "Never fear, Miss Milburn. I admit to having made one or two mistakes, but I shall get us out of here before long."

"I don't care about that," she cried. "We need only turn left by the nymph with the broken foot and then right at the lion to be on the way out. No, I meant that you're not going to quarrel with me, and I'll have to pay you fifty pounds."

"Oh." His eyebrows lifted in surprise. "It seemed like no more than an amusing game. I had not the least idea that our little wager distressed you so much."

"Well, it does. It will distress me if I lose, anyway."

He tugged at his ear pensively. Surely she could not be so poor that the loss of fifty pounds was catastrophic? He was about to retort briskly to that effect when the thought crossed his mind that this might be another attempt to goad him into a quarrel. If so, she would be disappointed. "What would be the consequence of losing such a sum?" he said in mild tones. "Would you starve? Be obliged to turn off servants? Have to sell the house?"

She gave him a watery smile. "Nothing like that. It isn't the money, because I have more than that sitting in the safe, and not earmarked for any of the tradesmen. No, it's the principle of it —

gambling, and *giving away* money for no good purpose. Forgive me for mentioning such a thing, Mr Leatham, but you don't exactly qualify for my charity, and you aren't supplying goods or performing a service. It's so... so *wasteful.*"

He had never considered gambling for such a small amount as anything other than a harmless amusement. How many nights had he sat down with his fellow officers and played for larger amounts than that, sometimes much larger? None of them had ever thought much about it, usually having an allowance from their fathers as well as their regimental honorarium. His own father's estate was not large, but he had never been short of the funds for whatever he wanted to do. This was the first time he had considered what it must be like to live in a different world.

"Were you... very poor?" he said eventually, hoping she would not be offended.

"Not at all," she said, looking up at him with a shy smile. "Oh, by your standards perhaps we were, but there was always enough money when Papa was alive. The trouble was that he *fussed* so about it, especially towards the end of the quarter, when all the bills began to come in. I used to help him with the accounts, so I knew that we had enough, but he would fret so, and it became ingrained, that habit of watching every penny, and never spending unnecessarily. So now *I* fret about the pennies, even though there is no need, and I can scarce believe that I am wasting *fifty pounds*, just because I was so ill-tempered as to be drawn into this scheme."

"I am very sorry," he said, and truly meant it. "I can see that it was ill-advised, but now that the bet has been offered and accepted, we cannot honourably withdraw."

"If you were a gentleman, you would allow me to win."

He laughed suddenly at the irony of it. "So now you want me to be a gentleman, do you? May I remind you, Miss Milburn, that you were the one who told me that I was *not* a gentleman."

She looked chagrined. "True, and I am not a lady, so there is no reason why you should waste your gallantry on me. I shall just have to pay up, and learn my lesson."

Her expression was so glum that his heart was touched. He picked up her hand and enfolded it in both of his. "There is a way out of this conundrum. We may not honourably call off the wager, but we may change the terms, I feel, so long as we keep to the spirit of the enterprise, and retain bets of equivalent value."

"What does that mean?" she said, looking up hopefully into his face.

For a moment, he was distracted by treacle-coloured eyes framed by long, black lashes. Her hair was almost as dark, a few wispy curls peeping out from beneath her fetching little cap. She was very fetching altogether just at that moment, her gown flowing over delightfully feminine curves not entirely concealed by her lace fichu. For a few long moments, he could not recall what he had been about to say. Gathering his wits, he cleared his throat and said, "It means that if I lose the bet, then I will pay you the agreed upon fifty pounds. If I win, then you may give me something of equivalent value."

Her eyes narrowed in suspicion.

"Nothing... nothing improper," he added hastily. "Your help. Advice, perhaps."

"Fifty pound's worth? That is a great deal of advice."

That made him smile. "It is worth as much to me, certainly. Miss Milburn, may I speak plainly? I must marry, and soon. That is my duty, and I have no wish to shirk it. I do not much mind who the lady is, so long as it is not Mildred. Mama has it in her head that it should be you, but I think we are both agreed that we should not suit. This leaves me in something of a quandary. How am I to find a wife? I have no skills in society suitable for the purpose. As you have so helpfully pointed out, I am not even a gentleman. Yet I am determined to overcome my deficiencies and persuade some intrepid lady to take a chance on me. Will you help me in this endeavour?"

"Are you serious? Whatever do you think *I* can do to help?

"You can assist me to become a gentleman, according to your precepts."

"Isn't your father the best person to advise you?" she said.

He heaved a sigh. "Perhaps, but he is such a gentle soul that he cannot bring himself to censure me, even when I need it. His lenience is, perhaps, why I find myself in this fix. I have no uncles or cousins I could trust enough, and my peers, those few men whom I count among my friends, are far away on foreign soil. But I have found a book, one that my brother Alfred bought, possibly for the same reason. It may well be that he was aware of the same deficiency in himself that I now find in my own character. The book is by the Reverend Dr John Trusler, and it is called *'Principles of Politeness and of Knowing the World'.* The heart of it was compiled by the late Lord Chesterfield, who was himself a consummate gentleman, so I feel certain that it will help me. By studying such a book, and putting into practice its precepts, I am confident that I shall improve my character immeasurably. Will you help me to practice? Please?"

"I will, if you think it would be useful," she said, but still she frowned. "There is a flaw in your scheme, however. In order to find yourself a wife who is not me and not Miss Beacher, you will have to go out into society and… well, do some courting."

"Indeed and you can help me there, too," he said eagerly. "This visit to Lady Narfield's, for instance… there will be a number of young ladies there. If you were to come with us—"

"No!"

"Now, hear me out, if you please. If you were to come with us, as Mama's companion, she would imagine us to be progressing towards a betrothal whereas in fact you would be advising me on choosing between the various young ladies, and ensuring that I behave as a gentleman should. If you have studied the book too, you will be able to say, *'Pay a lady three compliments before dinner, as chapter three instructs.'* Do you see?"

"Three compliments before dinner?"

He huffed in annoyance. "That is just an example I invented."

"Why would you do that?"

"Why, to show you how it would work. I have not read the book yet beyond the introduction, so I have no idea what it says."

"Then why do you talk about compliments?"

"Really, Miss Milburn! If you cannot see—" He took a long breath. "You are still trying to provoke me into an argument."

"It seemed worth a try," she said, with a throaty laugh. "Are you serious about this?"

"Perfectly. Will you do it? Help me with the book, and come to Narfield Lodge?"

"To settle my debt of honour I will do so, provided I'm satisfied that Lin and Poppy will have someone to watch over them. They aren't old enough to leave on their own."

"That is no problem," he said at once. "We can set Mildred to keep an eye on them." She spluttered with laughter. "Now, did you say you know how to get out of this place?"

"Turn left by the nymph with the broken foot and then right at the lion. Do you think there will be some lemonade on the terrace? I'm terribly thirsty."

"I am sure there will be," he said. "May I offer you my arm, Miss Milburn?"

"Why, thank you, sir."

Completely in charity, he followed her lead and they were outside the maze in two minutes.

16: Proposals

As soon as she descended from the Leatham's carriage that afternoon, Caroline knew that something was wrong. Susie's face as she opened the door told her as much.

"Mr Stratton's here," she sniffed.

"Today? It's not his usual day."

"Cooked it up between them, didn't they? Knew you were going to be out all day, and as soon as you were out of sight, there he was. They've been together in the parlour all day, and taking no notice of *me*, none at all. Holding hands and all sorts. They're there now, waiting for you."

"Ah." Caroline peeled off her gloves and hat, laying them on the hall table. Why was Susie so disapproving? She knew what was coming, and surely it was good news. It would mean the breaking apart of their little family, but for the best of causes. At least they would still have Poppy to look after. "Where is Poppy? She hasn't disappeared or done anything foolish?"

"No." Susie's face softened. "She's been good as gold, the little lamb. Tending her chicks, and the goat's arrived with the sweetest little kid you ever saw, so she's happy as can be. John

Christopher's been helping her settle the creatures into their pen."

"That's something, anyway. Can we have some tea in the parlour, please, Susie?"

"Aye, it's all ready, and a marmalade cake. I knew you'd want something."

The parlour door was open, so Caroline walked in without knocking. Lin and Mr Stratton were sitting side by side on the sofa, not holding hands, but with guilt written all over their faces. They jumped up at once, and Mr Stratton made a somewhat less fluid bow than usual.

"Miss Milburn," he said.

"Mr Stratton. What a surprise."

"Oh Caro, don't be angry!" Lin burst out. "You must have guessed... we've known for ages... Lester's asked me to marry him and I've said yes and *please, please* don't make us wait until I'm twenty one or I shall *die!"*

"I'm not angry," Caroline said. "Why ever should I be angry?"

"You'll say I'm too young and I'm *not*, truly I'm not."

"I've not said anything yet," she said, with a quick laugh. "But this is exciting news! I wish you both joy."

"So you won't stop us? You'll still be able to manage, won't you, even without my share of the money?"

Caroline went cold. Lin's dowry. *That* was why they were so nervous, and Susie was disapproving — Lin wanted her third of the inheritance. Or rather, Mr Stratton wanted it. No wonder he looked so guilty.

"Lin, let me talk to your sister alone," he said.

Reluctantly, she left the room and he closed the door behind her.

"Miss Milburn, I—"

"Caroline," she said, flopping onto a chair. "Or Caro. If we're to be brother and sister, then we'd better dispense with the formalities, Mr Stratton. Lester."

"Indeed." He sat, too, taking the same position on the sofa. "You are not, then, displeased with your sister's choice? You must know that I will cherish her for ever. I want nothing but her happiness."

"I am not displeased with her choice, but you want more than her happiness, I think. You want her dowry, too."

He flushed, and tugged at his neckcloth as if he found it too tight. "I cannot afford to support a wife on my earnings alone," he said abruptly.

"Then perhaps you should not marry until you can."

"That is what I have tried to explain to Lin, but she will not have it. A third of all this is hers, she says," he said, gesturing around the room, "and the funds invested too, and I cannot deny it. With the five thousand you were left by Mr Wishaw, and the money found in the garden, together with the value of the house, it must be worth over nine thousand in total, and Lin's share would be three thousand of that. It would be enough for us to marry upon. I have accommodation," he said, suddenly eager. "My uncle has been so kind as to offer us rooms in his house, and a partnership is not out of the question in a few years, so—"

"You have it all worked out." Caroline jumped to her feet and prowled restlessly to the window. John Christopher was hard at work in the kitchen garden, with Poppy sitting on the low wall that surrounded the forcing beds, a chicken in her arms as she talked animatedly to him. She, at least, was too young to be thinking of marriage. Her chickens and goats consumed her energy. Whereas Lin...

Dear Lord, three thousand pounds! How would they manage? Would the house have to be sold?

"Caroline," he said gently, coming to stand behind her. "She is almost twenty, and ready for marriage. I have never hidden my admiration for her, but I did not presume to court her formally. I *hoped*, of course, that in time... but you know what Lin is like! She made no secret of the fact that I had secured her affections, beyond all my expectations, and I... I could not deny my own regard for her. Naturally, she wishes to marry at once, but she tells me that you are her guardian, is that so?"

"It is. When Mama died, her will made our Romsey vicar guardian for all of us, but once I attained my majority, I was to have sole guardianship."

"Will you deny us?"

She knew at once that she would not. The rational part of her mind told her that six bundles of five hundred pounds apiece had now been found, and that would provide Lin's three thousand, with no need at all to sell the house or even broach the inheritance from Mr Wishaw. So long as Poppy did not marry for some time, they could survive well enough on the income from what was left. But the irrational part of her mind quailed at the prospect of losing so large a sum.

She said only, "It's not what I'd hoped for Lin, but if she is happy... and an attorney's wife is a step up from a linen draper's daughter."

"But a step down from the gentry she had become, is that it?"

"We're not gentry," she said, smiling. "I'm still making lace to sell, and if Lin and Poppy have abandoned their weaving for the moment, it's only because they are helping to put food on the table. I imagine they'll go back to their looms in the winter." She gave a small laugh. "Poppy will, anyway. Lin will be married by then."

The anxiety on his face lifted. "You will give your permission, then?"

"Yes, but there must be no rushing into this. You've only known each other a few months, after all. Let us say three months from now... October. That way, the vegetable beds will be fully dug over, and we will know exactly how much money we have to share out."

"Thank you!" he said with heartfelt sincerity, but neither his happiness nor Lin's brought Caroline much comfort. Their family was being torn apart, and their reassuring nest egg destroyed, and she could hardly bear it.

She went into the study, ignoring Susie who was just arriving with the tea things, and shut the door on all of them. Then she pulled out her account books. There at least she might find some solace.

~~~~~

The next day, a cavalcade paraded up the drive of Bursham Cottage. First came a curricle pulled by two white horses, then one pulled by black horses, and finally a barouche containing both Lord and Lady Elland. Caroline went out to greet them, as the two young men leapt nimbly down from their equipages, and Lady Elland waved cheerily. Her first visit to the cottage had been rather fraught, but in the company of her sons, she was perfectly amiable.
~~~~~

"Here we are, Miss Milburn, all of us!" cried Lady Elland, almost before the barouche had stopped moving. "Goodness, what a quantity of dust we have thrown up. That is the trouble with these sporting vehicles. There is nothing like a curricle for making a great cloud of dust."

"No dust if one drives—"

"— fast enough!" her sons said, grinning and bowing, almost sweeping the ground with their hats.

"We're very honoured," Caroline said. Susie had been dispatched to find Lin and Poppy, but if they were out weeding or cleaning the hen house, there was no way of knowing if they could make themselves respectable enough for visitors. It was so awkward having to deal with noble neighbours descending without the least warning. Life had been easier in Romsey, when there was only their work to consider.

Lord Elland descended from the barouche and then assisted his wife to alight, as footmen and grooms bustled about with the carriages. Caroline ushered them into the parlour, and allowed them to dispose themselves in chairs about the room. She soon learnt it was not a regular morning call.

"We are come to invite you—"

"—to a party!"

"C'est l'anniversaire de grand-mère!"

"Everyone is invited!"

"Anniversary?" Caroline murmured. "I don't quite understand."

"My mother's birthday celebration, Miss Milburn," Lord Elland said. "She is French, you see, and still speaks the language in preference to any other, so there is a great tendency to burst into French oneself when speaking of her. Kindly remember, you two, that Miss Milburn speaks no French."

The two young men rose and bowed again to her, although the room was a degree too small for such flamboyant gestures, and she was in great fear for Lin's vases of dried grasses.

"Your pardon, Miss Milburn."

"We will try to remember."

Susie brought tea and cakes, and the company ate and drank and talked about the weather, and the hope of a fine day for the birthday celebration. Eventually, Lin and Poppy bounced in, boasting clean gowns and scrubbed faces, and with just a trace of dirt beneath their fingernails. Poppy had a small, soft feather caught in her hair just behind one ear.

"Would you like to see my new baby goat?" she said as she bobbed a curtsy. "He is utterly adorable."

"How charming!" and "We should love to!" the two brothers said at once, and so the whole party drifted outside. Caroline was quite pleased to see that John Christopher had begun work on the rose garden, which had been choked with weeds. Even through the brambles and thick grasses, a few intrepid blooms showed their heads. The wilderness was beginning to feel like a proper garden at last.

Caroline found herself walking beside Lord Elland.

"Have you had any luck in your searches?" he said in a low voice. The missing documents... he must still be hoping they might be found.

"No. I've looked through all the drawers and cupboards, and part of the attic. I haven't given up."

"Ah. A pity. I should have liked Mama to have them for her birthday. If you should happen upon them, I trust you will return them to me?"

She didn't answer the question directly, but his persistence gave rise to interesting speculation in her mind, and perhaps an opportunity. He was a wealthy man, after all.

"They must be important to you, these documents," she said softly.

"To my mother's peace of mind, they certainly are."

"You might say they were of value to you, then."

He stopped, spinning round to face her, and she quailed at the look in his eyes. It was not anger — that would have been easier to bear. No, his expression was utterly contemptuous. She dropped her gaze, unable to withstand the disgust in his face.

"Miss Milburn," he said in icy tones, "you are very young, and therefore I make allowances, but let me be rightly understood — I do not submit to blackmail."

Her head shot up. "That wasn't what I meant!"

"Perhaps you did not intend it, but that is, in effect, what you implied. It is an insult to me to suppose that I would bow to such wrongful behaviour. Let me tell you the full story of these documents, and then you will understand. Abraham Wishaw came to me some five or six years ago, claiming to have papers from Italy which, he said, proved that I had no right to the barony. You will appreciate why this distresses my mother so, for it can only imply some insult to her reputation. Wishaw said he would keep the papers safe and not broadcast the contents to the world if I would pay him a sum of money every year, or a larger sum to buy them outright. I told him plainly that if he had such papers, he should submit them to the proper authorities —

to the House of Lords, who would determine the truth of the matter and what should be done about it. I told him, as I now tell you, that I will never bow to blackmail. He went away, but, so far as I know, he has not sent the papers to the Lords. Therefore, they are still in existence somewhere. If you find them, Miss Milburn, you may deliver them to me, if you wish, or you may send them to the Master of the Rolls in London, but I will never, ever pay you a penny piece for them."

"I'm very sorry, my lord," she said, trembling. "I never meant... Where I come from, everything has its price, so I thought... it was stupid of me."

"In *my* world," he said, "there are many things beyond price... integrity, loyalty, faithfulness, honesty. A man is nothing without honour."

She bowed her head, ashamed.

"There now, no harm done," he said in a softer voice. "You have had a great deal of responsibility thrust upon you at far too young an age, and no wiser head to advise you."

"I worry so much about money," she blurted. "I'm terrified of overspending our income, and one of my sisters will be marrying soon and—" She stopped abruptly, realising the foolishness of confessing all her fears to Lord Elland.

His eyes twinkled knowingly. "Ah! The attorney, eh? We suspected as much. It is not general knowledge, perhaps, but Grison happened to be patrolling the woods beside the road yesterday when a certain gentleman was taking his leave."

Mr Grison! She might have guessed it was him. A pity he couldn't mind his own business.

"So she will be wanting her share of the inheritance as dowry and you are worried that you might not be able to manage. Hmm. Miss Milburn, forgive me if my interference is unwelcome, but there may be an alternative to splitting the inheritance. If Mr Stratton were to live at Bursham—"

"But his employment is in Romsey, with his uncle!"

"He is a young man, still with his way to make in the world. There is a need for attorneys in Salisbury, also, and that is only a short ride away from Bursham. My own solicitor, for instance, is always lamenting the difficulty in obtaining a junior of a reliable disposition. If Mr Stratton were to apply to him, with a letter of recommendation from myself, naturally, and settle in here with you and your sisters… why, think of the advantages to all of you! You would have a man in the house to deal with any difficulties that arise, and to protect you and your sisters. And in a few years' time, when you and your youngest sister should both be married too, why, then the cottage may be sold and Mr Stratton may return to Romsey and his uncle, if he so wishes."

She could see the advantages at once. "It would indeed be beneficial to have a man in the house," she said thoughtfully. "Another man in the house, I should say. We have a manservant, but he is of little use as protection. He sleeps like a log at night and wouldn't hear an army of burglars if they stomped right through his room."

"Do you have many burglars?" he asked mildly.

"Somebody's found a way in twice now, and tried to get in a third time, but he failed. Nothing was taken, though. It was as if he was looking for something. Documents, maybe?" she said, looking straight at him.

He met her gaze squarely. "Not on my orders, Miss Milburn. If you ever find these papers, you will either give them to me openly or you will not, but I will no more condone theft than blackmail."

"Then I wonder what he was looking for?" she said.

"It is curious," Lord Elland said. "Very curious. But certainly you will feel much safer with Mr Stratton living in the house."

When Caroline hesitantly relayed this suggestion to Mr Stratton, he was momentarily struck dumb, the idea having never previously occurred to him. But he saw the advantages of the scheme as readily as she had.

"I have never been quite comfortable with the idea of three young ladies living alone," he said thoughtfully. "That is no reflection on you, Caroline, for you have done a wonderful job of managing the house and taking care of your sisters, but it is not ideal. But I do not know... there is my uncle to be considered... and for all Lord Elland's optimism, I might not be able to find employment in Salisbury."

Lin approved of the idea for another reason entirely. "That would be perfect! We could all stay together, and there would be no need to worry about dowries and so on, so we could get married at once! And then Lester would be here to look after Poppy and me while you are staying at Lady Narfield's house, Caro."

But Mr Stratton himself squelched that idea. "I believe Caroline is right to insist upon a delay, dearest. Hasty marriages attract any amount of adverse comment, and you will want to have time to put together your wedding clothes. It would look very odd if we get married in a great rush and I move in here at once. One must maintain the proprieties. But I think you cannot stay here alone while Caroline is away."

"There is no one we could ask to stay here," Lin said. "We have no relations we like well enough to have them in the house."

"Mr Leatham offered Miss Beacher's services as chaperon," Caroline said mischievously.

Lin and Poppy said, "No!" in unison.

Mr Stratton laughed. "I have a better plan. I shall take you both to Portsmouth to stay with my mother and father. They cannot wait to meet you, Lin, and this is the perfect opportunity. A week or two in Portsmouth being cosseted would do you the world of good, and Poppy too. What do you say, Caroline?"

"I think—"

"No!" wailed Poppy. "How can I leave my dear little chickens and my sweet goats?"

"I am sure John Christopher will—"

"No, no, no!" she cried, tears brimming. "He doesn't *care* about them the way I do! I *can't* leave them, I can't!"

Caroline was about to remonstrate with her, for it sounded like a wonderfully sensible plan which would set her mind entirely at rest while she was away. But Mr Stratton merely laughed.

"No matter. Mama must come here, then. She will enjoy a little stay in the country, I am certain of it. Perhaps Father will come, too, if he can take the time away from the bank. There now, that is all settled, and you can talk about wedding clothes together and all those feminine details. Caroline, be sure to let me know as soon as you have the date you will go to Narfield Lodge, so that I may arrange everything with Mama. There — is that not an ingenious plan?"

He beamed at them happily, and Lin wrapped her arm around his and rested her head on his shoulder, sighing happily. "How clever you are to think of it, Lester."

That made him beam even more widely.

But all Caroline could think about was how comforting it would be to have a man's broad shoulder to rest her head upon.

To be loved.

17: A Gentleman At Large

Charles soon put his campaign of becoming a true gentleman into action. He discovered, after a brief outbreak of hostilities, that Miss Milburn was not amenable to lengthy interruption when she had household tasks to attend to, but minded his presence less when she was working quietly on her lacemaking before breakfast. So each morning he and his book arrived at Bursham Cottage by seven or eight o'clock, and he was permitted to sit in the parlour reading while she worked. Then, if he came across a passage that confused him, she was on hand to discuss it with him.

'Modesty widely differs from an awkward bashfulness, which is as much to be condemned as the other is to be applauded. To appear simple is as ill-bred as to be impudent. A young man ought to be able to come into a room and address the company without the least embarrassment,' he read. He sighed, thinking of his own awkwardness in company.

"Do you think I am modest, Miss Milburn? Or is my reticence in company more like bashfulness?"

She looked up from her work, her hands falling still. "I've never noticed any bashfulness in you, Mr Leatham, and if you don't talk much, I assumed that was your sulky nature."

"My sulky nature? I am *not* sulky!"

"Aren't you? Then it must be arrogance, and feeling yourself to be above everyone else."

He almost exploded in anger, until he caught the wink of a dimple on her cheek. She was teasing him! Had she always done so, and he had just never noticed before, or was this part of a newer accord?

"Is that truly how I appear to others?" he said sheepishly.

She considered that carefully. "Do you know, I'm not sure quite how you appear to an impartial observer. We got off on such a poor footing that I've never thought of you as other than a very ill-tempered and ill-bred man."

"You are very rude, madam."

"I thought you wanted my honest opinion. If you don't, well, you'd best take yourself home."

"I beg your pardon," he said stiffly. "Your honest opinion is a little *too* honest for comfort. It stings, rather."

"That's how you improve, though, isn't it? By hearing the bald truth. When I was learning to make lace, if I went wrong, Mama told me exactly what I'd done and how to fix it. Then I practised until I could do it right without thinking about it. It has to become... what's the expression?"

"Ingrained? Second nature?"

"Yes! Second nature. Well, I don't really know what it means to be a gentleman, so you'll have to learn that from the book, and you'll need to practise and practise until you get it right. But if you ask my opinion on anything, then you'll get it, Mr Leatham, and not sugar-coated, either."

So he read, and considered the advice in the book. Sometimes he came across Alfred's notes in the margins, and it pleased him to think that his older brother had struggled with exactly the same difficulties, and he too had set himself to improve. He was following in Alfred's footsteps in more ways than one. Although he would not betroth himself to Mildred — in that at least their paths differed. But it was very difficult. Having learnt in one chapter to avoid false modesty, and be sure to address the company on entering a room, in the next he discovered that he must not be *too* forward, or put himself above others.

"So I must speak, but not too much, and not about myself. *'A well-bred man is easy and firm in every company, is modest but not bashful, steady but not impudent.'* How am I ever to achieve such perfection?"

"Practise, Mr Leatham. Practise. Just as you did when you were taught to ride."

"But that was a lot more fun."

She laughed and shook her head at him before turning back to her bobbins. It was soothing, he found, listening to the gentle clack of the bobbins, the pauses when she placed a pin with swift precision, then more clacking. As he pondered the relative merits of modesty and forwardness, and wondered how one might *'lean with elegance'* in a chair in a way that was neither stiffly upright nor lolling, he watched Miss Milburn as she went about her lacemaking, her clever fingers always busy. She bent slightly forward over her work, her face calm. The finished strips of lace looked so complicated, yet she never hesitated in reaching for the bobbins, or placing a pin. Her hair was usually tied up in a simple knot on top of her head, not a strand out of place, but he remembered her with gentle curls falling softly around her face, and a fringe of her own delicate lace edging her silk gown. She had looked... different, very different, and he had been intrigued, no doubt about it. And yet there was something mesmerising about this Miss Milburn, too.

The maid was deeply suspicious of his motives, feeling that a book was an inadequate excuse for being alone with her mistress for anything up to two hours, so she left the parlour door open, and spent an inordinate amount of time dusting and polishing in the hall, and peering into the parlour at regular intervals. Every time she did so, Charles realised that his attention had strayed from his book, and turned back to it with resignation. He was determined to master the art of being a true gentleman, as he would need to be when his father handed the reins of the estate to him. Even had the object been of less importance, it was pleasing to have a project under way, and to have a reason to rise from his bed at an early hour and stride down the long drive towards Bursham Cottage. Being busy was far, far better than kicking his heels for hours at a time and wishing he were back in the army. That life was gone for ever.

~~~~~

The Miss Milburns held a dinner to celebrate the betrothal of the middle sister to the attorney from Romsey, who was, it seemed, so besotted that he was about to throw over his position there and move into Bursham Cottage. All the Starlingford family were invited, even Mildred, who graciously agreed to accept. Even Charles' father was minded to attend, given the present spell of settled weather.
~~~~~

"It is a Saturday, too," he said. "We will be home before midnight. I do so dislike staying up until two or three in the morning. It destroys the whole of the following day."

"Does it?" Charles said.

"Ah, you young men! There was a time when I too could fall into bed at three in the morning and still be out riding by seven or eight, but nowadays I like my sleep at night, and a nap or two during the day as well. But it will be pleasant to dine with the Miss Milburns, and it is no distance, after all."

The small parlour was full when the Starlingford party arrived, and everyone was well known to Charles, excepting only the newly-betrothed attorney, which gave him the usual flutters of nerves. With a new acquaintance, he never knew quite what to say after the first greetings. Fortunately Stratton was a friendly man, well-disposed to the world and with an open, easy disposition that relieved Charles' fears. He was able to offer his congratulations, having read the appropriate chapter of his book and prepared a little speech in advance. *'There is a certain distinguishing diction that marks the man of fashion…'*, the book announced, going on to give some examples, which Charles had studied carefully.

His efforts were well received. Stratton immediately began upon a fulsome account of all his betrothed's manifold virtues and accomplishments. Charles was only required to murmur his agreement at suitable intervals, and before the fellow had completed his enumeration, dinner was announced and the company trooped into the dining room.

There were fourteen at table, and all agreed that the meal was enjoyable. Two full courses were served, with veal at one and turkey at the other, and a very tasty fricasée of rabbit, of which Charles was especially fond. The wine was greatly praised, the attorney taking the credit for selecting it from the late Mr Wishaw's extensive cellar. The only sour note was struck by Mr Ascot, the apothecary, who fell out with the middle Miss Milburn before the soup was removed, calling her a *'silly chit of a girl who should stick to growing parsnips'*. No doubt she had been expounding on the medicinal virtues of rhubarb again, and her half-formed ideas on the subject could not withstand the apothecary's greater knowledge of the healing arts. Still, it was rude to address her so, especially as the meal was in her honour.

Charles found himself sitting beside Miss Milburn, who was at the head of the table in her role as hostess, with his father on her other side. Even a week or two earlier, his heart would have sunk at the prospect of passing the whole meal at her side, and the difficulty of finding any common subject of interest. Now, he had devised a scheme for his conversation. He had reached the chapter of the book entitled *'Observation'*, wherein he had read that *'As the art of pleasing is to be learnt only by frequenting the best companies, we must endeavour to pick it up in such companies by observation.'* No one would describe a dinner at Bursham Cottage as one of the *'best companies'*, but nevertheless it was an opportunity to practise his observational skills, especially as he was directly opposite his father, surely a gentleman even by Miss Milburn's exacting standards.

So he watched as they chatted, and he was surprised to discover how broad a range of topics they managed to cover. First his father asked Miss Milburn her impressions of Valmont and the duke, which led them to a discussion of architecture, the growing of peaches, the construction of fountains and the style of Honiton lace. Often Miss Milburn set down her knife and fork, and gestured with her hands as she talked. Elegant hands, he decided, so quick with bobbins and pins, and so graceful shaping the air as she talked. Her hair was caught up on top of her head in a knot, with curls cascading down her back which tossed about as she moved her head this way and that. He thought he could watch those fascinating curls for ever.

Mrs Wenman was on his other side, and she was easy company, for she talked and ate in equal measure. She asked him about Valmont, but as her interest was largely in the ladies' gowns and embellishments, he was poorly equipped to satisfy her enquiries. After that, she began to tell him some story about her daughter, and, having nothing to contribute, he only half attended, and was glad to turn to Miss Milburn after a while.

Determined to put his observations to good use, he began, "Are you pleased that you decided to go to Valmont, Miss Milburn? I know you had reservations about the enterprise."

She looked at him suspiciously, but answered the question seriously. "My expectations were not high, and I cannot say that I enjoyed the day, on the whole, but it went off better than I'd feared."

"You should have told me sooner of your concerns regarding our arrangement," he said in a lower tone, although the conversation around the table was so animated that it was unlikely his words would be overheard. "I am not a monster, to hold you to an agreement so distasteful to you."

"Indeed you're not," she said, with a slight smile. "When we first met, Mr Leatham, I thought you capable of any outrage, but my opinion of you is much improved of late."

"Oh. Yet I still have a long way to go," he said, and meant it.

She smiled. "No one is perfect. We all have some way to go, so you're not alone in that. But that wasn't all that I feared from the day. I thought the Valmont ladies would look down their aristocratic noses at me, but they didn't, not at all. Nor did the duke. I thought him very gracious, and not at all high in the instep, didn't you?"

He gave a little laugh. "I never had the chance to talk to him, but from what I saw of him, he was—"

"Oh! That was my fault!" she said, eyes wide with dismay. "I told him something he didn't know about the *Brig Minerva*, and naturally he forgot everything else and you were never even introduced to him. I am so sorry."

"Naturally I am most disappointed that I cannot boast of having a duke amongst my acquaintance," he said. "You are far ahead of me in consequence now. May I pass you something, Miss Milburn? A custard, perhaps?"

She agreed to it, and he took a slice of cherry tart for himself, and for a while they were silent, busy eating. When the custard and tart were consumed, they sat on in silence. Mrs Wenman was still talking to Mr Christopher and his father was attending to Mrs Christopher, so Charles knew it was for him to continue the conversation with Miss Milburn, but his mind was blank. What on earth was he to say to her? But then he recalled that she had agreed to advise him on gentlemanly behaviour.

"Miss Milburn," he began tentatively, "I am at a loss. What now should I say to you? My conversational arsenal is exhausted."

She smiled, and said, "Then your preparations for battle were inadequate, Mr Leatham, for the evening is barely begun. There is the rest of dinner to be got through, then the time with the gentlemen, followed by tea and cards and supper... why, we might have another four hours of battle… I mean opportunity for conversation."

"I am woefully ill-prepared, I admit. The correct procedure is to retreat, regroup and await the supply train, but I fear such a recourse is impossible here. Whatever is to be done?"

"Why, we must resort to desperate measures, sir. We must each think of some detail of the other about which we are curious. Shall I begin? I should like to know about your brothers and sisters. There seem to be a great many of them, and one or other is mentioned in passing here and there, but I have never got them straight in my mind. Will you enlighten me?"

"With pleasure. I am one of six, with two older brothers, Alfred and Benjamin, and three younger sisters, Dorothy, Elizabeth and Felicity. My brothers are both dead, and my sisters are all married now."

"Alfred, Benjamin and Charles," she said, her eyes twinkling. "Dorothy, Elizabeth and Felicity. How… how *systematic."*

He sighed ruefully. "It was a tradition in my mother's family."

"Fortunately, there is an abundance of names at the beginning of the alphabet. There might be difficulties if there were more than a dozen children. Quentin? Ursula? I can't think of any beginning with X or Y or Z."

"Nor can I. Happily, each generation ground to a halt around George or Henrietta or Isabella." She laughed, and he was struck with how pretty she looked when she was not scowling at him, or frowning in displeasure at some misdemeanour. The curls on the back of her head danced about gaily as she laughed.

"Now it's your turn," she said. "Ask me something about myself."

"How do you get your hair to curl that way?" he said, mesmerised, "for your hair is ramrod straight naturally, is it not?"

She stared at him, then burst out laughing, so that conversation died down around the table and heads turned curiously in their direction. "Curling papers, Mr Leatham," she said under her breath. "Rags will do it, too, but we use curling papers, and very tricky it is too. I'm so glad you appreciate our efforts." And she went off into another peal of laughter, but there was no animosity in it, and he could not help laughing too.

"It was a foolish question, I daresay," he said.

"Not at all, just unexpected," she said, her eyes still brimming with amusement. "You are altogether unexpected, Mr Leatham. And I don't think your arsenal was quite as exhausted as you thought, do you?"

"Perhaps not," he said, laughing too.

From further down the table, his mother smiled and nodded at him encouragingly, but Mildred watched him unsmilingly.

Somehow, the rest of the evening passed by in a blur. The gentlemen talked of politics and the trouble in France, which was a subject in which Charles could engage with some authority. Then there was tea, followed by cards. Two tables had been set up in the study, while the remainder of the company settled in the parlour. Mrs Wenman played the pianoforte, while Miss Poppy and John Christopher talked together about chickens and goats and could not be separated. That left only Mildred, Miss Mllburn and Charles.

"Should you like to play cards, Miss Beacher?" Miss Milburn said. "We may all play vingt-et-un, or you and Mr Leatham might play piquet or backgammon, if you wish."

"Thank you, but I never play games of chance," Mildred said.

"Oh... but piquet and backgammon are more skill than chance, I should have thought. What about chess or—?"

"Thank you, but I have no wish to play any game."

"Of course. Then let us sit over here and you can tell me something about yourself, Miss Beacher."

"Thank you, but I usually spend Saturday evening reflecting upon the text for tomorrow's services. I have my Prayer Book with me, as you see. Do not let me keep you from Charles's company. I can see how eager he is to draw you into some amusement or other. I should not wish to interfere with his pleasure, I am sure."

So saying, she snapped open her Prayer Book, and commenced to read.

"What is it to be, Mr Leatham?" Miss Milburn said.

"Piquet," he said at once, "although I have a strong suspicion that I would be best advised not to play for money, not against you."

"I thank you for the compliment, but you are safe from me. We usually play for buttons here," she said with a smile. "Let me fetch the bag."

And so they played piquet for buttons, and he was right to be cautious, for she won handily, by more than one hundred buttons. Somehow, he did not mind at all, and as the carriage rattled homeward shortly before midnight, he reflected that the evening had not been half so dull as he had feared.

~~~~~
~~~~~

The day of Dowager Lady Elland's birthday party was drawing near. Mrs Leatham had warned the sisters to wear their best for the occasion, in compliment to the old lady, and this had caused some flutterings of alarm at Bursham Cottage. Caroline had her Valmont outfit, and Poppy was content to wear an old summer gown of Lin's with a newly refurbished bonnet, but Lin would not be satisfied until Mama's box had been raided and an entirely new, and highly fashionable, outfit created.

"I am an engaged woman now, so I must be more particular in my choice of clothing," she said, her chin lifting defiantly. "I must not bring discredit to my future husband."

"You're not married yet, Lin," Caroline said. "You should still look... *maidenly.* This fabric will make you look as grand as Mrs Leatham."

But there was no convincing Lin and so the gown was made, complete with matching bonnet and a Tyrolese cloak derived from a fashion magazine, although Caroline refused absolutely to trim the cloak with lace.

The day appointed for the Dowager Lady Elland's birthday party dawned fair and warm, and by the time they set off it was becoming very hot. They walked slowly up the long drive to Corranwater, trying to keep to the shade of the trees and being periodically coated in dust as the carriages of grander attendees bowled merrily past them. One carriage stopped, and Mrs Leatham's befeathered head peered out.

"Good day to you, Miss Milburn, Miss Elinor, Miss Penelope! We have room to take up one of you, if you should care to ride with us. Miss Milburn? Will you join us? Charles will make room on the seat for you."

Before Caroline could answer, Mr Charles Leatham's head appeared and the carriage door opened.

"I have a better idea," he said, with a grin. "I shall walk alongside Miss Milburn, and that way the younger Miss Milburns may both ride. Is that not a clever scheme?"

His mother agreed that it was, and as Lin and Poppy scrambled directly into the carriage without further ado, Caroline had no option but to acquiesce with as much grace as she could muster.

"There!" Mr Leatham said smugly. "Now I may discuss with you a passage I encountered this morning. It is in the chapter entitled *'Knowledge of the World'*, and it reads... wait a moment, for I have it written down, in the hope of being able to talk privily to you. Here it is. *'Observe the operations of your own mind, and you may, in a great measure, read all mankind.'* Do you think that is so? For it seems to me..."

He talked for the rest of the way, and Caroline had very little to do except to listen or to say *'Very true'* from time to time. They came eventually to the house, and were admitted and led right through it and out again into the garden. In the midst of the parterre was a stone pavilion constructed in the Roman style, with many pillars and a domed roof. There, on a large, ornate chair, sat the dowager, smiling serenely like a queen enthroned. She wore an exquisitely embroidered brocade, a fabric of the last century, but in the style of the present one, and a wig of incongruously dark curls. To one side, as if he were a courtier, stood Lord Elland. To the other side, the two sons, wreathed in smiles as they bowed and bowed again to new arrivals. Behind the dowager's chair, his face inscrutable, stood her personal footman, Lucien.

As they entered the pavilion, the butler announced them formally. Caroline made her curtsy and expressed her congratulations, and the old lady smiled and nodded. Then she reached into a box brought forward by the footman.

"En fête, je vous fais un cadeau," she said. Then she reached for Caroline's hand and placed something into it.

With a shock that rendered her speechless, Caroline recognised it. The gift was a netted purse, with a very distinctive tassel. It was exactly like the ones found at the cottage, holding five hundred pounds apiece.

18: A Birthday Party (August)

Caroline froze, staring uncomprehendingly at the purse in her hand. It was not exactly the same as any of the ones they had found, for they were all different in colour and pattern, but it was indubitably made by the same hand.

A nudge under her elbow brought her back to awareness.

"Shall we move on?" Mr Leatham murmured. "We are holding up the line."

Caroline bobbed a hasty curtsy to the dowager, nodded to Lord Elland, who was watching her quizzically, and allowed Mr Leatham to steer her out of the pavilion, across the parterre and into a much larger canvas pavilion where somebody thrust a glass of white wine into her hand. Then out of the pavilion into the blazing sun again, and onward to the shade of a massive fir tree, where Lin and Poppy came dashing towards them.

"Did you get one too?" Lin said. "She makes them all the time, apparently, in different colours and patterns. Then she gives them away on her birthday. There must be *hundreds* of them all over the county."

"Yes, of course," Caroline said, feeling stupid. "It doesn't mean anything, because everyone for miles around will have several of them."

"Exactly!" Lin said. "Although at first I was astonished, just like you. I think—" She stopped abruptly, throwing Mr Leatham a quick glance.

Caroline understood. "We can talk about it later." She gulped at her drink, and almost choked. Spluttering, she said, "Whatever is this?"

"Champagne," Mr Leatham said. "Try not to drink it too quickly. It is so hot today that lemonade would be more appropriate, but Aimée, Lady Elland insists on champagne, and Heaven only knows how Lord Elland got hold of it, or what he had to pay for it."

"Will there be anything to eat?" Lin said.

"Later," he said. "Once everyone is here, there will be a special cake, and then the footmen will move about with platters of those tiny pastry things and little balls of something or other. Very tasty but not exactly filling, unless one is so ill-mannered as to scoop them up four at a time. After that, there are games on the lawn, and finally, ice cream."

"I have never had ice cream," Poppy said wistfully. "It sounds wonderful, and I am so *hot.*"

"I'm thirsty, too," Lin said. "Let's go and get another drink."

~~~~~

The two ran off, and Charles found himself left alone with Miss Milburn. Gazing determinedly into the distance, he said, "I have no wish to pry, Miss Milburn, but if ever you want to talk about the purses that do not mean anything, you may be sure that I will
~~~~~

give the matter my full attention. I see my step-mother waving at us. Shall we go and brave Mildred's disapproval?"

"Does Miss Beacher disapprove of you? Or of me, perhaps?"

"Mildred disapproves of everyone and everything," he said. "It is very lowering to know that one will never, ever meet her exacting standards. She herself is perfect, so the rest of us must necessarily fall short."

"No one is perfect," Miss Milburn said. "I am sure Miss Beacher herself makes no such claim."

"She does not, but she is such a very *good* person."

"Is she?" Miss Milburn said. "I bow to your superior knowledge of her, but I'd have said myself that she's a sanctimonious prig."

He burst out laughing. "She is, of course, but then Ben was, too, so they were well suited. She would have made an excellent parson's wife, harrying the parishioners into harmony and plenty, or at least into silence, for it is impossible to disagree with her without appearing childish or unChristian. Lord, who are those two frights on the arms of the Alsager brothers?"

She turned to look, and laughed. "How uncharitable you are! I imagine those are the ladies they are to wed."

"Oh, excellent. I could not have wished for more suitable matches for them."

"Do you dislike them so much?"

"I do, because they have all the social graces that I so patently lack. If I had but a tenth of their charm, I should resent them far less, I assure you."

"You have your own charms, I am sure, Mr Leatham," she said. "Imagine how tiring it would be to live with all that... that *bounciness.* And as for the matching curricles, one with black horses and one with white... words fail me. Do you have a curricle, Mr Leatham?"

"If I lived in town, perhaps I might, but on country roads a horse is more sensible."

"How very prosaic of you," she murmured. "I do not think you can avoid Miss Beacher any longer. She is coming this way. You will excuse me, Mr Leatham. I must find my sisters."

Charles watched her go with some regret. Miss Milburn could be tolerable company sometimes, when she was not provoking him. Better company, at all events, than Mildred. He looked at his step-mother, champagne glass in hand, and Mildred, whose hands were empty, and sighed inwardly. Forcing a smile, he said, "Are you enjoying yourselves?"

His step-mother patted his arm. "Oh, indeed, never was there such a charmingly arranged celebration, and the weather so much kinder than last year. You will not believe it, Charles, but it rained all day last year, and not merely a fine drizzle, such as one does not much mind, but that heavy, drenching type of rain, where one is soaked through instantly. There were umbrellas, of course, but that never keeps one entirely dry, does it? So we huddled in the pavilion and told each other how much we were enjoying the occasion. Such a shame, to have so much rain."

"It was the Sabbath," Mildred said. "God disapproves of frivolity on the Sabbath."

"Oh, Indeed, but one must celebrate a birthday on the proper day," Mrs Leatham said. "We had all been to church beforehand, so I do not quite see... but still, I am sure you are right, Mildred dear."

"Excuse me, I must just have a word with Mr Christopher about his text for next Sunday." She dipped a curtsy and strode away.

Mrs Leatham sighed. "She is helping him with his sermons now," she said. "Poor man!"

"She likes to be useful," Mr Leatham murmured.

"True, but she is very *wearing,*" Mrs Leatham said. "I wish we could find her a husband. Oh, not you, dear, for you would suit her no better than poor Alfred would have done."

"Why ever did he offer for her?" Mr Leatham said. "I never understood that. With Ben, one could see the reasoning, for they were of like mind, but Alfred was no more suited to Mildred than I would be."

"You are quite right." She sighed again, more heavily. "Yet you must appreciate the position we were in. Your father had three sons, and there was not the least concern for the succession, for Ben was on the brink of matrimony, he had finally obtained a good living and Mildred would give him sons. The inheritance was secure, and Alfred could have taken his time to look about him for a wife. But then Ben died so suddenly, and you were away in the army and — forgive the indelicacy in mentioning such a thing, Charles, but there was no guarantee that you would survive. Indeed, we were in hourly expectation of receiving the news of your death. All depended on Alfred, and you know what he was like — all heart. He saw Mildred in distress, he saw his duty and he saw a way to relieve both. It was a generous act, but they were so different. He would not have been happy with her, any more than you would, and that is why I do not press you with regard to Mildred."

"It would do no good," he said. "It matters nothing to me whom I marry, except for Mildred. She is a very good sort of person and I wish her well with all my heart, but I shall *never* make her my wife, for I should surely murder her, or else kill myself. I wonder sometimes if Alfred—"

"*Hush!* It was a *fever* that killed him, both the physicians said so, and the coroner agreed. Poor, poor Alfred. My poor, dear boy!"

"I beg your pardon, Mama," he said gently, passing her a handkerchief for her tears. "It was a foolish thing to say. Naturally there is no question of... of anything other than the fever."

"No, indeed! A dreadful thing to suppose, and so cruel to poor Mildred. Alfred never wavered in his resolution to marry her, not for a moment. Poor girl! What a dreadful time of it she has had! She is not, perhaps, the most *comfortable* companion, but one must be kind to her, after all she has been through. We owe her that." She blew her nose. "Thank you for the handkerchief. When one cries, a man's handkerchief is so much better fitted for the purpose than the little scrap of lace we ladies are supposed to carry. You are such a comfort to me, Charles, and you seem to be getting along so well with Miss Milburn now. Is there...? Are you...?"

His answer was cautious. "I believe that her opinion of me is somewhat improved."

"There now! That is excellent progress, and she is to come to Narfield Lodge with us, I understand, so you will have the opportunity to improve her opinion of you even more." She laughed merrily. "We might even have you married by Michaelmas."

Charles saw no reason to disabuse her of the notion that he might yet marry Miss Milburn. Narfield Lodge would bring him within the orbit of a selection of suitable young ladies, and he could go about his courtship unhampered by his step-mother if she believed him already well along the road to matrimony. It was very satisfactory.

~~~~~

Caroline would have liked to walk down to the end of the reflecting pool and admire the fountain, but she felt she ought to stay close to Lin and Poppy. Lin, perhaps, no longer needed watching, for she would soon be a married woman, but Poppy was barely sixteen, and unused to company. So she abandoned the surprising champagne which got up her nose, handing her glass to a footman, and meandered about here and there, talking to this one and that one, but never straying far from her younger sister. She watched her talking to the Christophers, champagne glass waving about. She watched her grab another glass from a passing footman, only to spill half of it almost at once. She watched her say something to Lady Elland, who gave her a tight smile and moved away. And she saw the exact moment when the excitement caught up with her, and she went pale, swaying ominously.

Caroline was there in three quick strides. "Poppy? Do you want to sit down?"

"So *hot*, Caro. So… so…"

"Shade, that's what you need. A little sit down in the shade, under that tree there, where Mrs Leatham is. Come along." Taking her arm, she gently steered Poppy towards the tree, handing the now empty glass to a passing footman. "Almost there now. Just a few more steps."
~~~~~

Poppy stopped, swayed and then collapsed in a heap. Caroline was able to break her fall, but Poppy lay in a swoon on the lawn, her face as white as her gown.

"Stand aside, Miss Milburn." Mr Leatham loomed over them, his voice commanding. "Let us move her under the tree for now, shall we?"

Without further ado, he scooped Poppy into his arms and lifted her as if she weighed nothing. A few quick steps brought them beneath the spreading branches of the tree, where he gently laid down his burden.

"May I remove her bonnet?"

Caroline nodded, and with deft fingers he unfastened the ribbons, lifted her head and slid the bonnet off. "Your shawl, Miss Milburn, if you please. Can you bundle it up into a pillow? Good, good. There, now she will be comfortable. Where is Mama? Ah, there you are... your smelling salts, if you please." She already had the vial in her hand, passing it to him without a word. He waved it under Poppy's nose, and at once she coughed and moved her head.

"Oh, thank God!" Caroline cried.

Mr Leatham turned to her with a little smile. "She will do very well, Miss Milburn, never fear. It is only the heat, and perhaps the champagne also. The only danger with a swoon of this nature is that a lady may hit her head as she falls, and your quick thinking prevented that. Have you a fan with you? That would help." He looked round at the little crowd which had begun to gather, as crowds always do when there is some spectacle to be observed and talked about. "Where is a footman? Hoy! You there! Bring water, will you!"

"Monsieur?"

"Oh, for Heaven's sake! *De l'eau! Vite, vite!"*

"Oui, monsieur. Immediatement."

"Damned Frenchy!" he muttered under his breath. "He has been here long enough, you would think he would understand a civilised language by now." Then, in his usual voice, he went on, "Well done, Miss Milburn. Your fanning is having some effect. It is bringing a little colour to her cheeks."

Gradually, Poppy began to come round, although she was very confused at first to find herself lying on the ground with Mr Leatham bending over her. Caroline was able to reassure her, while Mr Leatham gave orders to servants and onlookers alike, moving the assembled crowd further back to give Caroline room to bathe Poppy's face with the cool water Lucien eventually brought. Lin arrived, and immediately elbowed Caroline aside to take over the position of senior nurse.

"She is still very hot," Caroline said quietly to Mr Leatham. "Would it give offence, do you think, if I ask Lady Elland if Poppy may rest indoors until she is well enough to go home?"

"There can be no offence in requesting help for one who is clearly unwell," he said. "Nor should any hostess deny a guest any succour that is theirs to offer. I have a better idea, however. Let me send for Mama's carriage, and we may take your sister home directly. She will recover more swiftly and completely in her own home."

"Indeed she would! That is a kind and generous offer, if Mrs Leatham will not mind."

Mrs Leatham did not mind. "Let me take you home at once," she said. "Charles can walk back with Mildred whenever it suits her, or I can send the carriage back for her."

"No, no," Mr Leatham said. "I shall take the Miss Milburns home, so that I may carry Miss Poppy into the house. She should not exert herself too soon."

"We have a manservant, Mr Leatham," Caroline said.

Mr Leatham laughed. "I fear your manservant is past the age of carrying a young lady about, even so light a burden as your sister. I will entertain no argument on this head. Mama, go and enjoy the party and you may tell me all about it later. Look, they are bringing out the cake now."

"If you are quite sure, Charles..."

"Quite sure. Miss Milburn, I shall order the carriage brought round at once. Pray continue to bathe your sister's face and fan her, do not allow her to attempt to rise, and allay her anxieties as best you can. I shall return in a very few minutes."

He gave her no opportunity to protest, but then she had no fault to find with his arrangements. They could have managed without him, naturally, but it was a great comfort to have a man take charge in such a masterful way in a crisis.

They waited, he returned in a very short time, scooped Poppy into his arms again — "Arms around my neck. Good girl! We will await the carriage in the hall." — and strode away through the crowds thronging around the pavilion, emerging now with plates of cake in their hands.

"Cake..." Lin murmured wistfully, as they rushed past.

Mr Leatham heard her, and stopped, turning around. "Would you prefer to stay, Miss Lin? My step-mother will convey you home later. You need not be in any alarm for your sister, for she is well on the way to a full recovery, and Miss Milburn will take excellent care of her."

"Susie will be there, too," Caroline said. "Our former nurse, Mr Leatham."

"That's true," Lin said, her face eager. "You won't mind, will you, Caro? You don't need me, do you?"

"With Mr Leatham's assistance, I can manage very well. Off you go."

Mr Leatham raised a quizzical eyebrow. "Do you wish to stay, too, Miss Milburn? I can arrange for a maid to travel in the carriage with your sister, if so."

"No, no. Let us go at once. Poppy is not heavy, but your arms must be aching, Mr Leatham."

"She is as light as a feather," he said with a smile, and she believed him, for there was not the least sign of strain in his expression.

They made their way through the house to the hall, where it was blessedly cool and Poppy seemed distinctly more alert. Then the carriage arrived, and again Mr Leatham lifted his burden effortlessly. Beneath his jacket, muscles bulged but as he conveyed Poppy to the carriage he was not even slightly out of breath. He stowed her safely inside, handed Caroline in and then climbed up beside the coachman for the brief journey home. Again, he would not hear of Poppy walking even so short a distance to the front door, but carried her into the house and then, at Caroline's direction, up the stairs to her room. Susie emerged from the back of the house as they did so, and at once took in the situation.

"Aye, this heat is something fierce. There now, my precious, Susie's here and you're quite safe. Thank you kindly, sir, but I can look after Miss Poppy from now on. Miss Milburn, there's lemonade cooling in the larder. Mr Leatham might like a glass after his exertions. Out, now, both of you."

Silently, they trooped back down the stairs.

"Would you like some lemonade?" Caroline said dubiously. "Or we have Madeira if—?"

"Lemonade would be very refreshing. Thank you."

She shooed him into the study, which was cooler, having had the shutters closed all morning, and fetched the lemonade.

"Mr Leatham, I cannot thank you enough for—"

He held up his free hand to interrupt her. "Say nothing of it, Miss Milburn. We have agreed that we should give up apologising to each other, so we should not waste words in foolish gratitude, either. What did I do to deserve it? Only what any man would do when seeing a lady in distress."

"You are very good, sir. I am very glad that you were on hand to take charge of the situation."

"Take charge?" He tugged his earlobe with a grimace. "Was I very managing? That was bad of me."

"You were very much the soldier," she said with a smile. "Lady Elland's lawn is not quite a battlefield, but I could certainly imagine you leading your troops in a commanding manner. What were you… a colonel?"

He gave a bark of laughter. "Nothing so grand! A captain only, and one moreover better suited to taking orders than giving them. Still, when there is a crisis, I know what to do, as a soldier."

"And as a gentleman also," she said gravely.

His face lightened. "Ah. Then I am making progress. Excellent."

19: Narfield Lodge

Little as Caroline wanted to spend two weeks as a guest of Lord and Lady Narfield, she had to admit it was very agreeable to don a new gown and spencer and bonnet, and watch her luggage be strapped onto the back of the Leathams' carriage.

There was quite a gathering on the steps of Bursham Cottage to wave them off. Apart from Lin and Poppy, Susie, Martin and Molly, Mr Stratton was there, together with both his parents, their manservant and maid, and John Christopher, who had left off weeding the front drive to watch the excitement. Nothing would do for Mrs Leatham but to descend from the carriage to make the acquaintance of the newcomers. The consequent greetings and polite enquiries as to journeys and homes and children and the state of the road delayed their departure considerably.

Eventually, however, Mr Leatham handed his step-mother back into the carriage, and then Caroline after her, just as if she were a lady too. He climbed in himself, settled himself beside Mrs Leatham's maid and the door was closed. With one groom riding beside the coachman, and another as an outrider leading another horse, they made rather an impressive cavalcade as they bounced down the uneven drive of the cottage, with Poppy and John Christopher running alongside, waving energetically.

"Your sister is feeling better, then?" Mr Leatham said.

"Thank you, she is. She's not quite her usual self, and likes to lie abed in the mornings and droops a little in the evenings, but I'm sure it won't take her long to be fully recovered."

"This continuing heat is excessively tiring," Mrs Leatham said. "I feel it myself, especially in the evenings, when one might hope for a respite. Poor girl! I do feel for her most sincerely. She will be much better once the heat wave has broken. A good thunderstorm would set her to rights, I am sure of it. When Mr Leatham and I were on our honeymoon — we went to Brighton, you know, and a rackety place it was too, even then, and it is worse now, so I am told, although we have never been back. Where was I? Oh yes, Brighton — the weather was just like this, so hot I was sure I would melt away into a puddle. I was all for packing up and returning home at once, for the countryside is always so cool and green is it not? But Mr Leatham did not wish to leave, having paid our accommodation for a fortnight together, and so we stayed, and it became hotter and hotter. But then there was the most tremendous storm of such thunder and lightning — I had never seen anything like it, and nor had Mr Leatham. It went on all night, but the next morning was beautiful, cool and clear and *so* refreshing after the heat. Now, we shall not need to stop in Salisbury, I hope, but we shall rest the horses at Alderbury."

"Oh, we are going on the Romsey road?" Caroline said.

"Are we?" Mrs Leatham said vaguely.

"We are," Mr Leatham said with a smile. "We turn a little to the south before the town, but Narfield Lodge is only some five miles to the west of your previous home, Miss Milburn."

After the grandeur of Valmont, Narfield Lodge was built on a far more modest scale, but it was still imposing in Caroline's eyes. Classical statues gazed austerely down from the lintel of every window, and the front of the house stretched out ornately arched and colonnaded arms to welcome arriving guests. There was no army of immaculate footmen, however, just two of them, supervised by a butler and housekeeper.

Four people emerged to greet them. Caroline recognised Mr and Mrs Narfield, whose estate bordered the Leathams' property, and Lady Narfield, the duke's sister she had met at Valmont. The fourth person was Lord Narfield, and a fine handsome man he was too, although he blinked at them rather vacantly as the introductions were made, as though he were not quite sure what they were doing there.

"I have had to drag Henry away from the orchard for the day," Lady Narfield said, laughing merrily. "Do not ask him about apples, I implore you, for once he begins on that subject so dear to his heart, he never stops. Shall we go inside? You will want to rest after your journey. Travel is so tiring in the summer, is it not?"

"Very true, my dear," said her husband, his eyes twinkling. "Everyone should travel in the winter, when the roads are impassable. That would be a much better arrangement."

"Foolish man!" his wife said affectionately, and the two went back into the house arm in arm, laughing together. Caroline was struck with sudden grief for her own dear parents, always so fond of each other. If only she could find a man just as devoted to her, and whom she loved in equal degree, then perhaps she could consider marriage. But where was such perfection to be found? Not in any of the men she had known, that much was certain. Lady Narfield undertook to show Mrs Leatham and Charles to their quarters, while Mrs Narfield led Caroline in a different direction.

"You will not mind sharing, will you, my dear?" she said, as she showed her into a very pretty room with the walls entirely papered with blue flowers, and hangings of blue and gold stripes. "We have put the eldest Miss Redpath in with you, since she is the nearest in age. Ah, here is Polly. She will help you unpack and change. We are all in the saloon, so come down whenever you are ready, dear."

Her box arrived almost at once, and Caroline was on her knees beginning to unpack before she'd thought twice. Polly giggled, and Caroline realised her mistake. "I'm probably supposed to let you do all this, aren't I?" she said ruefully.

"It's usual, miss."

"Well, it will go quicker with two of us, won't it?"

Polly nodded, and for a while they worked in harmony. But before long, the door was thrown open to reveal Mrs Narfield again, accompanied by a young lady dressed in the first stare of fashion, and a drably-attired woman who could only be a lady's maid.

"Here we are now, and is this not cosy? Jane, this is Miss MIlburn. Miss Milburn, Miss Redpath."

Caroline scrambled to her feet, and dropped into an awkward curtsy. Miss Redpath looked her up and down assessingly, before giving the minutest nod of her head in acknowledgement. Two footmen staggered in with her box, and then a second box, and yet a third. Miss Redpath unlocked them before carelessly tossing aside her spencer, gloves and bonnet, and sitting down on the dressing table stool to make delicate adjustments to her hair.

For a while, nothing was said, as the two maids laboured, Miss Redpath titivated and Caroline stood uncertainly to one side, wanting to help Polly but feeling instinctively that she should not.

After a while, Miss Redpath swivelled round on the stool to gaze at Caroline thoughtfully. "I hope there are plenty of entertainments planned for us. A ball, perhaps. Have you heard what is arranged?"

"No, I've no idea."

"I had no notion of leaving Cherleigh at all this summer, but Mama insisted, so here I am. She is planning a match for me with one of the Narfield boys, but I have no inclination for it myself. I had far sooner wait until the spring, and the season. There is a certain viscount who will be happy to see me again, and still unwed. Have you been presented, Miss Milburn?"

"Presented?"

"At court. I surmise that you have not. Is your father's estate near here?"

"My father never had an estate," she said. And then, because there was no point in hiding the facts, she went on, "My father was a linen draper in Romsey."

Miss Redpath gaped at her, almost as if she'd said he was a fishmonger. Rising, she said imperiously, "Leave that, Tomkins," and swept out of the room. The maid jumped to her feet, bobbed a quick curtsy to Caroline, then scuttled after her mistress.

Ten minutes later, she crept back in and began to repack all her mistress's clothes into the boxes. Two footmen came and carried them away.

Twenty minutes after that, when Polly had unpacked Caroline's modest wardrobe, offered to help her change and been rejected and gone away, a tap at the door revealed a homely face covered in freckles.

"Miss Milburn? I am sent to share your room if you have no objection."

"I have not the least objection in the world to sharing my room with any lady," Caroline said. "It seems, however, as if some ladies object to sharing with me."

The homely face nodded solemnly. "Miss Redpath is excessively particular in her notions, and the least little thing upsets her. Allow me to introduce myself... Louisa Law, governess to all five of the Miss Redpaths, for my sins."

"Caroline Milburn, lacemaker. Miss Redpath was disconcerted by the discovery that my father's estate consisted of a linen draper's shop in Romsey."

"Oh dear! Yes, that would do it. The girls are dreadfully stuck up, and nothing I do has any effect, I regret to say."

"Just as well I didn't tell her that my mother was the illegitimate child of a gamekeeper's daughter."

Miss Law laughed out loud. "Oh, splendid! Delighted to make your acquaintance, Miss Milburn. This visit is going to be more enjoyable than I had anticipated."

~~~~~

The saloon was not crowded, for it was far too large to be filled by only the dozen or so who were gathered there, but it was very
~~~~~

noisy. Little clusters of women chattered away together so volubly, that Caroline instinctively stopped on the threshold, trying not to wince.

"Miss Milburn and Miss Law, my lady," declaimed the butler, in tones loud enough to override the chatter. The room fell into silence, as a dozen pairs of eyes turned towards the door. Beside her, Miss Law seemed to shrink, and scuttled away into a corner like a mouse caught in the kitchen. Caroline felt that way, too. Just as at Valmont, she wondered what she was doing there. A lacemaker had no business mingling with these great people! But then she recalled that Lady Narfield had invited her personally, so how could it possibly be wrong? She straightened her back, and gazed back fearlessly at the assembled ladies.

But not all were ladies. Mr Charles Leatham was there, and there was one other man, and she recognised him. Of all the people in the world to be staying at Narfield Lodge! But she was glad she had not tried to hide her origins from Miss Redpath, for here was one who could reveal her secret if he chose. It was none other than the nameless man who had patronised Papa's shop, and epitomised the gentleman in her mind.

Lady Narfield rose and crossed the room. "Ah! Miss Milburn, do come and let me make everyone known to you. You know my sisters, Lady Henrietta Redpath and Lady Alice Wynne, of course, and here are their daughters..." There was a long list of names, and much curtsying and expressions of polite pleasure in the acquaintance, but Caroline could see from their faces that Miss Redpath had told her sisters and cousins of Caroline's lowly origins. She would make no friends there.

Then Lady Narfield led her to the gentleman she knew. He was older than she remembered, being above fifty now, she guessed, since his hair was quite white. But his face was unlined, and he smiled as he was introduced to her as Mr Wynne, husband to Lady Alice.

"Miss Milburn and I have met before," he said, making her a respectful bow. "I daresay you do not remember me, but I was well acquainted with your father for many years. I was very sorry indeed to hear of his death. How is your mother now?"

"She died two years ago, sir."

"Then you have suffered a double blow, and are sincerely to be pitied. To be orphaned at such a young age is a great tragedy, for your two sisters must be very young still, I fancy."

"Poppy is just sixteen, and Lin is almost twenty and shortly to be married."

"Now that is happier news! And do you still live in Romsey?"

They talked for some time, almost as old friends, and she found herself telling him all about their unexpected inheritance, and how contented her sisters were to be living in the country, Lin with her garden and Poppy with her chickens and goats.

"And you, Miss Milburn? Has country living brought contentment to you, too?"

"It's relieved me of many of my concerns," she said. "Money, of course, but also it's a comfort to know that Lin and Poppy are both safe and usefully employed in the garden. I don't have to worry about what they'll get up to next. But of course there are new concerns." Her eyes roved over the room as she spoke, at the unnerving collection of the fashionable and the wealthy.

"There is always something to worry over, if one is a natural worrier," he said, eyes twinkling. "You will grow accustomed,

Miss Milburn. Your father would be delighted to know of your good fortune and that your future is secure."

"Indeed he would," Caroline said, absurdly pleased at such simple but kindly words. It made her glad to feel she had a friend in such company as she now found herself, and he never once mentioned that his acquaintanceship with her father had arisen through the circumstance of having bought handkerchiefs and stockings from him. She saw no reason to modify her previous opinion of him as exemplifying every quality of the gentleman, and when another arrival led to an adjustment in the company, she took the opportunity to say as much to Mr Leatham.

"You would do well to observe his manner," she said. "Then you may tell me, if you will, if he is not the complete gentleman, and someone to inspire your enterprise."

He smiled, and murmured, *"'Whenever you go into good company, that is the company of people of fashion, observe carefully their behaviour, their address and their manners; imitate them as far as in your power.'"*

She laughed. "You are in a fair way to knowing that book by heart."

There was another round of introductions for Caroline to endure before dinner, as the sporting gentlemen were now returned from the field and the remaining guests had arrived, cousins to Lord Narfield. By the time Caroline entered the saloon, wearing her second best evening gown for the occasion, it was clear that everyone in the house was now aware of her humble heritage. Judging by the silence that fell as she entered, and the way so many of the occupants of the room avoided her gaze, she guessed that they had been that very moment discussing her.

Nevertheless, she was greeted cordially and given a prime seat near to Lady Narfield and one of her sisters, and gently drawn into their conversation. They were talking about the current fashion for trains, and the inconvenience of dancing with one.

"All that pinning and fussing about, and Lucilla is constantly tripping over hers," Lady Alice said. "Annabelle manages better, although she is the younger. What do you say, Miss Milburn? Do you not find this vogue for evening trains a great trial when dancing?"

"I don't know, my lady. I've never danced with one."

"Oh." She fidgeted uncomfortably with her fan, but then said smoothly to her sister, "I do hope you will have some dancing while we are here, Georgie. The young ones are wild for it, and we can certainly get up six or eight couples. Do you not think it an excellent scheme, Miss Milburn? You want to dance, I am sure."

"It might be amusing, my lady," Caroline said, without enthusiasm. There was little she relished less than the prospect of displaying her rustic dancing skills in front of this company.

"There, you see, Georgie? Miss Milburn would find it amusing to dance. You cannot refuse, I am sure, and Henry is so amiable he will make no objection. You may set up the card tables in the music room, you know, if the gentlemen insist on playing, and roll up the carpet in here. Come now, do let us have a little dancing."

"I can do better than that, Alice. We are to have a ball on Thursday week — what do you say to that?"

Lady Alice clapped her hands with glee. "What a good sister you are!"

A ball. Caroline sighed inwardly. Perhaps she could contrive to have the headache that night.

They sat down four and twenty to dinner, at so fashionably late an hour that Caroline's stomach was grumbling audibly, and she was very glad to find that the soup was distributed promptly. There was no delay in carving the joints, either, so her plate was soon filled with tasty morsels. She was seated between two gentlemen she had met only half an hour before, but one of them said nothing to her that didn't relate to the meal, and the other exhausted his conversational skills enquiring about her family and where she lived. Caroline didn't mind. She could attend to her plate, try to work out what the elaborate concoctions were that she was eating and also listen to the conversations of others as she pleased. Once or twice she caught the eye of Miss Law, not far away on the opposite side of the table, and discovered she was likewise neglected by her dinner companions. They exchanged sympathetic glances, the two lowliest and least regarded guests.

When the ladies withdrew, they went into the music room where most of the company clustered around a pianoforte and harp, with much lively discussion of pieces to perform, and who might be prevailed upon for a duet or to perform an Italian air. Caroline discovered Miss Law in a corner of the room with a piece of embroidery.

"I wish I'd thought to bring some work down with me," she said mournfully, sitting down beside the governess. "I can't bear to be idle."

"Nor I," Miss Law said. "Why not go and fetch your needlework, so that we may be cosy together in our quiet corner?"

It took no more than two minutes to run upstairs and fetch down her bag. Miss Law gasped when she drew out her lacemaking pillow and unpinned the bobbins.

"Oh, *lace!* How beautiful a piece! Did you make those frills on your sleeves? Oh, and your fan... may I? How clever you are!"

With such praise, all reserve between them was at an end, and long before the gentlemen joined them, the two women were firm friends. Caroline now had no apprehensions about enduring the long evenings. She need not fear to be drawn into card games for money she could not afford to lose, and she would be overlooked whenever there was music or dancing or any danger of public display.

She was not quite hidden from sight, however, so when the card tables were being made up, Lady Narfield called out, "Miss Milburn! Miss Law! Should you care to play?"

"Miss Law cannot play," Lady Henrietta Redpath said. "She must be free to attend to the girls, if they should need anything."

"As you wish," Lady Narfield said, "but Miss Milburn will oblige me, I am sure. It is only Speculation, you know, a very easy game, and I am sure Jane will explain the rules to you."

"Oh no, Aunt Georgie," Jane said at once, "for our table is quite made up and there is no room for anyone else. Miss Milburn would not fit in *here,* not in the least."

Lady Narfield looked disconcerted, and Lady Henrietta frowned at her daughter. "Nonsense, Jane! Another chair might be brought forward without the least inconvenience to anybody, and Speculation is all the better for more players."

"Thank you, my lady, but I have no intention of playing," Caroline said hastily.

"Oh, but I insist," Lady Henrietta said. "Jane is being foolish. You must play, Miss Milburn. Come now, do join the Speculation table. I shall be so disappointed if you do not. Take no notice of Jane! She is a thoughtless girl, but she means no harm, you know."

And although Caroline steadily refused, Lady Henrietta continued to lament it for quite twenty minutes, and to revive the subject periodically whenever a pause in the play permitted.

Caroline could not decide which was the more embarrassing, the daughter's rudeness or the mother's ill-conceived attempts to ameliorate it. She bent her head to her bobbins and wished she could disappear.

20: Observation

Caroline and Miss Law withdrew to their bedroom at the earliest opportunity, took turns behind the screen to change into nightgowns, put curling papers in each other's hair and then read aloud from the Bible for half an hour. They then knelt side by side at the bed and silently prayed. Caroline wondered what Miss Law prayed for. A new position, perhaps, with more agreeable charges. Or did she hope for a man to whisk her away from her life of servitude? Caroline's own prayers were filled with gratitude for her present state of comfort, the wish for happiness and prosperity for Lin and Mr Stratton, and the hope that the present occupants of Bursham Cottage may remain untroubled in her absence. She didn't mention any troubles explicitly, for surely the Good Lord knew all about the mysterious thefts, the boxes of money in the garden and the oddity of the Dowager Lady Elland's net purses, but she prayed very sincerely for the well-being of her sisters and the servants.

Miss Law went to check on the Miss Redpaths, returning almost at once with a gleeful grin. "Her ladyship is ringing a peal over Jane for her behaviour to you this evening," she said jubilantly. "I suspect you will be the target of Jane's contrition tomorrow. Prepare to be included in every activity as her bosom-bow."

Caroline pulled a face. "I wish all of them would just leave me alone. I don't mind being ignored. I don't feel I have any business in this company anyway."

"You have been invited, like every one else. Why should you be insulted and ignored? But if it truly makes you uncomfortable, you may be sure that Jane's attentions will last only as long as her mother's, and only then when Lady Henrietta is there to observe her. They will both forget about you soon enough, no doubt." She yawned widely. "Goodness, I am tired! I was up before dawn to finish packing the girls' boxes, and that bed looks so inviting, especially when compared with the dreadful hard bed in the attics which I was assigned originally. Shall I take the side by the wall?"

Without waiting for a response, she climbed in and fell asleep almost at once. Caroline lay awake for some time, torn between worrying about Lin and Poppy, and wondering how she was to survive two whole weeks of this misery. Once again, she wished she had listened to her instincts, and not allowed herself to be persuaded to move outside her own sphere. But she had promised Mr Leatham that she would help him in his quest to become a gentleman, and, since he had won the wager between them, it was a debt of honour.

So she told herself sternly that worrying never made anything better, and closed her eyes in a determined effort to sleep.

~~~~~

Charles saw at once that Miss Milburn was right — Mr Wynne was the consummate gentleman. His dress, his deportment and
~~~~~

mannerisms, his voice and his air of good breeding all defined him as a man who could mingle in the highest society in the land, would always command respect and yet was unobtrusive. He never put himself forward, yet he was deferred to. He never raised his voice, but others turned to listen to him. His opinions were considered and thoughtful, and he had no qualms about disagreeing with the majority view while firmly maintaining his own. By the time the gentlemen left the dining room, Charles knew that he had found the model upon which to base his own behaviour.

It was one thing to know whom he wished to emulate. It was quite another to perform the imitation. Even though he could see and observe the little distinctions that were so happily combined in Mr Wynne, he had no idea how to include them in his own behaviour. Accordingly, he set himself merely to observe. When an opportunity arose, he would share his observations with Miss Milburn and she might advise him how to proceed. His faith in her was so great at this point that he had no doubt of her ability to do so.

Accordingly, the first evening he had contrived to play whist at Mr Wynne's table, although he had been obliged to watch helplessly as Miss Redpath insulted Miss Milburn. She had disappeared before his card table disbanded, so he had no opportunity to speak to her that evening, but he fumed about it for hours, and woke the next morning still fuming.

He was sharing his room with an amiable young man who was a friend of one of the Narfield brothers. "J-j-just invited t-t-to m-m-make up the n-n-numbers," he said cheerfully to Charles. "Do you ride, L-l-leatham?"

Charles did, and had his horse in the stables to prove it. In no time, the two had made a firm arrangement to ride out every morning before breakfast. This proved such an agreeable exercise that they were late in arriving in the dining room and most of the gentlemen had already left. Charles felt a little self-conscious walking into a room almost entirely composed of ladies, but he saw his step-mother and Miss Milburn amongst them, and was about to join them when he noticed the disagreeable Miss Redpath was sitting next to them, and at once changed his plan. At least whatever antipathy had inspired last night's insult had dissolved into amity. He spotted Mr Wynne at the other end of the table, so that was where he settled when he had filled his plate from the sideboard.

"Do you have any plans for the day, Mr Leatham?" Wynne enquired politely.

"Oh… I have no idea. I shall just fall in with everyone else, I expect."

"Most of the young men are going out shooting. There are some snipe worth having in one of the coveys, apparently."

"Snipe!" Charles liked a day in the field as well as anyone, but he could not summon much enthusiasm for snipe. He reminded himself he was not there to enjoy himself, but to practise being a gentleman and to find himself a bride. He must not lose sight of his object. With this in mind, he said, "What are the ladies planning to do today, I wonder?"

"An outing to Southampton, I understand. A number of shops are to be visited."

Charles pulled a face.

Mr Wynne smiled gently. "Indeed, male company would be very much in the way. There is a tolerable library here, if you are minded to read."

"I have a book to read already."

"Then perhaps a walk in the gardens? It is a fine day, and there is a fair prospect of the New Forest from the ruined temple. For myself, Lord Narfield is to show me his orchard."

"You have an interest in apples, then, Mr Wynne?"

"Not especially, but Lord Narfield does, and it is a pleasure to him to have a willing listener. I always spend a day with him whenever I stay here."

This sounded excessively boring, but since the ladies were out of reach for the day, he might as well pursue his other object, and follow Mr Wynne about.

"Would he mind if I were to come along too?" Charles said.

"My dear sir, he would be delighted! Quite delighted!"

Entirely to Charles' surprise, he found the day diverting and the subject fascinating. Lord Narfield was slightly vague about who he was — "Do give my regards to your dear mother. I haven't seen her since we were in Bath last year." — but his knowledge of and enthusiasm for his subject was unbounded. Never had Charles suspected that the grafting of apple trees could be so interesting. He ended the day full of ideas for their own modest orchard at Starlingford, and a promise from Lord Narfield to answer any question that might arise.

Leaving his lordship still busy with his head gardener, Charles and Mr Wynne walked back towards the house, where an array of parasols and fluttering gowns on the terrace suggested that the ladies had returned from their expedition.

"Shall we go and make ourselves agreeable to the fairer sex?" Mr Wynne said, as they began the long walk across the lawn.

"It is a noble enterprise, but I fear I shall always fall short," Charles said gloomily. "The ability to be agreeable to a lady is not in my nature."

"It is a skill like any other," Wynne said affably. "Just as you have learnt to ride and to shoot and to play whist or backgammon, so you may also learn to be good company. It is merely another part of the gentleman's repertoire."

"That is the trouble, I do not know what a gentleman is," Charles said. "All I know is how to be a soldier. I am trying to learn, however. I have a book on the subject, and Miss Milburn is helping me." Then, in a rush of openness, he said, "She told me to observe *you*, Mr Wynne. In her opinion, you are the finest example she has ever seen of a true gentleman."

"I am flattered, for I make no claim to such extraordinariness. I follow only the precepts of ordinary politeness. It surprises me to discover that such straightforward and commonplace manners require an entire book to describe them."

"Ordinary politeness is perhaps within my grasp," Charles said with a frown, although honesty compelled him to add, "Most of the time, at least. My temper is not what it might be, and there I might fairly be censured, I know. But on common occasions, when I am not provoked, I trust I may be polite. But surely there is more to it? A gentleman must be more than merely polite, would you not say? His air, his appearance, his opinions… every aspect must be superior, and that is what I cannot grasp. Even when I feel I understand the principles espoused in the book, it is difficult to put them into practice. With a young lady, for example, I have not the least notion what to say, so I say nothing. How can I speak when I feel we have nothing in common? With a man, I may attempt a conversation, but a lady terrifies me, and yet I must find myself a wife, and soon."

Mr Wynne laughed. "Now *that* I understand. Our society does its utmost to raise each sex apart from the other, and then, by some miracle, the two are supposed to get along well enough in adulthood to fall in love and marry and spend their lives together. It is altogether too optimistic. I was approaching forty before I felt brave enough to approach the idea of matrimony, so I sympathise with your position, Mr Leatham. No book will teach you the skill of courtship, for every man must learn it afresh when he begins the quest for a wife, and the strategy will depend entirely on the lady. Some like to be complimented and flattered, some want ardour, some prefer a pragmatic approach..."

"Then what am I to do?" Charles cried. "The business is hopeless!"

"Not at all, not at all. My father gave me two pieces of advice when he introduced me into society, Mr Leatham, and I willingly offer them to you now, in the hope that they may be useful to you. Firstly, behave always in ways which are calculated to give pleasure rather than offence to the other party, without consideration of one's own wishes, just as we did today in allowing Lord Narfield to indulge his hobby. So when we reach the ladies, as we very soon shall, my first greeting will be to my hostess, if she is present, or failing that the highest ranked lady. After that, any lady who might be offended if not noticed, and then I shall look about for anyone who is otherwise unattended and might be glad of company."

"And the second piece of advice your father gave you?" Charles said urgently, for they were almost upon the ladies.

"To be myself at all times, not pretending to be either more or less than I am. We may speak more of this later, if you wish, but for now, observe what I do."

So saying, he moved smoothly towards Lady Narfield, bowed over her hand and began enquiring into the success of her day with every appearance of enjoyment. Charles took his cue from this, and found Lady Henrietta Redpath in the throng. He had only to mention the expedition to Southampton for her to begin a detailed recital of every shop they had entered, and the purchases acquired, and the inn where they had obtained a cold collation. He had very little to do except nod occasionally and murmur *'Really?'* or *'How fortunate?'* or *'Was it indeed?'* for her to continue. It was not interesting, but he recalled his book — *'However trifling their conversation, do not show them, by your inattention, that you think them trifling'* — and made a great effort to attend.

After a while, her disagreeable daughter sidled up and sat down next to him. He had no wish at all to talk to *her*, but he was mindful of Mr Wynne's words that he should talk to *'any lady who might be offended if not noticed.'* He suspected Miss Redpath to be a lady likely to be offended.

"Good day, Miss Redpath," he said. "I trust you are well?"

"Perfectly well, I thank you, sir. How kind of you to ask," she simpered. "Pray do tell us about your estate at Starlingford. Is it very charming?"

Charles had not been used to considering an estate as charming. Starlingford was a contradiction to him, a place filled with happy childhood memories but also the sorrow of his brothers' deaths. It was a burden and a chain that anchored him in place when he would far rather be free, yet its woods and pastures brought him a tranquillity he had never known anywhere else. It was his family home, and also contained the unwanted presence of Mildred. He never thought of it without pleasure, but there was also grief and regret. He could not put any of this into words, even had he wished to, so he talked instead of those things which might interest a girl of Miss Redpath's age — rooms and gardens and farms and the surrounding countryside. She listened with wide eyes, as her mother looked on smilingly.

Eventually the servants brought out refreshments and as the guests crowded around the pyramids of fruit and platters of meat, Charles was able to make his escape. Sitting unnoticed in a shady corner with her lacemaking equipment, he found Miss Milburn. Still in a gentlemanly frame of mind, he said, "May I fetch you some fruit, Miss Milburn? Or a drink, perhaps?"

She looked up at him with a mischievous smile which lit up her face. No one would ever say she was pretty, but when she smiled so, those dark eyes afire with merriment, she was handsome indeed, and there was nothing in her form to object to. In fact, she was rather a lovely young woman — when she smiled.

"How gallant you are today, Mr Leatham! A morning in the company of Mr Wynne has been most effective, I can tell. Whereas I have had less agreeable company, and I'm in high dudgeon as a result. If you are minded for an argument, I can certainly oblige you."

He laughed. "Sorry as I am to disoblige a lady, I am in too good a humour to quarrel with you today. But you speak of Miss Redpath? Is she more friendly today than she was yesterday?"

She nodded, her face rueful. "I could wish she wouldn't be, but her mother scolded her into it and so she's been clinging to me like a limpet all day."

"Barnacle," he said automatically.

"What?"

"Never mind. How did you escape her?"

"I told her I had the headache and must sit in the shade with some restful occupation."

"Oh, I am very sorry you have the headache. Might you not feel better if you were to lie down for a while?"

She gurgled with laughter. "I don't really have the headache, Mr Leatham. I told a little lie."

At once he said, "*'Remember as long as you live that nothing but strict truth can carry you through life with honour and credit.'* Oh… I beg your pardon, Miss Milburn, that was an offensive thing to say to you."

Fortunately, she took it in good part. "Not at all, for in general you're quite right, or rather, your book is quite right. I am impressed, by the way, with the amount of it you can quote at the very moment it's required. That shows an admirable degree of study. But I suspect the book refers to serious lies, where one pretends to be rich or well-connected or some such, and not the everyday little lies that make life tolerable. If a friend says to me, *'Does this gown flatter me?'*, am I supposed to say, *'No, not at all, it makes you look monstrous ugly and you should give it to your prettier sister at once'?* I should not have many friends if I spoke so. One may always find some little compliment to make. *'That is such an unusual colour'*, perhaps. Or *'What an elegant sleeve! Did you contrive it yourself?'* And sometimes, if one wishes to be left alone, one may pretend to have the headache."

He sat down abruptly beside her, tugging at his earlobe. "This is so obvious when you explain it this way, just as Mr Wynne's advice seems obvious, and yet all these years such things had never occurred to me. I must be very stupid. How will I ever be a proper gentleman and find a wife?"

"Not stupid," she said, patting his hand absent-mindedly, "but wrapped up in your own affairs, perhaps. Once you begin to look about you at the company, you will find out all sorts of interesting details about people which you can turn to your advantage. You would find out, for instance, that Miss Redpath and her mother are very keen to assist you in your search for a wife. Miss Redpath would very much like to be mistress of Starlingford. She has been plying your step-mother with questions about it all day."

"Miss Redpath?" he said. "No!" But when he looked across at the lady and her mother, he saw them watching him with narrowed eyes. As his gaze fell on them, they both smiled brightly, and Lady Henrietta waggled two fingers at him playfully. "Good God, that would be worse than Mildred," he said with loathing.

"Then do not pay her too much attention, or you may raise expectations."

"Miss Milburn," he said with feeling, "I thank you from the bottom of my heart. You are so wise."

"I? Wise?" But he thought she looked pleased, all the same.

21: A Ball

Charles found that the days passed very pleasantly. He rode each morning with Mr Smythe, satisfying the need of both gentlemen for exercise and a degree of freedom from the constraint of being constantly civil to strangers. After breakfast, he made it his business to be available to the young ladies if an escort was required, and conscientiously laboured to become thoroughly acquainted with all of them.

When he found himself with a spare hour or two, he sought out Mr Wynne, who was usually to be found in the library with the newspapers and a pile of books. He always politely set these aside, however, seemingly delighted to discuss gentlemanly behaviour or politics or the state of the roads or any of a hundred other subjects, as they arose. When Charles apologised for importuning him, Mr Wynne smiled and said it was a pleasure.

"Hmm. That sounds like precisely the sort of thing a true gentleman would say," Charles said. "You wish to please me by answering all my foolish questions, to the detriment of your own leisure time."

"You are quite correct," Mr Wynne said. "Nevertheless, it also happens to be the case that it is a pleasure for me too. I have no son of my own, and if that situation should be remedied in the future, I may not survive to see him reach adulthood and ask me such questions in his turn. Even if I am so fortunate as to have another twenty or more years left to me, I may be unable to do more than drool and pull my shawl closer about my shoulders by that time. So you are giving me something I may never otherwise experience, Mr Leatham, and I thank you for it."

The two were occasionally joined in the library by other bookish guests. Lord Narfield proved to be interested in more than apples alone, and could discourse at length on any number of scientific topics. Mr Julian Narfield, one of his unmarried brothers, was a lawyer with aspirations to enter Parliament, and he questioned Charles with great interest on his experiences of the war. Mr Thomas Redpath, uncle to the obnoxious Miss Redpath, was a man of some learning, whose spirited philosophical debates with the others Charles watched with amazement. His father, although well-read, was too private a man to display his own erudition, and his army friends had been men like himself, young, active and engaged in the serious pursuit of pleasure. He had never before been exposed to men of considered opinions, who were prepared to debate them at length and in good humour, acknowledging every sound point made against them. Charles had no ambition towards such learning for himself, but he could not but be affected by it.

He did not forget his principal task, however. When he found himself in company with Miss Milburn and the opportunity arose for private talk, he would ask her opinion of one young lady or another.

"What do you think of the Miss Wynnes?" he would begin.

"They seem like very pleasant, well-mannered girls," she said cautiously.

"But so young! The elder is barely seventeen. I should like a wife who can conduct a rational conversation. What about the Miss Narfields?"

"Very accomplished."

"All young ladies are accomplished," he said with a sigh.

"Except for me," she said, with a smile.

"You are accomplished, too," he replied seriously. "I have seen your skill at lacemaking, Miss Milburn, and in that area there is not a lady in the county to compare with you."

Her eyes widened, and she opened her mouth to make a retort, then thought better of it. In the end, "I thank you for the compliment, sir," was all she said.

That gave him pause for thought. He had paid her a compliment without the least effort, because it was something that was true. As with her examples of the friend with the unflattering gown, where she would find some little thing to praise, all he had to do was to speak the truth, which was perfectly consistent with the principles of gentlemanly behaviour. Once he had identified his future bride, therefore, he would be able to court her with perfect ease, now that he knew the way of it.

In the second week of their stay at Narfield Lodge there were some increases in the company, for with the approach of the planned ball, Lady Narfield felt the want of more young gentlemen to provide partners for the young ladies expected to attend. Amongst the newcomers was one Charles was especially glad to see, his cousin Will Leatham.

"So how are you getting along with the charming Miss Milburn?" Will said, as soon as they had an opportunity to be alone. "Am I to wish you joy?"

"Heaven forbid!" Charles said with feeling. "We should never suit. She is here only to advise me on which of the others to choose."

Will raised an eyebrow. "Truly? You contrived an invitation for her just so that she could point out that Miss So-and-so is tolerably pretty and has seven thousand pounds?"

Charles laughed at this description. "The invitation was none of my doing, I assure you. Lady Narfield took a fancy to her and invited her, or perhaps she wanted to invite Mama and thought Miss Milburn was her companion or some such. I cannot think she is very comfortable here, for the other young ladies thoroughly despise her."

"Because her father was in trade? Society can be very harsh. But if she marries well..."

"Who would marry her?" Charles said, with an indifferent lift of one shoulder. "She is a shrew, Will, destined to be a spinster aunt to the children of her sisters, who will all be terrified of her bad temper and avoid her as much as possible. Their parents will value her for the dreadful warning she embodies. *'Be obedient and good, or else you will end up like Aunt Caroline, unloved and alone.'*"

Will laughed but shook his head. "You are too hard on her, Charles. She seems amiable enough to me, and she has a very pleasing figure. Very pleasing indeed."

"Then you may have her, with my blessing," Charles said, with a careless laugh, but Will's words left him shaken. Amiable? Caroline? He had regarded her as unmarriageable for so long that he found it difficult to adjust his ideas. Now that he thought about it, however, he could not remember when they had last argued. Was she mellowing, or was he growing accustomed to her? He had begun to think of her as a friend, but as for anything more than that… definitely not. Recovering himself, he went on quickly, "You must tell me what you think of the Miss Narfields. The elder has a charming way with a Scotch air, although the younger is the pretty one."

"Why is it always the younger sister who is pretty?" Will said, pulling a wry face. "No doubt she has a lesser dowry on account of it. One may have the dowry or the handsome face, but not both seemingly. Not that I could aspire to either one, not in a gathering like this. Unless you should be so obliging as to break your neck on the hunting field, my prospects are very poor. Three hundred a year now and the hope of another five hundred later, if the present incumbent does not outlast me, which I believe he is determined to do. Seven years I have been waiting for that living, and still the old gentleman is hale. Did you hear about old Morton? Waited six and twenty years for *his* living, and when it finally came to him, he had barely got the pictures hung to his satisfaction when he was carried off with an apoplexy. Life is very unfair sometimes."

"It is a pity you had not settled on the church in time for us to give you Bursham St Matthew," Charles said. "If we had known, we would have kept it for you and not let the Christophers have it."

"You are very good!" Will said. "Not that it is a very great income — no more than a hundred and fifty a year. Is it Christopher's only living? I cannot imagine how he contrives, unless they all live on bread and dripping. The extra income would have been useful, even after the cost of a curate, but it is of no consequence. I shall do well enough when I have my two livings and a wife with some money of her own. A few thousand would set me up very comfortably."

That evening, Will made directly for Miss Milburn as soon as he had made his greetings to the matrons, and there he stayed, making her laugh with some amusing anecdotes and eventually leading her in to dinner. Charles was stuck between the two Miss Wynnes, who were scarcely able to string a sentence together, being barely out of the schoolroom. He laboured manfully to make conversation, but it was hard work, and all the more frustrating when he could see Will and Miss Milburn getting along splendidly.

When the ladies withdrew, Will pulled up a chair next to Charles. "Did you mean what you said earlier?" Will said eagerly.

"About what?" Charles said absently, as he poured port into his glass.

"About Miss Milburn. You have no ambitions there yourself?"

Charles' froze for an instant, decanter in hand. Will and Miss Milburn? Surely he could not be interested in a woman like that! Unbidden, the image of treacle-coloured eyes arose in his mind, eyes that brimmed with merriment as she teased him. And that delightful figure, softly curving so that the skirts of her gown swayed as she walked...

"Charles?"

Recollecting himself, he passed the decanter down the table and turned to Will, schooling his features into blankness. "I have no plans to marry Miss Milburn," he said firmly. And it was true, damn it! So why did he feel as if he had been punched in the chest?

"Then you will not stand in my way, if... I mean... too early to say, of course, but... she has such a good figure. I have always hoped... if ever I should be so fortunate... someone just like that. Do you understand me? I must say, she looks remarkably well with her hair done that way, and such a pretty gown. Even in such company as this, she looks remarkably well. And she is very practical. She has suggested some small improvements to my household arrangements..."

"Will, can you afford to marry on three hundred a year?"

"Of course not, but according to Aunt Daphne, Miss Milburn has two thousand pounds, as well as a third share in the house. That is another eighty or a hundred a year, and she can earn perhaps as much again with her lace. She would be able to find some economies in my management as well, I am certain of it. We should be comfortably situated, very comfortably, even without my second living. Of course, it may come to nothing. I should have to get to know her better and so forth. I shall not rush into anything, you may be sure. But if you do not value her, you will not object, will you? It can be nothing to you if I try to attach her."

Charles reminded himself that he did not value Miss Milburn in the slightest, and had no wish at all to marry her, but he had thought of her as *his* Miss Milburn for so long that the prospect of someone else marrying her was not one he could view with equanimity.

"Do consider whether she is likely to be a conformable wife, Will. She is an argumentative woman, and in your position... a clergyman cannot have a wife who is always running counter to his wishes."

"She has never argued with me, Charles," Will said smugly. "I get along rather well with her, in point of fact."

And Charles had nothing else to say, although his spirits were oddly low.

The evening before the ball, his step-mother drew him aside. "Have you engaged Miss Milburn for the first two yet?" she said in an urgent whisper.

"Does she plan to dance?" he said, surprised. "I should not have thought—"

"Really, Charles! Of course she plans to dance, and if she does not, then you must persuade her to do so. A ball is the perfect opportunity to secure her once and for all."

"Mama, I am not sure—"

"You must not begin to doubt your own mind, Charles. Now is the moment to make your move. She has had time to consider your offer and to think better of her refusal, and besides, you seem to be getting along perfectly well now, is it not so? Not a cross word between you. Although I do not think it was well done of you to draw her to the card tables."

"She is a capital whist player, Mama, quite wasted in her quiet corner with the governess. So long as she plays for fish, she is perfectly happy to—"

"Better in her quiet corner than mingling with the gentlemen. She was playing with Mr Julian Narfield last night, and I could see that he was rather taken with her. You will not advance your cause by exposing her to men of greater rank or wealth than is your lot. Ask her for the first two, Charles. Do it now, and then you can engage her for the supper dances later."

But when he obediently approached Miss Milburn, he found he was too late.

"You are very kind, sir, but I am already engaged for the first two to Mr Will Leatham."

"Oh. The second two?"

"Already promised to Mr Julian Narfield, and after that to Mr Edward Redpath. But there is to be a waltz later, and I shall *not* be standing up for that, so you may bear me company on the wallflowers' seats if you wish."

"Do you disapprove of the waltz, Miss Milburn?"

"No, but I don't know the steps, and I don't wish to expose my ignorance to the company."

"That suits me very well, for I have never attempted a waltz either," he said, with a smile. "We shall be preserving the company from my ignorance, too."

The day of the ball saw no excursions planned, for the ladies felt the need to spend the day resting and choosing their gowns and jewels. The gentlemen went shooting as usual, and for once Charles was free to go with them, enjoying tolerable sport. There was some relief in being only with gentlemen, and finding no need to be careful of his language or even to talk at all, if he had no mind for it. Even though he was learning to be more adept at dealing with ladies, he still felt more at ease with his own sex.

Dinner was a lively affair, for everyone was in eager anticipation of the ball. Even those who would not dance looked forward to a wider range of company. Charles wished he might be among their number, for dancing was not one of his favourite occupations. He always felt awkward and ungainly in the dance. However, it had been impressed on all the young men that there would be an excess of ladies, so he knew he must do his duty.

He had not yet secured a partner for the first set, and had thought perhaps he would observe just at first, but the sight of Will leading Miss Milburn onto the floor infuriated him. Instantly he looked about him for someone not otherwise engaged. The first young lady to catch his eye turned out to be the younger Miss Wynne, but as a distraction she was not a success. She was so busy minding her steps that she had nothing to spare for conversation, so that Charles had nothing to do except to glower at Will. After that, he danced with a Miss Smythe, and then with the youngest Miss Redpath, but although these two were happily able to talk and dance at the same time, they too failed as distractions, for there was Miss Milburn smiling brightly at her partner, and seemingly enjoying herself tremendously.

"Why are you not dancing with Miss Milburn?" his step-mother hissed at him, during a lull in proceedings.

"She was already engaged for half the evening."

"There you are, you see! You will lose her if you are not careful. Oh, I knew this would happen!"

"Have no fear, I have secured her for the waltz."

"Oh… the waltz… that is good, very good. Well done, Charles."

"Why are you so keen on her?" he said, suddenly curious. "Here are young ladies enough to please far more fastidious men than I am, all with better education and connections and fortune than Miss Milburn, yet you have never wavered in your support of her cause. Despite her unequivocal refusal, you continue to encourage me in that direction, and I cannot for the life of me understand why."

Her smile wavered and then vanished, to be replaced by a look of pure anxiety. "Charles, I shall be happy to see you settled, whomever you may choose, you know that. Even with Mildred, if your thoughts had run in that direction. If you should prefer another young lady above Miss Milburn, I should never dream of dissuading you. But…" She paused, chewing her lip nervously. "Consider my position, dear. I am five and thirty years old, and… and… let us be realistic… your father is almost twice my age, and therefore I am likely to be a widow before too many years have passed. I brought nothing into the marriage beyond my own self, and although your father has very generously settled a small sum upon me, it will give me only a tiny income, and I cannot bear to—" She gulped, then took a deep breath. "I cannot face the prospect of moving out of Starlingford into a tiny cottage with only a cook general and a maid of all work and no comforts at all, or else going to live with one of your sisters."

"That will never happen, Mama," he said gently. "I shall *never* force you out of your own home."

"But that is just the trouble," she said sadly. "It will *not* be my own home. It will be your wife's home, and naturally she will want to be mistress of it, and not have the former mistress underfoot, and I *completely* understand that. It is the way the world works, that the old mistress moves out when the new mistress moves in. All these young ladies here tonight understand that perfectly well. They see you as the future master of Starlingford, and themselves as its future mistress, and give no thought to me at all. But Miss Milburn is not like that. She has no notion of how our world works, and she will *need* me to advise her and guide her for years and years. *She* will not expect me to leave Starlingford, in fact, she will most definitely want me to stay." She heaved a sigh. "I am a selfish creature, Charles. You said it did not matter to you whom you married, so long as it was not Mildred. In which case, it might as well be someone who would suit *me*. Do you see?"

He took her hand, and gently kissed it. "I see perfectly, Mama, but I promise you this — I shall never marry anyone who would force you out of Starlingford. When I settle upon the female I should like to marry, I shall make my offer conditional upon it."

She laughed, and said, "Now you are being absurd! No rational woman would ever accept you on such terms."

"Then it will just have to be Miss Milburn," he said equably.

The next dance began, and he moved off to find some neglected female who would not despise his company for half an hour, but during the quiet moments of the set, he considered his step-mother's words. It was a relief to know her true reasons for preferring Miss Milburn, and their conversation left him unaccountably light-hearted.

22: A Waltz

Charles had the annoyance of seeing Will taking Miss Milburn into supper. He cursed himself for his stupidity in participating in the supper dance himself, for it meant he was obliged to accompany his partner in to supper. Fortunately, he spotted a free seat beside Miss Milburn, so he steered his partner in that direction and claimed the place for her. Supper was very convivial as a result. Will was in good form, Miss Tomkins laughed heartily at Charles's every feeble joke and Miss Milburn… Miss Milburn was delightful. Charles had to admit, rather grudgingly, that she was indeed perfectly amiable with Will. She smiled and teased him in a manner that, in any other woman, might be called flirtatious. Will was right in another way, too — she looked remarkably well. She wore only a simple topaz cross around her neck, and her dress was less elaborate than most, but the lace trimming was exquisite, even to his inexpert eye, and Mama's maid had dressed her hair charmingly. And those dancing eyes! For a fleeting moment, he wished she would direct her teasing at him instead of at Will.

When the musicians could be heard warming up again, Will said, "Miss Milburn, may I escort you to your next partner? Or sit with you if you are not dancing?"

"Thank you, Mr Leatham, but I believe this is the waltz, and therefore I am engaged to your cousin."

"Oh." For a moment, Will was disconcerted, throwing Charles a questioning glance. But he recovered quickly. "Then I shall leave you in Charles's care. Miss Tomkins, might I have the honour of this dance, if you are not otherwise engaged?"

She blushingly agreed to it, and Will led her away, with one last frowning look at Charles.

"Do you wish to watch the dance?" he said to Miss Milburn.

She shook her head. "It is so crowded and close in there," she said.

"True. These improvised ballrooms are always too small, are they not? Every house should have a proper ballroom, large enough for fifty couples, at least, do you not agree?"

She smiled at him, in a way that warmed him inside. "And have it standing unused for all but two or three days in the year? That would be wasteful indeed. The saloon and music room combined make a perfectly adequate ballroom, except that it is very hot and stuffy, and that is just a natural consequence of holding a ball in the summer."

"Indeed. Winter is a far better season for dancing, and with luck one might be snowed in and the ball could last for a fortnight."

She laughed, merely shaking her head at this sally.

"Shall we go out onto the terrace?" he said. "The air will be cooler and fresher outside."

"Oh yes! That would be very pleasant."

There were doors from the dining room opening directly to the terrace, so he offered his arm and led her outside. The terrace ran the full length of this side of the building, lit by lanterns. Although there were shadowy corners, Charles led Miss Milburn to a brightly lit spot where they were clearly visible from within, should anyone happen to look. She had not thought of it, but he was all too aware of the propriety of being alone with her.

She leaned against the balustrade, gazing out into the darkness of the garden, and for a while he chose not to disturb her reverie, content merely to watch her profile. Tendrils of hair curled round her face, and he was struck with the urge to reach out and touch them, winding them around his fingers. Such foolishness! Yet the urge was almost irresistible. Say something... he must say something... anything to break the silence.

"Are you enjoying your stay here?" It was a mindless question, but she turned to him with a ready smile.

"Oh yes! How could anyone not enjoy it? Although Lady Narfield's invitation to me was not entirely altruistic. She had discovered a whole chest full of lace from her mother-in-law's day... no, it must have been even earlier. Anyway, she wanted me to look through it all and tell her what I thought. So I had a very pleasant morning sorting through some exquisite pieces... the finest Bruxelles lace, and Flemish... some Italian convent lace... so beautiful!" She sighed. "If I could make anything half so fine, I should call myself a lacemaker. But we don't have the quality of flax now. Or at least, I can't get thread so fine."

"Your lace is beautiful," he said, with the utmost sincerity.

"You are very kind to say so. My lace fan has been much admired, it is true. I could have sold it a dozen times over."

Another sigh. "I suppose I don't need to sell my lace any more, do I? But I can't quite get out of that way of thinking. Your step-mother has been so kind to me, explaining how I should behave, and letting Cresset do my hair. I can't imagine how I'd have managed otherwise. I'm so grateful to her, although I have no idea why she should take so much trouble over me."

"She still hopes we will make a match of it," he said, with a deprecating lift of one shoulder. Then, his mind still on his last conversation with his step-mother, he went on, "Poor Mama! She wants me to marry, and yet she is so afraid of it, too."

"Afraid? Why?"

"Because when Papa dies, there will be a new mistress of Starlingford and Mama will have to leave her home."

Miss Milburn turned to face him, quivering with indignation. "That is abominable! This world we live in is so cruel to widows. When her husband is alive, a woman is a person of consequence but as soon as he is dead and buried, she becomes nothing — less than nothing! Poor and alone and neglected, and quite beneath notice. It is the greatest injustice."

"You speak warmly on the subject," he said. "Are you thinking of your own mother?"

"Yes, for once Papa died it was as if she shrivelled away, becoming so small and... and insignificant. The world saw her as nobody, so she became nobody. And poor! We had never been wealthy, but there was always enough money. Life was comfortable, even though Papa worried about it constantly. But then, after his death, suddenly we were poor and everything was a struggle and poor Mama could not cope with it."

"But you could," he said softly. "*You* became the head of the family."

"Someone had to," she said fiercely. "Someone had to decide if we could afford beef or not, or new boots, or whether we could afford to replace an old kettle. I was eighteen when Papa died, Mr Leatham, and the most difficult decision I'd made until that moment was whether to wear the green silk or the sprigged muslin for an evening party. I grew up very quickly, I can tell you. It was the physician's bills that finished us. Poor Papa was so sick at the end, and the physician came every day. How were we to know how much that would cost? And then, within months, poor Mama grew sick as well, and how could we deny her the care she needed, and the medicines? Lord, the leeches she endured! And it did no good in the end, for she grew worse and worse, and nothing helped, yet we still had to pay for it. What little money Papa left us went into fattening those leeches. We ended up in two rooms with only one servant, and the lace I'd made as a pleasant diversion was all that kept us from starvation."

"Had you no relatives to turn to?" he said.

"Several who came and tutted over us and offered useless advice and then went away again. None who had any real help to give us. One elderly aunt offered a home to one of us, as an unpaid companion, but we agreed that we must stay together at all costs. I worked it out that we could survive on Mama's tiny portion and our earnings for a few years, just until Lin should marry. She is so pretty, it was inevitable that she would marry sooner or later, and save us from penury."

"And now she is indeed to marry, although you are already saved from penury," he said, smiling.

"Yes! Although it is so hard to get used to the idea of not counting every penny," she said. "Perhaps one day I might even view the loss of fifty pounds on a wager as a mere trifle, and not panic quite so dreadfully. I was very bad company that day, Mr Leatham, was I not?"

He lifted her gloved hand to his lips. "To be wholly truthful, Miss Milburn, I enjoyed that day enormously."

"Even though you were never introduced to the duke?" she said suspiciously.

"Even so — although that *was* an annoyance at the time, I confess. No, our wager forced me to be civil to you for the whole day, and so I found myself with no lapse in temper with which to reproach myself later. Of course, I was ashamed of my inability to escape from the maze and we never did get to the pagoda, but otherwise I had a perfectly agreeable day."

"I'm very glad, and I enjoyed it too, on the whole," she said, her smile warming him inside in a most unexpected way. That he should ever be so grateful for Miss Milburn's approbation! It was an astonishing situation, yet so it was.

"We are rather alike, you and I," he said, surprising even himself with the thought. "We have both had to make difficult adjustments, which are for the good in one way, yet bad in another. You found yourselves pulled out of poverty to a life of relative ease, yet to a society not at all comfortable for you, and I—"

"—had to leave the army," she said. "You must miss it so."

"I do," he said quietly. "My life was settled, orderly… I went where I was bidden and did what I was told, and knew that it was *right*. There was a certainty to it that suited me. But all that is gone. We can never go back to the past, no matter how much we may wish to. We must accept the present for what it is, with all its trials and setbacks, all its frustrations. I was useful, once, Miss

Milburn. I was of value, in my small way, to my country and my King. Now I do nothing but shoot snipe and make meaningless conversations with people I have no wish to know and who have no wish to know me. One day, perhaps, I shall see this as a better life, but just at the moment it all seems so pointless."

"You see only the bad, but you have said yourself that such adjustments have both good and bad in them. You have left behind the regularity of army life, but you are also no longer at risk of immediate death, and that is surely a good. Everyone who cares for you must see it so. And then there is the fact that you are now the heir to your father's estate, you have fine prospects, although to be sure that only came about through the deaths of your brothers."

His throat tightened at her words. His brothers! His childhood friends, his unquestioning supporters, his most trusted allies... now he was alone. No... not quite alone, for there was one person above all others whom he regarded as a true friend, for she would never tell him false. That, above all, was her most endearing characteristic, that she would say what was in her mind, and not wrapped up in deceptive language.

The strains of the waltz drifted out from the open windows. To distract himself from such maudlin thoughts, he said, "Come, Miss Milburn, I would have you dance the waltz, for when will you again have such a perfect opportunity?"

"No... I can't... I don't know the steps."

"I shall teach you, but we will not expose my teaching or your learning to the world. We may dance out here, if you will."

She smiled, and again his insides turned over. What was she doing to him? And what was he doing waltzing with her? Such an intimate dance, and he was already in dangerous territory with her, yet he could not resist. In a little while, he would take her back inside so that Will could flirt with her, but for now, she was his. So he showed her the starting position, and she stepped towards him trustingly, not minding the arm at her waist, the hand holding hers tight, the closeness...

They danced, haltingly at first, as he whispered the steps and the changes into her ear, but then with greater surety as she mastered the intricacies of the movements. They turned this way and that, hands clasping and unclasping, one arm raised and then the other, but all the time with gazes locked. She smiled, she laughed when she went wrong, she laughed again when she executed some tricky movement perfectly. To his utmost delight, she hummed as she danced, so that the music was not merely flowing out from the ballroom, but was right there beside him, held fast in the circle of his arms...

In his heart.

He scarcely knew how it had happened, but in all the time he imagined he had been despising her thoroughly, he had been falling in love with her. Astonishing thought... yet it had happened so slowly, so imperceptibly that it had crept up on him unawares. What a fool he was not to notice it! Even more of a fool to pass her on so casually to Will. Fool, fool, fool...! Now he would have to watch Will court her, and how could he fail to win her? He had all the charm and easy manners that Charles lacked. What woman, even one so set against marriage as Caroline, could resist him? Dear, unpretentious Caroline would never refuse him just because he was only a clergyman with three hundred a year. And so capable a manager as she was, they would live very comfortably on it, and she would never regret the jewels, the carriages, the fine clothes that she might have had as Mrs Charles Leatham.

Deep inside, he knew that Will was a far better match for her. A country parsonage was exactly the right setting for her, one where she could be easy in the society such a position afforded. She would never be at home at Starlingford, mingling with the gentry of the parish and the fringes of the nobility. He had done the right thing, he told himself. So why did it hurt so much?

He never wanted the waltz to end, but end it did, with applause from within and a few figures emerging from the saloon to sample the cooler air on the terrace. They were not alone any longer. Yet their dance had brought them into one of the shadowy corners of the terrace, so they had privacy for just a few more precious moments. He longed to say something to her, something of what was in his heart, or at least something to acknowledge the momentous change in him, but no words came. That foolish awkwardness again. But he could not quite let go of her. His arm was still around her waist, and she made no protest.

In the end, she was the one to break the silence. "Thank you, Mr Leatham. I enjoyed that very much. And now you had better go back inside, and resume your efforts to find yourself a wife. You have a fine array of young ladies to choose from this evening."

Because he could not help himself, he said quietly, "But none of them please me as well as you do."

Then he pulled her a little more tightly towards him, leaned forward and gave her the lightest kiss upon the lips.

23: Welcome Home

Caroline couldn't quite believe what had happened. He had kissed her… actually kissed her! The tiniest, most delicate of kisses, so gentle it was barely felt, yet still undeniably a kiss. Her first.

He had been so easy about it. What had he said? *'None of them please me as well as you.'* Then he had touched her lips with his as if it were the most normal thing in the world. Before she'd recovered from the shock, he'd tucked her arm into his and led her back into the house.

"Who is your next partner?" he'd said. "Ah, Redpath, are you claiming Miss Milburn? Thank you for the pleasure of your company, ma'am."

A quick bow and he was gone, and Mr Redpath had offered his arm and led her onto the floor. The music started up, they danced, they stood, they danced again, they stood again. Perhaps they talked a little, but she had no knowledge of what either of them had said.

Afterwards, when he asked should he take her back to Mrs Leatham, or was she awaiting another partner, she murmured something about a headache, and made her escape up the stairs to her room. Then she sat on a chair and tried to work out what on earth had happened to her. Nothing had happened to her, that was her conclusion. Mr Charles Leatham had given her the briefest touch of the lips, and that was all. It had meant nothing to him, and it definitely meant nothing to her. She didn't like him any better for it, that much was certain. He was still an obnoxious man... although his ill-manners had been better concealed lately, it was true. He was learning some gentlemanly behaviour.

Eventually, Caroline decided that the shock of being kissed was quite enough to account for her state of mind. It was indeed shocking that any man should so take advantage of her. But she was not a green girl, to fall into a swoon or be overwhelmed by undesirable emotions. After all, it had not been the ardent kiss of a lover, more of a friendly peck. Nothing to alarm her. She would put it behind her, and meet Mr Leatham in future with equanimity.

Accordingly, she undressed, recited her prayers and climbed into bed, and when Miss Law returned, some considerable time later, Caroline was able to give a convincing impression of a young lady worn out by the exertions of the evening and fast asleep.

But she was not asleep. Long after Miss Law's breathing had subsided to the slow rhythm of one deeply unconscious, Caroline lay awake, mulling over that kiss.

It was the intimacy that most affected her, she decided. In all her two and twenty years of existence, no man had ever dared to venture so close to her. No man had ever placed his lips on hers in that familiar way. Once or twice a man had grabbed her hand, one had even pressed impassioned kisses on it, but she had been wearing gloves and he had been at arm's length, with enough space between them that she had not felt anything more than annoyance. She had snatched her hand away and told him not to be an idiot.

But Charles had not been at arm's length. His arm, in fact, had been around her waist, his other arm held her hand and when he had leaned forward and kissed her, it was as if he had breached some otherwise impenetrable barrier. Always there was a barrier between men and women, and now, with Charles, it was swept away. She felt... what did she feel? Vulnerable? Perhaps, but she trusted him. He had not gone further than that playful little kiss, in fact he had released her at once. Exposed, perhaps, but not in a fearful way.

For the first time in her life, she wondered what it would be like to be close to a man, to be more than friendly, to share one's life with him. To be married. Strange thought. But not an unsettling one.

She closed her eyes and slept.

~~~~~

The journey home was much the same as their outward journey. Mrs Leatham chattered on in a steady stream of reminiscences, while everyone else was silent. Cresset fell asleep, and the carriage was so comfortable that Caroline might have slept too, had it not been for the unsettling presence of Charles Leatham opposite her. Every time she dared to look in his direction, he was watching her, although she couldn't imagine why. Sometimes when he saw her looking at him, he gave her an odd, lop-sided little smile, which she couldn't explain.

Once, when his step-mother paused to draw breath, he leaned forward and said, "Are you quite well, Miss Milburn? Last night's dancing has not overwrought you?"
~~~~~

"I am quite well, thank you."

"You are so lucky to have such a robust constitution," Mrs Leatham said. "You are like Mildred in that respect. *She* is never ill, either. I have often wished that I had such strength, but I never have. Even in my days of youthful vigour, the least little thing would knock me up, and I am still of a delicate constitution, even now. Goodness, how I have worried your papa once or twice, Charles! Do you remember that dreadful fever I had three years ago—? You would not, of course, for you were not here. It was Alfred who bore the brunt of *that* trial with your dear papa. Truly they thought they would lose me, that time. But just when they had quite despaired, and even Liversedge had said there was nothing more that his skill could do for me, I rallied and here I am still. But I do have to be careful of my chest, especially in damp weather. Charles, do you recall the winter of...?"

She required no responses, even when a question was asked, and Caroline closed her eyes and thought about kisses and marriage and what it might be like to have a man underfoot all the time, one who was not Papa. A long time ago, when Papa's business was thriving, he had employed an old friend who was a tailor to do repairs and make shirts. He had lived in one of the attic rooms, and he was a sweet, mild-mannered man, but he was always there, at every meal and all evening, for he was not exactly a servant and no one wanted to banish him. After two years, he had gone to live with his sister, and everyone had breathed a sigh of relief. Since then, Papa had only ever had employees who lived out.

But marriage would not be like that, for a husband was not chosen for his skill with a needle. A husband, surely, would be like dear Papa, a gentle, smiling man, most of the time, who only got cross when he had to reconcile his accounts. And then she thought of Mr Charles Leatham as a husband, and had to smother a laugh. He was not in the least a gentle, smiling man, and he was cross almost all the time. Although, not so much lately, she had to admit, and when he'd asked after her health, his tone had been soft, as if he truly cared.

After resting the horses at Alderbury again, it came on to rain, and even Mrs Leatham's volubility could not withstand its depressing effect. They completed the journey in relative silence.

When they reached Bursham Cottage, the rain was so heavy that Mr Leatham would not allow Caroline to alight until he had procured an umbrella from the driver's box. The door opened, Martin emerged to take charge of her box, Lin and Mrs Stratton smiled at her, and she was ushered inside without time for more than the most cursory expression of gratitude to Mr Leatham, who had got himself thoroughly soaked on her account. She was whisked into the hall and the door closed on him.

"We should have invited them in for tea, or some such," Caroline said, frowning. "It seems rude to just dash away."

"They will want to get home, I expect," Mrs Stratton said. "There now, Lin, help your sister out of her wet coat. We have tea ready for you, and Molly's made strawberry tarts."

"I hope you're not too grand for strawberry tarts," Lin said, giggling. "I expect you've been living on lobster and champagne, haven't you? Tell us *everything!* Was it exciting? Did you dance every night?

Caroline laughed at the deluge of questions. "I'm certainly not too grand for strawberry tarts, the lobster was horrible and most nights there was no dancing, although there was a ball last night."

"Ooh!" Lin said, wide-eyed, and Mrs Stratton laughed.

"Let her get properly into the house before you pelt her with questions. There now, Miss Milburn, come into the parlour. Ah, here is Susie with the tea things. Thank you, Susie, just there, thank you. I shall pour, just for today, but tomorrow Miss Milburn must have her rightful place again."

Mrs Stratton was a pleasant woman, and her rounded figure and slightly old-fashioned clothes reminded Caroline forcibly of her mother. How wonderful it would be to have such a gently maternal person always on hand, someone to whom she might hand over most of the responsibility for the house and her sisters. How lovely to think only of her lace again! But they could never go back to the past. Mr Leatham was quite right about that.

The tea was poured, and Caroline was on her second cup and her third strawberry tart before she noticed. "But where is Poppy? Not still unwell, I hope?"

There was an abrupt silence. "Ah," Mrs Stratton said, putting her cup down carefully. "She is perfectly well. I expect she is with the goats. Comfort, you see."

"Why does she need comfort?"

"There was an *incident*. With John Christopher. Jane Wenman called yesterday with some little thing for the goats, and Susie went to find Poppy and caught her in the garden store with John and he was *kissing* her."

"Oh dear," Caroline said, trying not to laugh at the outraged expression on Mrs Stratton's face.

"And then, if you please, he had the cheek to say that it was all right because he wanted to marry her!"

"Heavens, no!" Caroline cried. "She is barely sixteen, and *far* too young to be thinking of marriage. I am not even certain she should ever think of it."

Lin spluttered in indignation, but Mrs Stratton shook her head sorrowfully. "She is a dear, sweet child, but no man of sense would want her for a wife, that much is certain. A doting man of wealth, perhaps, who could afford to indulge her whims, but where one would find such a man in these parts I cannot say. Society here is very confined. But John Christopher? The poorly educated son of an impoverished clergyman? He is only sixteen himself, and little better than a labourer, so hardly able to afford a wife, and Poppy would never cope with an army of children and one overworked servant. I sent John home until you decide what you want to do about the business, but I cannot see that he can continue working in the garden."

"No." Caroline sighed. "I shall have to talk to his father and see what may be done about it, and we shall still need a gardener. It is very awkward. I imagined we would have years yet before we needed to worry about Poppy and young men. It was the wandering here and there that worried me, and once she had her chickens and goats, I'd hoped we were safe. Ah well. It is a pity, but it can't be helped."

"You are very good to say so," Mrs Stratton said, "but I feel my own blame in the affair very strongly. I am not a green girl, and pray do not fly into the boughs, Miss Milburn, but you are very young yourself and not terribly experienced in the ways of the world, so *you* could not have been expected to notice anything amiss, but *I—!* I should have realised there was something between them. I should have been watching more carefully, for that is precisely why I was invited here, is it not? To keep an eye on your sisters, and that duty I have failed miserably."

"You cannot blame yourself," Caroline said firmly. "Poppy has always needed more watching than any normal person can provide, and unless she is locked up, or followed everywhere she goes, there is no possible way to keep her out of trouble. But she is such an innocent that I've always felt that she was safe, so it's disappointing that John Christopher took advantage of her sweet nature. And now, I suppose, she is head over heels in love with him and distraught because she cannot see him."

"She's not in love with him, Caro," Lin said. "She's fond of him, perhaps, but no more than she's fond of anyone who's kind to her. But she sees him as her special friend, who enters into all her feelings about her little creatures and helps her in a score of ways. She misses him dreadfully, and now she feels she has no friends at all except us, especially since she's not allowed to go to the farm any more and—"

"The farm? What's happened there? Was she making a nuisance of herself?"

"We don't know that anything happened," Lin said. "Mrs Neilson just said she preferred her not to come any more. She told us last week at church, but she didn't give a reason. Poor Poppy was very upset about that. She cried a great deal, and I don't know why Mrs Neilson should be so stuffy about her and talk about bad influences, because Poppy was helpful to them. That baby is always crying, and only Poppy could ever keep it quiet, and now it just cries and cries."

Caroline helped herself to another strawberry tart, and then, absentmindedly, yet another, while she thought about these difficulties. The others watched her carefully, but forbore to question her.

"I must talk to Poppy first," she said eventually. "But as to John... I don't know. Perhaps his father will have something to say about it on Sunday, but there is no question of marriage, none at all."

She found Poppy out in the pen that John had constructed for the goats, the kid in her arms. Her cheeks were streaked with tears.

"Caro? Did you have a lovely time?"

"I did, but what is this I hear about John?"

"Oh Caro, Mrs Stratton is very kind, but she doesn't understand!" Fresh tears coursed down her cheeks, blotched from crying. "John is my *friend."*

"I know he is, and an excellent gardener, but he mustn't kiss you, Poppy. It's not right."

"But he's so affectionate, and he's never had a good friend like me before — a girl. It makes him so happy, Caro!"

"I'm sure it does, dearest, but you mustn't let any man kiss you, not unless you intend to marry him. You don't want to marry John, do you?"

A long pause. "I suppose not."

"Of course you don't," Caroline said briskly. "You're far too young to think about it, and when the time does come, there have to be considerations of... of income and so on. John earns very little, certainly not enough to support a wife except in the most dreadful poverty. You don't want to be poor, do you?"

"Oh no! It was very disagreeable being poor and being cooped up in those two rooms and having to work all the time, because although I didn't dislike weaving, it was hard to do it all day, Caro."

"Exactly. You wouldn't want to go back to that."

"Oh, but I wouldn't have to, because we're not poor any more, are we? Lester said we're very comfortably off and we each get a third of everything, and that's why he and Lin can get married, so I could get married too, couldn't I? If... if I wanted to very much? Couldn't I?"

Caroline was silenced. There was no arguing logic with a mind like Poppy's, so in the end she just said, "Let us get Lin safely wed first, shall we? And then, perhaps next year, we'll see."

Poppy brightened. "Yes! But John can come back, can't he? I need him back, Caro. He's so good with the nanny goat, he knows just how to calm her when she gets cross."

"We'll see. I'll talk to him, and to his father, and perhaps we can find a way."

"Please, Caro! Please let him come back! I miss him." Another tear trickled down one cheek.

To distract her, Caroline said, "What is this about Mrs Neilson not wanting you at the farm any more? What have you done to upset her?"

"Nothing, I swear it! I was always good, and only went there after church, like she said, and Ruby never minded me holding little Mary, because she never cries when I hold her. But Mrs Neilson said I was a bad influence on the younger girls and I'm not to be friends with them any more and I don't know why, truly I don't!" Her voice rose to a tremulous wail, accompanied by another flood of tears.

"I shall go and see Mrs Neilson and ask what all that is about. Maybe Ruby could bring the baby here on Sundays, if Mrs Neilson doesn't want you to go there, for some reason."

"She's never liked me," Poppy said mournfully.

"Whatever the problem is, I'd better sort it out quickly," Caroline said. "We get all our milk from them, and it would be very inconvenient to have to go further afield for our supplies."

Caroline threw on her old cloak against the rain, and walked across the field to the farm. Before she was half way there, she heard the baby crying. Poor Ruby! Deprived of the one person who could manage to calm the child.

As she stepped carefully across the muddy yard, several of the men were gathered around a couple of heifers to one side. She gave them a cheerful greeting, and they shuffled their feet awkwardly. One or two nodded at her, but most avoided her eye. That was a bad sign.

A knock at the kitchen door brought one of the younger women to open it. With frightened eyes, she turned and called out, "Ma! It's Miss Milburn."

As soon as she saw Mrs Neilson's face, Caroline knew there was something very wrong. She had never been particularly friendly towards the sisters, but she had at least been respectful. But now she was plain angry.

"You'd best go home again," she said, standing on the threshold, hands on hips, as if to bar Caroline from access. "We don't want your sort here. Thought you were raised decent, but it's in the blood, ain't it? We're God-fearing folk in this house, and we don't want none of your immodest ways round here."

"Immodest?" Caroline said. "Whatever has Poppy done that's so upset you?"

For a moment, Mrs Neilson gaped at her, then gave a hollow laugh. "Well, if that don't beat all! You don't even know, do you? Don't know what that oh-so-innocent little sister of yours has been up to. Well, you'll find out soon enough. In about six months or so, by my reckoning."

"What?" Caroline whispered. "No...!"

"Aye, it's true enough. She's always liked babes, hasn't she? Well, see how she likes having one of her own. Good day to you, Miss Milburn."

She stepped back inside, slamming the door in Caroline's stunned face.

24: Of Marriage

That evening was full of tension. Poppy was tearful, while everyone else was too shocked to speak much. Mrs Stratton and Susie had marched Poppy upstairs and questioned her closely enough to determine that, yes, she was with child, and that John Christopher was responsible.

"They will have to marry," Mrs Stratton had said.

"I will talk to Mr and Mrs Christopher tomorrow," Caroline had said.

After that, there seemed little else to be said on the subject. Caroline's head was filled with questions, like what on earth they would do if John denied knowledge of it, or his father refused his consent to the match? And how was Poppy ever to be fit to be a mother, when she was still such a child in so many ways? It was a dreadful situation. How appalling that they, descended from illegitimacy themselves and yet risen above it, should find themselves in exactly the same situation as their grandmother Carter. And this time, there was no wealthy Mr Wishaw to support and protect his unfortunate offspring and her mother, only poor John Christopher, who had no money and no prospects for getting any.

Everyone went early to bed, although Caroline could not imagine any of them slept much. She herself was wracked with guilt, for should she not have protected Poppy better? Everyone knew how artless and childlike Poppy was, and here was the proof of how she had been neglected. Had there been signs of attachment that Caroline should have observed? Should she have suspected John from the start and kept them apart? She had been so glad that Poppy had her chicks and goats to keep her at the house and prevent her from wandering, but she had been afraid of the wrong thing. How foolish she had been! And yet could she have watched Poppy every moment? It would have been impossible. So her thoughts ran, and drove sleep from her.

At first light she rose, dressed and went down to her study. It was her refuge, the place where she escaped from the trials of her life into the restful world of the accounts. She had been away for two weeks, so there were neat lists of purchases from Mrs Stratton to be entered into the pages of her daily ledger, and less neat lists from Lin of supplies bought for the garden, and one scrap of paper in Poppy's hand, much blotted and crossed out.

She worked for some time, but her disordered mind must have made a mistake because the columns of numbers would not add up, no matter how she tried. She wrestled with it, reworked it, checked the original numbers and still it would not oblige her.

It was too much. She threw down her pen and burst into tears.

Just at that moment, there was a sharp rat-tat-tat on the front door. No Susie came through from the kitchen to answer the door, but the visitor, undeterred, rapped again, more peremptorily. With a sigh, Caroline wiped her face and went to open the front door.

Charles Leatham stood there, one eyebrow raised in surprise. Then his face changed to alarm.

"Heavens, Caroline, you look terrible. Whatever is the matter?"

He opened his arms and without a second thought she walked straight into them, with another burst of weeping. For a while he simply held her tightly, murmuring soothing nothings above her head, and gently rocking her. It was excessively comforting to be held so, she found, and although it was terribly improper, she was most unwilling to surrender to propriety when she had such a reassuring presence to draw strength from. It was just like the time that Poppy had fainted, and there Charles had been, taking charge and exuding authority. So she wept into his coat, and he asked no awkward questions.

After a while, he said into the top of her head, "Do you know, I cannot help thinking you would be more comfortable not standing on the front door step. Shall we go inside?"

She nodded and, with the utmost reluctance, let go of him. He crossed the threshold and shut the door firmly. "Now, what room were you in? In here? Good. Now you sit down just there, and let me call someone to attend to you."

Gently, he settled her in one of the chairs by the fireplace. There was no fire lit, only the lace screen to hide the empty hearth.

He reached for the bell, but she said quickly, "No, no! Susie isn't even up yet, I don't think. I'm all right now."

"You are not in the least all right," he said, in a tone that brooked no argument. "You must allow me to send for the physician."

"Oh, please do not! There is nothing at all wrong with me. At least, I am quite well. It is just..." She tailed off miserably. How on earth to speak of such things? And before a gentleman, too, and a neighbour who would inevitably despise her when he knew of it.

"Let me fetch you something... brandy perhaps, or—"

"At eight in the morning?" she said, with a sudden laugh. "Our reputation is already shot to pieces, without adding drinking before breakfast to the list of charges."

He looked at her quizzically but asked nothing about reputations, instead saying only, "You need something to steady your nerves, and I have always found brandy most efficacious. Or Madeira, or some such. Or tea, if you absolutely insist."

That made her laugh again. "There is some Madeira in the cupboard over there. No, the next one along."

"Ah." He occupied himself with pouring, and then brought a glass for her. He'd poured one for himself, she noticed. She sipped it gingerly, as if it might choke her, but finding that nothing untoward happened except for the usual warming effect of the wine, she sipped again.

"There, that will do you good," he said, settling himself in the chair opposite hers, the pristine, little-used visitor's chair. After a pause, he went on, "You are probably wishing me at Jericho, but I have no intention of leaving you alone when you are so out of frame, so we shall sit here quietly and get slowly foxed until one or other of your household arrives to bear you company."

That produced another small chuckle. "You are very good, sir. I'm sorry to weep all over your coat. I'm not normally so... so..."

"Lachrymose? I know it. You are the steadiest and most sensible person I know, so to see you brought so low is most concerning. However, we have long since agreed that we would not apologise to each other, so let us say no more of it. This is a very pretty screen. The lace is your work, I take it?"

"My mother's. She was the finest lacemaker in the county."

"What, better than you? That is hard to believe. But she taught you her skills, of course. It is a beautiful screen, and would be perfect in the dining room at Starlingford. If ever you wish to sell it, I would give you a very good price for it."

"I should never sell it. Oh! You came for your usual discussion of the book," she said, realising.

"Indeed I did, but unfortunately it has gone missing. I expect I left it at Narfield Lodge."

"You would forget your head if it wasn't stuck onto your neck," she said.

He gave a bark of laughter. "So I would. Soldiering suited me better, I believe, for I never once left my guns behind, or my sword, or my regiment."

"Or your horse?"

"One horse was shot out from under me, but I trust you would not count that in my disfavour. I left my batman behind, once, but luckily he caught up later. My colonel was far more forgetful than I, for he once left his wife, three children and their servants behind in London when he set off for the country, and it was only when he arrived and wondered where they all were that he realised."

"You are trying to cheer me up," she said.

"Is it working?"

"A little. It makes me feel much better to have you here to talk to, but as soon as you leave I shall be as blue as megrim again."

"Then I shall have to stay indefinitely," he said cheerfully, getting up and refilling his glass. "I hope your cellar is well stocked."

He was so kind that she wanted to cry again. He had asked nothing about what troubled her, and her scruples still prevented her from speaking of it. Yet that was absurd. It was not a matter that could be kept secret, for it would be common knowledge before too long. Once Charles knew of it, she would be quite sunk in his estimation, and somehow that distressed her almost as much as anything else. For a while she had moved in society as... not his equal, perhaps, but as one who was not too far below him. One who could aspire to friendship with him, at least. And if he were truly her friend, then it would not matter to him what Poppy had done.

Would it?

"Poppy is with child," she blurted. And then waited. Waited for his face to change, for him to glower at her disapprovingly. He would make his excuses and leave...

"Ah..." He set down his glass and steepled his fingers thoughtfully. "Yes, that would account for your lowness of spirits. That would certainly be enough to make anyone blue-devilled." He paused, with a questioning look in his eye. "May I ask...? Is it known... who the man is?"

"John Christopher."

"Oh." He let out a breath with a smile that may have been relief. "Well... that is all right, then. They will marry, and it will all be forgot in a few months."

"You suspected someone else?"

He pulled a rueful face. "One never knows. Your sister is such an innocent that anyone with ill intent might have taken advantage of her. But the Christopher boy… he is no great catch, but she will do well enough with him."

"How can you say so?" Caroline cried. "He is no older or wiser than she is! He has no fortune, no fixed employment… he is our labouring gardener, for heaven's sake! We pay him ninepence a day. It is certainly not enough to marry on."

"You would be surprised what people manage to marry on," he said with a smile. "But you are not thinking rationally, Caroline. If they marry, then they will not be setting up house for themselves. They will live either at the parsonage with his parents or here with you, at very little expense to anybody, especially as you will be saved the ninepence a day. He will get himself a proper job and contribute to the household expenses, and Poppy will have her own baby to look after and will be completely happy. Since Lin and her attorney will be living here, there will doubtless be another baby in the house soon, so any expense in engaging a nursemaid will be shared. *You* will be here, so the house will be well-regulated. And — perhaps the most important point — Poppy will be surrounded by people who love her unreservedly, and will protect her from the harshness of the real world. I would wager a hundred pounds that she has not spent any time crying over the shame of her situation."

"That is true!" Caroline said. "She is upset because John has been sent away. Once she has him back, she will be completely happy. She doesn't understand what she's done wrong, or why we're all so upset, and I'm not sure I can forgive her for it."

"She has all the innocence of childhood," he said. "Do not wish her any different. Be glad that she has her own protection from the cruelties of the world. I could wish that you had a little of her resilience, but you may depend upon my support, and Mama's."

"Do not speak for Mrs Leatham," Caroline said in a low voice. "*Your* support I'm very glad of, but don't hold your mama to anything she may not quite like."

"Very well," he said softly. "You will see her at church tomorrow. May I inform her privately of your sister's situation? Of course, if you prefer to keep such a matter secret, you may depend upon my discretion."

"You are very good, sir. You may tell her what you choose, but I should not wish the tale to spread beyond her ears just yet. It will be known everywhere soon enough."

He agreed to it, and as Susie appeared shortly afterwards, he took his leave. Caroline hardly knew what she felt about him. He had dealt with her news most generously, but that could not be depended upon. Once Poppy's situation became widely known, any friendship with the Leathams must surely be at an end. She had begun by resenting Mrs Leatham's insistent approaches, but had grown to like her very much, and even Mr Leatham… here she stopped, unwilling, even in the privacy of her own thoughts, to venture down that path. Ever since that wretched kiss, she had been tormented by ideas of matrimony, of the closeness that can only exist between a husband and wife who trust each other implicitly. Both Lin and Poppy, seemingly, had found such closeness, and something in Caroline yearned for it, too. It had been such a relief to have someone, even Charles

Leatham, to talk to about all her difficulties. Without his comforting presence, she would have been terrifyingly alone.

After breakfast, there was no help for it but to go to the parsonage to talk to Mr and Mrs Christopher. Such an awkward interview! They were shocked, of course, but Mrs Christopher recovered her composure quickly.

"But the cloud truly has a silver lining, for we shall have our first grandchild, albeit a little earlier than we had thought, and Poppy is such a sweet girl. Who could have the slightest objection to such a daughter-in-law? Indeed we had wondered..." She laughed, and went on, "This is quicker than we anticipated, but as soon as you and your sisters moved here we—"

"You mean you *wanted* them to marry?" Caroline said, astonished.

"Well... we hoped, let us say. "

Caroline stared at them, appalled. Looking back over the months since their arrival, she could see how the Christophers had pushed John into their lives, by offering him as a gardener, and then accepting Poppy as his friend. They had invited her to dinner the night that Caroline and Lin had dined at Starlingford! They had encouraged the match, in fact.

"But why?" she said, dazed.

"Why? Because we have not two pennies to rub together and too many mouths to feed, and there you are with a fine cottage and plenty of money. You gave John *five pounds* every time he dug up something from the garden, and that is riches to us. So yes, we encouraged John to think about Poppy. He'll be better off with her, and she'll be well taken care of, don't you worry. This is good for both of them."

Mr Christopher went off to talk to John, returning with the boy in tow and looking very sheepish. But he professed to a great willingness to marry Poppy as soon as it might be contrived. He then returned to the cottage with Caroline, was joyfully reunited with Poppy and they went off happily together to the parsonage to see about the banns.

Caroline was left to reflect on how to adjust their domestic arrangements to cope with the new situation, and to contemplate the prospect of her youngest and least worldly sister as a married woman and a mother. And beyond that, to wonder at the topsy-turvy world where the linen-draper's daughters were richer than the clergyman.

~~~~~

Charles walked home in a very contented frame of mind. Poppy did not concern him, for she would marry and have her baby and be happy, and in that alone he envied her. But Caroline! So distraught, and yet she had turned to him for comfort... she had confided in him. Even now, the dampness of the morning air could not chill him, nor anything at all dismay him, for Caroline had wept in his arms and poured all her troubles into his ear and he thought... he *hoped* at least, that she saw him as a friend. And perhaps that was enough, for now. A solid foundation, to be built upon in time.

He whispered the news to his mother, who was shocked to hear such a thing of John Christopher, distressed for Caroline and solicitous towards Poppy.

"What can we do to help?" she said at once, as he had known she would.

"Do not turn away from them," he said. "What else? There will be those who close their doors to all the Miss Milburns, but I
~~~~~

hope... I very much hope that we will not be amongst their number."

"So long as they marry," she said, looking at him anxiously. "If they should not..."

"They will marry," he said.

It seemed he was right, for at church the next day Poppy was there on the Christopher boy's arm, receiving the congratulations of all their friends on their forthcoming marriage. There were a few sour-faced groups casting them censorious looks and whispering together, but most of the congregation seemed pleased for them. The boy looked rather shamefaced, as well he might, but Poppy was radiant, as happy as if she had just landed a duke. Happier, probably, for it was hard to imagine her as mistress of a palatial establishment like Valmont. The vicar's son was about right for her.

As for Caroline, she too was surrounded by well-wishers, including Charles' step-mother. Charles managed no more than a tiny wave of one hand from some distance away, to be rewarded by a smile of acknowledgement. It was of no consequence, for he would see her tomorrow, when he made his usual visit before breakfast. He must hope to find her in higher spirits, and perhaps he—

"Nothing but trouble," a voice at his side muttered. It was Mr Ascot, the apothecary.

"I beg your pardon, sir?"

"Those Milburn girls. They've been nothing but trouble since the day they arrived. Interfering where they shouldn't and putting honest folk out of business."

Charles pondered these puzzling remarks, before remembering an altercation at Bursham Cottage, when Mr Ascot had been seated next to Lin at dinner. "Miss Elinor Milburn?" he hazarded. "Something to do with rhubarb, perhaps?"

"Aye, rhubarb and other things. Shouldn't interfere. I know I haven't had the supplies lately, not since my last apprentice left, but that doesn't mean—" He threw Charles a self-conscious glance. "Hmpf. No use telling *you* about it, I suppose."

He walked off before Charles could ask him what he meant.

Charles walked his step-mother back to their carriage where his father was already seated, and, surprisingly, Mildred.

"Not talking to your friends today, dear?" Mrs Leatham said to her.

Mildred pursed her lips in distaste. "I rather fear I am out of step with the majority in not offering congratulations for a certain event. I cannot bring myself to appear to condone such wickedness."

"Oh dear! Mildred!" Mrs Leatham said. "As Christians one must forgive—"

"Forgive, but not condone," Mildred said repressively, turning her head away to forestall further discussion.

They sat in silence as the coachman manoeuvred the carriage through the throngs leaving the church.

Charles tapped one foot impatiently. He hated to argue with Mildred, for it always ended with her quoting some Biblical text at him with unanswerable righteousness, but he could not be silent.

"I do not think it right to turn our backs on anyone who makes a mistake," he said. "We are all human, are we not? We all have weaknesses and foibles, and when we stray from the path of perfection, our *friends* stand by us. And even if one sister has strayed, it does not mean we should punish the rest too."

His step-mother glanced at Mildred, but she was still facing away from them. "Oh dear," Mrs Leatham said. "It is so difficult. One cannot object to persons who come from a station in life somewhat below one's own, not if they know how to behave and are... are *virtuous*, but... oh dear." She tailed off, with a helpless wave of her hands.

Mildred turned her head. "Persons with such a lowly background cannot be expected to know how to behave. That is why I advised against associating with them right from the start, and why *I* at least am not faced with such a dilemma. I shall treat the Miss Milburns as I have always done, as persons less fortunate than myself in terms of education and quickness of mind and position in society, and therefore possible objects of my charity and compassion, but not to be treated as an equal."

She closed her lips firmly, as if the final word had been spoken and the discussion was now closed. Perhaps in her eyes it had been, but Charles seethed inwardly. Loud and clear in his mind he heard Caroline's voice saying, *'I'd have said myself that she's a sanctimonious prig.'*

"Oh dear," Mrs Leatham said again, clutching her Prayer Book tightly. "Of course we should forgive the poor girl, for that is our Christian duty, and I hope I never shirk my duty. Even so..." Her voice tailed off, and a frown creased her brow, a rare sight. "Charles, I will be honest with you, and pray do not jump down my throat, but upon reflection I do believe Mildred has the right of it. Their reputations must be damaged. All of them. It is quite inescapable, and we shall have to consider how much we can have to do with them. None but the highest sticklers would cut them altogether, but the sort of association we have had until now... An alliance would be impossible, Charles, you must see that."

"You mean that after pushing me into Miss Milburn's most unwilling arms, you have now thought better of it? That is shallow, Mama, very shallow. If she had accepted me when I proposed, I should now be committed to the marriage and could not honourably withdraw."

"But she did not, dear," his step-mother said gently. "So now we must look elsewhere, for someone... unsullied. Someone whose behaviour will always be... upright."

Mildred smiled superciliously. *"'Blessed are they which do hunger and thirst after righteousness: for they shall be filled.'"*

"'Blessed are the merciful,'" Charles spat back.

"'Blessed are ye that weep now, for ye shall laugh. Blessed are the meek, for they shall inherit the earth. Blessed are the pure in heart, for they shall see God.'" She smirked in triumph.

Charles gave up the unequal battle to get the better of Mildred, and fumed all the way home.

25: Help And Support

Nothing more was said about the Miss Milburns, and it was not until dinner was at an end and his step-mother and Mildred had withdrawn, that Charles felt able to raise the subject. His father, he felt sure, would advise him.

"What do you think of the business with the Miss Milburns?" he began. "Are you inclined to be censorious, like Mildred? Or concerned about the possibility of taint, like Mama? What is your opinion, sir?"

"It is an interesting question," his father said. "There is much to be said on those points, but your view is different, I think."

"Why should you think so?" Charles said.

"If it were not so, you would hardly ask me for my thoughts on the subject," his father said in his mild way. "If you agreed wholeheartedly with Miss Beacher or Mrs Leatham, you would be satisfied and would ask no further. It is because you are *not* satisfied that you pursue the matter."

"Very well then," Charles said. "Let us suppose that to be true. I am dissatisfied both with Mildred's absolute condemnation of wrongdoing, and with Mama's wish not to be associated with it. I should like, therefore, to know your views."

"Do my views matter?"

"Of course they matter! I must always listen to my own father's advice."

"So it is advice you want, is it? Which you will take only if it agrees with your own wishes."

"Am I to take it that you will not help me?" Charles said in frustration. "You must have some opinion on right and wrong, sir!"

"Indeed I do, insofar as my own behaviour is concerned, but surely it is your own view that must prevail? Your step-mother must decide for herself how to respond to the changes in circumstance at Bursham Cottage, as must Miss Beacher, as must I. As must you, Charles. You know in your heart what is right and what is wrong."

Charles sighed heavily. "When I was at Narfield Lodge, I had the interesting experience of hearing Lord Narfield and some of his guests debating points of political or philosophical moment with great energy and articulacy. None of them hesitated to express an opinion in the most robust terms, or to admit when another made a good point. I had hoped that you might indulge me with a similar discussion, not in personal terms but in the abstract."

His father set his port glass down on the table. "That would please me greatly, but I give you due notice, Charles, that if you lose your temper, then the discussion will be over."

"Is *that* why you hold back?" Charles said, astonished. "You fear my intemperance? That is a dreadful indictment on my behaviour in recent weeks."

"It is not so much fear," his father said, eyes twinkling. "It is no more than a dislike of the ruffling effect of youthful energy. I have reached an age when I value calmness above everything — regularity, order, as many books as I can read and my favourite foods at dinner every night. Your step-mother manages everything to my liking, and neither Alfred nor Ben ever disturbed that tranquillity. But you are a very different sort of man, Charles. Not better or worse, you understand... merely different. You have more energy in your little finger than Alfred, Ben and I could muster between the three of us, and I have found it unsettling at times. However, you have been calmer of late, and perhaps we can rub along better now."

Charles shook his head ruefully. "You make me ashamed... or even more ashamed, I should say. I have been unbearable, I know it, and your forbearance is more than I deserve. Can you forgive me?"

"Only if you will pour me another port," his father said with a smile. "I cannot be philosophical without a full glass in my hand, you know."

"With the greatest pleasure, Papa."

~~~~~

Charles went to bed in a happier frame of mind. He felt as if he had grown up at last, for his father was treating him as an equal, and although he offered his son no advice, Charles found his mind clearer for the discussion. Or perhaps it would be more accurate to say that he understood his own mind better. Somehow, he could not quite say how, Caroline had become indispensable for his happiness, and he would not turn his back on her simply because she had a foolish sister.
~~~~~

The next morning he went early to Bursham Cottage and found her already at her lacemaking, a smile on her face.

"You are feeling better this morning. I am glad of it," he said simply.

"Oh yes! I was too ridiculous for words when you found me the other day, but they are to be married and all will be well, I am sure of it."

"They will live with you here?"

"Yes, although where we will all fit in, I cannot imagine, not with Lin and Mr Stratton as well, and the nursery. I daresay I shall be sleeping above the stables!"

"You will not be here long, I imagine," he said, eagerly. "You will marry and—"

"Marry? Me? You know better than anyone that I have no ambition for the married state." She laughed, not at all discomfited by the subject.

"I hope you will change your mind about that," he said slowly, watching her face carefully. "It would be a waste for you to dwindle into spinsterhood, the little-thought-of aunt to your sisters' children. You will marry, I believe, and rather better than your sisters."

She showed no sign of consciousness, merely laughing and shaking her head, but he was satisfied to have tiptoed around the subject. He knew he must approach one step at a time, but he was determined to bring her around to the idea in time, and then... then he could offer for her again.

In this beguiling scheme, he had forgotten about Will, but Will, it seemed, had not forgotten about Caroline. When Charles returned to Starlingford for breakfast, he discovered a letter from

Will announcing his intention to visit, which was followed, within an hour, by the man himself, all beaming delight and eager anticipation.

"This is very unexpected, Will," Mrs Leatham said, stepping around his large quantity of luggage in the hall to greet him. "Naturally we are quite delighted, but... are we to have the pleasure of your company for a long stay?"

"No, no, just until Saturday. I cannot obtain a replacement for the Sunday offices at such short notice, so I must return to do my duty. Well, well, this is pleasant, to be back here so soon. Ah, Miss Beacher! Your smiling countenance is not the least of Starlingford's attractions. You are well, I trust?"

He bowed over her hand, and, it was true, there was a smile on her face. Of course, he was a clergyman, which she must approve, but even so, it was such a contrast with her usual humourless expression that Charles was quite struck. Will could charm even the morose Mildred into cheerfulness.

Will had barely shaken the dust of the road from his boots before he wanted to walk to the cottage. If Mrs Leatham was surprised at such interest, she was too well-bred to mention it. Charles felt obliged to accompany him, telling himself that his motives were purely to facilitate introductions, since Will knew only Caroline. He need not have been concerned, however, for Mrs Stratton had whisked the two future brides off to Salisbury for some essential shopping against the happy days to come. Fortunately, Caroline was not part of the expedition. The maid showed Charles and Will into the study.

Caroline looked up in surprise. "Mr Leatham! And Mr Will Leatham. I didn't expect to see you again so soon, either of you.

Please come in. May I offer you some refreshments? Madeira? Cake?"

They accepted the Madeira and refused the cake. While she was pouring for them, Caroline said, "You find me struggling with my accounts, gentlemen. I can't get the numbers to agree at all."

"That is not like you, Miss Milburn," Charles said. "As a rule, all numbers bow to your superiority."

She laughed. "I wish these numbers would do so. There's something wrong, but I can't find my mistake. I have been in this room ever since breakfast, labouring away, but I cannot solve it."

"Then let us take you away from your desk for a while," Will said. "Shall we walk in the garden? The clouds have quite disappeared, and I am sure the sunshine would do you good."

Caroline fetched a bonnet and shawl, and they went out through the morning room door.

"That is a charming bonnet, Miss Milburn," Will said, offering her his arm. "Is it new?"

"It is. Poppy and Miss Stratton contrived it while I was staying at Narfield Lodge, and decided it was just the thing to wear with this shawl."

"Indeed it is," Will said gallantly. "You look most fetching in it. That style becomes you admirably, Miss Milburn. You would turn heads even in London attired as you are now."

"Thank you, sir," she murmured.

The path was only wide enough for two, so Charles was forced to walk behind and could not see her face, but he imagined her quizzical expression at such fulsome compliments. Still, Will's charm was powerful and she was soon chattering away to him as if she had known him for ever. He wanted to know all about the forthcoming marriage to the attorney, and she told him about the newest betrothal in the family, although without mentioning the reason for it, naturally. Will was suitably congratulatory.

They quickly exhausted the possibilities of the small pleasure garden, and the orchard held the tethered goats, so their steps led inevitably to the kitchen garden, where the Christopher boy was hard at work again. He lifted his hat and leaned on his hoe as they drew near.

"Mornin', Miss Milburn. Mornin', Mr Leatham, sir."

"Good morning, John," Caroline said. "Mr Leatham, John Christopher is the son of our vicar, and soon to be Poppy's husband. John, here is another Mr Leatham to admire your handiwork. Goodness, but everything has come on lately. Whatever are those great tall things?"

"Sea holly, miss."

"It's quite pretty, but... which part is for eating?"

"Oh, it's not for eatin', Miss Milburn. You soak the root in wine, and then it's good for dropsy. The endives there, you use the leaves. It cools the liver, and it's very good for hot fits of the ague. This one here, that's sweet marjoram, which Miss Lin uses for cold diseases of the head. It's fascinatin'. Miss Lin's been teachin' me."

"Has she, indeed," Caroline said. "John, is there anything grown here purely for the table?"

He frowned, thinking it over. "Molly takes some of the herbs, sometimes. Oh, and apples! Plums, pears, apricots! Plenty of fruit in the orchard. And some gooseberries over there."

"But no beans," she said crisply. "No peas. No asparagus. No cucumbers. No lettuce or artichokes or celery. It's all medicinal."

He shuffled his feet awkwardly. Poor fellow! He had had a difficult few days, losing his job, discovering Poppy's condition, finding himself about to be married, and now being harangued for something that was not his fault.

"I daresay Mr Christopher was only following orders," Charles said mildly.

He brightened and nodded. "Aye, just followin' orders from Miss Lin. I only did what she wanted."

"But what does she *do* with all this bounty?" Will said, gazing at the row upon row of abundant growth. "No one in the family has dropsy, I am sure."

"Bless you, sir, but it's not for the house!" He chortled with merriment. "She sells it to anyone who needs it. Gets a good price for it, too, even though she charges a bit less than Mr Ascot." Another chuckle. "Very clever, Miss Lin is."

"Oh!" Caroline burst out laughing. "Money *in*, not money out. *That's* why my numbers don't add up. I should have read Lin's records more carefully. But... charging less than Mr Ascot? Is Lin setting herself up as a rival apothecary, then? He won't like that."

"He does not," Charles said. "He was grumbling about it at church yesterday."

"Oh dear," Caroline said. "I'd better go and see him."

At that moment, Charles was struck by an ingenious scheme. "Perhaps," he said slowly, "you would permit me to undertake that duty for you, Miss Milburn? You have enough to do at the moment, and it might be the more easily settled between men. Mr Ascot is, I fear, the type of person who does not like to discuss business matters with a lady, and he has already raised the subject with me, so it will not look at all odd if I question him further about his concerns."

She looked at him with clear surprise in her eyes. Those treacle eyes! So beautiful, with their frame of dark lashes...

"That would be very kind of you, Mr Leatham. Papa was just such a man, I confess, and never talked about his business with us. Perhaps if he had— But there, that was just the way he was, and at least he allowed me to help him with the accounts, so where money is concerned, I am quite at ease. But I don't relish talking to Mr Ascot about Lin's activities, and if you are willing to help, I'd be very grateful."

When Will deemed it time to end the visit, he went on to Corranwater to leave his card for Lord and Lady Elland, while Charles walked into the village to call upon Mr Ascot. He found the apothecary very willing to unburden himself of all his grievances, and to listen to Charles' proposals. At the end of no more than half an hour, Mr Ascot had agreed that, if Miss Elinor Milburn should only desist from selling her medicines in contention with his own preparations, he would undertake to buy certain herbs and roots from her to supplement his own supplies, and also to engage John Christopher as his apprentice, for a modest fee which Charles himself would pay.

Charles then went back to Bursham Cottage to explain to Caroline all that he had done, to be thanked profusely and to enjoy a celebratory glass of Madeira with her. Despite Will's arrival and the niggling worry of his intentions towards Caroline, he felt the day had passed very satisfactorily.

It was not until dinner that evening that matters went awry. They were well into the second course and Charles was feeling quite mellow, when Will said brightly, "Charles and I went to Bursham Cottage today. The two younger Miss Milburns were out, but we were so fortunate as to find Miss Milburn at home. I thought she was in remarkably good looks. Did you not think so, Charles?"

"You called upon Miss Milburn?" Mildred said, in tones of astonishment.

"Why, yes. She was most agreeable, and told me all about her two sisters and their forthcoming marriages. One is to marry an attorney, and the younger is to marry their gardener. Not a great match, but she has money of her own, so they will do well enough, I daresay, and they are all to live at the cottage, so their expenses will be low."

"But—" Mildred said.

"He will not be a gardener for much longer," Charles said, trying not to feel smug. "I have today arranged for him to be taken on as apprentice to our local apothecary."

"Oh Charles!" his step-mother cried. "You have not!"

"Indeed I have. He was very happy to do it, too, for a modest fee."

"You paid him? Oh Charles! How could you?"

"Why should I not?" he said testily. "It is a small cost to me to help out a neighbour improve his prospects, and the money will come from my saved army pay, so it will not be a drain on the estate."

"It is not the money, dear," she said sadly. "Do you not see? If you pay Mr Ascot to train poor John Christopher, a man with no obvious claim on you, everyone will say that there must be a reason and look at poor Poppy and wonder."

Charles felt fury rise inside him. Angrily he tossed down the spoonful of stewed peas he had been about to eat. Four pairs of eyes watched him anxiously. Was he about to explode in rage?

With an effort of will, he remembered Caroline's grateful face smiling up at him, and the way she had laid her hand on his arm as she thanked him. Yes, he had done the right thing, and no one would convince him otherwise. Deliberately he reached for his wine glass, took a sip, set it carefully back on the table.

"It does not concern me what others might say," he said quietly. "My character is such, I hope, that no accusation of that nature could be given credence. I have a responsibility to exercise my influence for the good of the local people when they find themselves in trouble, and I will not be deterred from doing what I believe to be right by any concerns of what the tattle-mongers might say."

"But Charles—"

His father held up one hand, and the room fell silent. "My dear, let us hear no more objections. Charles is a man grown, and is perfectly capable of deciding such questions for himself."

"But Ambrose—"

"Enough, my dear. Is there any of that delicious braised calf's ear left? I should be very glad of another spoonful."

They lapsed into silence. When the servants came in, cleared the covers and set out dessert, Mrs Leatham, although slightly pink-cheeked, kept up a stream of small-talk to amuse Will, but as soon as the servants had withdrawn, silence again descended.

Charles had never before known his father to reprimand his step-mother, or to speak out at all in any matter under discussion. If it had been Mildred on the receiving end of such a reproach, he might have been tempted to gloat, but he could only sympathise with his step-mother, who had been used to speak her mind without reservation and now found that there were limits even for her easy-going husband.

Yet he could not but be pleased. Support from such a quarter was of all things the most unexpected, and yet the most welcome, too. He felt as he had once, after a particularly trying day in the field, when his colonel had singled him out for particular praise. *'Heroism,'* he had said, *'is not always spectacular or dramatic. Sometimes it is no more than dogged determination and a willingness to persevere even when all seems lost.'* Dogged determination... yes, he had a great deal of that. To be a good soldier... to be a gentleman... and now, to be a good neighbour and landowner.

But there was one more. To be Caroline's husband. Yes, he had enough dogged determination for that. And yet...

As he looked across the table at Will, he knew that he might already be too late.

26: Moral Guidance

Nothing material was said that evening until the elder Mr Leatham retired to bed. There being only three left at the whist table, for Mildred would not play, the cards were abandoned for the delights of the tea tray and the cake board.

"Charles…" his step-mother began, looking at him nervously.

"Yes, Mama?" He gave her an affectionate smile. "You may say whatever is in your mind, but do not ask me to withdraw my offer to pay for Christopher's apprenticeship."

"Oh no! I would not…! Your papa was so—! I would not go against his wishes, but I should like to talk about Miss Milburn, if that would not be disagreeable to you, because I do not believe her to be the right person for you to marry," she finished in a rush.

Will looked up from the cakes. "Charles has no intention of marrying Miss Milburn, Cousin Daphne. His very cunning scheme at Narfield Lodge was for her to help him choose a bride from amongst the offerings there. Although I do not think that worked terribly well, did it, Charles?"

"Oh," Mrs Leatham said. "No intention, Charles?"

"He says she is a shrew," Will went on complacently. "However, I suspect she is only ill-tempered with him, because he dislikes her so. She is perfectly amiable with me. These lemon cakes are delicious, cousin. Mrs Bendish has excelled herself."

"Oh." Her eyes were round as she gazed at Charles speculatively. "In that case... what do you say to Miss Narfield?"

"No."

"One of the Miss Wynnes? Although—"

"No, and not any of the Miss Redpaths, either."

"Oh. But Charles, you did say I might choose your bride for you? Did you not?"

He laughed. "I did, and you chose Miss Milburn. Now you advise against her, so we are at a stand, are we not?"

She fiddled with the fringe of her shawl as she said, "May a lady not change her mind?"

Charles smiled benignly at her, for he now had the inkling of an idea of how to deal with Will, who had not yet heard the full story of Poppy and John Christopher. Charles himself would not hold Poppy's misbehaviour against Caroline, but Will was a clergyman and might have misgivings on the subject.

"You may change your mind as many times as you like, Mama, but I only agreed to *offer* for Miss Milburn. Having done so and been rejected in no uncertain terms, you must now leave me to choose for myself. After all, there is less urgency now that Will is considering matrimony. That would relieve your mind, I am certain, and he does not seem to object to Miss Milburn, sullied though she is."

"Will?" Mrs Leatham said.

"Sullied?" Will said, a lemon cake hovering half way to his mouth.

"Has no one yet told you of the scandal embroiling the Milburn sisters?" Charles said blandly.

"Scandal?"

Mildred turned reproachful eyes on Charles. "That was rather remiss of you, Mr Leatham, not to give your cousin just a hint of the situation pertaining at Bursham Cottage before he called there this morning. I do not expect everyone to have my scruples about immorality, for my standards are very high, and you must do as you see fit, but your cousin is a man of the cloth."

"Immorality?" Will said, setting the lemon cake back on his plate. "Miss Milburn?"

"Not *that* Miss Milburn," Mrs Leatham said. "Not directly. It is her sister. Miss Poppy Milburn's marriage to the vicar's son is to be... rather hasty."

"Ah. So that was what you were talking about." Will glanced quickly at Charles, then hastily picked up the lemon cake again and took a nonchalant bite.

Charles sighed. "Now you are doing exactly what Mama feared. Let me set your mind at rest, Will. Poppy Milburn's condition is none of my doing. It may all be set at the door of the vicar's boy."

"Of course, of course," Will spluttered, through a mouthful of cake. "Never suspected... not a thought of such a thing... none at all, I assure you. No one could believe it of you."

"On the contrary," Mildred said calmly. "Everyone always thinks the worst of a neighbour. Only we, who understand Mr

Leatham so well, know the truth. His actions in supporting Mr Christopher may be misguided, but they are honourable."

"Thank you, Miss Beacher," Charles said, with only the slightest hint of sarcasm, making her a small bow.

"Misguided... yes," Will said thoughtfully. "It is an unfortunate situation, but if they are to be married... It will all be forgot in time."

"Such things are never forgotten," Mildred said.

"No, indeed," Mrs Leatham said. "I fear that all three girls must be tainted by association. Mr Stratton may even cry off his marriage to Miss Elinor. He has his own reputation to consider, and for you as a clergyman, Will..."

Charles said nothing, leaving Mildred and his step-mother to put the case to Will, which they did with great energy until they deemed it time to retire. Charles would have gone up too, but Will said, "Shall we play piquet for a while? And perhaps a brandy before bed?"

Silently, Charles prepared the card table while Will poured the brandy, and for some time they played without much conversation.

Then Will burst out, "What am I to do, Charles? Should I marry her or not?"

It was so tempting to answer such an appeal according to the wishes of his own heart. *No, you should not marry her! Run away and leave her to me.* But his conscience intervened.

"How can I answer such a question? You must make up your own mind, Will, as we all must, in the end."

"*You* do not regard her as beyond redemption, do you?" Will said. "You are still willing to call upon her and offer help to her family."

"Of course. There are behaviours which would cause me to drop an acquaintance, but not this. Miss Milburn cannot be blamed for the sins of her unfortunate sister."

"But it *is* a sin," Will said slowly. "Upon that point there can be no argument. The younger sister has sinned, and the older must bear some of her shame. As a clergyman, I cannot be seen to condone sin. And yet... she seemed so perfect."

"Do you love her?"

"What has that to say to anything? Marriage is not about *love*."

Charles' eyebrows shot up. "Is it not? I agree there may be other considerations, but surely there must be affection before anything else?"

"That is fine talk from the man who offered for Miss Milburn without the least affection," Will said, and Charles had the oddest feeling that his cousin was sneering at him.

"I was wrong to do so," he said quietly. "Miss Milburn quite properly told me exactly what she thought of *that*. Yes, there must be affection, Will. What other foundation can there be?"

"Why, money," Will said in surprised tones. "I cannot afford to marry without considerations of money, Charles. A woman with a little money of her own to bring to the marriage, and a certain attraction in her person, and not too high in the instep to look at a lowly clergyman with few prospects. Miss Milburn was perfect." He sighed. "How pleasant it would be to go about my daily round, knowing a woman such as that to be waiting for me at home."

"I can see the attraction in that," Charles said dryly.

"An undemanding woman who will run my house smoothly, attend to my every comfort and put a good dinner on the table every night, without waste or extravagance."

Charles was bemused as he tried to reconcile this view of marital bliss with argumentative Caroline. He had no answer, however, and so he allowed Will to run on in this vein until they were both ready to retire.

It seemed that Will was not deterred by Caroline's brush with scandal, and perhaps he would press his suit on her. Would she accept him? Charles could not determine the answer to that, knowing only that he would be utterly miserable if she did. His future lay in Caroline's hands. He had seldom been in such low spirits.

~~~~~

Caroline hummed as she worked on her lace. She liked having the house to herself, apart from the servants. Molly was busy in the kitchen, Martin would be out in the stables and Susie was somewhere upstairs, but everyone else was gone. Her accounts were balanced, and she was in harmony with the world.

Charles Leatham had come, as usual, before breakfast. He still didn't have his book about gentlemanly behaviour, but he'd wanted to ask her about the mill at Corranford, which the bailiff thought was not producing as much as it should. Not that Caroline knew a thing about mills, but she could listen while he explained it and ask the occasional question, and he had gone away much happier, and resolved to talk to the miller alone, without the bailiff present. He was a strange man, she decided, but a great deal less provoking than he'd been when she'd first known him.
~~~~~

In the middle of the morning, Mr Will Leatham called again. That was puzzling, for he'd paid his duty call only the day before, and since it was to be only a brief visit, she'd supposed she wouldn't see him again. Yet here he was, and not at all his usual unruffled self. He looked grave, and wandered about the parlour in a manner which reminded her of his cousin, although he didn't slap his gloves against his thigh in suppressed anger.

"You are alone today, Miss Milburn?"

"As you see. Mrs Stratton left this morning to return home to Romsey, and Lin has gone with her for a visit. Poppy has gone down to the vicarage to be instructed in the responsibilities of marriage, since she'll soon be entering that state."

He frowned. "Miss Milburn, I am sure you are aware of... of certain *rumours* regarding your sister."

"I never listen to gossip," Caroline said, in an acid tone. It was not true, of course, for she enjoyed a good gossip as much as anyone, but the circumstances of Poppy's marriage were no business of Will Leatham's.

"Oh, quite, quite. But as a friend to you all — I hope and trust I may claim that privilege — and also in my rôle as a clergyman—"

"I assure you, Mr Leatham, we are very well supplied with moral guidance from our own clergyman."

"True, but one feels... one cannot help but feel that in this case, where there is clear wrongdoing, there must be something amiss in the moral guidance he provides. Do you not agree?"

Now that was a very good point. The vicar's son ought to have the highest principles.

"If your sister had been properly taught from the pulpit, then this tragic outcome could have been avoided, one feels."

"Wait a moment," Caroline said. "Are you placing all the blame on Poppy for this?"

"Is it not the female of the species who holds to the highest standards of propriety and conduct? A young man will always be a little wild, if permitted, but a correctly instructed young lady will always be able to hold him in restraint."

Caroline jumped to her feet, boiling with anger. "Mr Leatham, I am far from being an expert on the subject, but I believe it is generally acknowledged that it requires the participation of two people to create a child. Poppy may not be blameless, but the heaviest responsibility for her present situation lies with John Christopher."

He had risen, too, and now his face was dark. "If that is indeed your opinion, then you stand in as much need of moral guidance as your sister," he said coldly. "It is always the woman who leads in moral matters, the woman who defines the terms of any connection. Surely you know this? It is the very reason that a woman who loses her reputation loses everything. If once she permits... liberties, then she is lost. In this case, the young man has chosen to wed, but if he had not—"

"You don't need to tell me what happens when a man chooses not to wed the woman he has dishonoured, Mr Leatham, for my own mother was the product of just such a union."

"You speak as if you are proud of it!"

"It does not embarrass me, for it was none of my doing. I am perfectly willing to accept censure for my own follies, but I will never be ashamed of my mother's birth or Poppy's mistakes. If Poppy, in her innocence, feels no shame in her situation, why should I do so? She made a mistake, she will wed and put it behind her, and there is an end to the matter."

"Indeed it is," he said stiffly. "I beg your pardon for proffering opinions so disgusting to you, Miss Milburn. Pray give my... my best wishes to your sister. To *both* your sisters. I bid you a good day."

Susie, who was more concerned than Caroline about propriety, had been hovering outside the open parlour door ready to show him out. That done, she came back into the parlour, and laughed.

"Lord, you look fit to burst, Miss Milburn! I ain't seen you so worked up since... well, since that Mr Charles was first coming here."

"Insufferable man! Horrid prig! Despicable, self-righteous, pompous, arrogant, self-satisfied, moralistic, smug, *horrible* man!" Caroline spat out, still pacing up and down.

Susie laughed. "Aye, he's all that and more, but aren't they all, these rich people? They think they're so much better than everyone else, but I'll bet they have their little mistakes, too, just like Poppy."

"That's true. The duke said as much," Caroline said, much struck. "He was talking about Mama, but he said such things happen even in the best-regulated families. Even in his, he said. So there is no need for Mr High-and-mighty Will Leatham to look down his supercilious nose at us." She sighed gustily. "Although I suppose he is right, and I should feel shame at Poppy's disgrace. Indeed, it is mortifying to have a sister in such a situation, but he need not have lectured me so. Trust a clergyman to preach morality!"

"At least we won't see him again, and that's a mercy," Susie said. "Can't have you flying up into the boughs like this."

"True. I am too upset for lace work now. I shall look over the accounts again, I think."

But before she could move from the parlour, another visitor arrived — Mr Charles Leatham, in some agitation. "I thought Will would be here. Is he here? Has he called?"

"He was here a few minutes ago, but he left in high dudgeon."

"Oh." Inexplicably, Charles' face lightened. "He did, did he?"

"I took exception when he told me I stood in need of moral guidance," she said crisply.

He burst out laughing. "So you rang a peal over him, did you? Wonderful!"

"Is it?" she said, smiling too. It was odd how his moods affected her. If he was cross, she was likewise cross, but if he was in good humour, so was she. "Oh, do sit down, Mr Leatham, and cheer me up, for I am still cross."

"My book has arrived from Narfield Lodge," he said at once. "Lord Narfield found it in his library, and a groom rode over this morning to bring it to me. Was that not kind? Oh, and Mildred's last remaining relative has died — her great-aunt in Harrogate. Mildred is now worth fifteen thousand pounds, can you believe it? She is quite upset about it."

"Upset about inheriting fifteen thousand pounds?" Caroline said.

He chuckled. "No, no, the death. I will say this for Mildred, she is not in the least mercenary. She seems to have been quite fond of the old lady, for all she had not seen her for years. She wrote to her every week without fail, and never got so much as a word in reply. She had no idea her great-aunt was worth so much."

"That is a very large dowry," Caroline said. "She will be snapped up now, I'm sure. Are you tempted, Mr Leatham?"

He smiled. "There is no dowry large enough to tempt me to marry Mildred Beacher. I mean no disparagement by that, for she is a very good person, and will make someone an admirable wife, but she would never suit me. She is altogether too moralistic for my taste."

"She should marry Mr Will Leatham," Caroline said lightly. "Heavens, is that a carriage arriving? So many callers and it is a Tuesday and not even a day when we might be supposed to be at home."

It was not a carriage, it was two identical curricles, one pulled by a pair of black horses, and one by a pair of white. But when Susie showed the Alsager twins into the parlour, they were not the bouncing, lively young men of Caroline's previous experience. These were two gentlemen so dejected and out of spirits that they could hardly speak.

"Oh, whatever is the matter?" she cried out. "What has happened? Your mama or papa? Not your grandmama?"

"Oh no! Nothing of the sort! Everyone—"

"—is perfectly well. We bring you—"

"—an invitation. To a party."

"A celebration."

Their faces were so long and their tones so gloomy that she was almost tempted to laugh. "A celebration? But that's good news, surely? What is to be celebrated?"

"Our betrothals," they said in unison.

"The Miss Harlings are to arrive for a visit on Monday."

"On Tuesday we are to propose to them."

"On Wednesday there is to be a betrothal party and—"

"—in March, after Easter, we are to marry."

"But... you're not pleased?" Caroline said. "I thought it had been agreed long since."

"It has." They nodded their heads. "But marriage... it is the end of *everything*."

Susie came in just then with tea and cakes, but although Mr Leatham tucked in with gusto, the two brothers wouldn't eat or drink a thing. Caroline had never seen them so miserable.

"Perhaps... I mean to say, if you truly dislike the Miss Harlings, then—"

"Oh, *no!* We like them very much."

"They are charming, and we have been great friends with them for years."

"For years and years. Ever since we were children."

"They understand that we must always be together, and—"

"—they feel exactly the same way, so we will share a house—"

"—and raise our children together, but—"

"—but... *married!* For ever. With no escape."

Mr Leatham set down his plate and delicately removed a crumb of pound cake from his breeches. "Is matrimony such a dire prospect? Since you will all live under the same roof, I cannot see that you will lose by it. The two of you will still go on as you always have, but you will now also have female companionship whenever you wish for it. You will always have a four for whist, and someone to smile at you over the breakfast table, or to drive out with you in your curricles, or to ride with. When you attend a ball, you need not dance with every hopeful chit just out of the schoolroom. If you want music in the evenings, the ladies will play duets for you, and if you want to read aloud, you will have a ready audience. I cannot see any disadvantages to marriage with an agreeable and sensible woman."

The twins stared at him, then looked at each other. "That is very true. How very perspicacious you are, Leatham."

They departed in much better spirits than they had arrived. When Caroline returned from seeing them out, she was amused to see Mr Leatham cutting himself another slice of cake. She took a slice herself, and only when she had eaten every crumb did she say, "You seem to have a higher opinion of matrimony these days."

He looked across at her with a smile. If only he would always smile! He was a handsome man when he was in charity with the world. "It is true, I have come to see the benefits of the wedded state. I am not at all as reluctant as I once was."

"So have you chosen a lady?"

"I have."

Why did that make her insides twist? "And have you spoken?"

"I have, but she refused me."

"Oh." Interesting, but who could it be? "I am very sorry for the disappointment that must cause you, for she must be rather special to make you positively want to marry her."

"She is very special indeed," he said softly. "Indeed, the prize is so well worth the winning that I shall not give up my campaign, and shall hope to change her mind before long. And now, Miss Milburn, I have trespassed upon your hospitality for far too long. I shall bid you good day, and hope I will not be unwelcome to call again before breakfast tomorrow, now that I have my book returned to me? We have a few chapters left to discuss, I believe."

Very special? How foolish to resent the unknown lady who had won his heart, yet she did. For when he married, he would come no more to see her, and how she would miss him!

Her throat was tight, but she managed to say, "You are welcome at any time, Mr Leatham."

He gazed at her for a long moment, and surely his eyes were unusually intense? Or was that merely the wish of her heart?

27: More Proposals (August/September)

She had to escape from the house, at once, before anyone else came to disrupt her day and destroy all her equanimity. As soon as Mr Leatham had gone, striding away down the drive, Caroline dashed upstairs for a bonnet, and hastened through the house.

"Susie, if anyone else calls, anyone at all, I am not at home."

Then she went out into the garden. The silence and the smell of pipe smoke from the rear of the wood store suggested that Martin was not as diligent in wood chopping as might be hoped. On another day, in a different mood, she might have stopped to reprimand him, but today she didn't care. All she wanted was to be out of the house, and for once she understood Poppy's need to disappear from time to time. Not into the woods, though! Poppy loved to wander far afield, but Caroline had no desire to go far. Just far enough to leave the house and all its responsibilities behind. Just far enough that she could *think*.

She passed through the small pleasure grounds and then the rather dishevelled patch that had perhaps once been a neat shrubbery. Beyond that was the area of former lawn where the goats were pastured today, and the orchard. It was not a hot day, the sun screened by dull, grey clouds, but there was a welcome coolness under the trees. The burgeoning fruits were growing large enough to weigh down the branches, but there was a clearly worn path winding through the trees and then, tucked away at the far end, a wooden seat that John Christopher had made. How many assignations had this seat seen, new as it was? Such a convenient and secret place for two lovers to meet and yet they were still in the garden. How many hours had Poppy spent here, unchaperoned, with John?

But she would not wallow in guilt. What was done was done, and today she had her own problems to consider. Her problem was tall and well built and handsome when he smiled. Which he had done frequently of late. Now she knew why. He was in love. And how had that happened, when he had seemed quite definitely *not* in love at Narfield Lodge? What was it he had said… *'None of them please me as well as you do'*… that did not seem in the least like a man in love.

Unless… unless he meant her? No, surely that was impossible.

But he had kissed her. Not a proper kiss, as a man in love might attempt, but the lightest peck on the lips. How it had tormented her, that kiss! It had kept her awake at night, wondering, for the first time in all her two and twenty years, what it might be like to be married, and have a man in her life as close and as intimate to her as her sisters were. She had thought about it and come to no conclusions. Perhaps it wouldn't be as terrible as she'd always feared. Mama and Papa had been happy, after all. Or perhaps it would be the surrender of everything that made her truly herself. To belong totally to a man… to one man in particular… to Charles.

She shivered. His words echoed in her mind. *'She is very special indeed.'* What did he mean… *who* did he mean? Could he mean her? Even if it were so, did she want to marry him? Did she love him? Impossible to say.

But of one thing she was very certain, beyond the least shadow of a doubt — she did *not* want him to marry anyone else.

~~~~~

Charles smiled as he walked home. He had believed it to be a huge mistake to go tearing after Will when he learnt he had left the house that morning. He knew his errand, and it could bring Charles nothing but torment to arrive at Bursham Cottage to find Will secure in his successful suit. Instead, he had found the most blissful situation — Will sent away on the wrong side of Caroline's temper, and herself alone and in need of his company. *'Sit down and cheer me up, for I am still cross,'* she had said, and he had managed to make her smile. How astonishing to be able to do so! They had come a long way since their first, infelicitous meeting.

And then the foolish Alsager twins had given him the perfect opportunity to hint at his own change of heart. Had she understood him? Surely she had! He had not been very subtle. It would be foolish to rush into it, but to give her a tiny hint so that she would not be unprepared… yet he had planned his campaign rather well, he thought. Will had upset his strategy somewhat, but he had now been routed and the field was left to Charles. All he had to do was to convince Caroline…

He was so lost in his own thoughts that he walked straight into the summer parlour without hesitation, and there discovered a scene as dramatic as it was incomprehensible. Mildred was seated on a chaise longue, a handkerchief to her eyes, weeping copiously, while Will knelt at her feet, her free
~~~~~

hand pressed against his cheek, his face mere inches from hers. As Charles stood gaping at them, Will released Mildred's hand and leapt to his feet. If Charles's suspicions had not already been aroused, Will's furious blush would have given him away.

"Ah... Charles..." Will began.

Recollecting himself, Charles made a hasty bow. "I beg your pardon. I shall retreat at once."

He turned to do so, but Will cried, "No, no! Stay, I beg you, cousin. You may be the first to congratulate us. Miss Beacher... my dear Mildred... has just this minute consented to be my wife."

Charles opened his mouth, realised that his astonishment was too great for speech and closed it again. How could a man who had left the house that morning determined to marry one woman now be betrothed to another? It was beyond all understanding.

"I see you are surprised," Will said, with a commendable degree of understatement. "I have long held Miss Beacher in the greatest admiration, as you know..." Had he known that? Will certainly had more tolerance of her prosiness than most. "...but my situation has always prevented me from speaking. Had I already received the preferment which will one day be mine, I should not have hesitated, but I could never ask her to so reduce her mode of living as to share my poverty. It would not have been fitting. But when I entered the house just now and Miss Beacher divulged her wonderful news... in the midst of our shared happiness at her good fortune..." Again he blushed. "...we... we became aware that we both harboured certain... *feelings* which could not... which need not be any longer repressed."

He paused, awaiting a suitable response from Charles. What could he say? He was stunned, and disappointed to find Will, for all his moralising to Caroline, was nothing but a fortune hunter. Fifteen thousand pounds! Yes, that would be more than enough to tempt an avaricious man to abandon a lady with only two or three thousand. Still he could not speak.

Will went on, "Miss Beacher, I now understand, has been very much distressed by... certain events. The death of her beloved Ben, of course, but also that Alfred felt obliged to offer for her, and everyone had been so kind that she had felt obliged to accept him. She has always hoped to find another man who would value her for her many good qualities and not marry her merely from duty."

That was a sentiment Charles could very much understand. "My dear Miss Beacher," he said, sitting beside her and handing her his handkerchief to replace the sodden one she held. "Why did you not say as much? No one should marry from duty alone, without affection. If they had known, Mama would not have... Alfred would not have..."

They would not have said so, but Mildred would have felt the weight of her obligation to them. Mama wanted an heir, and soon, and Alfred was a gentle soul who would do his duty, just as Charles had once thought to do. And Mildred, poor grieving Mildred, had accepted him in gratitude and despair but without love.

"Oh, Mildred," Charles said gently. "You poor, dear girl. And will my cousin make you happy?"

"Oh yes!" she said, through her tears.

"You are not accepting him because you feel you ought?"

"No. Oh, no, not in the least. I have always held him in the greatest regard. You must be aware that I have always been best suited to a life as a clergyman's wife, Charles. I would have done my best to make Alfred happy, and if you had... well, you never liked me, so it did not arise, but—"

"It was not a matter of liking or disliking," he said. "You are so good that you make me feel... unworthy. I could never be married to someone so superior to me in every way. Will is a very good match for you, and I shall like you very well when you are his wife and not here as daily proof of my inadequacy. I wish you both joy."

~~~~~

SEPTEMBER

The autumn rains began early, trapping Caroline indoors for day after day. In Romsey, she could still have dashed out between showers to do a little shopping, for the pavements dried quickly, but here in the country the inevitable consequence of rain was mud. If she were prepared to lift her skirts and not mind her fine new boots becoming caked in the stuff, she would have walked about as usual, and if she were minded to have the horse put to the gig and take Martin away from his work, she could have been driven about like a lady. But she would not do so, except on Thursdays, when she visited Starlingford and Corranwater. Then it seemed only right to take the gig, and as often as not she visited some of the shops as well, which pleased Martin greatly. Whichever village they were in, he always found a helpful boy to mind the horse while he went off to the inn to refresh himself until he was wanted again.

The Alsager twins were formally betrothed, and seemed not too dispirited by the prospect of matrimony. They departed with their mother to visit the Harling family, leaving their father and grandmother behind.
~~~~~

Poppy's marriage was fast approaching, and Mrs Stratton had helpfully undertaken to see about her wedding clothes. She had a seamstress in Romsey who would be making Lin's, and would be happy to make Poppy's, too.

"It will save you all a deal of sewing," she said cheerfully, "and if you will undertake to pay for the materials—"

"We have plenty of fabric," Lin said, bouncing with excitement. "Mama laid by a great quantity of silks and muslins and velvets and all sorts of wonderful things, and this is precisely what Mama's box is for, isn't it, Caro? We can use everything in it, can't we?"

"Not everything, Lin," Mrs Stratton said. "You must leave enough for Miss Milburn's wedding clothes."

"Oh, but Caro will never marry," Lin said cheerfully. "Will you, Caro?"

"Never say never," Mrs Stratton said. "Even if she does not, one third of everything in the box is hers."

Caroline said nothing, but Lin's words stabbed her like knives. That was her own sister's opinion of her marriage prospects — that no man would ever want her. Or perhaps she meant that Caroline would never want a man. Even a few weeks ago, she would have said as much herself, but now... No, she would not think of Charles Leatham. He must not be permitted to destroy her happiness. So she smiled and said nothing, and if the smile was a little strained, no one noticed.

Mr Stratton was now employed at Salisbury, and was living at the Wheatsheaf Inn until he married and would move into Bursham Cottage. There had been much discussion about bedrooms, but in the end it had been decided that there was no significant difference between any of the rooms and no need for any alteration. The two husbands would simply move into the same room as their wives.

If Caroline wondered just how well the arrangement would work in practice, she kept such thoughts to herself. Everyone spoke of it as though nothing would change, but for her, everything would change, for she would no longer be mistress of the house. Lin and Poppy, as married women, would take precedence over her, and she would have to defer to them. She would be obliged to hand over the keys to the linen and silver cupboards to Lin, and the key to the wine cellar to Lester Stratton. Lin would decide the meals and give orders to the servants. How many more servants would they need, now that they would have two men in the house and a nursery to set up? And what of the account books and the keys to the safe? Would Lester expect to take charge of the household finances? Caroline would be reduced to the status of the poor relation, and she must accustom herself to her destined rôle as spinster aunt to her sisters' children, she supposed, unless...

But no, she could not depend on finding a husband for herself. Such thoughts were foolish, however friendly Charles Leatham had become.

One day, when Caroline was in the still room with Susie and Molly, agitated voices could be heard in the kitchen — a woman's, high with distress, and a man's, loud and angry. Martin, remonstrating with someone. Then a baby's cry.

"Ruby!" Molly said. "She's here again."

"Ruby? And what do you mean, again?" Caroline said.

"She came here two or three times while you were off with your grand friends," Molly said. "Looking for Poppy."

"That baby won't stop crying, poor little mite," Susie said. "Where is Poppy, anyway?"

"Feedin' the chickens," Molly said. "I'll fetch her."

In the kitchen, Ruby was crying, the baby was crying and Martin was yelling at her. "You can't stay here, girl. You got to go back to the farm where you belong."

"Oh Susie! Miss Milburn!" Ruby cried. "Is Poppy here? Where is she?"

Susie lifted the wailing baby from her mother's arms. "In the garden, Mrs Neilson. Molly's gone to find her. Let me hold Mary for a while and you sit down and have a cup of tea. That'll make you feel better. There now, little one, hush your noise, for Susie's here now. Sshh, now, there's a good girl, for you're making your poor mama all upset. Sshhh... Martin, shoo, you're not needed here. Miss Milburn, would you mind? Just while I make the tea."

She held the baby out, a red-faced bundle of waving arms and kicking legs. Gingerly, Caroline took hold of it.

"Rock her a bit and talk to her. That'll soothe her."

Gently, Caroline rocked and murmured, "Hush, hush..." while Susie bustled around with the kettle and some mugs, and by some miracle, the child did indeed quieten down a little, although still weeping. Susie made tea and produced some cakes not long out of the oven.

The kitchen door flew open and there was Poppy. "Oh, the poor little mite!" she cried, whisking her out of Caroline's arms. "There now, little one, Poppy's here."

To Caroline's astonishment, the child instantly stopped crying.

"There now, that's better," Susie said, pouring tea. "Drink that, Mrs Neilson, and have a cake."

Obediently, Ruby sat at the big kitchen table and sipped and nibbled, and in between each mouthful she sobbed piteously.

"It's no good, I just can't make her stop cryin'," she wailed. "She cries all night and then I'm so tired I'm fit for nothin' the next day and Davy's mother shouts at me and says I'm useless, and I'm sure there's somethin' wrong with her. Davy says I fuss too much but how can I help it when she cries all the time? There must be somethin' wrong, mustn't there?"

"She's a fine healthy baby," Susie said firmly. "I've seen a few babes in my time, and your Mary's as fine and plump as any I've seen. When Miss Poppy were a babe, she were so thin you could see all her little ribs, and look how strong she turned out, and your Mary's a lot stouter than she was."

"That's what everyone tells me, but..."

"And everyone's right," Susie said firmly. "Now drink your tea, and eat a currant cake or two, and then we'll take you back to the farm."

Ruby seemed to shrivel into herself. "Don't want to go back."

"I'm sure you don't, but your husband's there so that's where your place is."

"I wish... I wish we could have a little place of our own, not livin' at the farm," Ruby said wistfully. "A cottage, be it ever so small, or even a couple of rooms somewhere, but out from Mrs Neilson's eye. I'd do better if she wasn't always watchin' me."

"Why can't you?" Caroline said, absentmindedly reaching for a currant cake.

"No cottages to be had, not that we could afford," Ruby said. "Davy's savin' up, but his pa don't give him much money. Bein' the eldest, he'll have the whole farm in time, but his pa says that means he don't get wages like his brothers."

"Well, there's something in that," Caroline said thoughtfully, "but if someone were to offer you accommodation elsewhere, rent-free, no one would mind that, would they? Somewhere close enough that your husband could easily get to the farm."

Ruby gaped at her, her expression such a mixture of hope and disbelief that Caroline wanted to cry. Stretching across the table, she took Ruby's hand in hers. "We have rooms above the stables. One end is the hay store, but the other end is fitted out for a coachman to live in. Just a couple of rooms, and some cupboards, but—"

Ruby burst into fresh tears. "You never would! Would you? Do that for us?"

"I believe I would," Caroline said. "You'd have Poppy here to help with the baby, and you can give Susie a hand with her work. I was wondering how we were to manage when we have Mr Stratton living here, and John Christopher as well. We'll need an extra servant. We could pay you ten pounds a year, to start with."

"You'd pay me?" she whispered. "My own money? Oh, Miss Milburn!"

~~~~~

Charles felt that his suit was progressing satisfactorily now that the threat of a rival had been removed. He could not have been more pleased about Will's betrothal to Mildred, for it removed two thorns from his side in one stroke. He continued to visit Caroline each morning, and was confident that she was now
~~~~~

firmly his friend. But how to progress from friendship to something more was a question that puzzled him. His book was annoyingly silent on the subject. He now knew all about cleanliness of person, absence of mind and sundry little accomplishments, but on the question of love and marriage not a word was said. He had resorted, in odd moments, to flicking through the pages of novels in case a proposal should be described therein, but so far he had had no luck. So he called on Caroline, and occasionally had the pleasure of meeting her over dinner, but was no nearer to a betrothal.

One morning before breakfast, he was in the parlour at Bursham Cottage, as usual. He had reached the last but one chapter of his book, on dignity of manners, and was finding it distressingly apt. *'If you discover any hastiness in your temper, and find it apt to break out into rough and unguarded expressions, watch it narrowly and endeavour to curb it,'* the book said uncompromisingly.

"I *do* endeavour to curb it," he said miserably, "but it is my greatest failing."

"Do you think so?" she said, looking up from her work with quick interest. "It seems to me that your temper is a great deal less hasty than it was. We have not quarrelled for weeks and weeks."

She smiled at him with such warmth that he was suddenly breathless. Oh, those treacle eyes, and the smooth, dark hair and creamy skin that he so badly wanted to touch. And her lips... such red lips, warm and mobile and oh so enticing...

He *would* speak. Here, now, when love for her flooded his veins and gave him the courage to brave even her disdainful refusal. He *must* speak, the need to touch her, to hold her was too powerful to be borne.

"Caroline—"

A knock on the door. The moment was lost. Perhaps it was just as well, because if she refused him again… all these delightful hours in her company could not be continued. She would be lost to him for ever, no more than a common acquaintance. Yes, just as well to be interrupted. A refusal would be too hard to bear.

It was Stratton, the attorney.

"Sorry to disturb you, Caro, but I plan to take Richmond to the farrier, and Martin wishes to take the cob along, too, but he thinks the fellow will want his bill paying."

"It is not Michaelmas yet, but we do owe him quite a large amount, what with your mama's carriage horses," Caroline said. "I'll have to get some money from the safe. Wait here a moment."

She returned in a very short time with a pile of coins, which Lester accepted before disappearing back to the stables. He did not know her well enough to notice anything amiss, but Charles did.

"Whatever is the matter?" he said quietly. "You are as white as chalk."

She turned wide, fearful eyes on him. "Come, and I will show you."

In the study, she led him to a corner and opened a cupboard door. Hidden behind it was the safe.

"Do you see?" she said, pointing at it.

"I see nothing untoward."

"Scratch marks, all round the key hole. Someone has tried to break into the safe."

28: The Silver Box

Charles stared at the safe. Now that Caroline had pointed them out, the scratches were obvious, and there were many of them. Not deep gouges, for the safe was constructed of the most solid type of metal, but enough to show that someone had laboured here with some determination.

"Is anything missing?" he said quietly, not wanting to alert the servants to the situation and create an alarm.

She shook her head. "The money box contains the exact amount it should hold, and apart from that, there is only the silver box."

"The silver box?"

"One of several dug up from the kitchen garden, each containing five hundred pounds of notes drawn on a London bank. The contents of the others are in the bank, but the silver box is locked, so it's stayed in the safe until I remember to take it to the locksmith."

"Curious. And who would know of this silver box? You and your sisters, John Christopher, the servants... anyone else?"

"Mr Stratton. And you, now," she added with a little smile.

Once again he was mesmerised. She was so lovely when she smiled, with a warmth in those dark eyes that quite unmanned him. He had to force himself to concentrate. “Hmpf. If the servants know, you may be sure that everyone in the parish knows, too. When did you last open the safe?”

“Not since before we went to Narfield Lodge. This is the first time I’ve needed more money than I had in my reticule. There were no scratches on the safe then, I’m sure. They’re so obvious I would have noticed, and what worries me most...” She paused, chewing her lip anxiously. “The previous time someone tried to break into the safe, there were—”

“This is not the first such occasion?” he said, anxiety making his voice sharp.

“No. The first time, someone just walked in while we were at church and the kitchen door was left unlocked. They searched the desk drawers and cupboards but nothing was taken. The second time, he broke in at night and found the safe, but again nothing was taken. We had all the locks changed, and the shutters made secure, and this is the first time he’s been able to get in since then. Mr Leatham, here’s what worries me... he must have been here for some time, working away at the lock with some kind of metal tools, yet there’s no sign of candle wax anywhere.”

“Your maid is very thorough, perhaps,” he said. “But you think he was here during the day?”

“Yes, and how could he do so without the servants knowing about it?”

“Ah.” He considered all the implications of that, and none of them were good. “Is it possible they forgot to lock up when they went to church, and someone got in then?”

"And how would anyone know to try the door on that particular day?" she said at once. "No, either the would-be thief was admitted by one or other of the servants, or..." She heaved a breath. "...or it was one of the servants who did this. And I think it could only be Martin," she added miserably. "Susie has been with us for years, since before Poppy was born, and Molly... I don't see Molly sitting here trying to break open a safe."

"Well, let us find out," he said grimly.

It took some determined searching to find Martin, who was fast asleep in the hayloft, but as soon as he was accused, the explanation came tumbling out.

"I never let no one in, 'onest, but... but I like to pop down to the Wheatsheaf of an evenin', just to 'ave a bit of a natter with the lads, and... and maybe a jug of ale, and Molly weren't 'appy to wait up to let me back in and I weren't 'appy to leave the kitchen door unlocked, so I took the spare key and... and I must 'ave dropped it somewhere, cos one time I 'ad it when I left 'ere and it were gone when I got back. I think someone must 'ave found it."

There was enough honesty in his face, as well as fear, for Charles to believe him, and Molly confirmed the story.

"Aye, 'e's that daft, an' so I told 'im, 'e'd lose 'is 'ead if it weren't screwed on," she said. "Lost the flamin' key, the daft fella, and too terrified to say a word about it."

"Any idea who might have taken it?" Charles said, but seemingly half the male population of Bursham St Matthew had been in the Wheatsheaf on that particular evening.

"I'll wager it was Grison," Caroline said darkly.

"Whoever it was, they did not succeed," Charles said. "We must give them no reason to try again. As much money as possible must be taken to the bank for safety. I am sure Stratton will be happy to undertake such a commission as soon as he returns from the farrier. Then we need only make it known that there is nothing left in the safe and you will not be troubled again."

Caroline agreed to it, so as soon as Stratton returned, she opened the safe and removed the silver box.

"I can deposit this directly into the bank's vaults," Stratton said. "There is no need to break it open."

"It is a delicate thing, though," Charles said. "Such a tiny lock! We might take a leaf from our thief's notebook, and try some tools to open it. Miss Milburn, may I borrow one of your hairpins?"

To his amusement, she blushed scarlet. "Not unless you wish to see my hair tumbled all down my back, sir," she said indignantly.

"While that would indeed be delightful, I shall not so embarrass you. One of your lacemaking pins would do perfectly well."

Still blushing, she scuttled away to fetch one, returning in a few moments rather more composed. How charming she was! And how much he longed to see her hair tumbled down her back and run his hands through it...

Breathing a little faster than normal, he sat down at the desk with the box and carefully jiggled the pin in the lock. It took some time, but he was patient and eventually the little lock yielded to his probing with a soft click.

"There you are, Miss Milburn."

"How clever you are! Thank you!" She raised the lid. Inside was a well-wrapped package, with several layers of oiled cloth to be peeled away. But then...

"Oh. It is not money at all, just papers. Letters... no... I don't know what these are. I can't read them."

Charles picked up a couple. "Latin, I think. Legal documents. Stratton? Can you make anything of them?"

"Not Latin," he said. "Italian."

"Oh!" Caroline cried. "Lord Elland's documents! That's what they must be. Something to show that he wasn't entitled to be the baron. He asked me for them, but I told him, quite truthfully, that I hadn't seen them. Apparently, my grandfather tried to get money from him with them but he refused to pay. He told me he would never submit to blackmail."

"Fine words," Stratton said grimly, raising his head from the documents he had been perusing. "But that is all they were — words. I cannot make out all of it, but these documents do indeed cast doubt on Lord Elland's parentage. It is very clear now what has happened here. Wishaw found these papers, and Lord Elland has been paying for his silence at the rate of five hundred pounds a year. That is what all those buried purses were about. And now that Wishaw is dead, his lordship is trying to recover the papers by whatever means he can."

"Lord Elland didn't try to break open my safe!" Caroline cried.

"No, but someone did so on his orders," Stratton said. "Grison would be my guess. Martin has doubtless told everyone at the Wheatsheaf about the interesting silver box in the safe. Grison drinks there too, so he would have heard the tale and reported it to Lord Elland. No doubt he spotted the key Martin had dropped and pocketed it. Caro, it is for you and your sisters to decide what to do with these. Everything in the house and grounds is yours, in law."

"But the documents belong to Lord Elland."

"Not so. These are only copies of register entries in Italy. You may choose whether to give them to Lord Elland, to send them to the House of Lords or... or to burn them."

"There is a fourth option," Charles said pensively. "There is a crime here — someone tried to break open the safe, and I should very much like to see that person caught and dealt with under the law. We could let it be known that the documents have been found, and entice Caroline's burglar into a last attempt—"

"No," Caroline said.

"—to retrieve them.

"But we will be waiting," Stratton said, with a sudden grin.

"No!"

"This is going to be so much fun," Charles said, grinning back.

Caroline threw up her hands with a sigh of resignation. *"Men!"*

~~~~~

They spent two days working out the details. Caroline left them to it, wanting no part of such foolishness. She had two weddings to prepare for, the coach house rooms to be cleaned up and furnished, Ruby, Davy and the baby to be settled in, and her own turbulent feelings to be ruthlessly suppressed. She veered each day between spikes of delirious hope and utter despondency, depending entirely on whether Charles smiled at her or not. Sometimes she was sure she saw something in his eyes that must
~~~~~

be admiration or even love, yet at other times he was coolly polite to her and she decided miserably that she must be mistaken.

The day arrived when the plan would be put into execution. The story they had come up with was that they had found some papers in a foreign language which they could not interpret. Lester had arranged for a linguist to call the next morning to determine what the papers were and advise what should be done with them. That would give the thief only that night to make a final attempt to steal the papers. Since it would defeat the object if the box were to be locked away in the safe, they put it about that the lock was damaged and until it could be repaired, the valuables would be kept in the bottom drawer of the desk. Martin was to tell everyone he met, including his friends at the Wheatsheaf, so that the story would be sure to reach the thief's ears.

There was still the possibility lurking at the back of Caroline's mind that Martin himself was responsible for trying to break into the safe, or for deliberately allowing a thief access to the house, but she could not believe he would be so dishonest. He was lazy, except for his care of the horses, but Mr Wishaw would not have kept him on for years if there had been any worse failings. It must be Grison, she thought, and since he and Martin cordially disliked each other, it seemed most likely that Martin was guilty of nothing worse than blabbing secrets and dropping the key.

The pretty silver box was locked away in the bottom drawer of the desk, and the household went about its evening. Caroline made her usual round of the house securing all the doors and windows, but when it came to the garden door in the morning room, she locked it but left it unbolted. When the conspirators arrived, they would be able to enter using the spare key. Martin returned from the Wheatsheaf, slightly the worse for drink, to report that Grison had been there. Then everyone went upstairs, Martin, Molly and Susie up the kitchen stairs to the servants' attics, and Caroline, Lin and Poppy to their more capacious rooms at the front of the house.

As soon as she had seen Lin and Poppy into their rooms, Caroline turned round and slipped into the box room. An hour later, from its tiny window she saw three shadows move silently across the rose garden to the morning room door. She didn't hear the lock turn or the door open and close, for Charles had carefully greased the locks and hinges, but she knew the conspirators were now in the house — Charles, Lester and John. Caroline slipped out of the box room again and took up her station at the top of the stairs to watch and wait and worry.

~~~~~

Charles was bubbling with excitement. He had not enjoyed himself so much for an age — not since he had left the army. How he had missed this kind of endeavour! Not the sneaking around in the dark, although he knew several acquaintances who regularly indulged, and not to catch thieves, either. No, it was the feeling that he was doing something worthwhile again, in bringing a criminal to justice. And naturally keeping Caroline safe and free from worry was an object, too.

The three disposed themselves around the study in dark corners. With the shutters closed, the room was black as pitch and Charles could see nothing until his eyes began to adjust to the faint moonlight penetrating the slats. They had agreed their strategy beforehand, or rather, Charles had told them what to do, and they had accepted his orders. Stratton was to station
~~~~~

himself between two cupboards near the door, so that he could block the miscreant's exit route. Charles, being the strongest and the most used to hand-to-hand combat, was to leap upon the fellow and pin him to the ground. John Christopher was to hide in the darkest corner, and strike a light when called upon to do so.

Then they waited.

The church clock had long since fallen silent before, finally, they heard a sound within the house. It was only the slightest noise, and might have been nothing but a mouse in the wainscoting. Then there was silence again.

Gradually, a slight glow emanated from the bottom of the door. Someone was standing outside in the hall with a candle or lamp. The door creaked, the light grew, the door opened and a lantern appeared, followed by the black shape of a man. He moved straight into the room, set the lamp down on the edge of the desk and moved round towards the drawers.

"Hold!" Charles yelled.

The man ran, but Stratton was there before him, blocking the door. Desperately the man pushed at him, Stratton slipped and fell with a cry, and the man lunged for the door.

Charles was upon him before he could reach it, hurling him to the ground. For a moment, surprise was on his side and he almost managed to pin the intruder down at once. But with a heave born of desperation, the man threw him off and then the fight was on earnest, with wild punches thrown, few of which met their target, and much pushing and shoving. The two rolled around on the floor, and first one chair crashed over, then another. Then there was an ominous smashing of glass and the light went out.

Fortunately, Charles had hold of the intruder's coat, otherwise he might have made a bid for freedom again. But the two were locked together, arms and legs flailing. Charles took a punch to the eye, but grimly held onto his mark.

Somewhere in the background Stratton was yelling, "Light! Light!" and John was yelling back, "I'm trying, dammit!"

Another solid punch caught Charles in the chest, and for a brief moment he had to stop to catch his breath, but he kept tight hold on the struggling thief. But then light flared up from the corner and he could see the terrified face of his opponent. Hauling him to his feet he prepared to land a final punch, but the man kicked him on the shins, disturbing his aim.

Now they were at the other end of the room, and breaking glass all around them suggested that they had ventured too close to the tray of glasses and the decanter of Madeira. Again Charles prepared to punch, but the man screamed in real pain and sagged against him, shrieking. Charles let go, and his opponent fell to the floor, screaming over and over again.

Stratton was there with a length of rope to tie him to the handle of the nearest cupboard. He was secured. The fight was over.

Out of nowhere, a small figure shot into the room.

"Charles? *Charles!*"

"Caroline?"

"Oh, thank God!" Crunching across broken glass, she hurled herself into his arms in a frenzy of noisy weeping.

He wrapped her in a tight embrace, and there he stood, amidst the wreckage of her study, grinning from ear to ear like an idiot. And when, after quite some time, her tears subsided and she lifted her head, rather shyly, to look at him, he discovered that the most urgent necessity — the *only* thing in the whole world that he had the slightest desire to do at that precise moment — was to kiss her, long and lovingly.

So he did, and, incredibly, she made no protest, returning his kiss with a great deal of warmth.

From time to time, when they surfaced to take a breath, there was activity going on in the room — the intruder being carried away amidst thumps and groans, chairs righted, some talk between Stratton and Christopher. But nothing was so important as Caroline and the wonder of holding her in his arms and kissing her and being kissed in return.

After minutes or hours, who could tell, the room was silent, and they were alone, with a single candle burning low on the desk. He gazed into those treacle eyes, and admired her creamy skin and that glorious mouth.

"Do you think we should run away to Scotland to get married?" he said conversationally, rubbing one finger gently over her lips.

"That's very romantic, but I've always thought it sounds like a dreadfully uncomfortable business," she said at once.

"It need not be," he said. "A post-chaise and four, and overnight stops at the very best inns, and we can take Mama for propriety." That made her giggle. "But if you dislike the idea, I can go to London and obtain a special licence."

"That's romantic too, but what's wrong with the banns like everyone else?"

"Because you are too special for such a mundane process," he said. "You deserve the best, sweetling."

She blushed enchantingly, and discovered something very interesting in the middle button of his waistcoat. "But I shall be getting the best, if I marry you," she said shyly.

His throat was tight, so he squeezed her a little and sighed. "Darling Caro... I was afraid you would never think well of me. I was a contemptible specimen of humanity until you taught me to behave like a gentleman."

"You were just angry, I think... at giving up the army life you loved, and having to marry to provide an heir. And I was angry too. We neither of us knew where we fitted in."

"I am still not quite sure, but we shall work it out together," he said. "You will teach me how to manage my land and tenants, and I... I shall sit at your feet and adore you."

That made her chuckle. "I wonder... agreeable as this is, do you think we ought to find out what happened to the man you caught? Whether he's all right, and who he is?"

"I think he just got cut by all the broken glass. He quietened down before the others hauled him away. I expect he is being bandaged up in the kitchen even now. As for who he is — it is that peculiar Frenchie from Corranwater."

"What, the elder Lady Elland's footman? Lucien, that was his name. Not Grison, then?"

"Grison must have passed on Martin's story to him, but it was the Frenchie all right."

"Well, I never!"

29: A Village Wedding (October)

Accompanied by Caroline and Stratton, Charles walked to Corranwater directly after breakfast. Stratton had sent a note by way of Martin to Lord Elland, so that he would be expecting them.

They were shown into the library, but Lord Elland was not there.

"I will inform his lordship of your arrival," the butler said, "but the household is a little disrupted this morning. Her ladyship the Dowager is unwell."

"I am sorry to hear it," Charles said. "We will not keep his lordship long, but if the household disruption is concerned with your French footman, we have information on that matter."

The butler's eyes widened, and he disappeared in as much haste as his station would permit to fetch Lord Elland. The baron seemed unusually agitated when he appeared.

"Miss Milburn, Mr Leatham, Mr Stratton. You have word of Lucien, my mother's footman?"

They had agreed beforehand that Charles would do the talking. He saw no point in wrapping the facts up in clean linen, so he said bluntly, "Lucien Claverie was caught breaking into Bursham Cottage last night with the intention of stealing certain items. You will find him in the care of the constables in Salisbury."

Lord Elland gaped at them, his mouth open in astonishment. *"Lucien?"* he said. "But why on earth—? Oh... did he think—? He supposed you had the documents which Mr Wishaw claimed to hold, I imagine. But you have not found them, have you, Miss Milburn? And perhaps there were never any documents to be found."

"Oh, but there were," Charles said. "They were buried in the garden, along with the several payments of five hundred pounds that you gave Wishaw to hold his tongue."

"I gave Wishaw *nothing!"* Lord Elland said, his eyes glinting in haughty disdain. "He tried to blackmail me, but I told him to send the papers to the House of Lords if he wished. I would never submit to blackmail, Leatham, as I told Wishaw, and as I told Miss Milburn when we discussed the matter."

"But you sent the footman to steal them for you."

"I did no such thing! Never would I stoop to such a level, and you insult me to suggest it. I can only suppose that Lucien wished to spare my mother any pain, and so bought off Wishaw, and then tried to steal the evidence."

"Where would a footman find five hundred pounds?"

Lord Elland went white, and sagged into a chair. "Dear God!" he whispered. "Then it must have been... good God, no!"

"It must have been the Dowager Lady Elland?" suggested Charles.

He nodded. "She must have valued her reputation more than her integrity, for which lapse may God forgive her. But wait… you said the documents were buried in the garden? Then you have found them?"

Charles nodded at Caroline, and she opened her reticule and drew out the bundle of papers. Lord Elland took them and began to read them. At first, he seemed puzzled.

"But these are only copies of the registry entries of marriage and birth, which I already have. There is nothing in these to…" His voice tailed off, he frowned, he reread one, and then he began to read more carefully, laying them out in some kind of order on the table beside him. Eventually, he looked up at them.

"You are aware of the meaning of these, I take it?"

Stratton coughed delicately. "My Italian is not strong, but with my knowledge of Latin I read enough to understand the doubt it casts on your birth, my lord. I have not discussed this with the others, however. We are agreed that we cannot determine the authenticity of these papers, but clearly they relate to your family. Thus the only proper course of action is to lay them before you, and leave it to your judgement to determine what to do with them."

"I shall send them to the House of Lords, naturally. That is the proper place for their import to be decided. But let me explain to you what they show. Here is the record of the marriage of my father, Edgar Alsager, to Aimée Dubray and the record of my own birth, and my two sisters. And then — the part of which I knew nothing — the record of the death of Aimée, and the marriage of my father to Marie Vautrin. And when I look more closely at the birth records, I see that Marie Vautrin is shown as the mother of all three children, which was not so on the copies I have."

"Then Marie was his mistress?"

"So it would seem. His wife's maid, most probably. His marriage to Aimée was childless, it appears, but when she died, he married his mistress and she assumed the identity of the first wife. They returned to England as the complete family, with a son and two daughters, and yet... they are all illegitimate. *I* am illegitimate. And the lady upstairs, who is indeed my mother, was once a ladies maid called Marie Vautrin, and not a virtuous woman at all."

He got up and rang the bell for the butler, asking him to request the dowager to come to the library. "Pray tell her that I have news of Lucien," he added.

She came, wearing another of her brocade gowns, and it was sad to see how eager she was for news of her footman. How many years had he been her faithful servant, speaking to her in her native French language and doing her bidding in all things? Naturally she was concerned for him. She started when she saw Charles, Caroline and Stratton sitting there, but she turned hopefully to Lord Elland.

"As-tu entendu ce qui est arrivé à Lucien?" she said, before she was properly in the room.

"He has been arrested," Lord Elland said, his voice harsh. "That cannot surprise you, *Maman.* You sent him to steal the papers that prove my illegitimacy and your lack of virtue. Fortunately, these gentlemen intercepted him."

She hissed in anger. *"Ai, tu es—"*

"In English!" Lord Elland said brusquely. "I know you speak it well enough, and do not deny any of it, *Maman*, for Lucien was caught in the act of stealing, and I have the papers here before me that prove your shame, and my father's guilt."

All the fight went out of her, like a pricked balloon. "It would not have mattered if Aimée had given him a son," she said, in a heavy accent. "That was all he wanted, *un fils*. But she died, and so he married me, and I thought... truly I thought that our marriage made the children legitimate. We had friends in that situation. I did not understand that in England it was not so, only in Scotland would it happen. England is harsh on bastards, as France is also. It was not until Edgar's father wished him to return to England that I learnt the truth. But there was a priest who suggested a way. No one in England knew the secret, and if Edgar had documents to show that the children were the legitimate issue of Aimée, and I were to take the name of Aimée... why, who would know? No one! And it worked, Edmund. You were accepted as Edgar's legal heir and now you are *le baron* and we went on very well until that little upstart Wishaw poked his nose in. *Ah bien! Alors maintenant le monde sait tout. Et Lucien?*"

"Lucien was slightly injured by broken glass," Charles said. "He is in the care of the constables at Salisbury."

"He must be brought before the magistrates, *Maman*," Lord Elland said more gently. "I shall speak for him, to explain his good character and his loyalty to you, but you must be prepared for him to receive a severe sentence for one who attempted to steal and offered violence when challenged. Mr Leatham has been injured, as you see."

"Nothing but a black eye and a few bruises," Charles said. "I have suffered worse, I assure you. I shall make no complaint against Lucien on that score."

"You are generous, sir," Lord Elland said. "And Miss Milburn also. You could have dealt with these papers in another, less principled, manner, and it is to your credit that you did not. I honour you for it." He bowed to her formally, which caused her to rise and curtsy in response. "Now it is for me to do my part," he went on. "I give you my word of honour as a peer— No, for I may not be that, indeed. Then I give you my word of honour as a *gentleman*, for I am still and always that, I hope, that I shall take these papers myself to London and lay them before the Master of the Rolls and await his judgement."

"Pft. *Honneur!*" Lady Elland said.

"Yes, honour," her son said gravely. "You may not regard it highly, but to me it is everything."

~~~~~

OCTOBER

It was a crisp autumn day, cool but sunny, when the eldest of the Milburn sisters entered the wedded state. The bride wore silk from her father's linen drapery and lace of her own devising, and carried a posy of late roses. She was given away by her cousin, Tim Carter, the Valmont gamekeeper. The groom wore a new coat for the occasion, and had allowed his valet four attempts at a fashionable arrangement of neckcloth before tossing them aside in favour of his usual knot. The groom's mother and both the bride's sisters wept copiously, and the church was as full as it could hold, with more well-wishers waiting outside to salute the happy couple. Afterwards, the bridal pair and their particular friends repaired to Bursham Cottage for a breakfast of hot rolls, buttered toast, tongue, ham and eggs, with the addition of wine and cake, and everyone else went to the Wheatsheaf to celebrate with the barrels of ale so generously provided by the groom. The
~~~~~

fields and craft shops of the neighbourhood were abandoned for the day.

Lord Elland did not attend the ceremony, but he called at the cottage to wish the couple well before they departed for their honeymoon. He was but newly returned from London, where he had been told in no uncertain terms that he would remain Lord Elland until his death, for His Majesty had made him so and therefore it was so.

"I asked if there were any circumstance by which that decision might be changed or revoked, and do you know what the Master of the Rolls told me?" Lord Elland said, his usually calm face alight with amusement.

"I can't guess," Caroline said.

"He said, *'Only by treason, Elland. Only by treason.'* And since I have no plans at present to attempt to overthrow the King's rule, I believe I am safe."

"And Mr Alsager will inherit in his turn?" she said.

"Yes, Edward will inherit. All he need do is prove that he is my legal heir, and since that is beyond all question, there will be not the least difficulty. So all is well that ends well. Although..." He paused, a frown crossing his face. "I feel as if my title is undeserved, as if it is not truly mine. I am not quite sure now who I am, or where I fit in to the world."

"Now you understand how I feel," Caroline said. "At the start of this year, I was a lacemaker struggling to survive. Then I found myself in possession of a house and a good income, and now I'm the wife of a wealthy landowner. It's a big change."

"You will adapt to it. Look at my mother — she was a lady's maid, yet I never once suspected she was not the cultured daughter of a diplomat that she claimed to be."

"It is a pity she wasn't aware that you could keep the title," Caroline said sadly. "It would have saved her a great deal of worry."

"True, but if she had done as she ought and told me the truth years ago, all that worry could have been avoided. She has been punished by her own deceit, whereas you, Mrs Leatham, have displayed the utmost integrity. But you were testing me when you brought those documents to me, were you not? You wanted to see how I would react."

"In a way. We agonised over it for hours, whether to send them to London ourselves, or to leave it to you to do the honourable thing. Which you did."

"But I could have tossed them on the fire. For a second, I was tempted, I confess, but I could never do it. It would have been despicable, to destroy the evidence of my own ignoble birth."

"It wouldn't have mattered if you had," she said. "You see, the documents were *not* the evidence. The real evidence was in the original registers in Italy. If you had destroyed those papers, we should have written to the Master of the Rolls to suggest where he might look, although it seems he wouldn't have cared anyway. But you passed the test."

"So I did," he said, smiling.

"And I, too, have a test to pass. My lord, all that money that your mother gave to Mr Wishaw, and which we assumed was ours — it grieves me to say this, for it is a hard thing to surrender so much money, but it is not ours to keep. It should be returned to her ladyship."

His smile softened. "It is a prodigious sum, yet it was hers to give and she gave it freely. I do not see why you should return it.

Keep it, with my goodwill, for the Lord knows you will put it to better use than she did. Ah, I see your husband is waiting to reclaim you. It is time for you to leave, I think."

"Yes. We're only going to the coast, a place called Lyme, but I've never seen the sea and Charles is determined that I shall."

"After ten days, you will be sick of it, I guarantee it," Charles said cheerfully, wrapping an arm around her waist. "You will never want to see the sea again. But tomorrow, you will be delighted by it, my dear, so go and put your bonnet on, for the carriage is on its way round."

The bonnet was put on, and the stylish matching pelisse, the carriage arrived, and Mrs Leatham, Lin and Poppy wept all over Caroline again.

"My dear, dear daughter!" Mrs Leatham cried, hugging Caroline very tight. "So very happy! So delighted! Always hoped you would make a match of it. Could not be more pleased for you both."

"Are you, Mama?" Charles said, smiling fondly at her. "I seem to recall a time when your enthusiasm for the match wavered just a little."

"Nonsense!" she said robustly. "That was just Mildred's influence. One never quite likes to argue with her, does one? No, I did everything in my power to push the two of you together, and was I not right? Is not Caroline the perfect wife for you?"

"You were absolutely right, dearest Mama," he said, kissing her cheek. "Thank you!"

With difficulty, the two extricated themselves from the crowd of well-wishers. Caroline was handed into the post-chaise, Charles climbed in after her and they bowled away down the drive.

"Well, that went off tolerably well," he said, untying the ribbons of her bonnet and tossing it ruthlessly aside. "There! Now I can put my arm around you and you can rest your head on my shoulder. See how comfortable that is, sweetling. We shall stay at Shaftesbury tonight, which is some distance from here, so sleep if you can."

"How can I possibly sleep when we are alone in a carriage, and not even a maid or a valet with us?" she said, snuggling into his arm with a sigh of contentment. "How ramshackle we are."

"They will join us later, but for a few days I want you all to myself. I am sure we shall manage perfectly well, at least until we run out of clean handkerchiefs."

"You will have to help me fasten my stays," she said. Then, raising innocent eyes to his, she added, "And unfasten them. But I daresay you will not mind that."

"I shall try my best not to mind that," he said gravely, but his eyes gleamed at her. "Are you happy, Mrs Leatham?"

"Oh yes! But I am not at all sure why you chose Lyme for our honeymoon. There are any number of seaside resorts you might have chosen, some of them much more fashionable. Brighton, for instance."

He pulled a face, which made her laugh. "Not Brighton," he said. "Will and Mildred are taking their honeymoon there."

"Are they? I should have thought one of the great cathedral cities would be more to their taste," she said, in genuine surprise.

"So should I, and perhaps Mildred would have chosen something along those lines, but Will is not quite so stuffy as she is. Now that he has her fifteen thousand pounds, he is minded to dabble in the fringes of the fashionable world."

"I hope she will not dislike it excessively," Caroline said.

"She has always been too pious by half," Charles said. "My cousin will teach her to enjoy life a little, and she will keep him from straying too far from his calling. They are well matched. As are we, sweetling."

"We are, aren't we, and yet I disliked you extremely in the beginning."

"I can hardly blame you for that, or for refusing my unmannerly offer. But, odd as it may seem, I think it worked for the best. We decided almost at once that we should not suit, and so we came to know and appreciate each other without any thought of marriage at all. We became friends, and I am convinced now that that is the only secure foundation for matrimony. Others may fall in love with a person on sight and decide to wed without much thought, but for us it was far, far better to become fast friends before thinking of love."

"Perhaps that is true," she said thoughtfully, "but for me there is no difference. My friends are those whom I love, and so, once you were my friend, love was unavoidable. Especially once you kissed me," she added punctiliously.

"At the ball?" he said, in tones of incredulity. "That made a difference? For it was the lightest of kisses, barely even worthy of the name."

"Perhaps not, but it started me thinking what it might be like to be close to a man. I'd never even considered the possibility before, you see, but that kiss set me wondering... what it would be like... to be married, and particularly, to be married to you."

"Well, if I had known that, I would have kissed you a lot sooner," he said.

She laughed, and said, “I have no idea why we are *talking* about kissing when we could be doing it. Can you think of a reason, husband?”

“Not a single one, wife.”

Whereupon a profound silence fell within the chaise, which lasted all the way to the first changing post.

THE END

The next book in the series is *The Apothecary.* You can read a sneak preview of chapter 1 after the acknowledgements. For more information or to buy, go to my website at http://marykingswood.co.uk/.

Thanks for reading!

If you have enjoyed reading this book, please consider writing a short review on Amazon. You can find out the latest news and sign up for the mailing list at my website at http://marykingswood.co.uk/. In case you were wondering, the book Charles used to help him become a gentleman is quite real. *'Principles of Politeness and of Knowing the World'* by Reverend Dr John Trusler is still available, thanks to the miracle of print-on-demand.

Family trees: Hi-res version available on my website http://marykingswood.co.uk/.

A note on historical accuracy: I have endeavoured to stay true to the spirit of Regency times, and have avoided taking too many liberties or imposing modern sensibilities on my characters. The book is not one of historical record, but I've tried to make it reasonably accurate. However, I'm not perfect! If you spot a historical error, I'd very much appreciate knowing about it so that I can correct it and learn from it. Thank you!

Isn't that what's-his-name? Regular readers of my books will know that occasionally characters from previous books pop up again. There are a few in this book. Lord Randolph Litherholm, the new Duke of Falconbury, made a brief appearance in *The Clerk*, the prequel to this series; his story will be told in book 6, *The Duke*. Lawyer Mr Willerton-Forbes and his flamboyant sidekick Captain Edgerton have been helping my characters solve murders and other puzzles ever since *Lord Augustus.* Keep an eye out for Mr and Mrs Elkington, unobtrusive guests at a dinner party here; you'll be seeing more of them in the next book, *The Apothecary*.

About the Silver Linings Mysteries series*:* John Milton coined the phrase *'silver lining'* in *Comus: A Mask Presented at Ludlow Castle*, 1634

Was I deceived, or did a sable cloud

Turn forth her silver lining on the night?

I did not err; there does a sable cloud

Turn forth her silver lining on the night,

And casts a gleam over this tufted grove.

Ever since then, the term *'silver lining'* has become synonymous with the unexpected benefits arising from disaster. The sinking of the *Brig Minerva* results in many deaths, but for others, the future is suddenly brighter. But it's not always easy to leave the past behind...

Book 0: The Clerk: the sinking of the *Minerva* offers a young man a new life *(a novella, free to mailing list subscribers)*.

Book 1: The Widow: the wife of the *Minerva's* captain is free from his cruelty, but can she learn to trust again?

Book 2: The Lacemaker: three sisters inherit a country cottage, but the locals are surprisingly interested in them.

Book 3: The Apothecary: a long-forgotten suitor returns, now a rich man, but is he all he seems?

Book 4: The Painter: two children are left to the care of a reclusive man.

Book 5: The Orphan: a wilful heiress is determined to choose a notorious rake as her guardian.

Book 6: The Duke: the heir to the dukedom is reluctant to step into his dead brother's shoes and accept his arranged marriage.

Any questions about the series? You can email me at mary@marykingswood.co.uk - I'd love to hear from you!

About the author

I write traditional Regency romances under the pen name Mary Kingswood, and epic fantasy as Pauline M Ross. I live in the beautiful Highlands of Scotland with my husband. I like chocolate, whisky, my Kindle, massed pipe bands, long leisurely lunches, chocolate, going places in my campervan, eating pizza in Italy, summer nights that never get dark, wood fires in winter, chocolate, the view from the study window looking out over the Moray Firth and the Black Isle to the mountains beyond. And chocolate. I dislike driving on motorways, cooking, shopping, hospitals.

Acknowledgements

Thanks go to:

All those fine people in Albany, Australia who restored the *Brig Amity*, and gave me the germ of an idea.

Shayne Rutherford of Darkmoon Graphics for the cover design.

My beta readers: Mary Burnett, Barbara Daniels Dena, Amy DeWitt, Quilting Danielle, Megan Jacobson, Melanie Savage

Last, but definitely not least, my first reader: Amy Ross.

Sneak preview of The Apothecary Chapter 1: A Visitor (May)

Annie was on her hands and knees in the cellar, counting bottles, when her life changed. Such a mundane chore, to precede so momentous an event. How could she have guessed?

She loved the feel of the bottles in her hand, heavy and solid. So many bottles… green ones, brown ones, blue ones, clear ones. Tall and thin, or short and squat, or lozenge shaped. Each one would hold a different type of medicine — tonics and sleeping draughts and healing receipts of one sort or another. A thousand different ways to heal, and already she knew several hundreds of them. Her uncle never tired of explaining his methods to her, and she never tired of listening. Ever since she and her mother had come to live with him, she had been her uncle's avid apprentice. His little apothecary, he liked to call her, in his jesting way.

Three boxes had already been counted, sorted and the bottles replaced, and she was just beginning on the fourth, when the door at the top of the cellar stairs creaked.

"Are you down there, miss?" came Betty's voice. Annie smiled. Betty hated the cellar, and would never venture down into the darkness unless compelled.

She sat back on her heels. "I am here, Betty. Am I wanted in the kitchen?"

"Mistress said to tell you you're to go upstairs and put on your blue muslin right away. Oh, and wash your hands and tidy your hair."

"Oh. Visitors?"

"Don't know, miss, but they's all a-twitter, mistress and your ma."

"Very well. Tell them I shall be there in a little while. I only have one more box to see to."

"No, miss! Right away!"

"An important visitor, then." That was interesting. The banker, perhaps? Or the landlord, although he usually only came at Lady Day.

Annie brushed herself down, raising a cloud of dust. No matter how often she swept out the cellar, there was always a great volume of dust. With a last, regretful look at the last box of bottles, she picked up her lantern and climbed the stairs to the kitchen passage.

Her aunt was waiting for her. "Well, now," she said, pinching Annie's cheek. "Yes, you need a little bit of colour. You've always been so pale. But never mind that now! Hurry upstairs and change, my dear, as quick as you can. He'll be back in an hour... less than an hour, now, and we must be ready. Gracious, I must send Wally round to Mrs Quaife for some cake or biscuits, for we have nothing... nothing suitable. What are you standing here for? Run, run!"

Annie flew up the stairs. The blue muslin was already laid out on the bed. Betty was rummaging in drawers, pulling out ribbons and gloves and handkerchiefs in a haberdashery whirlwind. Her mother had her jewellery box open, her thin fingers rifling through the contents, muttering, "No, no... not that, no... possible... no..."

"Whatever is going on?" Annie said, turning round to allow Betty to unfasten the back of her apron and gown. "Is it the landlord?"

Her mother looked up with amusement all over her face. "The landlord? Whatever gave you that idea? It is Mr Huntly."

"Mr Huntly?" Annie said blankly.

"Oh, Annie! You must remember him. He was so sweet on you but not a penny piece to his name. He could not afford a wife, and so your papa told him. He went away after that, but he was so sad, poor fellow."

"That was years ago! Seven... no, eight years ago, Mama. How should I remember him after all this time?"

But she did remember him. Not his face, perhaps, for his appearance was nondescript, but the way they had met. She had been walking up the High Street with Lavinia when he had emerged from the Angel, long legs striding, and almost bumped into them. He had stopped dead, gazing at her fixedly, then he had swept off his hat and bowed almost to the ground. It was so comical that she had wanted to laugh, and Lavinia *had* laughed. They had passed by without acknowledging him, naturally, but he had followed them all the way back to the vicarage. He had been in the congregation the next Sunday, but for several weeks he could do no more, for he had no acquaintance in common to introduce him to the society they moved in. When he had finally got his introduction, he had pursued her relentlessly for weeks… no, months, until he had plucked up the courage to speak to Papa. Poor man! He had gone away so dejected, Papa had said.

"But whatever does he want? Has he moved back to Guildford?"

"I think not," he mother said, with an gleeful grin. "Look at his card."

She pulled it from the pocket of her apron, and thrust it at Annie. *'Rupert Huntly, Esq. Willow Place, nr Salisbury, Wilts.'* she read.

"Willow Place. That was his brother's estate."

"It is his home now, and he is an esquire, do you see? A gentleman. What a fine thing for you, Annie!"

"Oh, Heavens, Mama, may a man not call on old friends without exciting speculation? He may simply live with his brother. He may even be married. Ouch! Too tight, Betty."

"We will find it all out soon enough, but he is not coming here to see *me*, you may be sure of that, even though he asked for Mrs Dresden and Miss Dresden. He has already found out that you are still unmarried, you see. I expect he made enquiries about you, and now that he knows you are single, he comes to call upon you. There now, that gown shows off your figure to full advantage. This necklace, I think, Annie, and the other fichu. Yes, the lace one, Betty, and then you must do what you can with her hair, while I go and change, too. Goodness, to be receiving morning callers again — why, it is just like the old days when your poor, dear papa was alive, Annie. I do so miss it."

"I know, Mama, but there is nothing to be done about it, and Uncle Tom has been kindness itself to us."

"Of course, of course, and I hope I am not ungrateful, dear one. Never that! But I may be grateful and yet still miss my old life, may I not?"

Uncle Tom had been called away to attend to a patient, so only the three ladies sat in the parlour to receive Mr Huntly. Aunt Hester was excited, her eyes bright with speculation. She had a fertile imagination, and so it needed only a male caller for her to be planning the wedding clothes. Annie's mother was, as always, outwardly serene, yet there was a certain flush on her cheeks all the same.

Annie herself was not sure what she felt. Excitement? Perhaps. Hope, certainly. To be married, and have a home and a family of her own! It was of all things the most desirable to her, and yet here she was, at the advanced age of six and twenty, still a spinster. So if Mr Huntly had matrimony in mind and could afford a wife, she would not rebuff him. Yet she dared not allow herself to consider it possible. He was an old acquaintance who was paying a courtesy call while in the town. Yes, that was all it was.

Betty showed him in, her eyes wide. "Mr Huntly, madam."

He was just as Annie recalled, although the skeletal frame of youth had filled out a little. He was still nondescript in appearance, but he was clothed rather better than she remembered, with well-fitted coat and breeches, polished top boots and a carefully arranged neckcloth. It would be too much to say that he was fashionable, but he certainly looked the gentleman.

They all rose, and Annie's mother stepped forward to greet him. "Mr Huntly, how kind of you to call on us. It is always pleasant to meet again with old friends."

"Mrs Dresden," he murmured, bowing, but even as he rose, his eyes strayed towards Annie.

"We have so much to talk about, but before you tell us all that you have been doing, my sister-in-law would be gratified to make your acquaintance. Hester, Mr Huntly visited us many times when my poor husband was still with us. Mr Huntly, my sister-in-law, Mrs Perkins. And... you will remember my daughter, Annie."

"Mrs Perkins." He bowed to her, then his eyes turned again to Annie. "I remember Miss Dresden perfectly." Another bow.

Annie curtsied composedly, but her heart was racing. His eyes! There was an intensity in them that could not be mistaken. This was not the courteous call of an old acquaintance passing through the town. He was here for her!

Her mother waved Mr Huntly to a chair and they all sat.

"Are you in Guildford for long, Mr Huntly?" was her mother's first question.

"I cannot say," he said. "That will depend on how long it takes for my business to be concluded."

"You are here on business, then?"

"Personal business, Mrs Dresden. Personal business." His eyes were on Annie as he spoke, so that she almost blushed. He was so direct! Impossible to misunderstand him. Before anyone could enquire further, he said quickly, "I was so very sorry to hear of the death of Mr Dresden, and the event was most unexpected, as I understand. Such a fine preacher. I always enjoyed his sermons enormously." He shifted on his chair a little, so that he was facing more towards Annie. "Miss Dresden, do you still attend your father's former church?"

"Occasionally, sir, but we are closer to St Mary's, and... it is distressing to Mama to—"

"Of course," he said quickly. "Naturally it must evoke memories of happier times."

Annie could see her mother drooping at this turn in the conversation, so she made a rapid change of subject. "You are not any longer living at Grantham, I understand, sir?"

"I am not. I have had... a change of circumstance. You will remember me speaking of my older brother, perhaps, Miss Dresden? The one who inherited my father's estate in Wiltshire?"

"I remember."

"He met a tragic demise earlier this year, and therefore I have assumed the responsibility for the management of the estate."

"That is sad news indeed," Annie said. "You have my condolences, sir. Was his illness of long duration?"

His lips quirked in a half-smile. "He was not ill. Herbert was aboard a ship from Ireland when it foundered off the coast of Cornwall. He was drowned."

"Not the *Minerva?"* Annie said, sitting a little more upright. "The same on which the poor Duke of Falconbury lost his life?"

He shook his head a little, albeit with a rueful smile. "I should have realised you would have heard of it. Everyone has heard of the drowning of the poor Duke of Falconbury. Well, Miss Dresden, my poor brother was also on board and also lost his life, which was just as precious to him as the young duke's was to him, but naturally no newspaper filled its pages with the death of Mr Herbert Huntly. That is the way of the world, that a duke is of more interest than a mere gentleman, and a great deal more than an able seaman. We all have our place in the world, do we not?"

His words were commonplace, but the look in his eyes told a different story.

Her mother said calmly, "The loss of your brother is a great tragedy, Mr Huntly, and the management of his estates must be irksome for you. Are you now settled permanently in Wiltshire, or shall you hope to return to Grantham one day?"

"My home is now at Willow Place," he said. "My brother had no son and so the estate fell to me. I had no wish for it and it was a wrench to leave my work, for I flatter myself I was beginning to make a name for myself as an attorney, but I daresay I shall grow accustomed, in time, to living as a gentleman. I have a few adjustments still to make to my style of living, but once that is accomplished, I daresay I shall be as contented as any man can be."

Once more his eyes fell on Annie, and he smiled at her with a warmth that made her blush and drop her eyes. Well! He could not have spoken plainer if he had dropped on one knee and offered for her on the spot.

Aunt Hester was naturally agog to know of his intention in calling, so she tiptoed around the subject by asking courteously if Mr Huntly had any other brothers, or any sisters.

"None now living, to my sorrow. I am the last of my father's children."

"And are you married, Mr Huntly?" Aunt Hester said.

His voice was heavy with meaning as he replied. "Not yet, Mrs Perkins. Not yet."

Annie's eyes were lowered, so she could not see whether he looked in her direction, but it scarcely mattered. She understood him perfectly.

The tea and some hastily procured cakes were set out, everyone ate and drank, the conversation reverted to indifferent topics and after precisely half an hour, Mr Huntly rose, asked if he might call again the next day and went away.

There was no time to discuss the matter. Aunt Hester was wanted in the kitchen and Annie had her bottles to finish counting. She changed out of the blue muslin gown, and went dutifully down to the cellar again to complete her task. Then there was an errand for her uncle, and then dinner, with the children's noisy presence. Only after that could the ladies settle to the agreeable task of discussing Mr Huntly, his person and manners and intentions. Annie said nothing, but when the two older ladies settled it between them that a summer wedding was very probable, she could not disagree.

Annie's uncle had gone out to a patient, but when he returned, the supper tray had been brought in, and his end-of-the-day claret had been poured, he said, "Well, Annie, so you have an admirer, it seems. What do you think of him, this Huntly fellow?"

"He is a pleasant sort of man, Uncle. Very well-spoken."

"True enough. He asked me very politely if he might call upon you and your mother. I trust I did right in telling him to come back in an hour?"

"Perfectly right, Mr Perkins," his wife said. "Annie had time to put on one of her good dresses. She looked very well, I thought."

"Annie always looks well," he said. Turning to Annie's mother, he said, "What say you, Mary? Will he come up to scratch, do you think?"

"What a vulgar expression, Tom! But it did seem... one would not wish to raise expectations too soon, but he *did* seem to speak in a most particular way."

"And to come all this way solely on Annie's account suggests the strongest attachment," Aunt Hester said.

"Do we know that?" Uncle Tom said. "That he has come here solely on Annie's account?"

"He said he was here on *personal* business," his wife said triumphantly. "And then he looked directly at Annie. What could be clearer?"

"Hmm." Her uncle looked at Annie thoughtfully. "He wished to pay his addresses to you once before, I believe, Annie, but your father sent him away. Were you... disappointed about that?"

"Oh no, Uncle. Papa knew best, and Mr Huntly had no great income then. It would have had to be a very long engagement."

"We don't know what his income is now, come to that. You send him to me if he starts talking about marriage, and I'll have it out of him. No point tying yourself to a man with the appearance of a gentleman unless he has the means to keep you respectably. I know a man in Salisbury who might tell us something about the family. I'll write first thing. But don't you go rushing into anything, missy."

"No, Uncle."

As she went to bed that night, Aunt Hester whispered, “Oh, Annie! Just think, you’ll soon be married.”

“I know,” she said, smiling.

She was still smiling as she climbed into bed and blew out the candle, for the glow inside her would not be extinguished. She would be married! What more could any woman want?

END OF SAMPLE CHAPTER of *The Apothecary*

For more information or to buy, go to my website at http://marykingswood.co.uk.

Made in United States
North Haven, CT
04 August 2022